8 Crime 2A
£2.99.   K
SIGNED

STRAN

STRANGERS

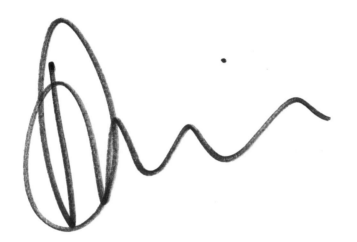

DAVID MOODY

First published in 2014 by Infected Books

A CIP catalogue record for this book
is available from the British Library

ISBN 978-0-9576563-4-5

www.infectedbooks.co.uk

Cover design by Craig Paton
www.craigpaton.com

www.davidmoody.net

FORTY-EIGHT MILES NORTH OF THUSSOCK

'You all right?'

He just looked at her, struggled to focus, took his time to reply. 'Sorry. Tired.'

'It's getting awful late. What are you doing out here at this hour?'

'Not sure. Lost, I think.'

'I'll say. Where you heading?'

'Can't remember,' he said, embarrassed, and he laughed like a child.

They blocked each other's way along the narrow pavement. The silence was awkward. Joan's dog Oscar tugged at his lead, keen to get home and out of the rain. She tugged back. He'd have to wait.

'I'm cold,' the man said, wrapping his arms around himself.

'I'm hardly surprised. Just look at you. You're not really dressed for it, are you?' Joan continued to stare at him. What was he... mid-thirties, perhaps? He looked about half her age. His nipples showed through his wet T-shirt and she couldn't help but stare. He was shivering, but that was only to be expected. She was cold herself, and she'd a vest, a blouse and a cardigan under her anorak. In the dull glow from the streetlamp between them, she thought he looked beautiful. 'You're not from round here, are you?' she asked.

'You can tell?'

'It's the accent,' she giggled. *What the hell are you doing, Joanie?* She felt foolish... silly, even, like she was back in school, flirting. There was just something about him... she knew she should get home, but she didn't want to go anywhere. Oscar whined and pulled at his lead again and she cursed him. 'I should really be getting back,' she said.

The man nodded, chewed his lip. 'Okay.'

'What about you?'

'Don't know,' he answered. 'Not sure.'

For a second she thought she detected an unexpected vulnerability in his face and she liked it. It made her pulse quicken, reminding her of times long-gone, times all but forgotten. Memories of youth clubs and dance halls... tongue-tied boys, all cocksure and confident with their mates, suddenly stammering with nerves when it came to asking her out. She remembered the makeup, the skirts, the dancing and the alcohol... knowing they were watching her, *wanting* her, knowing she had the power to make or break them with a single word, with just a look.

Stop. You're sixty-eight. You're a grandmother. Get a hold of yourself.

Normally she'd be wary of men like this, intimidated even. But not him. Not tonight. He was no threat, he was just... lovely.

'You're very pale. Are you sure you're okay? They said it's going to rain tonight, and you'll not want to be caught out here in just your shirt.' He didn't react, just stared. Oscar pulled again and this time she yanked his lead hard, making him yelp. 'Is there anyone I can call for you? Maybe get someone to come and pick you up?'

'No one.'

Joan half-turned away, then stopped. *You really shouldn't be doing this, Joanie.* She looked at him again. 'You're very handsome.'

He didn't say anything. Didn't react at all, just waited under the streetlamp, watching her watching him. She moved closer, then stopped again. She looped the dog's lead around the bottom of the lamppost then smoothed the creases from her skirt and moved closer still, tucking rogue strands of grey hair behind her ear. What the hell was she thinking? She didn't know anything about this stranger, hadn't ever seen him before. Her head was telling her to do the right thing, to just keep walking and get home. Douglas had said he didn't like her taking the dog out late at night like this, but he'd left her with no choice because the lazy old sod hadn't been prepared to get off his own backside and do it himself, had he? He didn't care anymore, not like he used to. To be honest, neither did she. They were bored of each other and had been for a long time. She pictured him now, back at home in front of the TV. He probably hadn't even noticed she'd gone out.

She decided she'd rather stay here than go home. There was something the way this man looked at her, the way his tall, muscular body made her feel inside, and those eyes... full of life, full of *promise*. She felt a warm glow inside become a burning need; a re-awakening of forgotten feelings she hadn't experienced in a long, long time.

Stop this, Joanie. Get a grip. You're missing Downton.

'I should really be going,' she said.

'Don't. Please.'

His unexpected protest surprised her. Delighted her. He took a single step nearer and they came together under the streetlamp glow, almost touching. He unzipped her fawn-coloured anorak then slipped his trembling hands inside and ran them all over her flabby body. And she reciprocated; holding him, stroking him... kissing him with lips that hadn't kissed like this in an eternity. He fumbled with his jeans while she struggled with her knickers. He gently lowered her down onto the wet pavement then ripped the gusset of her tights open as Oscar barked in protest and strained at his leash.

And who he was didn't matter. And who she was didn't matter. And the temperature and the time and the weather and the openness of where they were and what they were doing... none of it mattered. Because at that exact moment, there was only them.

In the morning they found the dog, still tied up, barking then whimpering. And close to Oscar, under the streetlamp, head in the hedgerow, legs sprawled across the blood-soaked pavement, mutilated, *violated*... they found his body.

The sun sneaked through between gaps in the clouds, dappling the ground with racing patches of vast shadow and light. The sky overhead was more grey than blue now, summer's last gasp disappearing fast. The end of August was in sight. Michelle didn't know where the last twelve months had gone and she didn't much care. As long as they'd gone, that was all that mattered.

The air smelled good out here, so very different. All around them were empty fields, nothing but space. The number of buildings had steadily reduced the longer they'd been driving, and now there were almost none. There were more trees than anything, huge pines which had been here forever, standing impervious and resolute, untroubled by the kind of trivialities and complications which had recently combined to make her life such an impenetrable cluster-fuck of hurt. The contrast with where they'd set out from this morning was stark. Back home in the Midlands, nature made way for man, but here the opposite held true. The road twisted and wound endlessly; the hills, rocks, rivers and forests dictating the way. *You've got to get used to this*, she told herself, *this place is home now*. But it was so very different to the sprawling suburban maze they'd left behind. Just a single road left to follow, no other traffic, no noise other than the car, just *them*.

She looked across at Scott. He'd been watching her soaking it all up. 'Told you you'd like it,' he said, slowing around a sudden sharp bend, then accelerating again as the road straightened and stretched out ahead of them. 'Look at all this space, Chelle. This is what it's all about, don't you think? We'll be happy here.'

Michelle smiled. 'I hope you're right.'

'You know I'm right. When have I ever not been?'

The souped-up Vauxhall Zafira's well-worn engine struggled to make it to the top of a short climb. Scott had been wanting to change the old heap, to trade-up to something better, maybe a Land Rover or an Audi, but that was out of the question right now and would be for a while longer yet. Their car was a necessary workhorse: boring but relatively reliable. Scott had grown to hate it. He'd paid extra for the fancy blue paint job and trim which had looked good back in the day, but it was dated now. That colour hadn't been available for years.

They'd already driven over three hundred miles today, overloaded with the five of them and a boot full of belongings, barely room to move. The removal van would bring the bulk of their things on Monday, but this was the stuff Michelle wasn't about to trust anyone else with, the important and irreplaceable. Photographs. Heirlooms. Documents and paperwork. Memories.

Scott changed down a gear to get over the crest of the deceptively steep hill, then put his foot down as the road sloped away again. It snaked for a couple more turns, then crossed a stone bridge over a river. Michelle thought it looked like something out of a fairy story. And in the distance now, beyond all the trees and fields, appearing to be at the very edge of everything, a snow-capped mountain range. Snow at this time of year! The sheer scale of the apparently never-ending landscape was hard to absorb. She couldn't remember ever being able to see so far ahead. 'Look at that. It's beautiful.'

Scott glanced into the rear view mirror. 'You don't get views like that in Redditch, eh girls?'

No response. He checked his step-daughters' faces for any flicker of reaction but there was nothing there. Tammy, headphones in, stared out of her window. Phoebe, two and a half years younger, had her face buried in a magazine. Eighteen month-old George sat between the two of them, strapped into his seat, fast asleep with his head lolled over to one side, bobbing with the movement of the drive, dribbling.

A signpost. The first for a long time.

Thussock 18

'Nearly there,' Scott said. 'Excited?'

'I guess,' Michelle answered.

'Try showing some enthusiasm then.'

'I am. This is a big thing though, Scott. I'm nervous.'

'Nothing to be nervous about. The kids are gonna love it here.'

'I hope you're right.'

'You've really got to sort out this negative attitude, love. You're doing my head in.'

'Sorry.'

'Focus on the positives... all this space and fresh air.'

'I know.'

'This is just what this family needs. Get us all on the right track again.'

'It's a big deal for everyone though, Scott, that's all. You too. You've only ever lived in Redditch.'

'Not true. I had a flat in Bromsgrove for a couple of years.'

'What, five miles down the road?'

'You're hardly a seasoned traveller yourself.'

'It's difficult with kids.'

'Tell me about it.'

'I travelled with Jeremy. We spent six months travelling around Europe with his job before Tammy was born.'

'Six months of sitting in hotel rooms, you said.'

'We did some sightseeing...'

'You said you saw more plastics factories than anything.'

'Yes, but—'

'Anyway, what you did or didn't do with your ex isn't important. It's where we are now that matters. This move is going to be good for all of us. The kids will be more secure.'

'Hope so.'

Michelle rested her head against the window and watched the world whip by. Another forest. Fields full of sheep. A herd of stampeding deer... she couldn't remember ever having seen deer before, not out in the wild like this.

This was a beautiful part of the world. Scott was right, she needed to lose the negativity and focus on the positives. A fresh start. A clean slate. A new beginning.

Half of the letters on the "Welcome to Thussock" sign had been worn away. *Please Drive Carefully* had been truncated to *Please Drive.* Michelle was tempted to make a joke out of it, but she thought she'd better not.

'Is this it?' Tammy asked from the back. It was the first time she'd spoken in an age.

'This is it,' Scott replied. 'What do you think?'

'You're frigging kidding me.'

'Language, Tam,' Michelle warned. 'You know how we feel about swearing.'

Tammy stretched across George and shook her sister's arm. Phoebe had nodded off. 'S'matter?' she asked, sitting up quick, still half asleep.

'Welcome to paradise,' Tammy told her, no attempt made to mute her sarcasm.

Scott ignored her. 'I thought you might like to see the town first,' he said. 'We'll do a full loop, then end up at the house.'

Tammy stared out of the window, her heart sinking. She'd been holding out some hope that Thussock might not be as bad as she'd expected, but it was all that and more. This place was... dull. Grey, scruffy and bleak. She'd taken a brief virtual tour on Google Earth last week, but the online images had failed to do the place justice. They'd looked pretty grim, but the reality was something else.

Sprawling council estate, maze-like lines of ugly, identical buildings? *Check*. Dilapidated playground and community centre? *Check*. Packs of feral kids hanging around on street corners? *Check*. Boarded-up windows, walls spray-painted with graffiti? *Check and check*.

Beyond the housing estate the road became slightly more congested. This, Tammy presumed, was the high street: the beating heart of Thussock. Except that today it looked in need of defibrillation. Every other shop was shut, most of their frontages an unloved mess of plywood and torn and faded posters, livened up by the occasional coloured flash of illegible vandal's scrawl. And the businesses still trading didn't look much better.

Michelle had seen something on the news last week about parts of South Wales which had been overlooked after the coal mines had closed. Once-thriving communities had slowly crumbled, left to decay like the useless machinery abandoned to rust around the mouths of the pits, all but forgotten. Now unemployment was high and morale was low. Public transport was minimal, public services non-existent. There were kids, she remembered hearing, who'd never travelled more than a couple of miles away from home. Christ, she hoped things weren't that bad here, but she harboured a sneaking suspicion that if she'd done find/replace on the newsreader's script and substituted *Thussock* for *South Wales*, few people would have noticed. *Stop it, Chelle,* she told herself, *this isn't helping.* 'I think it looks quite nice,' she said, knowing exactly how vague and non-committal she probably sounded.

'It *is* nice,' Scott told her.

'What the hell's that?' Phoebe asked, pointing at an ugly mass of metal rising up behind the nearest buildings, completely at odds with everything else: steel tanks and pipes, belching off-white exhaust fumes.

'Brewery,' Scott answered quickly. 'Quite a big one by all accounts. Thussock's on the up and up, I'm hearing.'

Jeez, Tammy thought but didn't dare say, *it's so tough living here they have to make their own booze to keep themselves permanently pissed.* The air around the site was filled with a noxious stink. Tammy and Phoebe just looked at each other, faces screwed up.

This place was like a town preserved in aspic: a relic of a thankfully long-forgotten time. Tammy felt a glimmer of hope for the briefest of moments when she saw a sign for a new retail development up ahead, but it was short lived. A number of redbrick units had been built in a horseshoe shape around a small car park and block-paved pedestrian area, but only two had so far been occupied. One was a Co-op supermarket (and she thought it sad that recognising the store's familiar green and white signage made her feel fleetingly positive), the other a cut-price clothing store. It was a chain she hadn't heard of before, one local to Scotland, perhaps? She couldn't imagine herself shopping there regularly. She'd already resigned herself to probably having to do all her shopping online. She hoped it wouldn't be long before they had broadband installed. Scott had told her they'd get it sorted straightaway, but she'd given up counting on anything he told her.

'That it?' Phoebe asked when they reached the end of the high street. Tammy thought the flat tone of her sister's voice perfectly described how she herself was feeling; a mix of disbelief and resignation. Disappointed and underwhelmed, but not entirely surprised.

'That's it,' Scott said. 'Perfect, eh?'

'If you say so.'

'Feels like we've dropped off the edge of the planet,' Tammy said unhelpfully as they drove up and over an unnecessarily ornate stone bridge. She looked through the gaps between grubby balustrades and saw a quiet stream where she'd expected a river. Big bridge, little trickle. It seemed to sum this place up perfectly.

'Come on you two,' Michelle said, doing what she could to keep their spirits up. 'It's not that bad. Anyway, it might be quiet around here, but Edinburgh and Glasgow are only about an hour away, probably quicker if we take the train.'

'So there's a station?'

'Of course there's a station,' Scott said.

'There it is,' Michelle added quickly, spying the distinctive Network Rail sign at the side of the road just ahead. She saw a largely empty gravel car park and a single platform, a tin shed wedged neatly between the two. So where exactly was the station? Wait, unless that shack *was* the station...?

'I think we missed your school,' Scott said. 'I'll double-back and try find it.'

'Don't bother,' Tammy grumbled. 'Let's pace ourselves. Can't take too much excitement in one day.'

'There's no need to be like that, Tam,' Michelle warned.

'You reckon?'

'Ignore her,' she told Scott. 'How about we just head for the house? I think we all want to see it.'

'Look, I know what you're thinking...' Scott said.

'If you knew what I was thinking you'd have kicked me out of the car,' Tammy said quickly.

'I know what you're thinking, but you need to give this place a chance, you all do. It's important. It's a fresh start for all of us.'

'But I didn't want a fresh start, remember? I was happy in Redditch.'

'Tammy, leave it,' Michelle said, feeling herself tensing, anticipating conflict.

'It was out of my hands, you know it was.'

'No it wasn't. You just decided you couldn't handle—'

'That's enough!' Michelle shouted, her voice loud enough to silence Tammy but wake George. 'Arguing isn't going to do any of us any good. We are where we are, and we're *all* going to make the most of it, right?'

No answer from the back.

'Right?' she asked again, a little firmer this time.

'Whatever,' Tammy said grudgingly.

'Just wait 'til you see the house,' Scott said, unperturbed. 'It'll blow you away.'

They kept driving until they'd left the town, then followed a wildly twisting road which narrowed to little more than a track in places. 'Where are we going?' Michelle asked, confused.

'To the house,' Scott replied. 'I found this route last week. I did some exploring. Thought I should get to know the area before you lot got here. Beautiful, isn't it?'

He was right, this was beautiful. In the space of less than half a mile the grey dereliction of Thussock had been well and truly left behind, hidden by the curves of the road and the undulations of the land and temporarily forgotten. The landscape opened up again. Scott followed the road as it meandered between two hills, one a lush, grassy mound, the other more craggy, covered in bracken and gorse. The greenery was just beginning to show the first signs of autumn browning.

Michelle, feeling unquestionably insignificant, dwarfed by the panorama, clung onto the sides of her seat as the car clattered along. An unseen pothole caused them all to lurch to the left. 'Don't fancy this route in winter much,' she said, already picturing long walks into town for supplies and then having to dig themselves out of snow-drifts.

Around the next bend, the road began to climb again. They were halfway up the rise when Michelle saw an odd-looking industrial construction in the distance. It was in the middle of an otherwise barren field alongside a forest, miles away from anywhere. And like the brewery in Thussock, it too appeared completely out of place. A tall metal tower loomed up over Portakabins and storage tanks. 'I'm going to see if there's any work going there,' Scott said.

'What is it? They drilling for oil or something?'

'Not quite. Fracking.'

'Whating?'

'Fracking. Something to do with drilling down to extract natural gas I think.'

'That's supposed to be dangerous, isn't it?' Phoebe said from the backseat. 'We learnt about it in geography. Causes earth tremors, I heard.'

'If it was that dangerous they wouldn't let them do it,' Scott said. Michelle just looked at him and bit her tongue. Christ, he could be so naïve at times.

'What's going on over there?' she asked, keen to end the debate before it began.

'Where?'

'Right over there,' she said, pointing out of her window. 'Past the fracking or whatever it is.'

Scott slowed down then stopped, perching the car almost at the very top of the hill. A well-spaced line of figures were walking across the countryside, scouring the fields, beating their way through bracken. And then she saw even more of them, so far they were barely discernible as people, their cagoules bright in the distant late afternoon gloom. Above them all hung a helicopter, appearing to match the methodical pace of the walkers down below. 'Probably looking for that woman,' he said.

'What woman?'

'Some old girl's gone missing. Heard it on the radio.'

'Sure she didn't escape?' Tammy mumbled.

'What was that?'

'Are we nearly there?' she asked. 'I'm desperate for the loo.'

Scott pulled away again. 'Very close.'

The sun bounced off the rippling surface of a small lake hidden between two low peaks. Scott wound down the window and all they could hear was the noise of the car and the rushing of the wind. 'Lovely,' Michelle said. 'It's so peaceful. Just what we need.'

'I walked up here from the house last week,' Scott told her, accelerating up one final climb. 'We're just over this rise.'

And he was right. Another couple of minutes and they'd reached a junction in the road, having completed a single large loop. He turned right, heading back towards Thussock, and in less than a quarter of a mile they were there. *Home.* He pulled up outside the house and stopped the engine.

Absolute silence. No noise from anyone. Nothing.

'Well?' he asked.

Michelle got out first and walked up to the front of the building. 'It's much bigger than I thought it would be.'

'Looks good,' Phoebe said, sounding surprisingly upbeat. Although Tammy didn't say anything, Michelle took her silence as a positive sign too.

The pictures Scott had shown her hadn't really done the house justice. It had been a farmhouse once, apparently, though all but a thin strip of land around the back had long since been sold off. Its grubby double-frontage appeared unloved and neglected, but she could definitely see potential. It had originally been rendered off-white, but over the years it had darkened to a uniform murky grey. There were three identical windows on the first floor and two more below, one either side of the front door. To the left of the house as she looked at it was a single-storey extension which, whilst it didn't exactly match either the colour or the overall look of the building, she thought looked spacious and useful. Over on the far right was a separate garage-cum-workshop. In front of the house was a large gravel driveway, big enough for several cars, and a patchy lawn wrapped around the side of the building. The place was massive. Far bigger than their old house.

'Happy?' Scott asked her.

'It's huge.'

'I know.'

'We'll have to put up some kind of fence to block the garden off. Stop George wandering off.'

'Plenty of time for that.'

'And maybe a gate across the drive. It's a bit open.'

'Christ's sake, Chelle, stop looking for faults.'

'I'm not. I'm just being practical.'

'Well don't, at least not for a few minutes. Just look at the potential of this place.'

'It's certainly got potential, I'll give you that.'

'Don't sound so surprised. See, you lot should trust me more.'

'We do trust you.'

'A place like this in Redditch would have cost a bloody fortune. Three times the price at least, I reckon.'

'I know. That's why we're here.'

'Probably because of the fracking,' Phoebe said.

Scott went to open the door. George was awake. He started moaning, then crying. 'Sort the lad out, love,' Scott told Michelle. 'I'll show the girls around.'

Michelle went back to the car and unbuckled George and lifted him from his seat. 'What do you think, Georgie?' she asked as she carried him to the door. 'This is your new home.' George buried his face in his mother's shoulder, too tired and grumpy to care. Michelle looked up at the house again, feeling like she was here for a viewing, not to move in. It was a lovely place, she had to admit, and though Thussock itself had been initially underwhelming, the surrounding area was glorious. *Beggars can't be choosers*, she reminded herself. *And though I'm not a beggar yet, for a while it was a close run thing.*

She took a breath – excited, nervous, heart fluttering with anticipation – and went inside. She could hear the rest of her family exploring already, their footsteps echoing from different rooms and different directions, but she couldn't see any of them. She was standing in a large square hallway with the staircase, the kitchen, and three other doors ahead of her. A downstairs bathroom, the ground-floor bedroom she and Scott would share, and the living room all looked like they hadn't been decorated in decades. Scott had already brought a load of their furniture up from Redditch, but rather than making her feel more at home, seeing their things in these unfamiliar surroundings made her feel even more disconnected. She ran her hand along the back of her sofa in the living room, and all she could see was the place in the house in Redditch where it used to be. She sat George down and left him to wake up fully while she continued to explore.

It wasn't a particularly well-planned house, she decided. In fact, parts of it looked like they'd barely been planned at all, just tacked on to cope. The girls and George all had rooms upstairs, but there was just a toilet up there, no bathroom, and down here there was no way into the dining room from the living room, nor from the dining room into the garden.

The others had met in the kitchen, an impressively well-sized room. 'So what do you think, girls?' she asked.

'It's big,' Tammy said, stating facts rather than expressing an opinion. That was usually a safer option.

'Bit cold, isn't it?' Phoebe said.

'That's just because no one's been here for a couple of days,' Scott said. 'You wait, there's a real fireplace in the living room. I had it going in the week. I'll stoke it up again later if I can find enough wood.'

'You could burn some of this furniture,' Tammy suggested. Much of the previous occupant's stuff had been left behind and whilst he'd already thrown a lot of it out, Scott had simply assimilated the rest.

'We might be able to salvage some of this,' Michelle suggested, looking at a dresser and gently pushing it, checking its sturdiness. 'Might even be able to sell bits of it.'

'Nah,' Scott told her. 'It's all crap. I'll burn the lot of it.'

'Might be some antiques here.'

'I told you, it's all crap.'

She shrugged her shoulders. 'Every penny helps.'

Tammy and Phoebe disappeared upstairs again to choose rooms, taking George with them. Michelle went to the kitchen window and looked out over the yard.

'So what do you think?' Scott asked.

She looked over her shoulder at him, then faced the window again. 'It's big. We'll be rattling around here.'

'That all you've got to say?'

'It's a lovely house, Scott. It will be, anyway.'

'Told you I'd see us right, didn't I? When I say I'm going to do something, I do it.'

'I never doubted you, love.'

'You're going to be happy here then?'

'We've only just arrived.'

'I know that, but just look at this place. Much more space than we had before. All those fields... the countryside.'

A pause. Careful consideration. Say the right thing. 'We are where we are.'

'What?'

'It's what I keep telling the girls. We are where we are, now it's down to all of us to make the most of it.'

'And we will. This is the start of a new chapter, Chelle. Turning over a new leaf, all that stuff...'

'Lay off on the clichés, love,' she said. 'Don't you know that's how ghost stories always start?'

'You're taking the piss.'

'Of course I am. I don't believe in ghosts. You should know that by now.'

Michelle walked around the battered wooden table which took up most of the kitchen floor. She went back through to the hall and looked up. She could hear the kids thumping on the floorboards above her. It sounded familiar and normal, though none of it felt normal yet. *It will in time*, she reassured herself. *Give it a chance.*

She followed Scott into the living room and peered through the rattling, single-glazed French doors into the overgrown back garden. It too had plenty of potential. Sort the lawn out, put in a couple of flower beds, maybe some decking or a patio by the house... The garden was certainly much bigger than the small square patch of grass they'd left behind. With no visible boundaries, no fence or wall, it seemed to go on forever, stretching towards the hills. Scott put his arms around her from behind. She flinched. 'You made me jump.'

'You wait, Chelle,' he said, 'once the rest of our stuff's in here it'll feel like home. The truck'll be here Monday afternoon.'

She nodded and gently freed herself from him, keeping hold of one hand for a few seconds longer. Her attention was caught by a pile of clutter in the corner of the room. 'What's all this?'

'Some of the old guy's stuff. I was going through it before I chucked it out. I'll keep the magazines for the fire.'

'You said you'd cleaned this place up,' she said, running her fingers along a dust-covered dado rail.

'I have cleaned it. You should have seen it before I started. Some rooms hadn't been touched in years. I swear, I was flat out all week. I dumped three loads at the tip. It's a sixty mile round trip, you know. There's still more down the side of the house to get rid of. Once that's all gone and the rest of our gear's in, we'll be sorted. This time next week...'

'I think it's going to take a while longer than that. It's not all about decoration and furniture, you know. The kids are—'

'The kids are going to be fine.'

'I know that, I'm just saying it'll take them time to adjust. In some ways it's been a bigger move for them than us. They've had to change school, leave their friends...'

'We've all had to make sacrifices. But I'll tell you something, Chelle, we've made a bloody good long-term move here. I was looking in an estate agent's window in town the other day. You should see the prices some of the properties like this one are up for. Once I've done it up, we'll make a killing on this place. We'll double the value of it in no time, I reckon. Think how much stronger a position that'll put us in.'

'One step at a time, love.'

'I'm serious. I've got big plans...'

'You've always got big plans.'

'What's that supposed to mean?'

'Nothing.'

'I'm gonna start down here,' he said, oblivious to her reticence. 'I'll knock the kitchen through into the dining room, make it more open plan, then I want a conservatory coming off the living room on the back and a decent-sized patio. All the windows need replacing, there's no double-glazing, it's all the original glass by the looks of it. Then I was thinking about extending our bedroom back and putting in an en suite, maybe even a walk-in closet if there's space. You'd like that. You always said you'd like more room for your clothes.'

'It'd be nice, sure, but I don't *need* more room.'

'Structurally the house is sound. The extension could do with a few minor repairs, but nothing much. I want to get someone in to look at the rendering.'

'Slow down, love.'

'The rendering's important. It's not just about keeping the place looking nice, you know.'

'I understand that...'

'We'll need to re-carpet throughout, but it's not worth doing that until I've done the interior alterations.'

'But...'

'Probably be a good idea to get the drive tarmacked too. The gravel's okay, but it's so bloody noisy, you know? And we'll be constantly dragging it into the house.' He stopped. She was staring at him. 'What?'

'Where are we going to get the money for all of this, Scott? Just because we've got a little in the bank at the moment, doesn't mean we can afford to let ourselves go wild.'

'You have to speculate to accumulate.'

'Yes, but the business is gone, remember? That money's all we've got to live off until we're earning again.'

'I don't see the problem. It's a sound investment. We use the cash in the bank to increase the value of the house.'

'Then what?'

'Then we've got an asset worth double what it is now. We'd never get that kind of return from a bank.'

'I know, you're right.'

'So what's the problem?'

'How do we live in the meantime?'

'We'll manage. We always do. Fuck's sake, wish you'd have a little more faith in me.'

'I do have faith in you.'

'I know what I'm doing.'

'I never said you didn't.'

'Change the attitude then.'

'I'm sorry. I just get the feeling we're on our last chance here, and I don't want to blow it.'

'We won't. *I* won't. I'm doing all this for you and the kids.'

'We just need to be careful.'

His expression changed. He looked hurt, then angry. 'You sound like you're having doubts.'

'I'm not. I'm sorry, love. I'm just tired, that's all. That was a hell of a drive. You must be knackered.'

'I'm all right. Getting used to it. It was a good run today, just on six hours. You should have seen it when I came up last week. Bloody nightmare, it was. Pissing down with rain all the way.'

'I just need some rest. I'll be fine in the morning.'

'As long as that's all it is.'

'I'm fine,' she said again, voice firmer.

Phoebe appeared in the doorway, holding her little brother's hand. 'George is hungry.'

'I'll see to him,' Michelle said. 'Can I have the keys, Scott. I need to get his food out of the car.'

Scott fished in his pocket and threw the keys to her. She left the two of them showing George the garden and went out to the Zafira. Tammy followed her.

'You okay, love?' she asked as she opened the boot and dug around for the remains of the picnic lunch they'd stopped and eaten mid-journey. 'What do you think?'

'It's a dump,' Tammy said, pulling no punches. 'He said it was a big house, but he never said anything about it being such a shitty big house. Have you seen the state of the bathroom, Mum?'

'No, not yet.'

'There's a tidemark round the bath that looks like it's been drawn on.'

'Come on, Tam, try and be positive.'

Phoebe appeared beside her and reached into the car for one of her bags. 'I'm being positive,' she said. 'I like it. I like my room. It's massive compared to the old place.'

'What have I got to be positive about?' Tammy argued. 'Bloody hell, Mum, thanks to your husband I've lost everything. My friends, my freedom...'

'Oh give it a rest. You haven't lost any of that. No one's died. You can still keep in touch.'

'You think? How's that going to work then? You think Katie's dad's gonna be happy to do the twelve hour round trip both ways so we can see each other of a weekend?'

'No, but—'

'Like I said, Mum, thanks to Scott, my life is screwed.'

'And like I said, it isn't. You'll still see as much of your dad, maybe even more of him. You know he works out this way sometimes.'

'I used to be able to walk to all my mates' houses. I could see Max's house from ours. Look around you, Mum, what can you see now? Bugger all. Just fields and hills and bloody trees. No people. None of my friends.'

Tammy wiped away a tear, angry with herself as much as anyone else. Michelle put a hand on her daughter's shoulder. 'I know it's hard, Tam. I know how it feels, honest I do. I'm doing the best I can here.'

'Problem?' Scott asked. They looked around and saw him in the doorway. 'Wondered what the delay was.'

Michelle shot him a quick glance – *don't get involved* – but it was too late. Tammy stormed off around the side of the house.

'What's her problem?'

'She just needs a little time,' she told him. 'She'll be okay.'

She squeezed past Scott and went inside to find George, following the whines. Thankfully he was much easier to placate than his older sister. *If only chocolate biscuits had the same effect on teenage girls*, she thought.

THE NORTH ROAD OUT OF THUSSOCK

The police officer stepped out into the road and flagged the old Ford Focus down. He'd heard it coming a mile off, its over-revved engine straining with effort. The driver cursed. He'd been too busy messing with his phone to see the flashing lights until it was too late. He braked hard, trying to make the sudden halt appear as controlled as possible. He wound down his window and wiped the spitting rain from his face. 'Evening, Sergeant.'

'How are we this evening, Mr Boyle? Driving a little fast, weren't we? In a hurry?'

'Just off to see a friend.'

'Ah, yes. And where would this friend be?'

'Up near the fracking site.'

'Is that right?'

'It's just Murray. You know Murray, Sergeant.'

'Oh, I know Murray all right. And what'll you two be getting up to?'

'Just a quiet night, helping him through his shift. Watch a few DVDs, have a couple of drinks, that's all...'

They'd been through this routine many times before. The sergeant peered into the backseat of the car where he could see a large black holdall. 'You don't mind if I...?' he asked.

'Whatever. Do you never get bored of this?'

'Never,' the officer replied. 'You do tend to bring it on yourself though, Mr Boyle, driving too fast on a road as quiet as this. Subtlety has never been a strong point of yours, has it?'

Boyle didn't answer, he just watched in his rear view mirror as the sergeant mooched through the holdall. A few cans of beer, some smokes, and a stack of DVDs. The officer looked at the covers of a few of them, then shook his head with disdain and dropped them back into the bag. He'd always had his doubts about this bloke.

'Are we okay here, Sergeant Ross?'

The sergeant leant into the driver's window. 'Aye, we're okay. Just take it easy. I know you're looking forward to watching your movies with your pal, but try and get there in one piece, won't you. Oh, and

I hope those cans are for Murray, not you if you're driving.'

'I'll just have the one.'

'I'd rather you had none. On your way now, Mr Boyle.'

Boyle pulled away, sticking to the speed limit until the lights of the police car were well out of sight.

'Aye, he's a fuckin' prick that one,' Murray said. 'Always has been. Always will be.'

Two DVDs and half the beer down and he was still complaining about Sergeant Ross. 'I swear, he's got it in for me. Always trying to catch me for sumthin'.'

'Were you speeding?'

'Yeah, but that's not the point.'

'It's *exactly* the point, you dozy prick. You know me, man, I'm as guilty of overdoin' it as you are, but I'm not so soft as to...'

Murray stopped and stared at one of the CCTV screens on the desk.

'What's up?'

He'd spent more time watching the DVDs on his laptop than the security cameras he was being paid to monitor. 'That's weird,' he said. He tapped the screen with his finger. 'Was that there before?'

'I don't know. Not my responsibility. You're the security man, not me.'

'Thanks for nothing, pal.'

Murray stared at the screen and used a keyboard and mouse to adjust the picture. His remit was to watch the fracking site, not the surrounding area, but the cameras had been set up with deliberately wide fields of view. *You know how it is, Murray,* his boss had told him. *There's always some eco-warrior dipshit banging on about us harming the environment. We just need to keep an eye out. Stay one step ahead of the game.*

'What is it?' Boyle asked, trying to make out the pixelated shape; a blurry mass at the bottom of a tree. 'Some kind of animal?'

'I've no idea. I think I should go out there and check. You coming?'

'It's pissing down and it's dark.'

'There's a flashlight and a spare waterproof in the cupboard. Come on, man. I don't want to go out there on my own.'

'Are you serious?'

'I'm serious. Come on.'

It was hard to work out where the shape was in relation to the security hut. Murray looked back and tried to orientate himself using the drill shaft at the centre of the site as a guide. This was definitely the right place. 'It was this way, man, I'm sure,' he said, flashing his torch around the wet grass.

'Well there's nothing here now, Murray. Let's get back.'

'Wait. Look!' Murray shone his light deeper into the dense copse of trees up ahead. There was something leaning against one of the larger trunks. Was that someone's head? A body slumped forward? He called out but there was no response. The two men looked at each other, then took a few nervous steps closer. Murray relaxed when he saw what it was. 'It's just a bike. Bloody hell, would you look at that. Just someone's bloody saddle bag.'

'What's anyone doin' out here on a bike at this time?'

'You'd be surprised. I could show you some clips on that CCTV. Folks get up to all sorts out in these woods.'

'Can't believe you thought that was a head. You fuckin' moron.'

'Least I got close enough to look,' Murray said. 'I wasn't the one hangin' back 'cause I was too bloody scared.'

'I wasn't scared. Like I said, you're bein' paid for this, not me.'

They were about to head back when something else caught Murray's eye, an unexpected flash of colour. 'Oh, fuck,' he said. This time there was no doubt as to what it was they were seeing: the crimson was jarringly out of place against the greens and browns. His torch illuminated a crescent-shaped pool of blood in the leaf litter. And there was more of it... another patch a short distance up ahead, a series of intermittent drips forming a trail. Murray continued forward, Boyle turned around and went the other way. 'Where the fuck are you goin'?'

'Sorry, Murray, I can't... I shouldn't even be here. Sergeant Ross has it in for me as it is. If he catches me out here then... I'm sorry, man...'

Boyle sprinted back to the security hut. Murray held his position on the edge of the forest, the dripping rain the only noise of any note, and waited a moment longer. He knew he didn't have any choice but to investigate. As his so-called friend had so succinctly put it, this was what he was being paid to do, and although whatever had happened here was technically outside the fracking site, he knew how suspect it would seem if he got this far then stopped. In the distance he heard Boyle's knacker of a car race away, blown exhaust echoing, tyres skidding on the gravel.

'Thanks, *mate*,' he grumbled to himself.

Deep breath.

Murray followed the blood trail deeper into the trees.

He found her in a patch of open space in the middle of the wood, lying on her side as if she was asleep. She was half-naked, a steady flow of still-warm blood running down the insides of her thighs, washing away in the rain. Porcelain flesh, hidden away through modesty for years but exposed for all to see now. Fawn anorak with blotting-paper blood stains. Steam snaked up from between her legs. She'd not been dead long.

Scott decided they'd start their first full day in Thussock with a trip into town. Despite their instinctive protestations – more for effect than anything else, just making their feelings known – both girls agreed to come. Other than cleaning and unpacking, there wasn't much else to do; the TV wasn't set up yet, and they'd no Internet connection. Scott had promised to get it sorted in the week but Tammy didn't know if she'd last that long. Less than twenty-four hours in and she was struggling with life offline. It felt like solitary confinement. The rest of the world continued to chat, message, share and update outside of her little bubble of disconnection, making her feel like she'd been blocked. Unfriended.

Another bloody "Welcome to Thussock" sign. They were taking the piss now, Tammy thought as they drove along the main road from the house into town. Scott pulled up outside a shed-like wooden bus-shelter. Michelle jumped out and checked the timetable for times and prices to school. 'I think we'll drive you in for the first week or so,' she told them when she got back into the car. 'Just until we've all got our bearings. The buses seem really infrequent. Don't want you two being late or getting stranded.'

'Oh, that's too weird,' Phoebe said unexpectedly.

'What, the buses?' Tammy asked, confused.

'No... over there. See that house?'

Tammy craned her neck and saw a bungalow with a pea-green front door and an over-fussy garden. It was nothing special. As unremarkable as the rest of Thussock. 'What about it?'

'Watch the woman.'

All of them, George included, now watched as an obese woman waddled out from around the side of the small house. She was wearing a long and distinctly unflattering cerise summer dress which clung to all the wrong bulges. Her bleached hair was cropped short. 'Don't stare,' Michelle warned, although she was as guilty as the rest of them.

'What about her?' Scott asked.

'Just keep watching...'

A car reversed out of a pre-fabricated garage adjacent to the bungalow. As the oversized woman in pink lowered herself into the passenger seat, an identically obese woman in blue got out and shut the garage door. 'Identical twins,' Michelle said. 'That's not weird.'

'It is when you live together and you're wearing the exact same outfits at their age.'

'Don't be so rude. I'm sure they're both lovely.'

The family watched, strangely spellbound, as the sisters pulled off their drive. The twin in the passenger seat saw them watching and gave them a nod of the head and a wave. 'Phoebe's right,' Scott said when they'd gone. 'That was weird.'

They followed the car into town. The twins turned off when they reached a small church hall, barely noticeable tucked away in the middle of a row of houses.

'Where exactly are we going?' Tammy asked.

'Thought we'd find your school first, then see if we can get some lunch,' Scott told her.

'Is it going to take long?'

'As long as it takes. Stop moaning.'

She slumped back in her seat. *And this is what my life has been reduced to: driving to look at a school on a Sunday morning.* Her friends Katie and Max had been planning to go to Merry Hill today, she remembered. Some shopping, then on to see that film they'd all been talking about last week. Most of her mates back home probably weren't even awake yet, still sleeping off the effects of the night before.

Thussock High School was a curious mix of the old and the very old; about eighty per cent decrepit to twenty per cent ancient, Tammy decided. *School's school,* Scott had told them both, spouting bullshit as usual. Did he ever stop to listen to the crap he came out with? *It's not where you go, it's what you do when you're there that matters*, he said. *You make your own chances*, that was one of his favourite nuggets of shite. Well, moving to Thussock would blow his theories out of the water, because Tammy knew beyond any doubt that the schooling here wasn't going to be as good as she'd had back in Redditch. For a start, the course options were severely limited. She'd had to choose

A levels she hadn't really wanted, and she was already concerned that would have an impact on her university choices in a couple of years time. She decided it didn't really matter what she went on to study at uni anymore. For Tammy, the *further* in further education now referred to the distance she could get from Thussock.

'What do you reckon?' Phoebe asked, standing at the fence along-side her, both of them gripping the railings like prisoners.

'Pretty grim. Matches the rest of this shitty town perfectly.'

'It might be all right.'

'It might not.'

A long, straight road ran through the centre of a large grey play-ground, stretching from the gate, deep into the main hub of the school. It looked like it had been built in the sixties: all concrete grey and sharp corners; modular and geometric; ugly, out-dated and drab. There were four temporary classrooms at the far end of the playground, and it was clear from the weathering of the flimsy-look-ing buildings that they'd proved to be far less temporary than had originally been envisaged.

Behind the bulk of the school buildings, visible in a gap between two blocks, they could see a more recently built leisure centre. Its cream, corrugated metal walls were a stark contrast to the rest of the campus. Tammy wondered if it had a fitness suite and a pool like the college she should have been starting at in Bromsgrove next week? She wasn't going to get her hopes up.

'We ready to make a move, ladies?' Scott shouted from the car. They ambled back. 'Hungry?'

'Starving,' Phoebe said.

'Then let's go and see what we can find.'

They left the car outside the Co-op supermarket, then walked the length of the high street. Scott and Michelle were at the front, Mi-chelle pushing George in his buggy, while the two girls followed at a distance. Michelle looked back at them. 'You two okay?'

'Fine,' they both answered, though the tone of their voices said otherwise.

'Do you think they're going to be all right?' Michelle asked, turn-ing back to talk to Scott.

'They will be. It's early days. Bit of a culture shock for them. Tammy's just sulking as usual.'

'Bit of a culture shock for all of us.'

'It's not that bad.'

'I didn't say it was. It's going to be very different here, that's all.'

'You all need to keep open minds. If you go into things with a positive attitude, they'll usually work out.'

'Is that right?'

'Yes it is. That's why I'm keen to get started on the house.'

Scott stopped walking suddenly and looked around.

'What's up?'

'That's it, I think,' he said. 'I think we've done the entire place.'

'We can't have.'

Tammy and Phoebe caught up. 'Why have we stopped?' Tammy asked.

'Because we've reached the end of the road,' Scott told her.

'You can say that again.'

'Didn't see many places to eat,' Michelle said.

'There was the pub,' Scott suggested.

'Didn't like the look of it.'

'Or the name,' Tammy interrupted. 'Fancy calling a pub The Black Boy. Sounds racist. Sinister.'

'There was a sheepdog on the sign,' Phoebe said. 'Probably named after a dog who saved a farmer, something like that.'

'There was a chip shop back a way,' Michelle said.

'You can't have chips for Sunday dinner,' Phoebe protested. 'It's not right. When we're with Dad, Nanny always cooks a roast dinner on Sunday.' Her voice cracked with emotion, an unexpected twinge of sadness taking her by surprise. She wished she was there now.

'Well you're not at your nanny's today, are you?' Scott said, oblivious. 'Looks like it's chips or nothing.'

'We could head back to the supermarket,' Michelle said. 'Get something to eat from there.'

'Too cold for a picnic,' Tammy said. 'The sun's gone in.'

'Then we can just take stuff back to the house.'

'What was the point of coming out then?'

'Give it a rest, Tam. Stop being so bloody argumentative all the time. We wanted you to see the school.'

'Why bother? We'll see it tomorrow, anyway. We should have stayed at the house and saved all the effort.'

'What effort?' Scott said. 'Haven't seen anyone else putting any effort in. Come on, let's go.'

Phoebe wasn't moving. 'You said we were having a Sunday dinner.'

'I know, but—'

'But you said...'

'What am I supposed to do? Just magic one up? Pull one out of my backside?'

'*You said...*'

Frustrated, Scott turned and started back towards the supermarket, walking at double pace. 'I'll get you your bloody dinner,' he shouted. 'Just stop being so bloody miserable.'

He was halfway back to the supermarket before the rest of them moved. 'I'll go and see what he's doing,' Michelle said. 'Make sure we get something decent to eat.'

'Bloke's an idiot,' Tammy said.

Michelle's shoulders slumped. 'Give it a rest, will you? I'm stuck between a rock and a hard place here. Scott's trying, you know. This hasn't been easy on him either.'

'Maybe he should have tried a little earlier. If he had, maybe we wouldn't have lost the house.'

'Tam, don't go there...'

'But it's true, Mum, you know it is.'

'And going on about it isn't going to help anyone. We are where we are.'

'Will you stop saying that.'

'Just deal with it. Both of you. Do me a favour and look after George. I'll go and see what Scott's up to.'

End of conversation. Michelle handed George's buggy to Phoebe then went into the supermarket.

'She always does that,' Tammy said.

'Does what?'

'Walks away when she doesn't want to hear what someone's saying. Does my head in.'

The sisters sat down on the stone wall around the edge of the car park, their brother parked between them.

'That school looked all right, actually,' Phoebe said. Tammy just looked at her.

'You serious? You must be off your head, Pheeb. It looked like a fucking hole, just like the rest of this dump of a place.'

'It is Sunday though, Tam. Everywhere's quiet on a Sunday.'

'You all right, girls?' an unexpected voice asked. They turned and saw a group of three lads and a girl standing on the other side of the wall. Two of the boys, Tammy quickly decided, were nothing special: all bad hair, cheap sports gear and exaggerated swagger. The one in the middle though, the tallest of the three, the only one who wasn't smoking, was quite cute. But she'd already decided there was an insurmountable difference between a quite cute boy from Thussock and a quite cute boy from Redditch. These people were alien to her.

'We've just moved here,' Phoebe said and Tammy glared and shushed her. Too much information.

'Never a good move,' the smallest of the boys said, his T-shirt flapping against his willowy frame in the wind. He looked colder than he was letting on. He had a sharp nose and small eyes and looked like he was scowling. 'Should'a stayed where you was. Fuck all happens here.'

Tammy struggled to work out what it was he'd just said. His accent was so strong, so unfathomable, that she had to replay the sounds over in her head a couple of times before she could make out the individual words and un-jumble them. 'We didn't ask to come here,' she said, not wanting to engage, but not wanting anyone to think she was here through choice either.

The girl leant over the wall and peered down at George. 'That your kid?' she asked.

'What do you think?' Tammy said, sounding more aggressive than she'd intended.

'Don't know, that's why I asked.'

'No, he's our brother.'

'He's cute,' she said, apparently unperturbed. 'I'm Heather.'

'Hey.'

'I'm Jamie,' the tallest lad said, introducing himself. 'This here's Joel and Sean.'

Tammy just nodded and grunted something that was hardly even a word. She turned back around to emphasise her disinterest and stared at the Co-op, hoping her mum would reappear and get them away from here. The automatic doors slid open and Scott emerged with a bulging carrier bag in either hand. For once she was relieved to see him. She could already sense the crowd behind her beginning to slope away, all cigarette smoke and put-on attitude. She glanced over her shoulder and made sure they'd gone.

'Were they giving you any trouble?' Scott asked.

'No,' she replied, indignant. Even if they were, she didn't need his help to deal with them.

Michelle watched the group disappear. She hated herself for sounding like such a snob, but she didn't like the idea of her girls mixing with kids like that. And she knew that attitude was unfair and probably wholly unwarranted, but for now that was just how it was. She wondered if she'd have felt different if she'd seen the same kids in Redditch?

'So what's for dinner?' Phoebe asked, more interested in her stomach than anything else.

'All kinds of crap,' Scott said. 'Mostly junk food, stuff that's really bad for you. That okay?'

'Perfect.'

'That's what I thought you'd say.'

They walked back to the car which was parked all alone, numerous empty bays on either side. Michelle strapped George into his seat while Scott collapsed the buggy and loaded it into the boot with the shopping.

'Wait up! 'Scuse me, sir!'

Scott looked around and saw one of the Co-op staff running towards him, waving furiously, already out of breath despite the relatively short distance he'd covered. He was in his late forties or early fifties, Scott thought, plump, and with a ruddy complexion and a shock of wild auburn hair which was just on the wrong side of being under control. He stopped short of Scott and stared at him with wide eyes, made to look even wider by the circular frames and magnifying lenses of his glasses. Scott was immediately on guard. He'd clocked this particular joker in the store, stacking shelves and collecting up trolleys and baskets with unnecessary enthusiasm.

'What's the problem?'

'There's no problem.'

The man, whose name was Graham according the name badge clipped onto his tie, just stood there.

'What then?'

'Eh?'

'What do you want?'

'Oh, right,' Graham said, remembering why he was there. 'You left your wallet in the shop.' He handed it over. 'Good job I was looking out for you, eh?'

Scott instinctively checked his pockets, then took his wallet from Graham's outstretched hand. He checked his bank cards and counted the notes at the back.

'It's all there,' Graham said.

'Cheers.'

'Don't mention it,' he said, and with that he was off again. He jogged back to the shop, suddenly veering off to the left to round up a rogue trolley he'd somehow missed when he'd last checked outside a few minutes earlier.

'Thank you,' Michelle shouted after him. Graham waved but didn't look back.

'Weirdo,' Scott said.

'That's a bit harsh.'

'Well, I mean... just look at him.'

'What about him?'

'Bloke his age, collecting trolleys for a living.'

'Don't be so hard on him, love. Looked to me like he'd got learning difficulties, something like that. Anyway, he's working, and that's got to be a good thing, hasn't it? It's more than either of us are doing at the moment.'

'What's that supposed to mean? We only just got here. Haven't started looking for work yet.'

'I know. I wasn't suggesting anything, I was just saying it's good to see people like him getting on so well, that's all.'

'Still a weirdo.'

Michelle sighed. 'He might be thinking the same about you. Look at it from his point of view, Scott. The folks here all know each other and they all know this place. Right now we're the strangers.'

The family's improvised lunch was just about sufficient. They ate in the kitchen, all sitting around the rickety table they'd inherited from the house's former owner. It started to feel reassuringly normal. 'It's like we're on holiday,' Phoebe said.

'Except you've got school tomorrow,' Scott reminded her.

'And you're supposed to enjoy holidays, remember?' Tammy said.

Michelle shook her head. 'Give it a rest, Tam.'

'You know what I mean, though?' Phoebe explained. 'It's like when you're stopping in a caravan, and it's home, but it's not home? You get it, don't you Mum? You've got all the same people around you and all the same stuff, but it's not home. Feels like it by the end of the week, though.'

'Remember when we went to the Isle of Wight?' Scott said. 'You two bottled it in the haunted house at that fair, remember?'

'I was only ten,' Phoebe protested. 'It was scary.'

'You should have seen your faces,' he laughed, remembering the way they'd both coming running back out through the entrance, barging through the queue still trying to get in. 'Priceless. You scared one woman half to death!'

'You were just as bad,' Tammy said. 'You wouldn't even go on the rollercoaster.'

'I wasn't feeling great. It was those chips. They didn't agree with me.'

'Yeah, right. I think you bottled it.'

'We all ate the chips, Scott...' Michelle said and he glared at her. The girls laughed and he had to admit defeat.

The conversation faltered. Michelle looked for a volunteer to help her wash up, but the girls were suddenly conveniently busy. They made their excuses and went up to their rooms, the idea of unpacking their belongings slightly preferable to dealing with dirty dishes. Only George remained, playing on the floor around Scott's feet as Michelle cleared the table. 'What did you say that for?' he asked.

'Say what?'

'The thing about the chips.'

'Oh that,' she said, shoving a handful of wrappers and scraps into a black sack. 'I was just messing about. I know you weren't well that day.'

'So why did you say it? Made me look stupid.'

'Sorry, love. I didn't mean anything by it.'

He got up quick, his sudden movement startling her momentarily. She was worried she'd offended him. He disappeared, only to return a few seconds later with paper, a pen, and his toolbox. He put the toolbox in the middle of the half-cleared table and took out a tape measure, then started studying the wall between the kitchen and the dining room, tapping it with his knuckles and peering into greasy nooks and crannies which looked like they hadn't been cleaned out in years. Michelle worked around him.

'It's not going to be that big a job,' he said.

'What isn't?'

'Knocking this wall through. Remember what I was saying about opening the kitchen out into the dining room?'

'I remember. Can we afford to do it?'

'Afford to do what? It doesn't cost anything to put a hole in a wall, Chelle.'

'No, but it'll cost to make it all good again.'

'A bit of boarding up and plastering, a lick of paint, that's all. I reckon I can have it done in a fortnight.'

'Sounds good.'

'Let me show you.'

'Can I just get the washing up sorted?'

'It'll only take a second.'

'Okay.'

She put down the plates and walked over to where he was standing. He started gesticulating like an excited kid, drawing imaginary lines on the wall. 'I'll take this much out, then you'll have double the space in here. Be perfect, won't it? I might put in another rad and shove a couple of extra sockets in here.'

'We could do with more plugs.'

'That's what I thought. Not sure yet, though. I might just wait and get it done when I get the house re-wired.'

'But like I said, can we afford it?'

'Will you stop going on about money all the bloody time? Christ, you're like a broken record.'

'I'm just worried, that's all.'

'I already told you, the money we spend on the house is an investment. So it'll probably cost a few grand to get these things done, but they'll all add to the value of the house.'

'I know that. We don't have a lot to play with though, remember? There's no rainy day fund anymore.'

'Can't you see what it's going to be like? Try and visualise it, Chelle. Getting rid of this wall will really open up downstairs, make it feel more like a home. It's too dark as it is, too many doors, not enough light.'

'I know. I *can* see it. It's just that—'

'I tell you, it's worth borrowing to get this done. We could take out a small mortgage on this place, release some of the equity.'

'Who's going to lend us money now, Scott? Come on...'

'Stop being so bloody negative.'

'I'm not. I'm all for being positive, love, but we also need to be realistic. If I wasn't being positive I wouldn't be here, would I?'

'I'm going to cost it all up, see what it'll take.'

'You don't listen to a word I say, do you?'

'I do. Your problem is you don't have any vision. Just try and picture it all done. It'll be amazing. I'm going to start looking for work tomorrow and once we're more established I'll get myself set up again and start doing a few building jobs on the side.'

'I thought you said you were done with running your own business?'

'Did you not hear me? *On the side.* I'll do stuff on the quiet. Cash in hand. This house will be beautiful.'

'I don't doubt you.'

'So what's the problem?'

She sighed and leant back against the table, choosing her words carefully. 'If you started on the kitchen, how long do you think it would take?'

'A couple of weeks if I'm working on it full-time. Might as well sort the wiring and the plumbing at the same time.'

'But what if you're working?'

'Don't know. A month or two, I guess. Evenings and weekends.'

'And once you've started, the kitchen will be pretty much out of action?'

'Not for the whole time. That's going to be inevitable to an extent, though, isn't it?'

'So what do I do about cooking? I can't cook in the middle of a building site.'

'We'll eat out.'

'We tried that this morning.'

'What the fuck's wrong with you? I'm trying to get this family back on its feet, you're just putting up obstacles.'

'It's just there's a serious lack of McDonalds, Pizza Hut and Burger King around here. We'll struggle without a fully functioning kitchen for a couple of days, never mind a couple of weeks or months, and I'm sorry if I sound like a broken record, but I'm really not sure we can afford to do all the stuff you're talking about doing in one go. I think we need to take our time, plan things carefully, save up...'

'And I think—'

Tammy burst into the room, mobile phone in hand, seething. 'Shit.'

'What's your problem?' Scott asked, annoyed he'd been interrupted.

'This stupid bloody house, that's my problem.'

She was gone again before either of them could react. Michelle followed her daughter from room to room. 'Tam, slow down,' she said, but Tammy was having none of it. She barged past her mother and went out the front door, slamming it behind her. Scott followed her out and chased her down the side of the house. She was coming back the other way now. He tried to stop her but she side-stepped him. 'What the hell's wrong with you?'

'Can't get a signal,' she yelled, holding up her phone as if it was going to make a difference. She stared hopefully up at the small screen, willing the 'Searching' message to disappear, desperate to see some signal strength.

'Have you tried upstairs?'

'Of course I've tried upstairs. I'm not stupid. I've tried everywhere.'

'Who the hell do you think you're talking to?' he shouted. She stormed off again, as much to put some distance between her and Scott than anything else.

'Just leave her,' Michelle said. She positioned herself between the two of them and put her hands on Scott's chest. 'Please, love. She's only doing it because she knows she'll get a reaction.'

'Too right she'll get a bloody reaction. I'm sick of the way she behaves. She's not the only one who's having to make adjustments, you know.'

'I know... you're right. But cut her some slack. Let her get used to the way things are now...'

'I'm not putting up with it. We've had this crap non-stop since we sold the old house.'

'Yes, and we probably will a while longer yet. She's hurting.'

'So am I.'

'Yes, but you're thirty-seven, she's not quite seventeen. We just have to give her some space.'

'She can have all the fucking space she wants around here. There's nothing *but* space.'

'Come on, love. Leave her to it. I'll go and see to her, then I'll come back and make us both a cup of tea. Okay?'

'She needs to sort herself out. Bloody prima-donna.'

'Let me talk to her, Scott. Please.'

Half a bar appeared, then a whole bar, then two. Tammy was well away from the house now, walking along the road into Thussock. She dialled out, desperate not to lose the precious signal strength. The call was answered quickly. 'Dad? Dad, can you hear me?'

'Tam? I was just thinking about you. How're you doing? You settled in yet? What's the house like?'

It all came flooding out. She couldn't help it. 'I can't stand this bloody place, Dad. The house is vile and there's nothing to do here, and all I want is to go home...'

'Whoa, whoa... slow down. We talked about this. You knew it wasn't going to be easy, but you need to be with your mum and your sister and George and—'

'It's not them though, is it? It's *him*.'

'Come on, Princess, we talked about this too. I know you don't get on and I know he's had his problems, but he's trying. You just have to give it some time.'

'Can't I come and stay at yours?'

'You know you can't. I'm not around much at the moment, and I can't leave you on your own. Anyway, listen, I was going to try and call you later. I'm in Switzerland for a few days in a couple of weeks. I thought I could arrange to fly back into Edinburgh instead of Heathrow, then I could come and spend a few days with you and Phoebe. I'll have to check with your mum first, but I thought it could be good. You can show me the sights.'

'There aren't any.'

'Well you've got about ten days to find some, okay?'

'Ten days... I don't think I'll last ten more hours here.'

'Of course you will.'

The phone crackled. She stopped walking. 'Dad? Dad... you still there?'

An anxious pause, several seconds too long. 'I'm still here.'

'The signal's rubbish up here. I don't get it. We talked all the time when you were working in Kenya.'

'And Nigeria last winter.'

'It's just this place.'

'Hey, are you ready for school tomorrow?'

'Suppose.'

'You seen it yet?'

'Saw it this morning.'

'And?'

'And what am I supposed to say? It's a school. School's school.'

'Big day tomorrow, though. Hope it goes well.'

'Just as long as it goes...'

'Come on, Princess, cheer up. It's not that bad.'

'It *is* that bad. Honestly, Dad, you won't believe this place when you see it. It's a dump, and the people are all retards and chavs.'

'They can't all be retards and chavs, I don't believe that.'

'Like I said, wait 'til you come here.'

'I'll look forward to it. I'll try and give your mum a call later, sort things out. But Tam, just try and be positive, okay. I know it's hard, but—'

'You don't understand.'

'I can't hear you... you're breaking up. Tam...? Tammy?' She could still hear his voice, but he couldn't hear her. Then he disappeared altogether. Three bleeps of disconnection sliced through the silence, emphasising the separation. She just stared at the phone thinking *it worked in Kenya and Nigeria... why not in fucking Thussock?* It made it feel as if her dad was further away than ever, almost like he was on another planet.

She'd walked as far as the wooden bus shelter. She sat down on the uncomfortable bench inside.

'No buses for another twelve hours or so, love,' Michelle said, startling her. She'd followed her from the house. She gestured for her daughter to shuffle up and sat down. 'Get to talk to your dad?'

'A bit. Signal went.'

'He okay?'

'Fine.'

'Do you want to talk?'

'No, I want to go home.'

'We are home.'

'You know what I mean.'

Michelle swung her feet under the seat, the tips of her toes scuffing the gravel. It was impossibly quiet. From here the side of the shelter obscured the house belonging to the twins they'd seen earlier, and the curve of the road had hidden their own place. She realised that apart from the shelter and the road, she couldn't see anything else man-made. The isolation was useful. She could talk freely here. 'It's all a bit shitty, isn't it?'

'You can say that again.'

'I'm sorry.'

'Why are you apologising, Mum? It's not your fault.'

'I feel responsible. I helped make the decisions.'

'No you didn't. This was all down to Scott, it always is. Stop making excuses for him.'

'I'm not. Look, Tam, I know it's hard. I think it's probably harder on you and Phoebe than the rest of us.'

'You reckon? I don't. I think you've got it toughest.'

'Me? How?'

'Phoebe and me still have a way out. I know Dad's not around much at the moment, but he keeps saying he's going to jack his job in so we'll be able to spend more time at his, and there's uni and we'll get our own places eventually. But this is it for you, Mum. You're stuck with Scott.'

'Come on, that's not fair. Don't say that.'

'I just wish you'd never married him. Things were fine before he came along and you and Dad split up.'

'The two things weren't connected, Tam, and you know it. Your dad and I just grew apart. It happens. We still get on, though, and that's just about the best we could have hoped for in the circumstances.'

'Spare me, Mum, I'm not a kid anymore. I've heard this a hundred times and I get it – you fell out of love and now you're just friends. I don't have an issue with any of that. It's Scott I have a problem with. He treats you like shit.'

'That's not true. He's been under a huge amount of pressure since—'

'It *is* true.'

'For all his faults though, Tam, I love him. He infuriates me and he does some bloody stupid things at times, but I love him. Besides, we've got George. You think the world of your little brother.'

'I do, and none of this is his fault. When he was born Phoebe and I used to think having him would make everything okay and bring us closer together, make us feel like a real family.'

'We are a real family.'

'Hardly.'

'Come on...'

'Anyway, I've realised I got it wrong. Having George didn't bring us all together, it just stopped you and Scott from falling apart.'

'That's rubbish.'

'It's not.'

There was no talking to Tammy when she was in this kind of mood. Michelle just put her arm around her shoulder and pulled her closer. She didn't know what to say for the best and so said nothing. There were no right answers, no easy solutions. Christ, with Tammy pulling her one way and Scott the other, it was a wonder she hadn't been torn down the middle.

After a few seconds, Michelle stood up. She reached out her hand and pulled Tammy out of the shelter. The twins were working in their garden across the road. They'd changed now, both of them wearing matching baggy jeans and complementary T-shirts. 'You were right earlier,' Michelle said, watching them. 'They are a bit weird.'

Tammy laughed and wiped her eyes. 'I don't get how they're happy wanting to look the same? If I had an identical twin I'd want us both to look completely different.'

'Jeez, two of you... imagine that. I struggle enough with just the one.'

'Shut up!' Tammy said, leaning against her mum.

Michelle was about to speak when a car shot past them. The driver braked hard, then put the car in reverse and came skidding back towards them. He wound down his window. 'Youse two ladies all right here?'

Michelle and Tammy looked at each other, both struggling with the accent. Michelle subtly positioned herself in front of her daughter. She didn't like the look of the man in the car. Unshaven, with a horrible, wiry ponytail and wearing a grubby denim jacket and faded football shirt, he looked like he'd been wearing the same clothes since the mid-eighties. His car, a battered old Ford-something-or-other, might have been impressive twenty-odd years ago, but it definitely wasn't now. The paintwork was patchwork, and the knackered exhaust made it sound more like a tractor than a car. The bodywork was spattered with mud, like it had recently been taken off-road. Inside was no better. The floor and dash were covered in all kinds of crap, the back seat full of DVDs and drinks cans, and the rear windscreen was more stickers than glass.

'We're fine, thanks very much,' Michelle replied. He kept trying to look around her. She couldn't tell if he was trying to eye her up or Tammy. Probably both, she thought.

'You lost?'

'We're not lost.'

'You new?'

'Just moved in down the road,' she said, inadvertently giving him more information than she'd intended.

'The grey house?'

'Uh huh,' she replied, not about to risk saying anything else, feeling increasingly uncomfortable. The way he looked at her... the way he kept licking his lips with his snake-like tongue...

'You know there's no buses Sunday afternoons?'

'We noticed.'

'You could walk back from here. S'not far.'

'We know, that's how we got here,' Michelle said, trying not to laugh. 'We were just getting a little air. Getting to know the area.'

'I'll give you a lift. Plenty of room,' he said and he leant across and opened the passenger door. The worn velour seat would have looked just as uninviting had she known him. Now she was really starting to feel uncomfortable.

'No, thank you,' she said firmly. 'Honestly, we're fine.'

'Ah, go on. I've always plenty of space for two lovely ladies. You're not out my way. Last chance...?'

'We're okay, thanks,' Michelle told him.

The man in the car nodded, pulled the door shut again, then put his foot down and disappeared in a cloud of gravel and dust. She might have been impressed, she thought, had she been Tammy's age and it had still been nineteen eighty-nine.

3

By mid-evening the tension in the house had reduced to a slightly more bearable level. Michelle had been working in the living room for the last hour or so, arranging the little furniture they had and leaving spaces for the rest of their belongings to be slotted in tomorrow once the removal van had been and gone. George was in bed, Phoebe had crashed out on a beanbag with her face buried in a book, and Tammy was sitting on an inherited sofa which, Michelle hoped, would be dumped outside by this time tomorrow. Scott was messing with the TV, had been for a while. He'd just about managed to get a decent signal. The picture was occasionally distorted by bursts of blocky digital static but, on the whole, it was watchable.

'Can't we get Sky?' Phoebe asked, not looking up.

'We can't afford it,' Michelle said quickly, hoping to nip the conversation in the bud before anyone could get any other ideas. She failed.

'I'll ask in town tomorrow,' Scott said.

'Just the basic package if we do. That's all we need,' Michelle warned.

'And the sports channels.'

'You had all those extra channels in Redditch and no one ever watched them.'

'I never had time back in Redditch. Anyway, I need to get the Internet sorted and the phone. Might as well get a bundle. It'll work out cheaper that way.'

'There's a free version, isn't there?' Tammy said. 'Hannah had something. Freesat, I think it was called. You have a dish and a box, but you only get the free channels.'

'Might be worth looking into?' Michelle said.

'Can't get the sports channels,' Scott said, still messing with the TV. 'Not worth it if you can't get the sports channels.'

'Can you even get satellite TV out here? Isn't it a bit remote?'

Phoebe put down her book and sighed. 'We're in Scotland, Mum, not on Mars. What, do you think satellites don't fly over here?'

'Haven't really thought much about it.'

Phoebe looked back down, then back up again. 'You know what, I actually think this place is going to be all right,' she said, surprising the rest of them. They all looked at her, as if demanding an explanation. 'I'm serious. I mean, it's not like being home, but I think we'll get used to it.'

'Speak for yourself,' Tammy grumbled.

'Good for you, Pheeb,' Michelle said. 'It's nice to hear someone being so positive. We need a bit of positivity around here.'

'We need a *lot* of positivity,' Scott agreed.

Nauseated by the sudden abundance of forced positive vibes, Tammy turned up the TV. It was the usual Sunday night shite they were watching, but it was a welcome distraction nonetheless. Without the Internet or a reliable phone signal, the TV felt like the only tenable connection she still had with the world she'd been forced to leave behind. Strange how reassuring it was seeing adverts she'd seen a hundred times before, and listening to theme tunes she knew note for note. Strange also how jarring it was when things weren't as she'd expected. When the national news bulletin ended and the announcer handed over to regional newsrooms, the graphics and theme music seemed all wrong – almost like what she remembered, but not quite. This programme was *Scotland Tonight*, not *Midlands Today*, and it would take some getting used to. The presenter's face was unfamiliar, she'd never heard of any of the place names, and the woman's accent was all wrong... Tammy stopped listening and thought about home again, no longer paying attention.

'That's horrible,' Michelle said. 'Absolutely horrible.'

'What is?'

Michelle nodded at the TV. 'They found a body.'

The picture threatened to break up again, then steadied. On the screen Tammy saw an area of woodland, criss-crossed with police 'do not cross' tape. There was a white forensic tent in the middle of the space. It reminded her of the gazebo Dad used to put up in the garden when he did barbeques before he and Mum split up. Officers in all-in-one white forensics romper suits worked around the scene.

'What happened?'

'Some poor woman,' Michelle said. 'Murdered.'

'So they found her, then,' Scott said. 'We saw them out looking yesterday afternoon, remember?'

The TV cut to a reporter loitering on the public side of the police cordon, the tent visible over his shoulder. 'The body was found late last night by a security guard. Cause of death has yet to be established, although we understand the woman may have been the victim of a sexually-motivated attack. An eye-witness described the body as being in a state of partial undress and having been badly mutilated. Falrigg is popular with fell runners and walkers and police are appealing for anyone who might have been in the area over the course of the last twenty-four hours to come forward. Formal identification of the body has not yet been made, and police have so far refused to comment on any links with the disappearance of Joan Lummock. Mrs Lummock of Glennaird has been missing since Thursday evening.'

'Nice,' Phoebe said. 'Is that far from here?'

'It's about a twenty minute drive,' Scott said. Michelle looked at him and he felt compelled to explain. 'The tip's not far from there, if I'm thinking of the right place.'

'Lovely area you've brought us to, Scott,' Tammy said, goading for a fight.

'Come on,' he protested, 'it's not like there were never any murders in the Midlands.'

'Ignore her, she's just cranky,' Michelle said.

'Damn right I'm cranky.'

'Shouldn't you girls be going to bed?' he said. 'Big day tomorrow. First day at your new school.'

'I'm sixteen, Scott, not six,' she reminded him. She changed the TV channel, then looked across at him. 'Sorry, were you watching that?'

'Ah, you're fine,' he said, and he got up and walked away. Tammy was past caring anyway. She scrolled through the limited channels until she found something completely dumb and inoffensive, and she switched off her brain and soaked it up.

4

The morning arrived too soon. 'Stop treating me like a little kid,' Tammy complained as they drove up the high street towards school.

'I'm not,' Scott said. 'I'm just checking you've got everything, that's all.'

'It's not like we've never been to school before,' Phoebe grumbled from the back. 'Just not *this* school.'

'Can't you just drop us here?' Tammy asked. 'We'll follow the other kids.'

'I told your mum I'd take you all the way to the gates, so that's what I'm going to do.'

'Jesus, don't. Just stop on the other side of the road or something. Don't take us right up to the gates.'

She looked across and he caught her eye. *He's actually enjoying this.* He stopped just short of the entrance to the school in the worst possible place. Hordes of kids swarmed past on either side. Tammy got out fast and slammed the door. Phoebe scrambled out after her, running to catch up. Tammy froze when she heard the car horn. Phoebe started to turn back, but Tammy grabbed her quick. 'Don't,' she said. 'He's just winding us up.'

'Have a good first day, girls,' they heard him shout. 'Stay safe and be good!'

'He's such a prick,' Tammy said, her face red with anger and embarrassment.

They followed the signs for Reception, sticking close to each other as they walked towards the main building, trying to avoid all eye contact. It was a walk of shame, everyone else stopping and looking at them, *staring* at them.

'It's like that horrible TV programme Dad used to watch, remember?' Phoebe whispered.

'Which one?'

'The one with the *local shop for local people*. You remember? The freak behind the counter who was married to his sister, and they were all played by the same blokes.'

'I remember. *League of Gentlemen*. Didn't like it.'

She was right though. Walking through the crowds this morning, Tammy felt like a social outcast. The kids seemed to part when they got close, like they didn't want to touch them. The feeling was mutual.

'There's that boy,' Phoebe said.

'What boy?'

'From outside the shop yesterday. Jamie, wasn't it?'

Tammy looked up but looked down again the moment she made eye contact. Boy was definitely the right word. He'd looked quite mature when they'd seen him yesterday but, standing there in his school uniform, he looked like just another kid playing at being a man. She kept her head down, but Jamie had other ideas, making a beeline for her. 'Hello again,' he said. Tammy ignored him. She didn't want to get overfamiliar with any of these kids. In fact, she didn't want to get familiar at all.

'Which way's Reception?' she asked, no time for small-talk.

'You've missed it.'

'Which way?'

'Go back the way you just came. First left.'

Tammy turned around and pulled Phoebe back through the heaving crowds. 'That was a bit rude,' Phoebe said.

'You're welcome,' Jamie shouted. 'Have a good day now.'

The corridor looked the same both ways. It was a long, symmetrical straight line with a set of identical double doors at either end. It didn't feel right. Hell, it didn't even *smell* right. Tammy couldn't ever remember feeling so out of place.

They missed the turn again, but found it on their third pass. Once they'd introduced themselves to the lady on the reception desk they, in turn, were introduced to the principal, to a couple more teachers who just happened to be passing, and then to Mr Renner, the school's one man pastoral team. Mr Renner gave them an embarrassingly brief tour of the school's facilities, then delivered them to their respective form tutors. Tammy looked over her shoulder as they were led off in opposite directions along the front corridor, watching her little sister disappear.

*

He'd never have admitted it, but Scott thought he was probably as nervous as the kids. After dropping them at school he'd driven back into Thussock to look for work. It was going to be no easy task, that much was clear. The brewery was laying off staff, not taking on, and though they told him he could try again in a month or so, the fracking company were only looking for engineers and specialists at the moment. Thussock didn't even have a job centre, it seemed. How was he supposed to find a job if the damn place didn't even have a bloody job centre? He toyed with the idea of driving to the next town, but it was too far and there didn't seem a lot of point. It would have been a hell of a commute if he'd found work there, and it would probably only have been financially viable if he'd managed to get a job requiring far more responsibility and commitment than he was prepared to give. He wanted something quick and easy: enough to put food on the table and still give him the funds and flexibility he needed to start work on the house, because the sooner he started working on the house, the sooner he'd be back on his feet again.

He parked up near the half-empty retail development they'd visited yesterday. He could see that crazy Graham guy, struggling to keep a snaking chain of shopping trolleys under control, and he thought to himself, *if a weird fucker like that can get a job here, surely I shouldn't have any trouble?*

Fuck it. There was nothing left for it. He was going to have to go door to door (if he could find any doors still open) and see if he could find anything that way. Chances were slim, but it was worth a try. And while he was there, he thought, he could try and find someone to talk to about getting Sky installed.

Nothing. Absolutely bloody nothing.

He went into a few places and looked through the windows of others, but no one had anything. The library didn't open until later, and the lady manning the tourist information kiosk had plenty of ideas of places to try outside Thussock, but next to nothing in the town itself. Scott stood outside the Black Boy pub, wishing it was a few hours later. He'd have propped up the bar for a while if it had been open. Pulling pints wasn't beneath him, and even if the landlord didn't have any work available, there was a chance he might know someone who did.

Christ, job hunting was tedious. His heart really wasn't in it. He wanted to work for himself again, to be his own boss and not have to answer to anyone else. It would be a while before that happened.

It was too soon to give up and go home, so Scott kept walking. Without the distraction of his family – their constant bickering and complaints – he saw more of Thussock this morning, things he'd missed previously. There was a small police station opposite the pub, a branch of a Scottish bank he'd never even heard of, and a betting shop that looked busier than pretty much everywhere else. A little further and he'd reached the bridge over the river. He stopped, leant over the balustrade, and peered down into the murky waters.

'Don't do it, son,' a man shouted, grabbing Scott's back and scaring the hell out of him.

'Wasn't planning on it,' he said quickly as the elderly gent walked on, laughing with his mates.

Scott realised he was almost back at the school. Bloody hell, he was rapidly running out of town. He thought about going down to the rail station, figuring that if he was going to have to commute, maybe public transport would be a better option. It wasn't what he wanted, but if there were no jobs here, what else could he do? Surely there'd be work in Edinburgh or Glasgow or somewhere between?

He stopped to cross a narrow side street, and had to pull himself back quick when a dusty builder's merchant's truck thundered past and swerved out onto the main road. He looked down the street to check there was nothing else coming and saw a sign on the fence the same as the logo on the side of the truck that had almost hit him. Walpoles. Strange name, he thought. The sign might as well have said 'Welcome to Dodge', because it looked pretty desolate down there. *Less the Wild West*, he thought, *more like the Numb North*, and he laughed at his own pathetic joke as he followed the track down into a decent-sized builders yard. Scott thought this place looked slightly more promising. The familiarity of bricks, tiles, cement and sand was welcome and, if nothing else, he figured he might be able to price up the materials he needed for the kitchen wall. The sooner he made a start on that the better. He'd heard what Michelle had said yesterday, but she was looking at it all wrong as she so often did.

And if he couldn't find work, which seemed increasingly likely, then wasn't this the perfect time to get done everything that needed doing to the house?

Walpoles looked like a typical builder's merchant's place: a dust-bowl of a yard with pallets of bricks, slabs, joists and various other mounds of material dotted all around. It looked scruffy and rough, as behind the times as the rest of Thussock, but it reminded him of the work he used to do and the business he'd built up from nothing then lost. Three hundred and fifty miles away from home he might well have been, but a brick was a brick wherever you found it.

He couldn't see any prices. He walked over to a pallet loaded with sacks of plaster, the whole thing still wrapped in plastic like it had just been delivered. 'Help you there?' a gruff, barely understandable voice asked. Scott turned around and saw a short, stocky, balding man standing behind him. He wore a grubby blue polo shirt with the 'W' from Walpoles embroidered on the breast pocket.

'Just looking, thanks.'

'Not the kind of place folks usually browse, this,' the man said, and Scott thought he should explain.

'Just pricing up. I've bought a house not far outside town. Got a few alterations planned.'

'You in the trade?'

'Yes and no.'

'What's that supposed to mean?'

'I was,' he answered, 'until I moved up here.'

'You in the grey house?'

'Haven't heard it called that before, but yes, it's grey. Needs a lick of paint.'

'On the road into Thussock.'

'That's the one.'

'Willy McCunnie's old place.'

'Was it?'

'Aye. Poor old Willy. Terrible, that was...'

Scott paused, uneasy. 'You sound like you know something I don't. You gonna tell me a horror story or something? Something bad happen there?'

'Not that I know of. Lovely guy, Willy.'

'What happened to him?'

'He died.'

'Oh.'

'Ninety-two he was.'

'Oh,' Scott said again.

'Cancer.'

'Right.'

'So what're you doing?'

'What?'

'To the house. What you plannin'?'

'Complete overhaul by the time I'm done. The place needs gutting. Heating, wiring... Got some structural stuff to do first. Couple of walls to knock through, that sort of thing. Probably replace the kitchen and bathroom, maybe add a conservatory... like I said, pretty much a complete renovation.'

He nodded thoughtfully. Scott waited for him to say something, and had to wait a little longer than was comfortable. 'You need to talk to Barry,' he eventually said.

'Barry?'

'Barry Walpole. This is his yard, see. I don't know what terms he's doing at the moment. We just shift stuff about for him, he likes to do all the figures and the sellin' himself.'

'I'm not looking for any favours.'

'Good. Barry won't do you any.'

'So where is he?'

'Just gone out in the van to kick a supplier up the arse. Bugger short-changed him.'

'Not a good move?'

'Nope. You don't upset Barry. You should come back later.'

'Okay. Any idea when he's due back?'

'Nope.'

'Right.'

'Give it an hour.'

'Okay. Is there a number I can get him on?'

'He has a mobile.'

'Great.'

'But he leaves it here. Doesn't like carrying it.'

'Isn't that why they're called mobiles? So you can carry them around?'

'Like I said, give it an hour.'

Scott turned to leave. He wasn't getting anywhere. He started back towards the driveway and passed a grubby caravan he'd barely noticed on the way in. It was obviously being used as an office, and equally obviously had been parked in the same spot for some considerable time. There were piles of bricks propping it up at either end, the tyres were flat, and the curved roof had been stained green by fallen leaves and bird muck from the overhanging trees. In the window was a handwritten sign. It simply read 'Driver wanted'. Scott looked back at the man and pointed at the sign.

'Talk to Barry,' he said.

'Warren says you're lookin' for work?'

'That's right.'

'And you've got experience?'

'I can drive a truck, if that's what you mean.'

'It's not. You know about the trade?'

'Absolutely. I've had more than fifteen years experience, both working for myself and being employed on plenty of sites. Small scale domestics right up to large corporates. I was a project manager with—'

'Fair enough. That'll do.'

Barry Walpole chewed the end of an already well-chewed pen and watched him. Scott could handle himself, but Barry was an imposing character. Six feet tall and probably the same wide, he'd had to turn sideways just to get through the caravan door. The floor had groaned under his weight. The usual fitted furniture had either been stripped out of the van or had worn out, and Barry sat on a threadbare swivel chair behind a desk piled high with unsorted papers. There was a filing cabinet in one corner and a key cabinet screwed to the wall. The door of the key cabinet swung open several times and he slammed it shut as though he was swatting a nuisance fly. He took a swig from a mug of coffee, then put the cup down on a mountain of invoices. The silence was increasingly uncomfortable. Scott felt obliged to try and fill it. 'So, how long have you been in business here?' he asked.

'Long enough.'

'Trade good?'

'S'all right. Shouldn't complain but I usually do.'

'Getting any business from that fracking thing over the way?'

'Nope,' he said and he leant forward and stared into Scott's face. 'Listen, this is one of those interviews when I ask the questions, right? So tell me this, why you here?'

Trick question? 'Because you need a driver...?'

'No, not here, *here*. Why d'you come to Thussock? Warren says you've bought Willy's old house. Why d'you do that?'

'We wanted a change of scene. A change of lifestyle, I guess.'

'Just you and the missus?'

'Three kids. One son, two step-daughters.'

'You from the Midlands, ain't you?'

'Yep.'

'Then I call bullshit.'

'What?'

'You heard me. I don't buy it.'

'I don't really care if you—'

'Look, man, I don't really give a shit who drives the bloody truck for me. Thing is, I don't do bullshit, that's all. No one moves their entire bloody family to a place like Thussock for the fun of it. Be straight and honest with me and we'll get along fine. If you ain't, then we won't get along at all.'

Scott took a deep breath. Obnoxious fucker. Did he really need this? He was on the verge of walking out. For fuck's sake, this was just some two-bit driving job. This Walpole bloke could shove it if he was going to be this anal. But he stopped himself. It was pride swallowing time. He needed cash, and this would do until he found something better or got the business up and running again. *Lay it on thick*, he thought, *make him think you're pouring your heart out*. 'I took on too much. Over-stretched myself. Lost a couple of blokes, defaulted on a loan payment and the bank threatened to pull the plug. I wound things down before they could wind the business up. Same old same old... happens all the time.'

Barry nodded and chewed his pen again. 'It don't take much these days. Never trust banks, me. Try and avoid them.'

'Bit late for business advice now.'

'So why Thussock?'

'Why not?'

'I could give you a hundred reasons.'

'Fair enough. Distance, I guess. We wanted a clean break. It's over three hundred miles. Six hour drive.'

'You runnin' away?'

Scott shook his head. 'Like I said, clean break. Fresh start.'

'So how do I know you're not gonna throw a wobbler and disappear? Go back to wherever you're from?'

'I won't. We bought the house. Sold the assets of the business and paid cash. We want to settle here. Every penny we own has been sunk into that place.'

Barry rocked back on his chair again. 'There's not a lot of work going round here right now.'

'I'd noticed.'

'You might have had it shitty in Birmingham or wherever you're from, but it ain't much better up here.'

'I didn't expect it to be.'

'I need someone I can rely on, understand?'

'I get it.'

Barry locked eyes with Scott and wouldn't look away. Scott held his gaze, figuring this was some kind of bizarre initiation test. It was. 'It's important to be able to look the other fella in the eye,' Barry said after he'd been staring a little too long.

'Is it?'

'Absolutely. Key to a man's soul.'

'That right?'

Barry didn't answer. He hunted around the desk for a scrap of paper to take down Scott's details. 'You're a lucky bugger, Scotty lad. Right place, right time, an' all that.'

'You're giving me the job?'

'I'm giving you a try-out. When can you start?'

'As soon as.'

'This afternoon?'

'Why not. I'll need to go home first, tell the missus. She'll need the car to get the kids from school.'

'Fair enough. Pick up some ID, your bank details, national insurance number, drivin' licence, all that crap, and make sure you're back here by one.'

'A good day all round then,' Michelle said at dinner. 'All our furniture's in, you two have settled in at school, and Scott's got a job.'

'I wouldn't say we're settled in,' Tammy said quickly, keen to put her straight.

'No, but your first day's over. That's something.'

'Made any new friends?' Scott asked.

She glared at him. 'Hundreds. You?'

He ignored her sarcasm. 'They must think I'm stupid. I can't understand a bloody word they're saying half the time.'

'What's your boss like?' Phoebe asked, wolfing down her dinner.

'Miserable bugger,' Scott replied. 'Huge, he is. Gave me a right grilling too. Asked all kinds of questions about why we'd moved and why we're here.'

'Were you honest with him?' Tammy said.

'Give it a rest, Tam,' Michelle said, interrupting before the conversation degenerated into another fight.

'Is it a nice place?' Phoebe asked him.

'Is where a nice place?'

'The place you're working?'

He shrugged. 'It's a yard. They're all dumps. It's not that far from your school.'

'And they liked you?'

'They want me back in the morning, so I guess so. That reminds me, you'll have to drop me off, Chelle. You can do it when you take the kids to school. And I'll need picking up after five. Okay?'

'No problem. It'll be nice to have the car. I was going to walk into town with George anyway.'

'What for?'

'Shopping, register us all at the doctor's surgery, that kind of thing. All very exciting.'

'More exciting than school,' Tammy moaned. Michelle ignored her.

'It's all coming together nicely,' she said. 'If things are going this well after a couple of days, just think what it'll be like in a few weeks.'

Later, lying in bed together, lights out, Michelle felt Scott's hand on her under the covers. She'd almost been asleep, but she was awake again in seconds. 'Hello you,' she whispered.

'Hello you.'

'You all right?'

'I'm fine.'

He slipped his hand under her nightie uninvited, cupped her breast.

'Starting to feel good, isn't it?' she said.

'It is to me.'

'I'm not talking about my boobs, I'm talking about us... about being here. The girls seem more relaxed tonight, and you've managed to find some work. I've got a good feeling. This is going to work out, you know. If you'd said a couple of months ago that we could have all this, I'd never have believed you.'

'I don't let you down, Chelle. You should know that.'

'I do. It's just that sometimes you have to take a few steps back to start moving forward again, don't you?'

'Nice cliché.'

'It's true. Seriously, love, if you're happy, I'm happy and the kids are happy, it doesn't matter where we're living. I'm really proud of you, you know... just walking into a job like that.'

'It's no great shakes. I'm just driving a knackered old truck around, delivering bricks and shit.'

'It's a start. You never know, your boss might let you have stuff cheap, make it easier to do all the things you were talking about doing to the house.'

'Doubt it. You haven't met Barry Walpole.'

'I'm sure he's lovely.'

'He definitely isn't. You are, though.'

His compliment took her by surprise. Before she could react she felt him kiss the side of her face. He climbed on top and pushed against her. 'I'm tired, love,' she said.

'I'm not.'

THE YOUTH HOSTEL AT GLENFIRTH

It never ceased to amaze Mairead how little respect folks had for the property of others. This building was here for the good of the community as a whole, and yet people seemed perfectly content to use and abuse the facilities without a care.

The old farm had stopped being a farm more than two decades ago now. After falling into disrepair, the one remaining habitable building, this two bedroom cottage, had been renovated and re-opened as a very basic youth hostel, catering to the needs of visitors attracted to the area by the hills and the hiking. On the whole people usually abided by the basic rules of the facility: pre-bookings only, clean the place when you leave, collect and return the key to Mairead down the road. But the girl who'd used the place last night hadn't returned the key and Mairead needed it back as three lads from Newcastle were due later this afternoon. She had better things to be doing with her time than chasing around after bloody kids who thought the world owed them. She'd put all her cleaning stuff in the back of the car before she set out. *If the lass couldn't be bothered to hand back the key*, she thought, *then she sure as hell won't have cleaned up.*

The cottage door was open. The building was cold, but then again, it usually was. Mairead leant in and called out. 'Hello... Hello, is anyone here?'

No answer.

Agitated, Mairead put her Hoover down by the door. This had happened all too often this season. The remains of a meal had been left on the table. Slovenly. It made Mairead cross. And she could smell tobacco too. Bloody hell, how large did she have to make the *No Smoking* signs? There was one stuck on every interior door. Was that not enough?

The kitchen could have been worse, she supposed. There was a little washing up left on the draining board, and a pile of clothes which had been washed and rinsed but never hung out to dry.

'Hello...' Mairead shouted again. 'Are you here, Miss? I've come for the key. I'll have to make a charge for the state of the place. It's really not good enough.'

She picked up a waste-bin and carried it over to the bedroom door. She knocked and waited for a reply. When she moved again, the floor was tacky beneath her shoes.

Mairead looked down and saw blood. More blood than she'd ever seen before.

5

'It's not my fault. I didn't take your order. No good shouting at me, mate.'

Kenneth Potter pointed accusingly at Scott. 'Then who else am I going to shout at? And I am definitely not your mate. Good grief, what's Barry doing employing folks who can't even load up a van right?'

'Listen...'

'No, laddie, you listen. Barry and I go back a long way. I taught him and most of the men who work in his yard. I've never had any problems before, and I don't understand why I'm having one now. Fence panels, concrete, sand and fence *posts*. Did you not stop to think? Christ's sake... how am I to repair a fence if I've not got any bloody posts? Should I just balance the bloody fence panels on their side and hope the wind doesn't blow them over? I mean, come on... it's not rocket science.'

Scott bit his lip. He'd been warned about this little fucker. He wondered if the blokes at the yard had done this on purpose, screwing up Ken Potter's order as some kind of fucked-up initiation? Or had they done it to get back at Potter himself? He'd noticed them all muttering to themselves when the order had come through. *Ah well, I've handled worse. Remember that job in Alvechurch when they set your boots in the concrete...*

'Well?' Potter demanded. Scott knew he had little option but to take this one on the chin and head back to the yard to get the missing posts.

'I'll go and get the rest of the order,' he said, making little effort to disguise his frustration. 'I might as well unload what I have for you, then come back. It'll take about an hour.'

'I'll not sign for any of it.'

'Whatever.'

'Anything you leave here remains your responsibility until I've received everything I've ordered, understand?'

'Loud and clear.'

Scott started to unload the truck, working around Potter who watched him, arms folded, eyes following his every move. No one was going to pinch any of this stuff. As Potter himself had said, what good was a fence without posts? And anyway, there was no one else here. No other houses for miles.

The morning had been going reasonably well until then. He'd had a number of small loads to deliver, all going to folks in locations which seemed to be both miles from the yard and miles from each other. He'd been starting to think that this job, although hopefully only temporary, might not be as bad as he'd originally expected. Out here alone in the truck he had time to think, to try and work everything out. At home there was always something – *someone* – who wanted something from him, but his time out here was almost his own. His mobile signal dropped regularly and Barry Walpole didn't believe in satnavs, apparently, so it looked like most of the time it was just going to be him, his maps and the open road. It was surprisingly relaxing. It could have been a lot worse.

The job was way beneath him, though. He'd managed complex projects before now where he'd had to coordinate large numbers of staff and trades to hit specific deadlines, so this was easy by comparison. Getting five bags of sand to one location, then a number of timber joists to the next... it was all straightforward. But one thing had taken him by surprise, and that was the sheer scale of everything. Before they'd come here, he'd imagined Thussock and the surrounding area to be twee and small. The reality was very different. The landscape was immense, unending. This was a vast, sprawling place, often with many miles between communities, sometimes between neighbours. In the half hour or so it had taken him to get to Kenneth Potter's house from his last drop off, he'd seen only two other cars and a solitary hiker walking along the side of the road. He'd driven along an otherwise empty road which ran along the foothills of a mountain he couldn't even see the top of. Even the largest landmarks back home would be dwarfed by this enormous mound of rock. It was awe-inspiring, strangely humbling.

The practical differences between this place and Redditch had been hammered home last night when he'd tried to get petrol. It was past ten, and the only filling station in the town had been shut. He'd managed to get online using his phone, and had located another station some thirty-five miles away. He'd probably had enough in the tank to get there, but he'd decided not to risk it. It was strange just how isolated it had made him feel. What if that one was closed too, or what if he got lost and took a wrong turn which led him down another endless road where he might have run out of fuel and ended up stranded? He'd given Michelle the money instead, leaving her with instructions to fill the car up in Thussock later.

When he got back to the yard, Barry Walpole was waiting for him. 'What the hell's goin' on? I've had Ken Potter on the phone, tearing a strip off me.'

'It's not my fault,' Scott protested. 'No good shouting at me. I never loaded the bloody van.'

'You should 'a checked it 'fore you went out.'

'It's my first day. I didn't know the routine. You should have told me if I was supposed to check the bloody load first. I assumed it would have already been done. What's the matter with you people?'

'It'll be your last day if you don't bite your lip. You know who you're talking to?'

'Yeah, someone who's accusing me of fucking up when I haven't. I'll load the fucking van myself next time.'

'Next time? You think there's gonna be a next time after this?'

Scott marched away, ready to leave this power-crazed arsehole and his bumbling staff behind and not look back. Warren blocked his way through. 'What?' he yelled. Warren looked past him and at Barry.

'My fault, Baz.'

'What?'

'I said it's my fault. I got the manifest wrong, not him.'

'Ya bloody idiot. Get 'em on the truck.'

Scott watched Warren scuttle away then glared at Barry, waiting for an apology that didn't come.

'You've a quick temper and a foul mouth, Scott. You should fit in nicely here, long as you don't piss me off. I'll come with you and make the drop at Ken's. I'll phone him now and say we're on our way. We'll give him a hand with his fence, make up for the delay.'

Barry returned to his caravan office, leaving Scott alone in the middle of the yard, stunned by the ineptitude of pretty much everyone he'd so far met in Thussock.

The drive back to Potter's house seemed to take twice as long second time around. Maybe it was the fact Scott knew this trip was unnecessary, or maybe it was just because Barry was with him. Whatever the reason, Scott would have rather done this on his own.

'Ken's a good friend, but he's always been a bit of a bugger,' Barry said. 'It's 'cause he was a teacher. Taught most folks round here, actually. He likes things done jus' right, know what I'm saying?'

'I get it,' Scott said. He could see why he was such good friends with Barry. They were both angry old bastards, both cut from the same cloth.

The goods Scott had delivered earlier were where he'd left them on the verge, but there was no sign of Potter himself. He'd expected him to come charging out of his house again at the sound of the truck's engine, ready to berate Barry for employing this useless southerner. In fact, he'd half expected him to be out in the road, clock-watching. Scott parked up then waited as Barry marched up to the front of the house and hammered on the porch door. 'You in, Ken?'

No response. Barry looked back at Scott, then knocked again. When the door remained unanswered, he took a few steps back then peered in through a downstairs window. Scott got out of the truck and stood beside him. 'No sign?'

'Daft sod's probably asleep.'

Scott felt as if he'd found a hole in time, a wormhole letting him stare back into the seventies. Everything about this house was so... *antiquated*. Yes, that was definitely the right word. He'd had the same feeling when he'd first walked into his own house – the grey house, as Barry had called it yesterday. Paint was peeling from the metal frames of Potter's windows, no uPVC or double-glazing here. Was it that this place was struggling to keep up with the modern world or, as Scott was beginning to think, was it just not interested in catching up? No one in Thussock was concerned about keeping up with the Joneses. Christ, from here you couldn't even *see* the Joneses.

Barry knocked the door again. Still nothing. 'This don't make sense. He was spitting feathers on the phone.'

'Shall I just start unloading? I'll shift all his stuff round the back. Get us back in his good books.'

'Good idea, Scotty. You get to it. I'll keep trying.'

The driveway continued up the side of the house and, at the far end of the drive, Scott saw that a section of fence was missing. There was a pile of old rotten panels there too, dumped out of view behind Potter's heap of a car. He went through the gap in the fence, wondering why Potter hadn't answered. He might have fallen asleep as Barry suggested, all the exertion of his vociferous complaining tiring him out. He might have been out walking his dog (if he had one), or visiting a neighbour (though he didn't seem to have any of those either). After the noise and bluster of earlier, his non-appearance was irritating more than concerning.

At the back of the house was an ugly concrete patio which hadn't been touched in years. It was covered with mottled, ground-in dirt, dotted with patches of moss and persistent weeds which had patiently forced their way up through the narrowest of cracks. Potter obviously wasn't particularly interested in maintaining his property to any great extent. Judging by the state of the rest of the house, he was only fixing the fence because it had collapsed.

Scott looked at every place he saw with builder's eyes. Maybe if he could get on the right side of Potter he could give him his details and quote for some of the immediate repairs which needed doing? From the outside décor and style, he thought the house was probably built in the twenties or thirties. There was a large patch of rendering missing from around one of the windows, and an equally large damp patch under the eaves of the roof (which sagged in the middle somewhat).

'Mr Potter?' he shouted, looking in through a back window. 'You here, Mr Potter?'

The interior decoration looked as dated as everything else. The sitting room floor was cluttered with piles of newspapers and stacks of books, all centred around a grubby, well-worn armchair which was angled towards a TV so old Scott thought it looked steam-driven. He rapped his knuckles on the glass and shouted again.

When Scott turned around, he noticed something strange in one of the flowerbeds. In contrast to the house itself, the rest of Potter's garden was reasonably well-tended. The lawn had recently been mowed and the beds were a riot of colour, and that made it harder to understand why he could see what he was seeing. It was a bare foot, toes pointing upwards. He took a step forward then hesitated, uneasy. Had Potter had an accident out here?

'Scott, I don't know where the hell he's—' Barry started to say, stepping through the hole in the fence. He stopped speaking when he saw it. 'What the hell's that?'

The two men walked further down the garden together in silence. The body in the flowerbed was definitely not Kenneth Potter. It was a young girl, and it was clear even from a distance that she was dead. Scott didn't get too close because he didn't need to. He could tell from her ice-white skin, her frozen expression and her unblinking eyes that she was gone. For several seconds all he could do was stare deep into those eyes, unable to look away.

From where they were both standing, a large Rhododendron bush obscured much of the girl's body, covering her chest down to her feet. Barry moved slightly, trying to get a better view, but not sure if he should. He leant down and moved part of the bush away, immediately wishing he hadn't. 'Jesus...' he said. 'Bloody hell...' He staggered back, tripping over the straps of a discarded rucksack and ending up on his backside on the grass, scrambling away. Scott helped him up.

'You know her?'

'Never seen her before.'

Scott looked back at the house, half expecting Ken Potter to appear, gunning for the two of them. The mad bastard must have done this girl in, then made a run for it.

'What the hell happened?' Barry said, still backing-up.

Scott moved around to see what Barry had seen. He kept his eyes on the girl's face, and it felt for a moment as if he and the corpse were the only two things left in the world. He looked down at her feet – one wedged in the mud, still wearing a thick hiking sock, the naked toes of the other still pointing skywards – then at her legs. And then, much as he didn't want to, much as he knew he shouldn't, he lifted his eyes further.

Fuck.

It was hard to make out exactly what he was looking at. He didn't mean to stare, but it was impossible to look away. Between the girl's pale white thighs was a mass of blood, torn tissue and pubic hair. Still wet. Glistening. Maybe still warm. It looked like blood had gushed, not trickled, from her horrific eviscerations. There were pools of it in the flower bed, crimson puddles under her buttocks. And yet, despite having crushed the plants where she'd fallen, there were no immediately obvious signs of a struggle. The blood was strangely contained.

Scott walked away from the corpse, his head spinning. 'We need to call the police,' he said, tapping his pockets and checking for his phone. He'd left it in the truck. He turned to go fetch it.

'Where you going?' Barry asked.

'Phone. In the truck.'

Barry followed him, not wanting to be left alone with the dead girl. 'Wait... Ken wouldn't have done this.'

'Then who did?' Scott demanded, grabbing his phone from the glovebox. He checked the screen. No signal. No surprise.

'No, no... this isn't right... He's panicked, is all. Someone else did this and Ken's found her and panicked.'

Scott shook his head and tried the phone anyway. Christ, why hadn't he spent more time thinking about the practicalities of dragging his family to the ends of the Earth like this? Shitty phone coverage, fuel stations about half a tank apart, blood-soaked bodies dumped in forests and retired school teacher's back gardens... He went back towards the house. 'I'll try the landline.'

'What if Ken's in there?'

'Then you can talk to him. He's your mate.'

Scott tried the back door. It was unlocked. He opened it but paused before going inside. If he hadn't had Barry with him, he thought he might have just got back in the truck, driven away and pleaded ignorance later.

'Anyone here? Mr Potter... you in?'

He was standing in the middle of the kitchen, a room as antiquated and untidy as the rest of the house. Strange. There was a half-drunk mug of tea on the counter and an unfinished sandwich, just a couple of bites taken. He touched the side of the cup and it was still warm. Had Ken Potter simply decided to kill that girl right in the middle of his lunch? And there was only one drink and one plate of food... had she turned up unannounced? Had he murdered her on a whim?

'Ken,' Barry shouted, his voice echoing. 'You here, Ken?'

'I reckon he's long gone.'

'I'll phone for help,' Barry said, squeezing past and going out into the hallway. He looked around constantly as he picked up the telephone and called the police. Scott followed him out and listened to the empty house around them. He was sure they were alone. Potter had clearly done what he'd done then made a run for it. Strange, then, that he hadn't taken his car.

'Well?' Scott said as Barry replaced the receiver.

'Sergeant Ross says he's on way. Says he's stuck dealing with something else first. We best wait in the truck. Don't want to be takin' any chances.'

It was more than an hour before the police arrived. Barry knew each of the men in uniform personally. Sergeant Dan Ross was clearly in charge – older than the others, grey haired, and, it seemed, in no mood to take any crap. With him was PC Mark Hamilton, half the sergeant's age, but just as professional, and PC Craig Phillips, an altogether more relaxed officer. He remained with the two men in Potter's cluttered living room while the others secured the scene and waited for back-up to arrive. Barry excused himself and went to the toilet leaving Scott with PC Phillips.

'I knew he was a wrong-un,' the PC whispered. Scott was shocked by his lack of professionalism. 'Can't say I'm surprised. My old man always said he was capable of it.'

'Capable of what?'

'Doin' what he's done. You pissed him off at school and you knew you was in trouble.'

'He taught you as well?'

'Very few folks round here Ken Potter didn't teach. Half of Thussock would have been out in the streets celebrating if he'd been the one found dead in the flowerbed.'

'So what happens now?'

'Big one, this is,' the officer explained, giving away too much information but apparently unconcerned. 'We've got everyone working on it. Ties in with the others.'

'The others?'

'Aye. Glennaird and Falrigg. Joan Lummock? You must'a seen it on the news.'

'I saw something...'

'Never thought it'd be Ken Potter, though. Sick bastard. Still, we'll have him before long. He won't get far. Everybody round here knows him. I'll look forward to seeing him banged up. Might sell a few tickets to that one.'

6

It was almost ten by the time Barry dropped Scott home, the questioning at Potter's house having gone on for some time. Scott had managed to get the briefest of messages back to Michelle after she'd picked up the girls from school, but the brevity of their conversation had inevitably raised more questions than it answered. *There's been an incident*, was all he told her. *I have to give a statement.*

'What happened, love?' she asked the moment he was through the door. 'I've been going out of my mind.'

He looked up. Phoebe was at the top of the stairs. Tammy appeared in the living room doorway. 'Not in front of the kids,' he said and Michelle shooed the girls away then followed him into the kitchen. She fetched him his dried-up meal and a drink and put them down in front of him. He just stared at his food.

She held off for as long as she could, wanting to give him a chance to get over whatever it was that had happened, but after a couple of minutes she could wait no longer. 'You going to talk to me?'

'I found a dead body,' he said, and the combination of such unexpected news being delivered so abruptly, so tactlessly, took her by surprise.

'You... you found what?' she stammered.

He looked up at her face, a mask of seriousness but with a definite hint of disbelief, bordering on a smirk. 'You heard me. I made a delivery, but one of the blokes at the yard fucked it up. I had to go back to the same customer's house later with the boss and...'

'What had happened to him?'

'Nothing. He'd gone. Done a runner. Left a girl in his back garden, badly fucked up.'

'What do you mean?'

'What do you think I mean? He'd cut her up, Michelle. Looked like he'd had his way with her, then cut her up. Sick fucker sliced her fanny to pieces.'

Michelle visibly recoiled, again both because of what he'd said and how he'd said it. He took a couple of half-hearted mouthfuls of food, then shoved the plate away.

'Want me to cook you something fresh?'

He shook his head. 'Nah.'

'Want a beer or something?'

Another shake of the head.

'Want me to—'

'I want you to shut up, Chelle,' he said. 'Give me some space.'

'Sorry.'

He looked at her, watched her watching him. 'I've been answering questions all day. Just don't want another load, that's all.'

'I understand.'

'It's not your fault.'

How could it be my fault, she thought but didn't dare say. She could only imagine what he'd been through today, this coming on top of everything else. She sat down next to him and cautiously put her hand on top of his. When he didn't react, she held it a little tighter.

'How did the girls get on at school?' he asked.

'Fine. Both miserable as hell, complaining about the kids and the teachers and how much homework they've got. They've settled in quick. That's exactly how they were in Redditch.'

He managed half a smile and seemed to relax slightly. 'George all right?'

'He's fine. He missed you tonight, though.'

'I'll see him in the morning.'

'That's what I told him.'

'I think I will have that beer,' he said, and Michelle got up to fetch it from the fridge. She took the lid off the bottle and handed it to him. He gestured for her to sit back down. 'And what have you been doing with yourself today?'

'Oh, just pottering around the house, unpacking. Not a lot else to do yet. We're going to go out tomorrow, George and me. Get signed up at the doctors and see if I can find something for him to do. He needs to get out and mix with other kids.'

'I know.'

For a short while longer, neither of them spoke. Michelle almost did a few times, but she didn't want to put her foot in it. He did this too often, distracting her with trivialities to keep her from asking about the big stuff. Scott picked at his food and she cleared her throat. 'Look, love, I know you've had enough and I don't want to do anything that's going to upset you, but I just need to know a few things about what happened today, okay? I'm not asking you to tell me everything, I just want to know that you're all right and that we're going to be okay here.'

'If there was a problem I'd tell you.'

'I know you would. It's just that—'

'We're going to be okay.'

'It's just that I feel really out on a limb here, emotionally as well as physically.'

'I get that.'

'Do you?'

'Yes, and like I said, we're going to be okay.'

'But this girl... the police...'

Scott drank more beer, then put the bottle down. 'What's the problem? What more do you want me to say? Look, I'll spell it out for you, shall I? I made a delivery first thing, but some dickhead at the yard hadn't loaded everything up right. The uptight arsehole I was supposed to be delivering to had a fit, so I went back to the yard. I went back out to his house later with Barry Walpole, and he'd disappeared.'

'And that's when—?'

'That's when we found the girl, lying in a flowerbed, with blood all over the place and her cunt torn open. Okay?'

Michelle choked back a startled sob. 'I'm sorry.'

'So we phoned the police and waited a fucking age for them to turn up. It's not like Redditch here. I get the impression there's only half a dozen of them, and they didn't know their arses from their elbows. Took for-fucking-ever to get everything done, so that's why I'm back so late. Oh, and I've still got a job, if that's what you're worried about.'

'Of course it's not. I don't care about the bloody job. I'm just interested in you.'

'Nothing to worry about. Think about it logically – this girl gets sliced up and Potter goes missing the exact same time. He probably did that body in the woods we saw on the news too.'

'You think?'

73

'One of the coppers practically said as much.'

'So who was he?'

'Ex-school teacher. Bit of a bastard from what I hear. Bit of a sick fuck, actually...'

'Why did you have to be the one who found her?'

He looked at her, surprised. 'Luck of the draw? What does it matter? I didn't do it. It's got nothing to do with me.'

'I know that, but people here don't know us, do they? They don't know anything about us other than the fact we're new to the area. I've had enough of people whispering behind my back. We came here to get away from all that.'

'This is different.'

'It sounds like everyone knew this Potter guy.'

'They all know each other, fucking inbreds. Anyway, they didn't know him like they thought they did, did they? Fuck's sake, he carved up a girl in his back garden...'

'We just have to make sure they don't start pointing fingers.'

'Why would they?'

She paused, choosing her words carefully. 'Sometimes you can be a bit aggressive, Scott. You can fly off the handle.'

'Only if I'm pushed.'

'I just don't want you doing anything you'll regret. Anything *we'll* regret.'

'Who the fuck do you think you're talking to?' he demanded. Michelle swallowed hard. Nervous. Scared.

'My husband. Look, Scott, you know I love you and I'll always support you...'

'Is there a but coming here?'

Another deep breath. She didn't know how he was going to react, but she had to say this. More to the point, he needed to hear it. 'We've had to make a lot of sacrifices for this family, and we don't have a lot left to give. Personally, love, I've got nothing left. I know what happened today was out of your control, but we have to deal with it in the right way and not alienate ourselves. There's nowhere left for us to go now.'

'What's going on?' Tammy asked. Scott and Michelle both looked up. They hadn't noticed her standing in the doorway.

'How long have you been listening?' Scott yelled.

'Few minutes.'

'And what did you hear?'

'Not enough by the sounds of things.' She turned and faced her mother directly. 'What's going on, Mum?'

'It's nothing. Just give us some space, Tam.'

'Bullshit.'

'Tammy, watch your language.'

'Don't speak to your mother like that,' Scott said, staring straight at her.

'Why not? You do,' she said, staring straight back. She flinched when he pushed his chair back and went to stand up, but she stood her ground. Michelle put her hand on his arm.

'Tammy, please,' she said. 'Just leave it. It's none of your business.'

'It is though, isn't it? How can it not be?'

'Look, Scott had some trouble at work and—'

'Already? You've only been there two days, Scott.'

'It wasn't his fault.'

'You always say that. You always defend him.'

'It's true.'

'You always say that too. We've been down this road before, Mum, remember? You kept telling me then that everything was fine and there was nothing going on, then you put the house on the market.'

'Tam, leave it...'

'No, I won't. It's him again, isn't it?' she said, nodding at Scott but unable to bring herself to even say his name. 'Everything was fine until *he* got home. He's back for five minutes and you're shouting at me and treating me like a kid again and—'

'Do what your mother says,' Scott warned. 'Leave it. Go back to bed.'

'I'm sick of this,' Tammy continued, clearly in no mood to do either. 'I'm sick of the way you keep messing with our lives. You think you're the only one who matters.'

'I'm the only one who keeps this family functioning,' he told her.

'You're the one who ruined everything. You screwed things up for all of us. It's your fault we're here, your fault I had to leave everything that mattered to me.'

'You don't know what you're talking about, you silly little bitch.'

'Scott, don't...' Michelle protested.

'Did you hear what he called me? Mum, did you hear what he just called me?'

Scott leapt up and sprung at her, grabbing one arm and pinning her up against the wall. 'I'll call you a lot worse if you don't shut up. Now take a hint and keep your bloody nose out of things that are none of your business.'

Michelle pulled her husband away from her daughter, squeezing into the gap between them. She turned around and gently pushed Scott back into the kitchen, not wanting to wind him up more than he already was. She looked back over her shoulder at Tammy who remained pressed up against the wall, tears rolling down her face, more through anger than fear.

'Go, Tammy,' she mouthed. And Tammy didn't want to, but she did.

7

Michelle's heart sank when she woke up next morning and re-membered everything that had happened the night before. All she wanted was to close her eyes and go back to sleep for another few hours, maybe even a day, perhaps a month or more. She'd gone to bed after she and Scott had finished talking – *shouting* – and he hadn't said a word when he'd come in hours later. Then he'd got up this morning and it was like nothing had happened. She'd expected that. She'd grown used to his mood-swings and tempers. Strange to think that she'd actually found his volatility attractive when they'd first got together. It had been a stark contrast to Jeremy with his steady caution and dreary predictability. It had been exciting for a time. It had made her feel alive. Not anymore.

She worked like a bloody trooper first thing; washed and dressed before the others were even awake, and she'd had the house cleaned and breakfast on the table before the first of them had made it down-stairs. Normally she liked to be up first, to make the most of the qui-et before the usual domestic storm, but today there were things she needed to think through. What exactly had happened at that man's house yesterday? Why was it always Scott?

Once the kids were downstairs she was distracted. She refereed a couple of minor skirmishes between the girls, helped George with his porridge, and kept all three of them out of Scott's way. It was a delicate balancing act. She thought she deserved a bloody medal but her efforts went unnoticed as usual. All they had to think about was themselves, she was the one who kept it all together. She stared out of the kitchen window, eating a piece of toast she didn't want but thought she'd better have, watching birds turn impossible angles in the grey sky. She envied their freedom, their manoeuvrability.

She dropped Scott at work then took the girls to school. Then, with the three of them out of the way for the day, she turned around and looked at George strapped in his travel seat behind her. 'So what do you reckon, sunshine? Shall we go see if there's anything for a big man like you to do in Thussock?'

*

Chores first. She had a list of them. This was the last one.

'I'm sorry, I can't remember my postcode,' she said to the woman behind the counter. 'I've not been there a week yet.'

'Well without your postcode, madam, we can't register you and your family as patients here. I'm a receptionist, not an address look-up service.'

'There's no need to be sarcastic. People call it the grey house, you know it?'

'Oh, I know it all right, Willy was a patient here.'

'Can't you check his old records then? Get the postcode from there?'

'That'd be a breach of customer confidentiality, I couldn't possibly do that.'

'He's dead, isn't he? I don't reckon he'd be too bothered.'

'Hardly the point now, is it?' The sour-faced woman just smiled, the knowing smile of someone sitting behind safety glass who couldn't be throttled or punched. 'Why not take the forms with you and bring them back when we're less busy.'

Michelle looked over her shoulder. The spacious waiting room was empty but for two patients, one reading a dog-eared magazine, the other coughing and wheezing constantly. She turned back and eyed-up the ice maiden behind the counter again, knowing this was a battle she wasn't going to win. More to the point, it was a silly, trivial fight she didn't need. She picked up the five forms. 'Thanks for nothing. I'll be back.'

'Don't mention it,' the receptionist said. Michelle was on her way out when the woman called her back. She was holding up five plastic phials. 'Oh, and the doctor'll need urine samples with each form, and he'll need to see all of you in person before he agrees to take any of you on as patients. That all clear?'

'As crystal. Thanks again for all your help.'

Michelle took the phials and walked away. With the forms, the phials, the car keys, her handbag and George, she was struggling. Unsighted, she crashed into a man coming the other way and managed to drop everything but her son. The man, late fifties, short with grey hair, horn-rimmed glasses and a close trimmed beard, quickly picked everything up for her. 'New patient?' he asked.

'Hopefully. How can you tell?'

'The forms and the piss-pots,' he said, grinning. He folded the papers and dropped the phials into her open bag. 'I'm Doctor Kerr. Nice to meet you.'

'Nice to meet you, too,' she replied, trying to juggle everything so she could shake his hand.

'Alice give you a warm welcome, did she?'

'Alice?'

'My charming receptionist.'

'No, not really.'

'True to form,' he sighed, then he leant a little closer. 'She's very efficient and remarkably thorough, but her interpersonal skills are bloody awful.'

'I'd noticed.'

'I inherited her from my predecessor. She's been here longer than this building. I think they built it around her.'

Michelle laughed. 'I can believe that.'

The doctor tapped her arm, ruffled George's hair, then walked on. 'Be seeing you soon, then.'

'I'm sure you will.'

'Alice, the light of my life, how are you this morning?' she heard him say at the top of his voice. She didn't hear Alice's response.

'See, George,' she said as she carried him back out to the car, 'they're not all complete aliens here. Most, maybe, but not all of them.'

The Thussock Community Hall was a one-storey rectangular wooden building with a flat roof, situated on the outermost edge of a grassy recreation area close to the main housing estate. Probably the only park in Thussock, the recreation area itself was little more than a large, odd-shaped field with a rectangle of tarmac dropped right in the middle, upon which sat a slide, a roundabout, and a row of three swings. One of the swings didn't have a seat, and the graffiti-covered slide had seen better days.

Michelle had spotted the play area from the road first and she'd figured that if she hoped to meet like-minded parents with kids of a similar age to George at this time of the day, this place was as good as any to find them. She'd felt like a weirdo, loitering and looking for kids. Fortunately she discovered that a parent and toddler group was in session in the hall next door. Going into the timber-clad building felt unexpectedly daunting, like she was stepping into the lion's den, but she was getting used to it. If she was honest with herself, she hadn't felt completely comfortable since she'd left Redditch.

A wide entrance corridor ran from the front door into the main hall. Off it were several more doors: a half-empty storeroom, a small kitchen, and male and female toilets. A particularly gruff-looking woman headed Michelle off before she could get through. Michelle tried to make conversation but received only the most cursory of replies. The woman's responses were little more than a bullet-point list of dos and don'ts: the times, the rules, the cost. She wasn't as bad as the doctor's receptionist, Michelle thought, but she wasn't far off.

Michelle paused and took a deep breath before going into the hall. She felt self-conscious... on edge. There were chairs around the edge of the room and in the centre a group of between fifteen and twenty children (they didn't stay still long enough to count) were playing with, and occasionally fighting over, a mass of well-worn toys. She let go of George's hand and gave him a gentle nudge. Unsure at first, he gravitated towards a sit-in car similar to one he had at home and climbed inside. Within minutes he was settled – already playing with several other kids. Michelle sat by herself on a wooden bench at the side of the room and watched him. She almost envied him. *Nothing matters to kids*, she thought. *Who you are, the things you've done, what you've been through... none of it counts for anything much. They see someone roughly the same shape and size as them and they play, simple as that.*

The same definitely couldn't be said for adults. It wasn't a problem specific to Thussock, of course, but it seemed particularly prevalent here. There were plenty of other parents in the room, almost exclusively mothers and (she presumed) grandmothers, but none of them seemed particularly keen to welcome a stranger. No one was going out of their way to be rude – plenty of folk had acknowledged her when she'd arrived – but those nods and mumbled hellos were the full extent of their interaction. There had been a roughly equal number of people sitting on all sides of this room at first. Not now.

Now, apart from a couple of other stragglers, there were two larger groups of women on either side of the kitchen serving hatch, leaving Michelle on her own at the other end of the hall.

You're just paranoid. It's perfectly natural. You're the new girl. It's up to you to make the first move.

Clutching her purse, she walked up to the hatch. 'Could I have a cup of tea, please?' she asked the first lady she made eye contact with.

'What's that?'

'A cup of tea, please.'

'It's your accent,' the woman grunted as she poured Michelle's drink.

'How much do I owe you?'

'Fifty pence.'

Michelle gave her a pound. 'Keep the change for the funds. Can I take a biscuit for my boy?'

'That'll be twenty pence.'

Michelle gave her another fifty, despite having already overpaid. *Keep trying*, she told herself over and over. 'We're new here. Just moved here from Redditch.'

'Thought we'd not seen you before.'

The woman was almost monosyllabic, as if small-talk in Thussock was taxed.

'Nice hall you have here.'

'It does the job.'

'Do you meet here every day?'

'Monday, Wednesday and Friday mornings, Thursday afternoons.'

Michelle just nodded, her questions now beginning to sound as forced as the woman's replies. The door into the kitchen opened, and another woman put her head through. 'Do we have more fruit juice in the stores, Sylvia? I can't find any.'

Sylvia – the woman Michelle had been talking to – appeared to visibly relax when she talked to her friend. 'I've not seen any. I thought Bryan was supposed to keep everything stocked up. He's bloody useless, that one. I can see why Betty's the way she is.'

'Don't get me started on Betty, love. You'll never believe what she's gone and done now...'

They moved out of earshot. Michelle stopped listening but kept watching. Sylvia was unrecognisable now, all the frostiness and reticence gone. She was laughing and joking with her friend and Michelle couldn't help wondering, *are they laughing at me?* She picked up her tea and George's biscuit and walked away.

She was getting better with the accent, but people were still occasionally hard to understand. She was sure she'd just heard someone mention Ken Potter's name. Wasn't that the man whose house Scott had been delivering to yesterday? The man who...? She stopped herself from jumping to conclusions. *They might know him.* Her ears better attuned now, she listened in. 'S'terrible,' a young mum cradling a new-born was saying to three friends gathered around her. 'We were just saying this morning how we'd seen him in town at the weekend, carrying on like he owned the place as always.'

'Funny bugger,' one of the other girls said. 'I always said there was something wrong about him.'

'You say that about all the blokes in Thussock.'

'Aye, that's 'cause they're all no good!' a third girl joked. The women laughed, and Michelle sidled a little closer, sipping her piss-weak tea.

'Terrible business, that,' she said. She half-expected the entire room to fall silent and for everyone, even the kids, to stop and stare at her, like a clichéd scene from a horror movie. But they didn't. Instead, one of the women acknowledged her with a subdued 'aye', then turned back and continued talking to her friends. She closed the circle, moving ever-so-slightly to her left, positioning herself so she had her back to Michelle, preventing her from edging into their group. The snub was subtle but definite. Their conversation continued, the accents a little stronger than before, harder to make out. Michelle couldn't clearly hear what they were saying, but she managed to pick out a few choice phrases amongst the mutterings. 'No one else's business... Folks should mind their own...'

Each of these knock-backs, although individually insignificant, were beginning to wear her down. She took her tea and George's biscuit back over to where she'd been sitting. *It's only natural*, she told herself, *it's not personal. I'll take my time. We're here in Thussock for the long-haul. There's no rush...*

George saw the biscuit before he saw his mother. He came running over, babbling excitedly in child's half-speak about his game and his new friends. Michelle perfectly understood her son's mix of full words, truncated words and nonsense, and the fact she was so tuned-in to his immature language was reassuring. She wasn't alone.

Biscuit demolished, George didn't have any reason to stay. He ran off again and Michelle was so focused on him that she didn't notice someone sitting a few places to her left. 'You've not been here before, have you?' the woman asked. Michelle looked up fast. 'Sorry, did I startle you?'

'A little,' Michelle said. 'I'm sorry. I'm miles away this morning.'

'Don't worry about it. So are you new to the area?'

'Just moved in. My husband's been up here for a couple of weeks getting the house ready, but the rest of us came up this weekend just gone.'

'And how are you finding it?'

'Oh, fine...' she said, deliberately evasive.

'Really?'

'Yes. Why? You sound surprised.'

'I am. Thussock's a bit of a dead end if you ask me.'

'I was trying to be polite.'

'I shouldn't bother. You're not from round here, are you?'

'You can tell?'

'The accent kind of gives it away.'

'We're from the Midlands. Redditch.'

'That by Birmingham? I was gonna say you sound like you're from those parts.'

'Not a million miles away.'

'No, a million miles away is what you are now.'

'What do you mean by that?'

'This place. It can feel like another planet.'

Michelle felt herself relax. 'You don't know how relieved I am to hear you say that. I thought it was just me. Just us.'

'Ah, no. I was exactly the same when I first arrived. I moved here with my folks almost ten years back. Thussock definitely takes some getting used to.'

'You can say that again.'

'I remember thinking how everybody else seemed to know what

was going on but me. It was like they were all in on some big secret.'

'That's exactly it.'

'There's no secret, though. Sorry to disappoint you.'

'That's a relief.'

'And you will get used to it.'

'I'm not so sure...'

'No, you will. Once you get tuned in to this place you'll be all right. It'll all start making sense in no time.'

'I hope so.'

'It *will*. Trust me.'

Michelle thought she was probably just saying that to make her feel better. 'I'm Michelle, by the way,' she said. 'Michelle Griffiths.'

'I'm Jackie. Is that your boy?' she asked, pointing at George.

'That's him. That's George.'

'Oh, but he's adorable.'

'When he wants to be. Where's yours?'

'I've two, right over there,' Jackie said, nodding over towards the diagonally opposite corner of the room.

'Are they twins?'

'Yep. One of each. Sophia and Wes.'

'Christ, you've got your hands full.'

'Don't even go there. They're a bloody nightmare. I mean, I love them to bits, but they make my life hell.'

'It doesn't get any easier, believe me.'

'Thanks for that,' she laughed. 'You've other kids then?'

'Two girls from my previous marriage. Fourteen and sixteen.'

'I remember being sixteen.'

'Me too. I was an absolute bitch. I know where my Tammy gets it from.'

'Boys and cider, that's all I was interested in. Couldn't be doing with lessons and rubbish like that.'

'How old are you now, if you don't mind me asking.'

'Twenty-four.'

That made Michelle feel old. She was half as old again. 'And when did you move to Thussock?'

'When I was fifteen. I tell you, I made my parents' lives hell when they dragged me here. I was a little shit before I came here, understand, but this place brought out the worst in me.'

'You're not making me feel any better...'

'I'm sure your girls will be fine.'

Michelle laughed. 'I'm sure you're right.'

'Ah, Thussock's not so bad. Nothing ever happens here, sure, and there's bugger all for the kids to do, but it's okay.'

Michelle watched George. He was lying down now, colouring in, more crayon ending up on the floor than on his paper. She was enjoying this conversation. She didn't want to put her foot in it or say the wrong thing, but she couldn't help asking. 'You say nothing much happens here, but what about that murder?'

'Terrible thing, that,' Jackie said, her voice as hushed as Michelle's. 'Between you and me, I always had my doubts about that Potter bloke.'

'I wouldn't know...'

'Never did anything wrong that I know about, it's just there was sumthin' about him... bit creepy lookin'. Dez says he never trusted him.'

'Dez?'

'My other half. Potter taught him at school.'

'Oh, right.'

'I'd never have had him down for a serial killer, though.'

'A serial killer?'

'Have you not heard? Dez says there're two more deaths they're pinning on him. Some fella last week, and a woman in the woods over last weekend.'

'I saw that on TV.'

'She was all cut up like that girl in his garden, apparently. One of Dez's mates found the body. He does security up by that fracking place near Falrigg. Dez was with him just before he found it.'

'How d'you know about the body in the garden? I didn't think the police had said anything about how she'd died.'

'Dez was talking to Alan.'

'Alan?'

'He works for Barry Walpole.'

'So does...'

'Your other half?' Jackie said, surprising Michelle.

'Yes. How did you know that?'

'I thought it might be, didn't want to presume, though. He said there was some new bloke from Birmingham started there.'

'Redditch.'

She shrugged her shoulders. 'Same difference. Everything's south from here.'

'Suppose. Scott's pretty shaken up by it all.'

'I'm not surprised,' Jackie said. She watched Michelle and noticed that her demeanour had changed. 'Sumthin' wrong?'

'No, it's nothing.'

'Come on, spit it out.'

Michelle sighed. 'It's just the way you knew who I was by default. I'm not used to living somewhere where everybody knows your business like that.'

'It's not like that here, honest. Thing is, you're always gonna get a few folks who like to stick their nose in, and you'll get that wherever. The difference here is that Thussock's so small, people can't help noticing change. No one's watching you or spying on you, nothin' like that.'

'I *think* that makes me feel better...'

'Look at it from the other side. My Dez starts talking about this bloke with a Brummie accent who's just started working at Walpoles, then I find myself talking to someone else with the same accent here. No spying, just common-sense.'

Michelle relaxed. Slightly. 'You're right. Sorry. It's been a big thing moving here, that's all. We're all on edge.'

'Nothin' to be sorry about.'

At the far end of the room, a woman wearing a shapeless smock-top and baggy jeans clapped her hands three times. The kids – all bar George – looked up, the oldest of them already starting to get up and put their toys away. 'Is this us?' Michelle asked.

'Aye.'

Michelle pushed herself up from her seat and winced.

'You hurting?'

'Hurt my wrist last night. It's nothing.'

She went to take her cup back to the kitchen. Jackie took it from her. 'Here, let me take that.'

'Thanks.'

By the time Jackie returned from the kitchen, having made a detour across the room to collect the twins, Michelle had George ready to leave. 'Will I see you here again?' Jackie asked.

'I'm sure you will. George had a great time, didn't you George?' He tucked himself behind his mother's leg, avoiding answering. 'Thank you, Jackie.'

'Thanks for what?'

'For the chat. For not making me feel like a complete social leper.'

'All I did was come across and start talking rubbish to you.'

'That was more than anyone else has done. It was what I needed.'

'I told you, I know what it's like. And like I said, it *will* get easier.'

'I'm sure you're right.'

'Listen, there's another session here on Friday morning, maybe I'll see you then?'

'That'd be good.'

'There's a Thursday afternoon group too, but I don't bother with that one.'

'Why's that?'

'Don't like the folks there. Bit strange.'

'Stranger than this lot?' Michelle whispered.

'Believe it or not, yes!' Jackie replied, also whispering. Michelle's laughter filled the hall, her noise loud enough to warrant a few sideways glances.

'I might see you Friday, then.'

'Sure.'

She went to walk away, then stopped. 'Listen, d'you fancy meeting up for a coffee some time?'

'Yeah, definitely.'

Michelle hesitated. 'Where exactly do people go for coffee around here?'

'Usually Mary's.'

'Mary's?'

'Aye, Mary's café in town. If you want Starbucks or Costa, anything fancy like that, then you're lookin' at an hour's round trip.'

'You're kidding.'

'I wish.'

'Right, a date with Mary it is then.'

'Ah, bugger the expense. Just come around to mine. I'm only five minute's walk from the café, so if you don't like my coffee, we can still go to Mary's. Here, let me give you my number.' Jackie scribbled her phone number and address on the torn off corner of a red gas bill, then handed it over. 'I'm stuck at home with the twins most of the time. Dez has the car, so you've a good chance of catchin' me.'

'Excellent. Look forward to it.'

'Aye, me too.' One of Jackie's twins yelled out, fighting over a toy with the other. 'Got to go,' she said. Michelle just smiled, scooped up George, and headed for the door.

8

Scott tried to keep on the road and away from the yard as much as possible, but it was a quiet day for deliveries. As well as himself, Barry Walpole and Warren, there were two other members of staff working today, far more than was necessary. A wiry-framed man in his fifties called Alan shifted slabs, and Chez, a streak of piss and wind who could only have been in his late teens or early twenties, helped. Alan, who Scott really wasn't sure about, seemed to have an unhealthy preoccupation with the dead girl in Ken Potter's garden. He kept pressing Scott to talk about her, and when he didn't oblige, Alan just made stuff up instead. It wasn't just him, they were all seriously pissing Scott off. He was glad when lunchtime arrived, though his relief was short-lived when Barry shut the yard and disappeared off with the truck. That move in itself took him by surprise. *This is the twenty-first century*, he'd protested, *businesses don't shut for lunch anymore.* Then Warren made a point he found difficult to counter: they'd barely had any custom all morning, what were the chances of missing someone at lunch time? The others all went home to eat leaving Scott alone, stranded.

When they returned, just after half-one, Alan had news. There were still no customers and Barry hadn't yet come back, so Scott, Chez and Warren were a captive audience.

'Shona McIntyre,' he announced excitedly.

'Who?' Warren asked.

'Shona McIntyre,' he said again. 'That's her name.'

'Whose name?'

'The girl Barry and him found in Potter's garden yesterday.' There was something about the way Alan dismissively avoided using Scott's name which rankled him. It was almost as if he wasn't there.

'Never heard of her,' Chez said. Scott said nothing. He knew no one.

'And?' Warren pressed.

'And what?'

'That all you got?'

Alan shook his head and continued. 'The missus says she wasn't local.'

'So what was she doing at Potter's?' Chez asked.

'Been out hiking, apparently. She was a student, Marj reckons. It was on the local news. Involved in geography or geology, she was, sumthin' like that.'

'But why was she at Potter's house?' Scott asked, repeating Chez's question. 'It doesn't make sense. Took me long enough to find that bloody place yesterday.'

'Maybe she was lost?'

'So did she get lost and walk there, or did Potter pick her up and take her back to his?'

'Not sure what you're alludin' to,' Alan said, his tone a little aggressive. 'You need to be careful what you're sayin'. Ken Potter's a good man. I've known him years. He taught me and both my kids, he did, and he never did nothin' he shouldn't. He didn't do nothin' to that girl.'

Scott couldn't help himself. The words just came out. 'So who did then?'

They turned on him as one. 'I reckon you'd be the best person to answer that,' Chez said. 'You're the one what found her.'

'Piss off. It had nothing to do with me. Anyway, Barry was with me. You think Barry did it?'

Alan cleared his throat. 'Barry was with you second time,' he said, 'but you was on your own when you first went there. An' you had a run in with Ken.'

'Fuck's sake,' Scott said, his temper rising. 'Sure, I had an argument with him, but that doesn't mean I cut up that girl and left her in his back garden, does it? What do you think I am, some kind of madman?'

'I don't know what you are,' Alan said. 'I don't even know *who* you are. Now Ken Potter had his moments, but he weren't no pervert and he weren't no murderer. We've all known him for years. You ain't even been here a week.'

'I didn't say he was a murderer or a pervert, I just said I don't understand. It doesn't make sense.'

Alan walked up to Scott, his body language suddenly hostile. 'Fact is, mate, you need to be careful when you're throwin' accusations around in a small place like Thussock, 'specially if they're as serious as the things you're sayin'. I don't know what happened at Ken's house or why that girl was there. It's my thinkin' someone did her in and dumped her body, then Ken found her and panicked. Ken can be a bit of an arse at times, but he's no killer.'

'How do you know?'

'What?'

'I mean, how much do you really know about each other? You're quick enough to say how little you know about me, but what about you lot? Chez, do you know what drives Alan wild in bed?'

'Fuck off. What d'you think I am, a fucking perv?'

'That's my bloody point. You just don't know. We all think we know other people, but you never do really, do you? For all you know, Ken Potter might really get off on slicing up young girl's fannies. Whatever floats your boat, eh?'

Alan was about to say something, but he didn't get a chance. Barry Walpole came at Scott from out of nowhere, grabbing him by the scruff of his neck and slamming him against the side of the caravan which rocked precariously on its piles of bricks. Scott tried to fight him off, but Barry had surprise and weight on his side. 'Watch what you're sayin' you little bastard,' he hissed.

'I'm sorry, Barry. I didn't mean—'

'Watch what you're sayin', and watch who you're sayin' it to, right? This place isn't like where you're from. Folks here are less forgivin', understand?'

'I understand.'

Barry let him go and staggered back. Scott massaged his throat and chest.

'To be fair,' Chez said, doing what he could to calm the suddenly volatile atmosphere, 'I don't think he meant nothin' by it. He just... Barry? Barry, mate, you all right?'

The men crowded around their boss at first, then they backed away. He wiped his eyes. He was crying.

'S'matter, Barry?' Alan asked cautiously.

'Looks like you was right, anyway,' Barry said, looking straight at Scott.

'What do you mean?'

Barry composed himself. His anger faded slightly. He looked pained... devastated. 'They found him.'

'Found who?' Warren asked, though he thought he already knew.

'Ken.'

'Where?'

Barry paused again. Took deep breaths. 'He's dead. Sam Adamson's kids found him on the train track north of Thussock. Silly bastard killed himself.'

'Can't believe it...' Alan mumbled.

'Nor me, Al,' Barry said, the emotion draining from his voice. 'I don't know what was goin' through Ken's head to make him do what he just did, but I'll still stake everythin' I have on the fact he did nothin' to that girl.'

Scott kept his mouth shut and went back to work, knowing that whatever he said would be the wrong thing.

9

Michelle was glad to get out of the house again. By Friday morning she'd had enough. She'd spent most of their first week in Thussock unpacking everybody's stuff, trying to make it feel like home, but she was already climbing the walls. It had come to something when an appointment with the doctor was a highlight.

The receptionist was just as fearsome as last time but Dr Kerr, fortunately, was as friendly as she remembered, perhaps even more so. He seemed in no rush to deal with the rest of the patients in the waiting room and was content to sit and talk for a while. He seemed to be more interested in her house than her health.

'He was a smashing lad, Willy,' he said.

'Who?'

'Willy McCunnie. The chap who lived in your house before you.'

'Oh, right.'

'He spent almost as much time in this surgery as me near the end, you know. Lovely fella. Was cancer that finished him off. Such a shame.'

'Sorry to hear that.'

'Ah, well, he was past his prime,' the doctor said, navigating his computer with ponderous speed, looking from keyboard to screen after virtually every key press. 'We're practically neighbours, you know.'

'Are we?'

'Yes... May and I live just down from Jeannie and Lou.'

'Who?'

'Jeannie and Lou. The twins. You must have seen them. Lovely girls.'

'We've seen them,' she smirked.

The doctor checked her blood pressure and measured her height and weight, then checked George over too. Dr Kerr had been talking constantly throughout the appointment and Michelle wondered if he'd listened to anything she'd said. He had. He'd taken it all in. He'd been doing this job for so long he made it look easier than he should have, to the point where it seemed he was no longer concentrating. It took Michelle by surprise when his expression suddenly changed and became more serious. He looked straight into her eyes and held her gaze. 'Your wrist,' he said. 'I noticed it was tender. I could see from the way you were holding it.'

'I twisted it the other night.'

'A bit accident prone, are you?'

'No more than anyone else. Why?'

'Just that you've had a lot of little injuries recently.'

She shifted awkwardly in her seat. 'It's par for the course when you have kids. Always on the go, you know how it is...'

He smiled. 'I know how it is. Is everything all right at home?'

'Fine. It will be once we're settled, anyway.'

'Good,' he said, smiling again. He adjusted his glasses and looked at his computer screen, struggling to control the cursor with the mouse. 'Fluoxetine. Now, how long have you been taking that?'

She struggled to remember. 'Six or seven months, I think. Maybe a little longer.'

'Things been tough?'

'Very tough.'

'The depression any better?'

'I'm getting there.'

'Is that why you're here?'

'No, we just wanted to register as patients and the lady said I had to book an appointment so...'

'No, not here, *here*. Is that why you moved to Thussock?'

'Partly.'

'Do you want to come off the pills?'

'Eventually. Now's really not the time, though.'

'Why not?'

'New house... my husband's got a new job and the girls have started a new school...'

'Fair enough. Got enough to last you a while?'

'A few weeks.'

'Will you come in and see me again when you're running out?'

'Okay.'

'And in the meantime, don't do anything silly. If you're feeling low, come straight back and see me. Take no crap from Alice. Call at the house if it's out of hours.'

'Thanks. I'm not about to do anything stupid, you know.'

'Glad to hear it.'

'I think I'd have already done it by now if I was.'

'I get that impression. You seem like you have your head screwed on, Michelle.'

She wasn't sure how to respond to that. 'Thanks.'

He paused and looked at the screen again, doing all he could to make his next question sound as casual as possible. 'And how are things between you and your husband? You've been under a lot of pressure, I imagine.'

'You don't know the half of it.'

'I'm sure that's true. You're okay, though?'

A moment of hesitation. 'We're okay.'

'And *you*?'

'I'm okay.'

'I'm looking forward to meeting the rest of the family.'

'They're great kids.'

'I've no doubt. Just remember, if you need to see me, I'm only a little way down the road.'

'I will,' she said. 'Thanks.'

And Michelle watched the doctor as he added to his notes, and all she could think was *he knows*.

Michelle phoned Jackie and arranged to skip the toddler group session and do coffee together instead. She didn't feel like spending time with the sour, stony-faced women in the community hall. She felt like going back home even less.

Jackie's terraced house was right on the main road through town, protected from the traffic by a waist-high wire-mesh fence and a narrow sunken pavement. Over the years the constant fumes had blackened the front of the building. Half-hearted attempts had been made to clean patches, but that had just spread the muck about. The whole building was dirty-looking.

Michelle drove past then took the next left and pulled up behind a car she thought she recognised. It was an old Ford Focus. Dirty and full of crap, it was splattered with mud and its exhaust was hanging off. It took her a while to remember where she'd seen it before. It had been less than a week, but it felt much longer. When she saw the man who'd stopped to speak to her and Tammy at the bus-stop last Sunday evening, it clicked. He emerged from Jackie's front door and gave way to Michelle. Shifty-looking bugger, she thought. He was wearing the same faded football shirt as before, the same denim jacket too.

'Sorry,' she said as they side-stepped each other and both did a double-take. The man made less of an effort than she did, brushing up against her.

'No apology necessary,' he said, staring for a little too long. 'You must be Michelle.'

The seedy man made her flesh crawl, but she did what she could not to let it show. 'That's right. How did you...?'

'Psychic,' he said quickly. He broke into a huge smile and an over-exaggerated laugh which seemed to fill the entire street. 'Not really. I'm many things, lover, but psychic ain't one of them. Jack'll tell you.'

Michelle looked up and saw Jackie standing on the doorstep, wearing a short dressing gown and not a lot else. 'Piss off, Dez,' she said. 'That useless bugger is my other half,' she explained as she beckoned Michelle inside. 'Really landed on my feet with that one, eh?'

'Nice to meet you again,' Michelle said, turning back around, but Dez had already gone. A couple of seconds later his car raced past the front of the house at a ridiculous speed, the noise of its tired exhaust taking an age to disappear.

'Again?' Jackie asked, puzzled. Michelle explained as she followed her into her small, cluttered house. They went through into the kitchen, every available bit of work surface covered with crockery, saucepans and food.

'I was having a bit of trouble with my eldest last Sunday evening. She had a strop and walked off. I was sitting in the bus shelter with her, trying to get her to come home, and he stopped to check we were okay. I think he was just concerned.'

'You reckon? Perving, more like. Funny, though, he never said anythin'.'

'Probably forgot about it 'til now. I had.' Michelle thought she should try and steer the conversation into safer waters. 'So what does Dez do?'

'As little as he has to,' Jackie answered quickly as she filled the kettle.

'And you're okay with that?'

'Don't have a lot of choice, really. As long as he brings enough money in, I've learned not to ask too many questions.'

'Like that, is it?'

She laughed. 'I'm making it sound worse than it is. Dez isn't scared of hard work, but he can't hold down a regular job to save his life. He does odd jobs for people, helps folks out, all cash in hand. Everybody knows Dez.'

Michelle couldn't help asking. 'What kind of odd jobs?'

'Whatever needs doin'. Look, I know it sounds dodgy, but it's all kosher. He just does things different to everyone else, that's all. People jump to the wrong conclusion too easy about Dezzie.'

'Sorry, I...'

'I didn't mean you, love. He gets it all the time. Just this Saturday gone Sergeant Ross stopped him for no good reason. Mind you, he was off to see his mate with a load of beer and knocked-off DVDs in the back of the car. Dez don't exactly help himself.'

'What do you mean?'

'Ah, he asks for trouble half the time. Carryin' on like he'd a load of hard-core porn stashed away or worse.'

'And he hadn't?'

'It was a stack of Star Trek videos. Him and his mate Murray, that's the guy who works up on the fracking site by Falrigg, are proper geeks. Sergeant Ross thought Dez was into sumthin' mucky, fact is him and Murray were just plannin' a Star Trek all-nighter.'

Michelle laughed at the ridiculousness of the story, then took her coffee from Jackie and followed her into the living room where the children were playing. The room was scattered with toys. *Scattered.* She thought that was a good word to use to describe the whole house; everything where it had been last used, nothing where it should be. She picked her way through the chaos to get to a seat, having to shift newspapers, TV listings magazines, remote controls and toys so she could sit down. Jackie took them from her. 'Sorry about the state of the place,' she said, noticing Michelle's wandering eyes. 'Fast as I clean it up, Dez and the kids trash it again.'

'You should see my house,' Michelle said quickly, worried that she'd caused offence. 'We've still got a load of boxes to unpack. It takes forever. It took me weeks to get everything ready for the move and it's going to take twice as long to sort it all out at this end.'

'You sure you want to?'

'What?'

'Unpack? I mean with everything that's happened here since you arrived? Ken Potter killing that girl then doin' himself in... your other half finding the body... you sure you're safe here?'

'You taking the piss? Tell me you're taking the piss?'

'Course I am,' Jackie laughed. 'Jeez, you're easy to wind up. I was just messin' with you. Like I said the other day, I know what you're goin' through. Thussock takes some getting used to.'

'You can say that again.'

'Actually, it's not the place, it's the people. Most of them are all right, it's just that when they've lived here all their lives, they've never known nothin' else, you get me? What's wrong to us is normal to them. Dez has got these cousins on his dad's side what live right up in the Highlands, miles away from anyone else. He took me up to meet them once – just the once – and I swear they were the weirdest buggers I've ever met. Had their own words for things, like they was talkin' their own language. Kept a bloody pig in the bathroom.'

'A pig in the bathroom? You serious?'

'Absolutely. Thing is, they didn't have nowhere else to keep it and it was a downstairs bathroom so it kinda made sense. Point is, sittin' having a piss with a pig lookin' up at you was normal in their house. If they came to your place they'd be freaked out if you didn't have no livestock in your bathroom. You get me?'

'What're you saying? The further north you go, the more screwed up people are?'

Jackie just shook her head and smiled. 'I'm sure you had your fair share of fuck-ups down south too.'

'You can say that again. I could tell you a few tales.'

'Then we'll do that one night. We'll get some drink in, get rid of the kids and the men, then sit here talking bollocks 'til we've drunk so much we've forgotten our own names. Probably do us both good, that would.'

'I'll hold you to that,' Michelle said, feeling herself slowly beginning to relax. Being here felt reassuringly, unexpectedly, normal. She drank her coffee and watched the children. They were tolerating each other, warming to one another's company. In her book, that was good enough.

'So your man's at Walpoles?' Jackie asked.

'Yeah. Driving work, mainly.'

'That Barry Walpole can be a bit of a bugger at times.'

'Can't all men?'

'You're not wrong there.'

'Scott's a typical bloke. Never tells me anything about work.'

'Ah, he'll be fine, I'm sure. Thing about Barry is he's a big fish in a small pond, you know? Gets himself on every committee he gets wind of, jus' 'cause he reckons he's some big businessman or sumthin'. Likes the sound of his own voice.'

'I get that impression.'

'But he's not the worst,' she added. 'Unless you rub him up the wrong way or try to short change him, then he'll come gunnin' for you.'

'You're not making me feel any better, Jackie. There's no one more stubborn than my other half.'

Jackie, still barely dressed, pulled her dressing gown tighter around her and watched Michelle drinking her coffee and watching the kids. She waited a few moments longer, the silence getting ever louder, before asking another question. 'What are you doin' in Thussock, Michelle? You don't seem the type, no disrespect, nor your family neither. You're better than this place. Why sell up and move here?'

Michelle looked anywhere but at Jackie. How much did she tell her? 'Scott's business went belly-up. We needed a fresh start.'

'Yeah, but there's fresh starts an' there's fresh starts. You didn't need to come out all this way, did you? Or if you did, why not keep going that little bit further and go somewhere that's not such a bloody dead end?'

'Housing's cheap here, and we're short of cash. *Really* short of cash. Scott's a builder. He's going to do up the house and then...'

'And then what? Housing's cheap around these parts because there's more folk movin' out than in. They did up a load of houses on the other side of town a couple of years back an' half of them are still empty. So are things really that bad, Chelle?'

Still avoiding eye-contact, Michelle looked past Jackie and out of the window, watching the slow trickle of eye-level traffic driving up and down Thussock high street. She wiped away a tear. 'Yep,' she answered, voice cracking, 'things really are that bad.'

'Want to talk about it?'

'I can't.'

'Why not?'

'I'm not supposed to.'

'Says who?'

'It's complicated.'

'I'll not tell. Honest, Chelle, I'm no gossip. I don't talk to many folks, and Dez never listens to anythin' I tell him.'

'Honestly, it's very boring. You wouldn't want to hear it.'

'Maybe it's not about me wanting to hear it, though? Maybe it's all about you gettin' stuff off your chest? I seen it in you from when we first started talking the other day. You're holding onto things. Carryin' stuff for other people.'

'You're wrong, Jackie. It's been a tough few months, that's all.'

'No disrespect, love, and tell me to mind my own business if you want, but I think it's more than that. I was with this bloke once... he liked to drink. Never let me do anything. When things went wrong – an' they usually did 'cause he was pissed most the time – he'd blame me, tell me it was all my fault. Thing is, when you hear that stuff for long enough, you start thinkin' it's true.'

'Scott's not like that.'

'I didn't say he was.'

'Like I said, it's complicated.'

'And like I said, you'll do yourself no good holdin' onto it all.'

'It's the kids more than anything.'

'What d'you mean?'

Michelle was crying freely now, fishing for a tissue from her hand-bag. Jackie threw a half-empty box across the room to her. 'They're the ones who are struggling most. It's not fair. We make the mistakes, they pay the price.'

'They're not stupid, though. They know what's what, do kids. They know more than we give 'em credit for.'

'So what happened, Jackie?'

'What about?'

'You and your fella? The one who drank?'

'My dad happened. See, I thought he'd washed his hands off me on account of him not likin' Kevin. Turns out he knew exactly what was goin' on... he'd worked it all out long before I had. I went to see Dad when I couldn't take no more, an' he beat the shit out of Kev. Nearly bloody killed him. Took nearly two years, but it got sorted in the end. This kind of stuff always does. I reckon it's better just to take a deep breath and deal with it.'

'It's not that easy,' Michelle said, wiping her eyes furiously, cursing herself.

'Why not?'

'You wouldn't understand.'

'Try me.'

'I've staked everything on coming here and trying to make things better, Jackie. I need to give it a chance.'

'Makes sense,' Jackie said, drawing her legs up and watching Michelle over the rim of her mug. 'But that just reminds me of sumthin' Dad used to say.'

'What was that?'

'He said things don't get better, people do.'

Michelle didn't say anything at first. 'I could do with a drink,' she said eventually.

'Another coffee?'

'No, a *drink* drink.'

'Bit early for that.'

'Shame.'

'One night soon, yeah? We'll have that session we were talking about.'

'You're on.'

Another pause. Michelle sensed more questions were coming, but did nothing to encourage them. 'So is that it then?' Jackie asked after a while. 'Your man's business went tits up? That's all you're gonna tell me?'

'That's about it.'

'I heard what you said about housin', but couldn't you just have downsized, sumthin' like that? Why d'you move so far? You got family up this way?'

'No, none.'

'What then?'

Michelle paused again, knowing she shouldn't say anything, but also knowing Jackie was right. This wasn't her burden, why should she have to carry it? 'Scott and I had a fight,' she said, still unsure. 'Can't even remember what it was about now. Anyway, he got wound up and left the house in a temper.'

'And...?'

'And he had an accident. Kid just walked straight out in front of him and he hit her.'

'Jeez...'

Michelle was shaking her head. 'She was only six. They said it was her fault, that she shouldn't have been out on her own. I mean, Scott was cleared and everything, but I still can't help thinking...'

'...that if you two hadn't been fighting, it might not have happened?'

'Something like that.'

'Shit, Chelle, I'm sorry.'

'Problem is, most folks aren't so forgiving, especially those who knew Scott and knew what he's like. They decided he was guilty before he went to court, and even afterwards they still blamed him. We had bricks through the window, graffiti on the garage door... That's why the business went under, Jackie, and that's why we're here.'

Sophia, Jackie's little girl, waddled over to her mother and handed her a remote control. It was sticky. Jackie wiped it clean on her dressing gown. 'Beebies,' Sophia said, and Jackie switched on the TV, thankful of the interruption.

'Thank Christ for children's TV, that's all I can say,' she said to Michelle.

'Tell me about it. George watches the same two DVDs over and over. It does my head in, but it's worth it. I'd never get anything done otherwise. It's the only time he leaves me alone.'

'Aye aye,' Jackie said, pausing as she flicked through the TV channels, fighting off Sophia who tried to get the remote control back so she could put on the channel she'd asked for. 'Look at this. We've made the news.'

Jackie's television was too big for the room. It dominated one corner and, once it was on, its size demanded it be watched. There was an aerial shot of the train line on screen, pictures taken last night before the track was reopened. The police were out in force again with their garden gazebos and protective suits, unspooling miles more 'do not cross' tape. It reminded Michelle of the footage they'd been watching the other night, when they'd found that poor woman in the woods. Maybe Potter had something to do with that too? 'It's a terrible thing.'

'From what Dez says, I don't think Ken Potter was the type.'

'Is there a type?'

'Who knows. You never really know folks though, eh? Just goes to show.'

'I guess,' Michelle mumbled, distracted by something she was reading at the bottom of the screen. '*Another* body?'

'What?'

'They're saying there's more of them, look. Potter, the girl in his back garden, the woman in the woods last weekend, and two more.'

'Shit, really?'

'Look. Some guy in a village last week, and another one found between Falrigg and Potter's house. Jesus, your man's been busy.'

'Someone in the shop was sayin' last night that Ken Potter used to go walking out on Falrigg. I heard the woman there was killed the same way as the girl in his garden. They're saying he did the same thing to both of them, apparently. Messed with them... mutilated them. Loads of blood, I heard. Nosy old cow in the post office said he sliced them up and left them to bleed out. Said it was sexual...'

'Careful, Jackie,' Michelle said, lowering her voice and nodding at the kids. 'You never know what they'll pick up on.'

Jackie nodded, but continued anyway. 'You heard what he did, didn't you? Threw himself in front of a train, apparently. I tell you, Chelle, it's properly rattled some folks round here. They don't know what to do with themselves.'

'It all feels so close,' Michelle said. 'Too close.' She watched the TV footage of the police operation; helicopter patrols, house to house enquiries, support drafted in from other forces... 'Back in Redditch everything felt like it had some distance, you know? There was always hundreds of other people around to cushion the blow. Always some space between you and the rest of the world. It's not like that here.'

'Beebies!' Sophia screamed, and Jackie changed channel, the perma-happy presenters and brightly designed sets of children's TV immediately replacing the grim reality of the Thussock murders. It was a relief, and for the next few hours Jackie and Michelle drank coffee, ate junk food, and alternated between kids' programmes and banal daytime TV. Michelle revelled in the mediocrity, feeling herself beginning to properly relax for the first time since arriving in town.

'There's a cinema in Thussock?' Tammy said, not sure how she'd managed to miss something like that. 'What's on?'

'Don't know. I heard about it yesterday,' Michelle explained as Scott parked the car. 'It's around here somewhere. Let's go and have a look.' Before anyone could say anything else, Michelle was up out of her seat. She ushered Phoebe out onto the pavement then leant inside and plucked George from his booster. She moved with far more conviction than the rest of her family. 'Come on,' she said, looking back at them, 'what's the matter with you lot?'

'We're coming,' Tammy said. 'Jesus, what's the hurry?'

Michelle took the handle of George's buggy from Scott then lowered her son down and strapped him in. 'No hurry, I just want us to have a nice day out together, that's all.' She was off before any of them had a chance to respond.

They were looking for bright lights and neon, and so walked past the cinema twice before they found it. It was little more than an entrance between two shops, barely signposted and hardly lit. Three white steps up into a small, dark foyer, it looked more like an office than a cinema. Tammy's heart sank when she saw it. She cursed herself for getting her hopes up. She should have known better by now. 'This it?'

'Guess so,' Scott said as he and Phoebe studied the 'now showing' poster.

'Any good films on?' Michelle asked hopefully.

'Film,' Phoebe corrected her, 'not film*s*. There's only one screen.'

'You're kidding me,' Tammy said, moving closer and running her eyes down the listing. This was like one of those fleapit cinemas she'd seen when they'd been on holiday to the coast: single daily showings of films which had done the rounds months ago in Redditch. 'Seen, seen, seen,' she said, 'don't want to see...'

'Well this is a bit of a let down,' Scott said. 'I'd got myself all psyched up to see something decent.'

'Any kids films on this afternoon?' Michelle asked hopefully.

'No films on this afternoon,' Phoebe told her. 'There's a horror movie on at eight tonight, and some historical rubbish on tomorrow.'

'No films on a Saturday afternoon?' Scott said, barely able to believe it. 'How can they expect to make any money when they're not showing films at peak times? It's a bloody joke.'

'Maybe it's not about making money,' Michelle. 'Look around, love, there's hardly anyone here. I think it's got more to do with not losing cash.'

'Great,' Tammy said, feeling herself getting wound up again. 'What now then?'

'Food,' Michelle replied quickly, determined to keep her family positive and occupied. 'Follow me.'

Jackie had given Mary's café a tentative seal of approval yesterday, though it had more to do with the lack of alternatives in Thussock than any great culinary recommendation.

'I'll drive us somewhere else,' Scott said when they reached the café.

'Why?' Michelle replied. 'What's wrong with this? We live in Thussock now... we need to start giving places like this a chance. Besides, George is cranky. He needs to eat. Jackie said it was okay here.'

'Jackie? Who the hell's Jackie?'

'Just a friend.'

'Since when?'

'Since I met her at the toddler group. I did tell you.'

'You said you'd been to a group, you never said anything about any friend.'

'Does it matter?'

'Yes, it matters.'

'Please don't argue,' Phoebe groaned. 'I'm hungry.'

'It's Mary's or nothing,' Michelle said.

Tammy leaned against the window of the café and peered inside like a miserable tourist on a wet bank holiday weekend. 'I'll go for nothing then,' she said. A sideways glance from her mother shut her up.

'Not an option. We need to eat and I'm having a day off cooking.' She looked around at their miserable, long faces. 'Come on you lot, stop being so bloody negative all the time. I'm making an effort, so you can too. Anyway, this place might be good. You might be surprised.'

'Yeah, right,' Phoebe mumbled as she followed her inside.

'They might struggle to fit us in,' Scott said sarcastically as he looked around at all the empty tables.

'Stop it,' Michelle said. 'It's only just turned twelve. It'll get busier.'

The café looked as trapped in time as the rest of Thussock, perhaps even more so. The uncoordinated décor was a collision of out-dated fashions left over from different decades: part fifties milk bar, part eighties greasy spoon café, part something else entirely. They heard a dog yapping somewhere in the building. 'A dog running wild in a café,' Scott grumbled. 'Not a good sign...'

They sat near the window. The interior of the café wasn't particularly large – optimistically overcrowded with too many tables, Michelle thought – but she wondered if they might have picked the wrong seats when a large-hipped woman burst dramatically through a dated beaded curtain and made a big deal about getting all the way over to them, weaving clumsily around the furniture. Michelle cringed, but she relaxed when the woman broke into a broad and genuinely friendly smile. This, she decided, had to be Mary McLeod. She certainly fitted the description Jackie had given her: very heavy makeup, stacked-up hair, barrel-shaped.

'Afternoon. What'll I get for yous all?'

Scott studied a dog-eared laminated menu card. The pictures were faded and the prices had been adjusted for inflation in ballpoint pen. The choices were limited, but he'd expected that. *No specials today*, he thought, *just ordinaries*. Typical straightforward, unadventurous meals with bugger all in the way of flair or garnish. He was initially disappointed, then relieved. He didn't want much, actually, just a good, hot, cheap meal to fill him up. No pretentiousness, just decent food. 'I'll have an all day breakfast with a side of chips,' he said, pushing the boat out.

'The same but without the chips,' Phoebe added quickly.

'Lasagne,' Tammy said, choosing the least dodgy-looking dish she could see.

'Chicken nuggets and chips for George, and I'll have a baked potato with cheese and beans, please.'

Mary scribbled furiously, concentrating hard. 'Drinks?'

'Three teas, one coke and an orange juice,' Michelle answered automatically, without needing to think or consult the others. Mary nodded and scribbled some more. She was about to walk away when she stopped and turned back again.

'You the new family?'

'We just moved here...' Michelle started to answer before Mary interrupted.

'The grey house?'

'That's right.'

'I thought as much. I could tell from your accents that you weren't local, and I'd heard you'd two girls and a boy.'

'Jesus,' Scott said. 'There's no privacy in Thussock.'

Michelle glared at him. Mary didn't seem to mind. 'News travels fast. Anyway, it's lovely to meet yous all. I'm sure you'll be very happy here.'

'Why does everyone call it the grey house?' Phoebe asked, waiting for some mysterious explanation. Mary just looked at her.

'Because it's grey.'

'It's quite a change from where we were before,' Michelle said, desperately trying to build bridges, not burn them. 'It's going to take a little time to get used to things, but we're liking it here so far.'

'That's just grand,' Mary said, her wide smile revealing nicotine-stained teeth behind lipstick-scrawled lips. 'But you've had quite the first week of it by all accounts, haven't you?'

Scott looked up. She was looking directly at him. 'What do you mean by that...?'

'Ah, don't worry,' she said, resting her hand on his shoulder. 'We're not all gossips here. It's just that when you live in a place as small as Thussock, word gets around whenever anything out of the ordinary happens. Warren from Barry's yard comes in here most mornings for something to eat. He said Barry had given you some work, and then, of course, he told me about all that terrible stuff going on with Ken Potter.'

'It's not been the best of starts,' Michelle agreed, getting in quick before Scott could say anything.

'Things'll calm down for yous all, I'm sure,' Mary said, looking round the table at the faces looking back at her. She ruffled George's hair. 'Right then, lets go get your food sorted...' and with that she disappeared back through the beaded curtain into the kitchen.

There was an awkward silence around the table. 'Seems friendly enough,' Michelle said.

'I'm not having people knowing my business,' Scott said angrily. Michelle tried to calm him. She reached for his hand but he snatched it away. 'It's a frigging joke,' he hissed. 'Who the hell do they think they are?'

'Don't get angry, love, they don't mean anything by it.'

'I'm not having it. It's like living in a bloody horror film round here... people getting killed and everyone knowing your business.'

'You're too cynical, suspicious of everybody.'

'I've got every bloody right to be. I've been let down too many times. I don't like people sticking their noses in. It makes me feel uneasy. I don't know anything about anyone here, but they all seem to know a lot about me.'

'But that's only to be expected, isn't it? We're a large family from way out of the area, and we've moved into the middle of a small, tight-knit community.'

'Inbred, more like,' Tammy said, listening in.

Michelle sighed. 'You're as bad as each other. They don't know about *us*. All they know is that we've moved into the grey house, as they all insist on calling it, and they know what happened with you at that chap's house this week.'

'I'm going to paint that bloody house next summer.'

'I'll help you,' Tammy said, surprising them both.

'You serious?'

'Anything to get rid of the grey. It's like living in a morgue.'

'Don't say that,' Michelle said, lowering her voice again as Mary returned with their drinks. 'It's not that bad.'

'Here we go,' she said, handing the drinks around and getting them right. She put the orange juice down in front of George. 'You're a big strong lad, aren't you?'

George just looked at her, then looked at his mother. 'It's your accent, I think,' Michelle explained. 'He has trouble understanding us sometimes, never mind anyone else.'

'Ah, he'll get used to us,' she laughed, 'and we'll get used to him. Won't be long with your food now.'

'See,' Scott whispered, 'it's like the bloody *Wicker Man*.'

'The what?' Phoebe asked.

'*The Wicker Man*. It's a horror film. A policeman moves into a place like Thussock, and it turns out they're all a bunch of screwed-up devil worshippers.'

'What, a bit like *Hot Fuzz*?'

'Sort of. *The Wicker Man* came first though. The original's a classic. In the last scene the policeman is—'

Michelle put her hand on his. 'Come on, love, this place is nothing like that. I don't think Phoebe wants to know about horror films.'

'I do,' she protested.

An elderly couple came into the café and sat down at a table nearer the counter. Mary's voice drifted out from the kitchen. 'That you, Edie?'

'Aye, that's us,' a decrepit-looking, grey-haired woman replied.

'The usual for yous two?'

'Aye.'

'Be a few minutes, love. Got a big order on.'

'There's no rush, Mary. We've all day.'

At least that was how Michelle thought the conversation went. It was difficult to make out. The locals' accents became broader and harder to decipher when they were talking to each other. 'You do realise that's how George is going to talk, don't you?' Tammy said. 'Did you think about that when you dragged us all up here? He's going to end up with a Scottish accent.'

'Nothing wrong with that,' Michelle said, though she wasn't entirely sure how it made her feel.

'Not if you're Scottish,' Tammy added unnecessarily.

The food was good. In fact, it was better than good. The only person who'd left anything on his plate was George, and his dad was now finishing off his few remaining nuggets and chips.

The café was getting busier. A group of lads had appeared, making more noise than the rest of the diners combined. Michelle noticed the way Tammy tried not to make it obvious she was watching them and, at the same time, how they were gawping at the girls. 'You know them?' she asked. Tammy sank into her seat, embarrassed at being seen out with her family. It wasn't cool.

'They're from school,' she replied. 'The cocky one's Jamie. I've been beating him off all week.'

'Lucky you,' said Scott. She just glared at him.

'You think? Look at the state of them.'

'That's a bit harsh.'

'Whatever.'

'Want me to have a word, tell them to back off?'

'Don't you dare,' she said quickly. 'I'd die. I can handle myself, thanks. The last thing I need is you getting involved.'

'Yeah, but if they're causing you problems.'

'Don't Scott, just don't.' She shook her head in despair. He just didn't get it, did he? She was relieved when Heather, the girl who hung around with these lads, came into the café. Tammy had spoken to her a couple of times in class during the week just gone and was quietly pleased when Heather spotted her then changed direction and came straight over.

'All right?'

'Yeah, you?'

'I'm good. These your folks?' Heather asked. 'Nice to meet you all.'

'Get your arse over here, Heather,' Sean, one of Jamie's mates, hollered across the room. 'You got any cash on you?' Heather turned around and glared at them, stuck her fingers up out of sight of Tammy and her family, then turned back again.

'Sorry about them,' she said. 'Bunch of morons.'

'They're fine,' Michelle said. 'I'm Michelle, by the way.'

'Heather.'

'You two in the same class at school?'

'For some subjects,' Tammy mumbled, still embarrassed.

'You settling in?' Heather asked.

'Getting there,' Michelle replied. There was an awkward silence. Michelle sensed Heather wanted to go but didn't want to appear rude. She tried to make it easier for her. 'You'll be wanting to get back to your friends.'

'Hardly friends,' she laughed. 'That there's my brother.' She pointed to Jamie.

'Oh, right.'

'What you doing today?' Tammy asked suddenly. Heather shrugged.

'Not a lot. Hanging around town for a bit, I guess. Want to come?'

Tammy was up and out of her seat in a heartbeat. 'I won't be long,' she said to Scott and Michelle. 'I'll keep in touch.'

'Where will you be?' Michelle asked.

'Your place ain't too far from mine,' Heather answered quickly. 'We live on the estate. We'll walk back together later.'

'Be careful,' Scott warned. 'Don't do anything stupid.' But they were already gone. A few seconds later and the three boys left too. Scott looked concerned, Michelle less so.

'We have to let her do this,' she whispered to him. 'If we're going to settle in here, she has to make friends and have some freedom.'

'Yes, but those lads...'

'Are just normal lads, same as you were at that age. Besides, I think she'd eat them for breakfast.'

'I don't know. I'm not happy about this. What about all the trouble there's been here?'

'Ken Potter's dead, remember?' she whispered. 'That's all done now. And besides, it's Saturday lunchtime and they're in the middle of town. They're safe.'

'Ah, don't worry,' Mary said. Michelle looked up, startled. She hadn't even realised she was standing next to their table, never mind that she was listening in on them. 'Those boys are all noise, no trousers. They'll give it all the attitude they can, but they're good lads at heart. Now, can I get yous all anything else?'

'No, we're done, thanks,' Michelle said. 'Lovely meal.' She meant it. The food had been perfect, just what she'd wanted despite all their original reservations and protestations. Funny how the satisfaction of a full stomach made them all feel a little more settled.

Michelle loaded George back into his pushchair then waited outside with Phoebe as Scott settled the bill.

*

They passed Tammy on the way home. She was walking along the side of the road with Heather. Jamie, Sean and Joel were following close behind. Tammy did what she could to pretend she hadn't noticed the car, even when Scott beeped the horn, wound down his window and shouted at her.

Heather and Jamie lived on the grimy-looking council estate Scott had driven them through when they'd first arrived in Thussock. They could see it looming in the distance. Tammy said nothing about what she'd thought of the place that day. Back then it had seemed like something out of a documentary made in the seventies: rows of identical houses which might have been considered tasteful and modern when they'd originally been built, cutting-edge, but which were now hideously dated and impractical. All Tammy had seen last Saturday had been the overgrown gardens and the kids sitting on walls outside squat and ugly apartment blocks. She had to admit it didn't look quite so bad today. Framed by the mountains in the distance and fields on either side, the place didn't look as sprawling and endless as it initially had. Maybe it was because last week she'd been at the wrong end of a six and a half hour car journey? Maybe it was because she was on foot now and had time to look properly? Or then again, maybe it was because after a week here her standards were already slipping?

They stopped at the recreation ground, way before they reached the estate. At first Tammy was reluctant to hang around here. Loitering in kids' playgrounds – that was the kind of thing chavs did back home. She'd given up on street corners years ago. Was this really what she'd been reduced to? Still, when she weighed up all her options and considered the alternatives, this was probably the best way of wasting time she could find. She quite liked Heather. She'd been talking inconsequential crap non-stop since leaving the café, going on about her boyfriend Chez (*he's nearly twenty, you know*), and how many times they'd done it (*he fucked me here by the swings one time... it was lush*). Tammy was starting to think Heather could be shaped, that the only reason she was rough like this was because of a lack of similarly-aged female company. She decided she'd stick with her for a while and see how things went. Anyway – and there was no way she was going to say this out loud or admit it to anyone – she quite liked

113

Jamie. He could be a real dick at times and he was way less mature than the boys she was used to back home, but he was quite cute. The best of a bad bunch. Better than nothing.

Tammy and Heather sat talking on opposite sides of the slowly spinning roundabout, occasional one-footed pushes keeping them moving. Behind them, Jamie and his mates chucked stones at the metal bins down the side of the community hall. 'Hey, Graham,' the weasel-faced one – Joel – yelled. Tammy looked up, still spinning around, and saw a man walking across the bottom edge of the recreation ground at speed, head down, doing all he could to ignore the torrent of abuse Joel was now hurling at him. He had a Co-op carrier bag clutched tight to his chest and he refused to look anywhere but directly ahead. Tammy thought he looked familiar.

'Who's that?'

'Just Graham,' Heather told her. 'Bit of an odd-ball. Works at the Co-op. Mops the floors and collects the trolleys.'

That was where she knew him from – he was the one who'd found Scott's wallet and brought it out to him.

Joel ran after Graham, sprinting down the hill and cutting him off, blocking his way through. 'Where you goin', Graham mate?'

'Home,' Graham said, head still down, refusing to make eye-contact. He tried to side-step Joel, but Joel anticipated and got in his way again.

'What's in your bag? Got any food?'

Graham clutched the bag tighter. 'Just my dinner.'

'Leave him alone, Joel,' Jamie shouted, his intervention surprising everyone.

Joel looked up and grinned. 'Just chattin' wi' me mate.'

Graham tried to pass him again, this time managing to get through. Joel ruffled his hair as he passed, then watched him walk away, now so fast he was almost running.

And again, Tammy's heart sank. *Is this really the best I can do? Hanging around in a park, watching a moron hurl abuse at the village idiot?* It hurt. Christ, she couldn't remember ever feeling so low before, not even when Mum and Dad had first split up. She walked away, trying hard not to let Heather see she was crying.

'Wassup Tam?'

114

'Nothing.'

'You missing home?' she asked with surprising perception. Tammy nodded, then the floodgates opened. 'Come on,' Heather said, getting up and putting her arm around Tammy's shoulder. 'Let's go back to mine.'

They walked towards the estate, passing Joel as he came running back up the hill they were walking down. 'Lesbians,' he shouted at them.

'Fuck off,' Heather shouted back.

'That's my sister, you prick,' Jamie said, and he booted Joel in the backside then chased him around the back of the community hall.

Tammy managed to get a text through to say where she was going, then phoned Michelle a few hours later, asking for a lift home. 'Have you seen the car keys?' Michelle asked.

'I've got them,' Scott said, tapping his pocket. 'Why?'

'Tam needs picking up.'

'I'll get her.'

'It's okay. It's just around the corner.'

'Did you not hear me? I said I'll get her. Give me the address.'

Michelle did as he said. It wasn't worth arguing.

Sunday afternoon. Michelle didn't know how much more of today she could take. George had picked up a cold – probably from the change of surroundings or mixing with new kids, she thought – and he was making life hell for everyone, moaning and grizzling and constantly demanding attention. Tammy and Phoebe were bickering about something, probably nothing, and now Scott was making a hell of a noise downstairs. She dumped George in with the girls and went to see what he was doing. She found him in the kitchen, shifting furniture. She tripped over a bucketful of tools he'd left in the doorway.

'What are you doing, Scott? I nearly crippled myself just then.'

'What's it look like I'm doing?'

He didn't give her time to answer, just swung a sledgehammer at the wall between the kitchen and dining room. It hit with a deep thud which resonated throughout the entire house. Everything in the kitchen shook. It snowed with dust. She dived for the still wet washing-up on the draining board, re-wiping and shoving plates and dishes into cupboards, cringing as the sledgehammer hit again. And again. And again.

She covered up what she could, then waited in the doorway for him to stop, watching the knee-level hole in the wall getting bigger and bigger. Already there were mounds of plaster and broken brick on either side.

'What?' he said, panting with effort, pausing for breath.

'You pick your moments.'

'Don't talk to me like that.'

'Well I've tried being tactful and that doesn't seem to work. I thought we were going to wait a while.'

'This needs doing.'

He turned his back on her, adjusted his safety goggles, then swung the sledgehammer again. Three more hits and he stopped, conscious she was still there and still watching.

'What's your problem?'

She just looked at him, seething. 'A bit of notice would have been nice.'

'I told you, this is the most important job. This needs doing first.'

'I thought we were waiting,' she said again.

'Waiting for what?'

'Waiting to get back on our feet, to get some cash behind us again. I thought you'd at least wait until we'd finished unpacking.' She peered through the hole. 'The carpet in the dining room's ruined.'

'We were gonna change it anyway.'

'That's not the point. We can't afford to change it, not yet. You know that. We talked about it.'

Three more hits. After the third strike Scott waited for the dust to settle.

'I don't know what your problem is,' he said.

'Where do you want me to start? Summer's over, Scott. With a bloody great hole in the wall we'll lose the heat.'

'Not when I've finished.'

'But you said it would take weeks.'

'Let me get on with it then. I don't know why you're being so cranky, love. I'm doing this for us.'

'If you were doing it for us, you wouldn't be doing it now.'

'It'll be worth it.'

'How many times have I heard that before?'

'I mean it.'

'You always mean it. This is the central part of the house, Scott. How am I supposed to cook meals in the middle of a building site?'

'You're exaggerating. It won't be that bad.'

'You try it then.'

He looked at her again, face more serious. 'I'm at work all day. Cooking isn't my job.'

She swallowed hard. 'It isn't my job either, but I do it because we need to eat. Same as all the cleaning I do, and the laundry and everything else.'

'Damn right too. You're sitting at home all day anyway,' he said, lifting the sledgehammer to start again. 'You'd be bored otherwise.' Michelle bit her lip. He just looked at her, waiting for a response, but knowing he wouldn't get one. 'Oh well, I've started now. Can't leave it like this, can I?' He swung once more, then stopped again. She was still there. 'Well?'

'Why do you keep doing this to me, Scott?'

'Keep doing what? I don't know what you're on about.'

'You keep undermining me, taking away the little control I've still got.'

'Now you're just talking rubbish. You're paranoid, love.'

'I'm not. You put the house on the market without consulting me, made an offer on this place without me even seeing so much as a picture. You do it on purpose, don't you?'

He turned his back on her and started hammering on the wall with more force than before.

Another hour and he was knackered. He had to stop. He stood back and admired what he'd done. He'd made good progress, managing to knock a roughly door-shaped hole through into the dining room. He'd cleared some of the rubble too, but he'd have to finish the rest after work tomorrow. If only Michelle could see things the way he did. She just didn't share his vision, always thinking about things in boring, practical, day-to-day terms. *You need to take chances from time to time*, he kept telling her. She was the one who was always banging on about wanting them all to eat together in the dining room eventually. Well, now she could carry their food straight through from the kitchen.

She was back again, hovering in the doorway. 'Looks the business, doesn't it?' he said, but she didn't seem to hear him. 'What's up with you now?'

'Have you seen Tammy?'

'No, why?'

'She's gone.'

'What do you mean, gone?'

'What do you think I mean? She's not here.'

'Well have you tried her phone?'

'She's not answering.'

'She must have said something. She'll have told Phoebe.'

'Phoebe's been in with me and George for the last hour.'

'But she must have said something?'

'If you really want to know, last time I spoke to her she said she

119

was sick of your bloody noise and she wanted out.'

'When was that?'

'Just after you started knocking hell out of the house.'

'And you didn't think to say anything? Bloody hell.'

Scott kicked his bucket of tools into the corner of the kitchen and grabbed his jacket.

'Where are you going?' Michelle asked.

'Where do you think? I'll go and look for her.'

'All due respect, I think it'd be better if I—'

'*I'll* go. Keep trying her mobile. Let me know if you hear from her. Wait here in case she comes back.'

'What else am I supposed to do?' she said as he barged past her.

Scott ran out to the car and drove towards Thussock. It seemed the most likely place for her to have gone. The sun was out, but it wasn't a particularly warm afternoon, so he couldn't imagine her wanting to walk out in the open for too long. If he didn't find her in town, he decided, he'd follow the road around the back of the house and loop around the fracking site.

The road ahead and behind was empty. He could see most of the way into town and there was no sign of any pedestrians or other traffic, let alone Tammy. Thussock was quiet at the best of times, and this afternoon it was dead. A bloody ghost town.

They'd been so busy fighting and knocking shit out of the kitchen that neither Mum or Scott had heard her tell them she was going out with Heather, Jamie and Sean. *Screw 'em*, Tammy thought. *If they can't be bothered with me, I can't be bothered with them.* She thought it strange how her perspective had changed overnight. Yesterday the idea of hanging around outside the community hall hadn't appealed in the slightest, but being here today was a blessed relief, infinitely preferable to being in that bloody house with those bloody people.

'That your dad?' Jamie asked, watching the Zafira disappear into town at speed.

'Step-dad,' Tammy corrected him quickly, staring until she was sure he was out of sight.

'He out looking for you?'

'Probably.'

120

'Should you tell someone you're here?' Heather asked.

'Can't be bothered,' Tammy immediately replied. 'Might do them some good.'

'What?'

'Might make them sit up and listen if I'm not there.'

'You reckon?'

'Probably not. They're not interested in me. It's frigging stupid, I don't wanna be here, and I don't think they even want me here. Doesn't make any sense.'

'I can relate to that,' Heather said.

Tammy leant against the frame of the swing without a seat, listening to the endless emptiness of Thussock. 'So is this really all there is to do around here?'

'Pretty much,' Heather said, checking her phone.

'Drink, Tam?' Jamie asked, and he took a small bottle of vodka from his inside coat pocket. She took it from him, unscrewed the lid, and knocked back a large slug. 'Jeez, careful.'

'I'm used to it,' she told him, and she was.

'It's not that, I just don't want you neckin' it all.'

Tammy took another gulp then passed the bottle back. 'I've been drinking this stuff for years. Takes the edge off. My mum would go mental if she knew.'

'Aye, aye,' Jamie said, walking to the furthest edge of the tarmac play area. 'Here he comes.'

Joel was speeding towards them on his bike, his thin sports jacket splayed out behind like a superhero's cape. He skidded to a halt in front of the swings, his back wheel churning up dust.

'Wassup with you?' Jamie asked.

Joel struggled to breathe. 'Another one,' he panted.

'Another what?'

'Body.'

'Grow up, Joel,' Heather said. Joel shook his head furiously.

'I swear, Hev, they found another body. Dead woman, this time.'

'Where?'

'Alderman Avenue. Right by your place. Neighbour found her this morning.'

'Who?' Tammy asked.

'Angela sumthin'.'

'No idea,' Jamie said, but Heather knew who he was talking about.

'She that woman with the weird name? Polish or sumthin'? The prossie?'

'That's her,' Joel said.

'So what happened?' Jamie asked

'Like that girl your dad found,' he replied, looking at Tammy.

'Step-dad.'

'Whatever. Anyway, Mark says she was all fucked up like some-one'd been messin' with her. Fucking sicko if y'ask me.'

'Who's Mark?'

'My mum's boyfriend. I trust him, though. He don't usually lie to me, not about stuff like this.'

'Stuff like this? You make it sound as if it happens all the time here.'

'Only since you got here,' he said without thinking. 'Shit. Sorry. Didn't mean to say you was involved or nothin'...'

'I'm not.'

'I don't get it,' Heather said.

'Don't get what?' Tammy asked.

'People were sayin' Ken Potter killed that girl at his house then he did himself in.'

'So?'

'So if this Angela whatever-her-name-was is fresh—'

'Fresh?' Tammy said, puzzled.

'If she's only just been cut up, then maybe Potter didn't do it?'

Bored of hanging around with the boys, Tammy and Heather later walked arm in arm along a footpath which ran parallel with the high street, tucked out of sight behind the buildings. To their left; open space, green and empty. To the right; the backs of shops and offices, wheelie-bins and cluttered yard spaces. Tammy hadn't been down here before. With all the talk of murders and perverts round here, she thought they were taking an unnecessary risk. But it was worth it. Being hidden down here meant Scott would stand less chance of finding her.

They talked about nothing of any importance, and that suited both of them. A sudden stench took Tammy by surprise. 'What's that smell? That's horrible.'

'The brewery,' Heather explained. 'You get used to it. Depends which way the wind's blowing. Sometimes in summer the whole bloody town stinks like that for days.'

'Great. Just when I thought things couldn't get any better.'

The footpath dipped. A narrow metal footbridge crossed a small stream, then the path climbed again. They passed a bench under a lamppost, another popular place for hanging out, it seemed. Most of the seat's struts were broken, the worn grass littered with cigarette butts. A wire-mesh waste bin was a third full of beer cans and bottles. The footpath curved right then ran parallel with a grey stone wall. 'There's a cut through in a minute,' Heather said, checking her phone again. 'Brings us out by the Co-op.'

Tammy followed her down a dingy alleyway. They emerged at the far end of the high street, close to the supermarket. Heather made straight for the shop. 'I'll wait out here for you,' Tammy said.

'You sure?'

'I'm sure. I've got no cash.'

'Right then. Back in a sec.'

Tammy had been waiting at the side of the road for less than a minute when a car – just about the only car she'd seen apart from Scott's – screeched to a halt in front of her. She'd seen it before. She'd seen the driver before too. Bloody creep. He wound down his window and leant across to talk to her. 'You all right out here, love?'

'I'm fine,' she answered quickly. 'And I'm not your love.'

'Let me give you a lift home.'

'No, thanks. Mum said never to accept lifts from strangers.'

He laughed then licked his lips. 'That's the thing, though, I'm no stranger. I know your mother. I met her this Friday just gone. She was at my house. My name's Dez.'

'Bullshit.'

'I swear, that's my name!' he said, grinning at her now.

'You know what I mean. You don't know my mum. You saw me with her last week.'

'It's true, I tell ye. Come on, sweetie, let me give you a lift back. Looks like it's gonna rain.'

'Do you think I'm fucking stupid?'

'I think you've a fucking foul mouth on ye.'

'Leave me alone. Bloody creep.'

'Ah, come on... don't be like that.'

Tammy started to walk away. Dez followed in the car, crawling alongside the pavement, making her feel even more uncomfortable than she already did, like she was on the game. 'Will you just piss off?' she hissed at him.

'I'm just lookin' out for you is all,' he said. 'You can't be too careful these days. I hear there's been more trouble down on the estate.'

She stopped walking and bent down to talk to him, leaning into the window like the hooker he obviously thought – or hoped – she was. *Thank Christ for those two slugs of vodka*, she thought, *Dutch courage*. 'Did you not get the message? Fuck off and leave me alone!'

She caught his eye – watching him watching her – and it made her feel sick. The way he looked her up and down, lingering too long on all the places he shouldn't, licking his lips like she imagined he wanted to lick her... she'd had blokes back home who were way out of this lame fucker's league; blokes with money and style, not some washed-up hillbilly prick in a grubby football tee and a knackered old car. 'Last chance,' he said, not giving up. 'Like I said, just looking out for you.'

And then it struck her, and she pushed herself away from the car and staggered back. Was it him? Was he the one? Was this the sick bastard who'd done all the killing...?

'Did you not hear the lady, Dezzie? Leave her alone or I'll have a word with your Jackie when I see her next.'

Tammy spun around and saw a young man behind her. He was tall and relatively good looking by Thussock's low standards, and he had his arm around Heather. She turned back when the pervert in the car sped away, his knackered exhaust filling the air with ugly noise. 'This is Chez,' Heather said, introducing him.

'Hope you didn't mind me butting in,' Chez said. 'That Dez is a frigging idiot. Fuck knows why Jackie puts up with him.'

'I was fine,' Tammy replied, indignant. 'But thanks, anyway.'

'You related to Scott?'

'Unfortunately. He's my step-dad. Why, you know him?'

'I work with him at Barry's yard.'

'Lucky you.'

The conversation stalled. Chez and Heather exchanged less than subtle glances and Tammy knew what was coming. 'Look, Tam,' Heather said, 'I'm going to head back to Chez's for a while. Do you mind?'

'You're welcome to come,' Chez said quickly, but it was pretty obvious she wasn't.

'No, I'm fine. I'll head home in a while.' Then she remembered something. 'Is there a phone box around here? My mobile's crap and I want to try and call my dad.'

'Everybody's mobile signal is shite here,' Chez said. 'You not got a phone at home?'

'Don't want everybody listening in.'

'Fair enough. The nearest phone box is the only phone box. It's by the café. You know it?'

Of course she knew it. It dawned on her that she'd been staring at the damn thing through the café window yesterday while they'd been eating. 'I know it. Thanks.'

'Sure you'll be okay, Tam?'

'I'm sure.'

'See you at school tomorrow?'

'Yep. See you then.'

Tammy watched the two of them drift away. They had a complete lack of urgency about them, like it didn't matter where they were going or how long it took to get there. The way they walked across the main road without even bothering to check for traffic seemed to perfectly sum up the listless pointlessness of life in Thussock.

Tammy found the phone box without any problems, glad to be doing something positive at last, not just hanging around. This call was going to be difficult, but she was resigned to that. Hearing Dad's voice would only emphasise how far from him she was but she had to do it. She needed reassurance that the old world she'd left behind still existed and that, maybe, she had a chance of getting back there. It felt like a fucked-up version of the Wizard of Oz, like she was stuck here trying to get back to Kansas. The place was full of munchkins, witches and other oddballs all right, but there was no yellow brick road running through the middle of this shit-hole.

She checked her pocket for change. Jeez, this felt so antiquated. She couldn't remember when she'd last needed to use a phone box to make a call. Finding enough loose coins had been an ordeal in itself. She did all her shopping online or used her bank card, rarely ever used cash. In the end she'd helped herself to a handful of silver and a couple of pound coins from the change pot Mum and Scott kept on the kitchen windowsill. Scott had been so busy knocking seven shades of shit out of the wall he hadn't even heard her take it.

The phone box smelled bad. It was an ugly metal and glass box, not one of the old traditional red ones. The glass was covered in graffiti, names and tags and Christ knows what else scratched onto every panel. She couldn't make out any of it. She didn't know why she was bothering to look.

Do I put in the money first or pick up the receiver? It took her a while to remember the order of things. She dialled Dad's home number from memory (she thought it made sense to try his landline first – less expensive), then hung up and dialled again when she realised she hadn't dialled the area code. She was so used to them all living within the same few miles radius...

A pause which dragged endlessly, then the click of connection and the phone finally started ringing out. She'd often phoned Dad around this time on a Sunday afternoon before. Although he was out of the country most weeks, he didn't usually leave until late Sunday or early Monday. He'd had an agreement with his employers to spend weekends at home so he could be available for her and Phoebe. When he and Mum had first split up and the atmosphere between them had been at its most volatile, reassuring weekly phone calls on a Sunday afternoon had been the norm.

Connected.

'Hello...'

'Dad, it's me, Tammy. I just wanted to—'

'...you're through to Jeremy. I'm sorry I can't get to the phone right now, but if you leave your name and number after the tone, I'll do my best to get back to you...'

The realisation she was talking to an answering machine, not her dad, hit Tammy like a punch to the gut: the sudden elation she felt at hearing his voice disappearing in a heartbeat. For a moment she felt embarrassed, then frustrated, then angry. She waited for the message to finish, listening to her father's voice for as long as she could, before unloading after the high-pitched tone as instructed. All her emotion, all the pent-up frustrations... everything came pouring out. 'Dad, it's Tammy. I need to talk to you. Please pick up if you're there. I'll try your mobile in a minute but I still can't get a decent signal in this crap-hole so I'm calling from a phone box. I need to talk to you, Dad. I need you to come and get me. I can't stand it here. I feel... I'm really...' She stopped talking; a brief pause to try and regain her composure. *Don't get upset.* 'Dad, I'm really not happy here. I know it's only been a week and I know you said I needed to see how things were after a month, but... but I really want to come home.' She stopped again, the word *home* making her feel desperately sad and empty. She was trying hard not to cry again, but once she'd started it was impossible to stop. The tears came so hard and so fast it was difficult to keep talking. She didn't know if he'd even be able to understand her. 'I can't stand it here, Dad. It's so backwards... so weird. The people are strange. It's like being stuck in the past. I don't like the school, can't do all the courses I wanted to, and there's all kinds of stuff going on around here. I bet you've seen it on the news... It's not safe here, Dad. *We're* not safe.'

She didn't know how long she had before the recording ran out, but she kept talking anyway. 'Scott's acting like a jerk as usual. He's been fighting with Mum again. I don't trust him. I don't like being around him, Dad. I never know what he's going to be like. One minute he's fine, the next he's—'

Something slammed up against the door of the phone box behind her. Her heart racing, still holding onto the phone, desperate to stay connected, she slowly turned around.

She screamed out loud when she saw him.

It was that oddball Graham from the Co-op, all wild hair and staring eyes, and he was leaning up against the glass, masturbating. His lips and tongue left greasy drooled smears, as if he was trying to French kiss her through the glass. Tammy screamed again and dropped the phone, cowering back in the corner, but Graham wasn't going anywhere. She locked her arms and held the door shut, stopping him getting inside. He remained completely unfazed, leaning against the phone box with one hand, stroking his cock with the other. She tried to look anywhere but at his dribbling erection and ginger pubes.

Their eyes met again. He was just staring at her... lusting after her. The initial shock began to fade slightly and she was left feeling... Christ, she didn't know what she was feeling now. She wanted to get out and run, wanted to slam his cock in the door... But he was all right, wasn't he? It wasn't his fault. He was just a bit simple...

Stop. What the hell are you thinking?

He wasn't so bad. He was still wanking in front of her in broad daylight, of course, but so what? Graham wasn't the brightest spark, but then again, she didn't really know him... didn't know anything about him. He probably didn't mean her any harm, he just wanted to hold her, to be held himself. Poor guy. It had probably been a long time since anyone had shown him any affection, if ever. She looked into his hazel eyes again, magnified by the lenses of his glasses, and she wondered if she'd misjudged him. He had a lovely face actually... kind and gentle, innocent... She wondered if he'd ever kissed a girl like her and—

—and then he was gone.

In a flurry of barely-controlled movement, someone rugby tackled Graham, sending him flying across the pavement. The two men came to rest in a tangled heap against the wall of a pharmacy. Immediately brought crashing back to reality again, her head all over the place, wondering what the fuck she'd just been thinking and why she hadn't panicked and run, Tammy continued to hold the phone box door shut. Could this horrifically fucked-up place possibly get any worse? The scratched glass, almost opaque with graffiti in places, now covered with Graham's semen and drool, was difficult to see through. Who was out there? Was it Heather's boyfriend, Chez? Was it Jamie? That creepy guy Dez again? She felt relieved and disappointed in equal measure when she spotted Scott's car parked across the street, the door open and the engine still running. Without hesitation she ran over and climbed in, pulling the door shut behind her.

On the pavement outside the shop, Scott grappled with the pervert who'd been flashing at his step-daughter. He already had a distinct height, weight and strength advantage over Graham, but he wasn't holding back. He wanted to teach this sick little bastard a lesson. On top of him now, pinning his arms down with his knees, one hand wrapped around his throat, he threw punch after undefended punch at Graham's face. Scott's hand stung but he kept pounding, splitting Graham's lip and breaking his nose, blood all over the place. When the pain in his hand became too much to stand, Scott stood up and staggered away, panting hard. Graham lifted himself up onto one elbow, struggling for breath, blowing bloody bubbles from one nostril and from the corner of his mouth. Scott ran back at him again and kicked the sick fucker in the gut, feeling real satisfaction when the tip of his boot struck bone. 'You stay away from my family, you dumb cunt, understand?'

Graham was crying... whining... but still trying to get up. Scott grabbed his collar and lifted him 'til their faces were just inches apart.

'You understand me?'

Graham nodded. Scott spat in his face, then dropped him back down.

Where the fuck was she?

Scott looked around and panicked when he couldn't see Tammy. He couldn't see anyone, thankfully. Then he spotted her sitting in the passenger seat of his car and he ran over.

She was sobbing. 'I'm sorry... I just wanted to talk to Dad...'

Scott wasn't listening. He turned the car around in the road, bumping up the opposite kerb, missing Graham's outstretched foot by just a few inches, then accelerated hard.

'You stupid, selfish little bitch. Your mum's been going out of her mind. What the fuck did you think you were doing?'

'I'm sorry...'

'You need to sort yourself out, you hear me?' No response. 'I don't give a shit who you think you are, I'm in charge here. Got it?'

'I get it,' she said, her voice barely audible over the noise of the straining engine.

Once she was sure the car had gone, Mary McLeod unlocked the café door and went outside. She'd seen everything. Graham had had it coming to him, silly bloody idiot, but that had been a hell of a beating he'd just taken. She'd been too scared to get involved. By the time she thought about phoning the police, that horrible, miserable man from Birmingham had gone.

She looked up and down the street. There was no one else around. Just her and Graham.

She tried to pick him up and help him walk, but he was too weak. He was really in a bad way, and the silly sod still had his trousers around his ankles. 'What are we going to do with yous, Graham? You're in a real mess, lover. Let's get yous over the road and get yous sorted.'

She pulled him close and tried to pick him up again, but she couldn't cope with his weight. He groaned with pain, his mouth next to her ear, his breath tickling the side of her face. She liked that. 'What would your old mum think? I kept telling her when she got ill that you'd be all right, and you had been 'til now. What d'you have to go and do that to that girl for, love?'

Mary didn't have the strength to get him into the café, but she couldn't leave him here. She didn't want to leave him, didn't even want to let him go for a second. In a series of hefts and grunts, she managed to shift his bulk up onto the front step of the pharmacy, the sunken doorway giving them a little privacy.

And she sat him there with his back to the door, one side of his face a mass of purple bruising, blood dripping from his nose, trousers still around his ankles, his hard penis still upright and erect. She kissed him and ran her fingers through his mop of hair. 'You poor love.'

And he looked up at her with wide, staring eyes, and he pulled her even closer.

12

Scott had barely spoken since he'd got back to the house with Tammy. It was late now, almost eleven, and he was still hammering in the kitchen. Michelle had learnt to keep her distance at times like this, and though the circumstances tonight were wholly different, there had been plenty of times like this before now.

Phoebe and George were, thankfully, managing to sleep through. Michelle crept upstairs to check on Tammy. They'd talked – argued – when she and Scott had returned from Thussock. Tammy had accepted she'd been way out of line, but Michelle understood her daughter's frustrations. She was feeling them herself. She gently knocked on Tammy's bedroom door, then let herself in. 'You still awake, love?'

Tammy was lying in bed with her back to the door. The curtains were open, moonlight flooding in. Michelle tiptoed around the room and crouched down. Tammy's eyes were wide open and she clutched a tissue in her hand. She continued to stare into space before slowly looking over at her mother.

'I'm sorry,' she said.

Michelle shook her head. 'What's done is done. That's not why I came up. I just wanted to see if you were okay.'

A pause. The noise downstairs had stopped. They held their breath and waited until it started again.

'Of course I'm not okay,' Tammy answered, sniffing back more tears. 'I don't think I'll ever be okay here.'

'You've got to stop talking like that, love. We are—'

'—where we are. I know. Give it a rest, Mum.'

Michelle sat down on the bed, her legs tired from crouching. She stroked Tammy's long hair. 'I'm sorry.'

'What have you got to be sorry about? You haven't done anything wrong.'

'Doesn't feel that way.'

'It's not you... it's *him*.'

'Please don't...'

'But you should have seen him. You should have seen the way he attacked that bloke, Mum. He scared me more than anything else.'

'I know Scott's got a temper, but—'

'He just kept punching him and punching him... there was blood everywhere.'

'No matter what you think about what he did, Tam, it was for the right reasons. He was trying to protect you, trying to keep you safe.'

'But I don't feel safe. Not around Scott.'

'You have to keep things in perspective. Think about how he was feeling, how worried we both were...'

Tammy sat up, held her mother's gaze. 'This was different, Mum. It was like he'd gone insane, completely lost it. It makes me wonder...' She allowed her voice to trail away, not sure if she should continue.

'What, Tammy?'

'It makes me wonder about the body he found in that garden, that's all.'

'What are you talking about?'

'It just makes me wonder if he's as innocent as he makes himself out to be.'

'That's just rubbish...'

'Is it? Hell of a coincidence. All this stuff happened since Scott got here.'

'You can't talk like this, Tam.'

'Why not?'

'Just listen to yourself. You're saying Scott's a serial killer? Seriously?'

'But you know better than anyone what he's like, what he's capable of.'

'Yes, but—'

'I don't want him to hurt you more than he already has, Mum. You need to do something because next time might be too late.'

Michelle got up fast, her head full of thoughts she didn't want to think, certainly didn't dare vocalise. This was too much. On top of everything that had already happened, this was just too much...

The hammering downstairs had stopped. She rushed back down to Scott.

13

Not even six o'clock yet. It was barely even light. Scott had hardly slept. His arms felt like lead from all the work he'd done yesterday, he had to go to work in a couple of hours, and now some selfish fucker was banging on the front door at this hour. Michelle rolled over onto her back and groaned something he couldn't make out. 'I'll get it, shall I?' he said. *Fucking useless family.*

Scott grabbed yesterday's dust-covered T-shirt and jeans off the floor and put them on again. The noise at the door continued. *If they wake George up*, he thought, *I'll have this fucker's balls.* He felt in the mood for a fight. *Another* fight.

He fumbled with the chain and the lock, then yanked the door open. The man on the doorstep surprised him. They'd met before at Kenneth Potter's house. 'Scott Griffiths?' Sergeant Ross asked. Scott didn't immediately respond with anything other than a bemused mumble and a nod of the head. The officer spoke again. 'Scott Griffiths, I'm arresting you on suspicion of the murder of Graham McBride. You are not obliged to say anything, but anything you do say will be noted down and may be used in evidence. Do you understand?'

Scott looked at him, blank. Was this a joke? 'Who the fuck's Graham McBride?' he said, then realisation dawned. Last night. Tammy. The pervert outside the phone box with his dick out. Scott's legs weakened. 'Shit...'

'Do you understand, Mr Griffiths?'

'I understand,' he said, still not sure he did. 'Murder? But I didn't... It wasn't my fault. He was exposing himself at my step-daughter and I just...'

'I need to remind you that you're under caution, sir.'

'What the hell's going on?' Michelle demanded. Scott looked around to try and explain but he couldn't speak, could barely even begin to process what was happening. His mouth was dry. 'Scott?' she said. 'Scott, what's this about?'

He just looked at her, then looked at the police officer, then shook his head. He felt numb inside... didn't know what to do, what to say... Had he killed a man?

Sergeant Ross moved aside to let one of his officers cuff Scott. Scott didn't resist. Didn't do anything. 'Get him in the van, Hamilton,' the sergeant ordered before turning his attention to Michelle. 'Mrs Griffiths?'

'Yes...' she said quietly, watching in stunned disbelief as they led her husband away.

'We've witnesses who've identified your husband as being involved in an altercation with Mr McBride yesterday afternoon, during which Mr McBride sustained serious injuries. I'm sorry to have to inform you he's since died from those injuries.'

The sergeant continued to talk, and Michelle continued to listen, though nothing she was hearing was making any sense now. She wanted to protest but what could she say? Scott had been in a fight yesterday, but he'd told her he'd just knocked the other man about a bit... just enough to scare him. Then she remembered how Tammy had described the incident. Jesus, exactly what had Scott done?

George was crying now. Tammy was downstairs. She was at the bottom of the staircase, just behind her mother. 'Mum, what's happening. Are they—?'

'Go and see to George,' Michelle interrupted, screaming at her daughter to move. But it was too late. Phoebe already had George and they were all crowded into the hallway now, watching Scott being bundled into the back of a police van and driven away.

The sergeant told Michelle in no uncertain terms to stay home and wait for news. All she could do was watch as the convoy of two patrol cars and the van turned right out of the drive and headed for Thussock.

Tammy shut the door. Michelle leant against the wall, then slid down to the floor and stayed there, feet sticking out across the hallway. Numb.

'What's going on?' Phoebe asked.

'They took Scott,' Tammy started to explain.

'Took him where?'

'Where d'you think? The police station.'

'But why?'

'You tell me. You never know with Scott. I think he—'

134

'He's there because he tried to protect you,' Michelle screamed at her.

'I'm sorry, Mum, I just...'

'This is *your* fault. If you hadn't disappeared yesterday, none of this would have happened.'

Tammy's visible shock turned to anger. 'It's not my fault. How is any of this my fault? Come on, explain it to me... I had to get out of the house because I was sick of the noise and the atmosphere – not my fault. The local pervert decides to flash his dick at me – not my fault. Scott decides to beat the crap out of him – not my fault. You marry a fucking idiot who makes all our lives hell, treats you like shit and knocks you about, then drags us the length of the country away from anyone and anything that matters to us when *he* fucks up – that's not my fault either.'

Sobbing, Michelle got up and walked into the kitchen, her head spinning. Tammy followed her. Phoebe – eyes wide, nervous as hell, still holding onto George – didn't move.

'Scott messed up,' Michelle said. 'I get it.'

'No, Mum, you don't. Scott messed up *again*. We all get hurt because of him *again*. It's not the first time and it won't be the last.'

'You've got him all wrong.'

'No I haven't. It's you who's wrong. You're the one in denial. Scott ruins lives, it's as simple as that. Yours, ours, that bloke from yesterday, that little girl...'

'It was an accident. Stop bringing her up. There's not a day goes by when he doesn't—'

'No one else matters to Scott but Scott, don't you see that?'

'That's not true. What happened with that little girl could have happened to anyone.'

'He didn't stop. Bloody hell, Mum, he didn't stop. He hit her and he didn't stop.'

'He went back...'

'It was too late. She was already dead.'

'We've been over this a million times. He made a mistake. He accepts that now. He paid the price.'

'No, *we're* paying the price.'

'Look, I know you resent him and—'

'I don't resent him, Mum, I *hate* him. I hate him for what he's doing to you.'

'And I *love* him. I know what he is and what he does, but I love him.'

'Jesus, that's pathetic.'

'Well it happens to be true. Please don't fight against me, Tammy. I need you and your sister. I don't know if I can go through all this again.'

'Do you think he did it?'

Tammy's question floored Michelle for a moment. She answered instinctively, though with enough hesitation to reveal a trace of doubt. 'No.'

'You know what he's capable of. You more than anyone. He's hit you enough times...'

'He's not a murderer. He might be many things, but he's not a murderer.'

'Who are you trying to kid, Mum?'

'Tammy, just leave it,' Michelle yelled. 'I can't handle this, not now. We're right on the edge here, in case you hadn't noticed.'

'He's already been responsible for one death...'

'You think I don't know that?'

'But he never takes responsibility. He always finds someone else to blame or finds a way to squirm out of it.'

'Please, Tam... please just stop.'

'No, Mum. You need to face facts and—'

'There's nothing I can do, can't you see that? Christ knows I've already tried. I don't have a way out, love. There's nowhere left for me to go. I've got nowhere left to run to.'

14

The processing brought back all kinds of foul memories Scott thought he'd buried forever. It was a different police station with different officers who wore different badges and spoke with different accents, but their routine and intent was immediately familiar and the helplessness he felt took him straight back to that day. The noises. The smells. The way they looked at him and spoke to him, *at* him. And in his gut it felt just the same too. He knew what he'd done to that poor little girl as soon as he felt the van hit her and bump over her tiny, fragile body, and he knew what he'd done to that pervert last night too. But should he have just let that freak wave his dick at Tammy until he'd got bored? Christ, imagine what they'd have said if he'd just sat back and not done what he'd did. No, he'd had to do it. He'd been right to do it.

After the frantic activity of the last hour, time had now slowed to an unbearable crawl. All kinds of thoughts ran through Scott's mind as he waited in the cell, all kinds of buzzwords and phrases he'd heard used before: *reasonable force, self-defence...* but nothing fitted his circumstances. He was fucked. He kept thinking he should try and put up a fight to clear his name, but what good would that do him? It was fighting that had got him here. Part of him thought he should just accept what was coming, to confess to whatever they charged him with in an attempt to cooperate and hopefully reduce the hell he knew he was inevitably facing. Just get it over with...

And then things changed again.

Everything suddenly stopped being quite so uncomfortably familiar and became even more uncomfortably unpredictable. He knew this wasn't how things were supposed to be, that the police were turning a blind eye and playing fast and loose with procedures, but why? Was it, as he suspected, a clichéd case of locals closing ranks to deal with an *outsider* who, they'd decided, had harmed one of their own? Or was this just the way things were done up here? Whatever the reason, it was playing out like a scene from a bad TV drama: just him and a plain-clothes officer facing each other in a grey and featureless room. The door was slightly ajar. There was someone waiting outside.

'I need a lawyer,' Scott said, remembering the TV routine. 'I'm not saying anything until I've got a lawyer.'

'On his way,' the officer said. He looked to be in his mid- to late-fifties, grey-haired, with a bulbous, purple-tinged, drinker's nose. Scott could see straight through him, trying to act all casual and matey, like he'd just decided to stick his head around the door on the off chance Scott felt like a chat or maybe confessing... save them all a load of hassle. This guy really seemed keen to live up to all the clichés: world weary, jaded, been around the block a few too many times... Scott might have risked taking the piss if he hadn't been so bloody frightened. *This your last week in the job, officer? One final case to crack before you hand in your badge for good? Do you keep a bottle of whiskey in your desk drawer? Do you live alone? Wife got bored and found someone else because in all your twenty-plus years together, you've always really been married to the force...*

'Who are you?'

'My name's Detective Inspector Litherland. I thought we might try and help each other out, Scott. Your brief's going to be a while getting here. That's the problem with living somewhere like Thussock, as I'm sure you've already discovered. It takes forever to get anywhere.'

'I'd rather wait.'

'Your prerogative, of course. Don't be too hasty, though. You scratch my back, and all that shite...'

'Nice. What is this, *Taggart*?'

'You're in no position to take the piss, sunshine. I'd be very careful if I were you. Believe me, you're in a shitload of trouble right now.'

Scott bit his tongue. He knew the detective was right. He swallowed hard and looked away, not wanting him to see how nervous he was. But then again, it wouldn't have taken a body language expert to work that out. The back of his shirt was drenched with sweat; dark, wet rings under both armpits. He constantly chewed the ends of his fingers.

'Okay, Scott,' the detective said, 'I'll lay things on the line for you here, just so you know what we're dealing with. Graham McBride is dead, and we've several witnesses who saw you beating seven shades of shit out of him shortly before he died.'

'No comment.'

'I'm not really asking for your thoughts just now, sunshine, I just need you to listen. Absorb and understand, okay? Now, as I was saying, you were seen kicking seven shades of shit out of Mr McBride—'

'He was harassing my step-daughter. He had his dick in his hands for Christ's sake. He was wanking himself off. She's not even seventeen... what would you have done?'

'Calm down, Scott, I'm not here to—'

'Sure I punched him a couple of times, but I didn't do enough to kill him.'

'Medical expert, are you?'

'No, I—'

'Or is it that you checked Mr McBride was okay after you finished beating him up? Oh no, that's right, you didn't. You left him at the side of the road, barely even breathing.'

'It wasn't like that. I didn't—'

'Slow down, and calm down. Take your time. As I said, listen to me first, then we'll talk. You see, my biggest problem right now is that it's not just Mr McBride we're talking about here. Poor old Graham's not the only death we've had to deal with recently.'

'I don't know anything.'

'Think carefully, Scott.'

'I told you, I—'

Litherland raised his hand, silencing Scott mid-sentence. 'Remind me again, how long is it that you and your family have lived in Thussock?'

'We moved here last Saturday.'

'By we, I take it you mean your family?'

'Yes.'

'So what about *you*? How long have you yourself been up here?'

'I came up about a week and a half earlier to get the house straight. Wait, what are you saying? Do you think I—?'

'I'm not saying anything. My job's not to suppose, it's to prove. You see, I'm just trying to work out what's going on around here. Look at it from my perspective... until these last few weeks, there'd only been one murder here in eight years. Now in the time since you first got here, seven people have died. Heck of a coincidence.'

'And that's all it is, a coincidence. I don't know anything.' He stopped, still trying to make sense of all of this. The woman in the woods, Potter, the girl in his garden, that nutter Graham McBride... 'Wait... seven people?'

Litherland picked up a folder full of papers, then sat down opposite Scott. If he was trying to intimidate him, it was working. 'Giles Hitchen,' he said.

'Never heard of him.'

'You sure? Think carefully, lad.' The detective pulled out a glossy photograph from the folder and passed it to Scott. He looked at it briefly, then put it down on the table. A young guy sprawled across a pavement on his back, his head and shoulders hidden in the hedgerow, legs naked and drenched with blood. What was left of his shredded penis hung between them. The gore was astonishingly vivid: a crimson scrawl across the monotone.

'I don't know anything about this,' he said. 'I've never seen this man.'

'Joan Lummock.'

Another photograph, this one even worse. A woman in her late fifties, her skin discoloured by the first signs of decay, lying on a bed of blood-soaked leaf litter. He recognised the location from TV reports he'd seen. This was the woman they'd found in the forest last weekend. Again, same as the last picture, she was naked from the waist down. What was left of the rest of her was hard to make out; a vile, bloody mess instead of a vagina. Scott could barely stand to look.

'I don't know anything,' he said, simply and emphatically.

'Took us a while to find poor Joan,' Litherland continued. 'She'd been missing a day or so by the time we got to her. None of this ringing any bells?'

'I heard about her on TV, but that's all.'

A third photograph. A dead man in walking gear, anorak on top, waterproof trousers wrapped around one ankle. He was slumped against a wall inside a particularly cramped looking house, his groin eviscerated.

'David Ferguson. Retired. Recently widowed. Father of four. His youngest, Karen, did admin work here at the station for a while. David was found like this up at the youth hostel near Glenfirth.'

Scott looked into the dead man's face, his lifeless eyes staring at nothing. His glasses were at an awkward angle, half-on, half-off. It was easier to focus on them than on the rest of the bloody corpse.

'How many times do I have to tell you, I don't know anything about this.'

'I'm not so sure.'

'I swear!'

Unperturbed, Litherland continued. Another photograph, this one depressingly familiar. 'Shona McIntyre. You must remember poor Shona?'

'Of course I do. She's the girl Ken Potter—'

'—she's the girl you found in Ken Potter's garden,' Litherland said, correcting him.

Next photograph. Barely a body to be seen in this one, but Scott knew exactly what it was. Parts of Ken Potter lying on and around the train track.

'Notice anything?' Litherland asked. When Scott didn't immediately respond, the detective elaborated. 'See, we thought old Ken might have been responsible for some of what's happened, but it's not looking likely. Look at his legs, Scott.'

Scott held the photograph, his hands shaking. It was hard to make out any of Potter's remains. 'Can't see his legs.'

Litherland took the photo from him and tapped his finger next to a bloody chunk of flesh beside the tracks. 'That's a foot, see?'

Scott saw. It was like one of those old 'magic eye' optical illusions he remembered – pictures hidden in patterns. Once he'd been able to make out part of it, the rest of the image seemed to come sharply into focus. There was a bare foot, an ankle, then the bottom of a leg, crushed and dismembered below the knee. It almost made him gag.

'I see it.'

'He was half naked, just like the others. We're waiting on confirmation, but it's looking like he was dead before the train hit him.'

'Jesus.'

'Happened on a stretch of track not far from Barry Walpole's yard. You've been working for Barry, haven't you?'

'Yes, but—'

Before Scott could finish his sentence, Litherland showed him another photograph. A young woman. Dyed hair, faded pink. Tattoos. Lying in the corner of someone's lawn. Mutilated like the rest of them. He felt like he was going to vomit.

'Angela Pietrszkiewicz... think I'm saying that right.'

Scott looked away. 'I've never seen her before. I don't know who she is...'

'You sure about that? Angela was found yesterday morning. Mother of two, she was. Two little kiddies. Neighbour heard them crying, then we found Mum a couple of streets away. We did door to door enquiries. Only lead we got was that she was heard talking to some bloke...'

'I was at home with my family all day yesterday. Ask them. I was with them the whole bloody day.'

The detective paused ominously. 'Yes, but I didn't say she was killed yesterday, did I? I said she was *found* yesterday. We're estimating the time of death as being sometime Saturday evening.'

'I was at home again.'

'You sure, Scott?'

'Yes. Course I'm sure.'

'Thing is, with Thussock being such a small and close-knit community, folks tend to notice things that're out of the ordinary. You and your family, you've been attracting more than your fair share of interest just by virtue of being here. No fault of your own, of course, that's just the way it is.'

'I was at home, I swear.'

'You've quite a distinctive car. Ordinary, but distinctive. Blue Zafira, isn't it? Seven-seater? One black wheel arch?'

'Yes...'

'Noisy old thing, eh?'

'What of it?'

'Well I've a number of folks who're saying they saw your car driving around the estate where Miss Pietrszkiewicz lived on Saturday evening, around the time we think she was probably killed.'

'No... no, that's not right.'

'Oh, so they're all lying are they?' He glanced at a page of notes.

'Jean Morris of Strathway Crescent says she saw a "large blue car driving up and down the road at speed", said it was making "a heck of a noise, like its exhaust was knackered". And do you know Dez Boyle?'

'Never heard of him.'

'Well he seems to know you. Dez says he saw you driving around there too. Think very carefully, Scott.'

'Wait... Tammy, my stepdaughter.'

'What about her?'

'She was at a friend's house. I picked her up in the car.'

'And what time was that?'

'I don't know... around half-eight, I think.'

'And where exactly does your daughter's friend live?'

'Wayfield Close.'

'Backs onto Alderman Avenue, that does.'

Scott shook his head. 'I wouldn't know.'

'Miss Pietrszkiewicz was found on Alderman Avenue. Litherland paused, looked at Scott again. 'So tell me, did you drive straight from your place to Wayfield Close?'

'Yes.'

'You positive?'

'Yes. Wait... I might have taken a couple of wrong turnings... that estate's like a maze. I got a bit lost.'

'So you *didn't* drive straight there?'

'You're twisting my words. I went straight to the house. I hadn't been there before and I took a wrong turn, but that doesn't mean I did anything to that woman.'

'You can see where I'm coming from though, can't you Scott? Here's me telling you about a murder on Saturday evening, and that you were seen in the vicinity, and there's you telling me you weren't there, but wait, maybe you *were* there and you were just driving around the place on your own.'

'I wasn't just driving around...'

'I think you were. It's not the first time, is it?'

'What?'

'Angela Pietrszkiewicz was a sex worker, Scott. You've a history of using prostitutes. Done for kerb crawling near to the Hagley Road in

Birmingham. You dirty little bastard.'

Scott put his head on the desk. This was getting worse by the second. 'That was a mistake,' he said. 'It was almost ten years ago. It was a one off.'

'Hardly. Mrs Morris said she'd seen your car before, a week or so back. Had you been that way before? Perhaps before the rest of your family arrived in Thussock?'

'No comment,' he mumbled.

'I think you'd been to see Angela previously, hadn't you, Scott? I think you paid Ms Pietrszkiewicz for sex.'

'No comment,' he said again, because lying was safer than telling the truth.

'So, apart from taking advantage of vulnerable young women, paying for sex and cheating on your wife, are there any other bad habits you think you should tell me about? Because there is something else interesting on your record...'

'Stop it. You're just twisting everything. This is all circumstantial. You're trying to make me out to be some kind of—'

'I'm not trying to do anything,' Litherland interrupted, 'except find out who killed all these people and stop them before they kill anyone else.'

'I need my lawyer,' Scott mumbled, barely able to form cohesive words now.

'I really think you do.'

'I had nothing to do with any of this.'

'What about Graham McBride?'

Scott started to sob involuntarily. He tried to stop himself, but that just made it worse. 'We had a fight,' he managed to say. 'I already told you.'

'That you did, aye. We know you were involved in his death, though whether you caused it or not is something the coroner's going to have to decide, and we should have her findings shortly.'

'What would you have done?' Scott asked, pleading almost. 'He exposed himself in front of my step-daughter. I did what anyone would do. Are you a parent? Do you have kids?'

'That's irrelevant. But for the record, yes, I do have kids and yes, I'd have certainly done something if I'd caught a man flashing at my

144

daughter. I'd maybe not have killed him, though.'

'But you know why I did what I did, don't you? I saw red. You do these things for your kids.'

'Not so good with other people's children though, are we, Scott?'

His heart sank. A few barely suppressed tears became an uncontrolled flood. 'This has got nothing to do with what happened back home. I made a mistake and I've been punished for it. Believe me, there's not a day goes by when I don't—'

'When you don't what, Scott? You see, I'm having trouble tying a few things up here. You've a history of lying to the police and—'

'And I've paid the price for that. Jesus, please...'

'You knocked a girl down and killed her, then just drove on.'

'I panicked.'

'Doesn't change what you did.'

'I was gone for a matter of minutes. I wasn't thinking straight. I didn't know what to do. I turned straight around and drove back but by then...'

'By then other folks had got to her. By then it was too late.'

'It didn't make any difference. She was already dead. I did it. It wasn't my fault, but I did it.'

'That's why you're here, isn't it? That's why you moved to Thussock.'

'How could we stay in Redditch? She lived on the same street as us, for Christ's sake. We knew her parents. I'd got people throwing paint at the house, people badmouthing me all over the place.'

'Hardly surprising.'

'I'm not going to argue. If I could turn back time I'd do it in a bloody heartbeat. My business went down the pan... I lost almost everything.'

'Not as much as the family of that poor kiddie though, eh? Or the relatives of any of the people who've died round here recently either.'

'I didn't do any of this. I punched that guy in the face, yes, but I didn't have anything to do with any of the others.'

'Then who did? I tell you, Scott, it's causing us some real problems. We're a small rural force, and our resources are stretched as it is.'

'Then stop wasting them on me.'

Litherland looked at him for a few seconds, weighing him up. 'This killer,' he said, 'whoever he is, is a devious little fucker. He's not leaving a bloody trace, you know. Not a single clue. No footprints, tyre tracks, fingerprints... So you can see why we're following up every lead, and why you're so interesting to us.'

'This has got nothing to do with me,' Scott sighed, exasperated, wishing he could find some way of convincing the detective but knowing he probably wouldn't.

'Sick little bastard, we're dealing with here, Scott,' Litherland continued, not finished yet. 'I do hear what you're telling me, but I can't dismiss your involvement. You saw poor Shona's body so you know how sick what's happening here really is. These people have virtually been bled dry, their bodies mutilated. Excuse my language, Scott, but I think you can probably understand how bloody angry this is making me. I've innocent people being abused then murdered in my town, and I'm gonna put a stop to it.'

'It's horrific,' Scott said, 'but I don't know how else to tell you... it's got nothing to do with me. You can't accuse me of—'

'I'm not accusing you of anything yet. I'm simply pointing out my concerns and asking you to clear a few things up. Surely you can see where I'm coming from? I might not have all the forensics I need yet, but alarm bells are ringing as far as you're concerned and you've said little to convince me otherwise. Look at it this way, the killings only started after you arrived in Thussock.'

'It's coincidental.'

'Lot of coincidences, though. You're the one who found Shona, Ken Potter died not far from where you're working, you're seen driving around on Saturday evening when Angela Pietrszkiewicz was killed and you'd already paid her for sex, you've confessed to beating the shit out of Graham McBride...'

'It's all circumstantial. It's not even that, it's just bullshit. I want my brief.'

Litherland stood up, pushed his chair under the table and collected up his gruesome, blood-spattered photographs. 'Fair enough, Scott. I'll have you taken back to your cell, then we'll do this all over again when the duty lawyer arrives.'

15

PC Mark Hamilton couldn't remember anything like this ever happening before. Not anywhere, and certainly not in Thussock. Born and raised in the town, he'd gone off to university then spent several years travelling before coming back home. He'd managed to get himself in (and out) of various dodgy situations whilst abroad and had seen more than his fair share of trouble in other postings around the country. He'd dealt with inner-city gangs, drugs traffickers, fraudsters, deviants – the whole gamut of shysters and bastards and society's dregs. But not here. Not in Thussock.

Travelling had initially broadened Mark's horizons and had made many of the people he'd left behind seem infuriatingly blinkered and self-obsessed. Being away from the town for so long, though, had also made him feel unexpectedly protective of the place. All his mates on the force thought he was out of his mind when he'd accepted the posting and come back here, but he knew what he was doing.

The crimes which had recently been committed in and around the town were unprecedented in their number and ferocity. The killings were wanton, brazen, indiscriminate, and apparently motiveless. He was glad they'd got that slimy fucker Scott Griffiths locked up in the cells. Cocky bastard. Hamilton had had his eye on that one since they'd first met at Ken Potter's house. Sergeant Ross felt the same about him, he knew he did. There was something about Griffiths which just didn't ring true. There was no denying he was a suspect. More to the point, right now he was the only suspect.

PC Hamilton walked down the high street, making a point of acknowledging all the faces he knew, and making even more of a point of acknowledging the few he didn't. He stopped and talked to several folks, letting them drive the conversations, reassuring them that everything possible was being done when the topic of conversation inevitably strayed towards recent events, going as far as to discreetly tell one or two of them that they did, in fact, have someone in custody.

In reality, this morning's foot patrol was little more than an impromptu public relations exercise. Thussock didn't particularly need much policing at this time on a Monday, but Sergeant Ross had taken great pains to stress the importance of maintaining a visible presence until they were able to go public about Scott Griffiths.

PC Hamilton was thirsty. One of the things he liked most about foot patrols like this was the freedom. In uniform he could come up with a viable reason to go just about anywhere, and right now Mary's café was calling to him. Mary McLeod could gossip with the best of them and she was always willing to share anything she'd heard on the grapevine. If she knew how he'd used the titbits she'd inadvertently dropped into conversation before now she'd have been mortified, of course, so he kept things light and informal. To Mary, PC Hamilton was still the snotty nosed little kid she used to have to shoo away from outside the café with his mates in the school holidays.

He made a beeline for the café, figuring that even if Mary didn't have any information for him today, she'd almost certainly have a mug of tea and maybe even a bacon sandwich if he played his cards right. His stomach growled at the prospect of food. He'd been on his feet since they'd brought the suspect in for questioning, and he'd likely be out a few hours longer yet. He needed sustenance.

Strange.

The café was closed. The lights were off inside.

If there was one thing he knew about Mary McLeod, it was that she never closed the café. Running the place was more than a job to her; since her husband Derek had died it had become a way of life. She lived alone now and relied on her regular customers for company more than income.

Was she ill? Worse, was she… ?

His frustration quickly gave way to something more serious. Given everything that had happened over the last few days, Mark feared for Mary's safety. Griffiths had fought with Graham McBride outside the chemist opposite. What if she'd seen them? What if Griffiths had caught her watching and done something to her? Hamilton hadn't been on duty last night when McBride had been found. He didn't know if anyone had seen Mary since. He cupped his hands around his eyes to see in through the window but it was too dark inside. He knocked the door then tried the handle. It was open.

'Mary? Mary, you in? It's PC Hamilton. It's Mark…'

Nothing. He took a few steps inside and called out for her again.

The place was deathly silent. He looked hopefully at the beaded curtain through which she always loved to make her dramatic entrances, but it just shifted with the breeze from the open door.

Wait. What was that?

He was sure he could hear movement in the back of the café and he went through to the kitchen. No sign of anyone. He knocked on the door between the private and business parts of the building – kept shut as always – then pressed his ear against it. There was definitely something in there... he could hear a faint scraping, scrabbling noise.

He pushed the door open and had barely taken a step forward when Mary's yappy little dog – Horace, he thought its name was, or was it Milly? – came running at him. It swerved between his legs and pelted past, whimpering rather than barking. Hardly a guard dog, it was little more than a tiny, highly-strung ball of fluff which generated a lot of noise and shit and served no other purpose. His girlfriend Meryl called it Mary's rat on a rope whenever they saw her out walking it in town.

The dog's unusual behaviour heightened PC Hamilton's concern. He noticed it had clawed deep grooves into the very bottom of the door in its desperation to get out.

'Mary?' he called out again. 'Mary, are you here? Is everything okay?'

He went deeper into her living area – her small private kitchen space built on the other side of the café pantry – then stopped. The place smelled awful, truly rank. His pulse began to race. She was dead, he was sure of it now. He'd seen the bodies of a couple of the other victims and the memory of their brutal and senseless mutilation was seared onto his retinas, all he could see. He'd been one of the first on the scene when those kids had found what was left of Ken Potter on the tracks, and he'd been there when Angela Pietrszkiewicz had been found too. She'd been stripped to the waist... violated... He prepared himself to find another body here, then panicked. *What if the killer's still here?* He leant against a wall and steadied himself. *Wait, it's okay... the guy from Redditch is in the cells...*

PC Hamilton trod in something moist and he froze as it squelched beneath his boot, fearing the worst. The smell hit him before he was

149

able to reach across to the curtains and let in some light. Dog shit. Gross. He gagged. Bodies he could just about cope with, but the smell of dog shit got him every time. And the floor was covered in it, scattershot diarrhoea courtesy of that vile little creature he'd just let out. He kicked off his boots rather than risk treading shit through the rest of the house, then picked his way through the canine mine-field. Christ, why did people bother with dogs? Meryl had a cat, and as much as he despised the needy little fucker, at least it always took itself outside to crap then buried the evidence afterwards.

'Mary?' he shouted again. He edged down her short hallway then looked into the living room. The curtains were open. No Mary. More importantly, no body.

Upstairs.

He climbed the steps slowly, his sock-clad footsteps making little noise. He tried to think of as many possible explanations for the situation as he could: Mary's just overslept, she's ill, she's had a heart attack, she's fallen out of bed and broken something, she's just not here... He focused on those slightly more palatable options and tried to block out the idea of finding her like Angela Pietrszkiewicz yesterday, covered in blood, with every last shred of dignity barbarically stripped away.

Onto the landing. Still nothing but silence. He worked his way along, room by room. The bathroom was empty, as was the back bedroom. The door to Mary's room was ajar. He took a deep breath then knocked and pushed it open. 'Mary?'

He didn't look until he had to, not knowing what he was going to find.

The relief was immense.

Mary was sitting on the floor at the foot of her bed, wearing a loose, open dress and very little else. She looked up at him and smiled and he felt himself relax. 'Thank Christ you're okay,' he said. 'Did you not hear me shouting?'

'No, sorry.'

He looked at her again, then looked away with embarrassment when he realised how much of her flabby body was on show. She'd been grossly overweight for as long as he'd known her, so large that she'd scared him when he was a kid; a grotesquely made-up, moun-

150

tainous monster. He'd vivid memories of her catching him and his mates playing around by her bins one time. His mates had got away, but she'd managed to grab him. He could still remember the smell of used cooking fat and cigarettes and the feel of her pudgy hands on his shoulders, greasy from working with cooking oil all day, every day.

'Is everything all right, Mary?'

He made himself look again. She was on the floor with her legs splayed, everything on show. *No knickers*, he thought, and he tried not to stare but he couldn't help himself, his eyes drawn to the parts of her he wanted to see least.

'Cold,' she said. She lifted her head and looked at him. She'd got the most beautiful eyes. He'd never really noticed them before. They were deep brown. Warm. Welcoming. Irises almost as dark as her pupils. She had a kind, motherly face, but she'd always covered herself with too much makeup for his liking, tried too hard with her hair and clothes, like she was clinging onto long gone youth. For crying out loud, she'd gone to school with his mother. She was no spring chicken.

But today Mary looked... different. He felt the awkwardness melting away.

PC Hamilton remained in the bedroom doorway, watching her watching him. He couldn't put his finger on what was different about her today. In fact, he decided, there wasn't anything specific, she just looked... right. Motherly. But it was more than that. He took a few steps further into the room then stopped and knelt down next to her, wanting to help, wanting to be sure she was okay. 'You sure you're all right?'

Mary lifted a hand and touched the side of his face. 'Fine,' she said, her voice an alluring, airy whisper.

He tried to move, but he was rooted to the spot by her serene beauty. His mouth was dry, his pulse quickening. He'd never thought of Mary in this way before. It was hard to accept, but he realised he wanted her.

What the hell? Don't be stupid, man. She's old and greasy... this is Mary from the café for crying out loud...

But there was no denying the attraction. She still had her hand on

151

his face and he leant against her touch, then he pushed himself even closer and kissed her cheek and revelled in the closeness. Her smell... oh, her smell... words couldn't express how it made him feel inside. So natural, so *right*. He felt a burning in his gut now that he fought hard to ignore. He wanted her, but he knew that was ridiculous. *I'm twenty-seven, she's got to be almost seventy...* It wasn't going to happen. Not here. Not now. Not Mary. It was wrong on every conceivable level.

But that burning was getting stronger. He couldn't understand it, but he couldn't dismiss it either. He'd known her for more than twenty years, but had never appreciated her like this before. Why hadn't he seen it until today? And she felt it too, he knew she did. The way she looked at him, the way she touched him... The way her breathing had changed: light with frequent fluttering gasps now, like the way Meryl's breathing changed when they made love together. Not when they fucked while her dad was out and not how it was when she was on about having kids again and sex was contrived, but how they connected in those rare moments when circumstances and emotions combined and collided perfectly, when they had the kind of sex that made him feel alive, more than human.

He knew Mary would make him feel that way this morning. He wanted her and he knew she wanted him. She had her hand on his crotch. There was a wet patch on the front of his uniform trousers.

PC Hamilton peeled Mary's dress completely open. She shuffled around and lay down flat on the floor for him, her saggy breasts parting as gravity pulled them in different directions, a roll of fat hanging down over her waist as if she was wearing a string belt beneath it. The sudden shared passion was undeniable. She opened her legs. Moist. *Ready.* That excited him even more and he hurriedly stripped, kicking off his trousers and underwear. He crouched down beside her, cock hard, still not understanding why but knowing that all he wanted was Mary.

No foreplay. No words.

My god, he'd never seen anything as beautiful as this woman at this precise moment. The roadmap of broken veins on her thighs, her breasts like bags of grain, the mole on her hip the size of a coin, her unkempt bush of wiry grey pubic hairs, streaks of cellulite...

And nothing mattered but the two of them. Nothing mattered but the sex.

He sat astride her and she took him deep and hard.

16

Word spread fast about Scott. But then again, word spread fast about everything in Thussock. Tammy and Phoebe didn't go to school and Michelle didn't take George to toddler group. She spent the morning pacing around the kitchen, waiting for the phone to ring. The routine had been as familiar and frightening for her as it had for Scott; the endless waiting for news, the complete helplessness. The police had been as vague and unhelpful as expected. 'Stay at home, Mrs Griffiths,' was all they told her. 'We can't give you any information. We'll contact you as soon as we've anything to tell you.' A couple of phone calls with the lawyer they'd assigned to represent Scott followed, and Jackie called Michelle once the news reached her, but that was it. The gravity of the situation was undoubted, the outcome uncertain.

But as the day progressed, a strange sense of normality began to prevail. An engineer arrived to install a satellite dish and connect the TV. Michelle hadn't even known Scott had arranged it. He never told her anything. Sometimes she felt like she hardly knew him.

By seven o'clock, frayed tempers and nerves had begun to repair. Tammy, Phoebe and George sat with their mother in the living room watching TV, catching up with the channels they'd missed. The doorbell rang and Michelle was out of her seat in a heartbeat, guts immediately churning again. It was Jackie, and she didn't know how that made her feel. She was equally relieved and disappointed. 'Come on in, Jackie,' she said.

'Only if you're sure. I didn't know whether to come round or not.'

Michelle eyed up the bottle of wine she'd brought with her. 'You should *definitely* have come.'

After introducing her to the girls, Michelle took Jackie into the kitchen. The TV noise drifting through the house made everything feel deceptively normal. 'Dez was in town yesterday afternoon,' Jackie said. 'He said Graham was acting weird. It's not his fault, but that fella's never been quite right, you know?'

'I know, but that doesn't mean he deserved to...' She didn't finish her sentence. Couldn't finish it. Jackie put her hand on Michelle's and topped up her already generous glass of wine. 'You not drinking?' Michelle asked.

'I'm driving. Anyway, I bought this for you. Figured you'd be the one in need of alcohol.'

'It's appreciated. I can't tell you how much.'

'Like I said, love, I know where you're at.' Jackie watched Michelle, not knowing what she should say, or even if she should say anything at all. The building site state of the kitchen was a convenient distraction. 'That's quite a hole you have in your wall there.'

Michelle laughed into her wine glass. 'That's Scott for you. Impulsive. Selfish.'

'And is there a plan, or did he just feel like putting the wall through?'

'Oh, there's a plan okay. It's his plan, though. All on his terms, his timescales. He decides he's putting the wall through, so he puts the bloody wall through.'

Michelle drank more wine and wiped her eyes. Jackie continued to watch her, wondering if she was just making matters worse by being here. Should she just butt out and bugger off back to Dez and the kids? 'Look, love, do you know what they're saying?'

'What who're saying?'

'Folks out there?'

'I couldn't care less.'

'I think you should. You and your girls need to be ready, I think.'

Michelle finished her glass and poured another. 'I can imagine the kind of stuff. They're saying Scott killed that Graham bloke.'

She looked at Jackie. Jackie looked away. 'It's worse than that. Way worse.'

'Worse. How can it be worse?'

'They're saying he killed all of them, Chelle. Thing is, all this only started when you moved to Thussock. Folks are putting two and two together and are coming up with all kinds of answers.'

Michelle laughed. Not a quiet, nervous laugh, this was a full-on belly laugh which filled the house. The girls even heard her over the TV. 'That's fucking hilarious,' she said.

'I thought you needed to know. I think you and your girls need to be aware. People think your husband's the killer.'

'Let them think what they like, Jack. We're all in the dark here. I don't have a bloody clue what Scott's capable of anymore.'

'You can always come and stay at ours if things get bad here, love.'

'Things already are bad, Jack. Though to be fair, they were bad before we got here. I thought this move would help, but it's just made things worse. It must be something to do with me...'

'It's not you, Mum, and you know it,' Tammy said. Neither of them had noticed her in the doorway. 'We should pack our stuff tonight and get out of here. Go back home. Granddad's always saying we can stay with him.'

'That's not the answer, Tam, and you know it.'

'Then what is, Mum? Stay here with him until there's nothing left of any of us? You should have seen him with that bloke last night. Scott was like a maniac. For what it's worth, I don't know if he had anything to do with all the other deaths, but I'm worried. I'm worried if he carries on like this it'll be one of us next. He's made threats to you before, Mum, and he's right on the edge. I think we should cut our losses and get out of here.'

Jackie stayed for hours. Michelle put George to bed then she, Jackie and the girls sat in the living room together and talked about nothing all evening, deliberately avoiding any difficult topics of conversation. It was relaxing. It was *liberating*. There was no mention of Scott, other than when Tammy remarked on how different the house felt when he wasn't there. 'It feels normal, Mum, don't you think? No one's shouting. We're not treading on eggshells. I've got satellite TV, we've finally got the Internet, and you're half drunk. If things could be like this all the time, I might even feel like staying in Thussock.'

17

A little over twenty-four hours after driving him away, the same police car returned and dumped Scott back outside his front door. Michelle hadn't been home long from taking the girls to school, figuring the sooner they got back into routine, the better. She rushed outside to greet him, her legs weak with nerves, not sure how she felt. 'You're back. You okay, love? What's going on?'

Scott didn't answer. Couldn't answer. He walked straight past her and went into the house, sitting down at the kitchen table without uttering a word. Michelle hesitated and watched him from the doorway, trying to gauge the situation, unsure what to do or say next. Should she just pretend nothing had happened? It would probably be for the best, but she couldn't do it. As much as he would inevitably need space after what he'd been through, she needed answers. She moved closer, then sat down opposite him. When he didn't react, she cleared her throat. 'What happened, Scott?'

He looked straight at her. 'You know what happened,' he said, his voice unemotional. 'The pervert I beat up died. They decided I killed him. Apparently I hadn't.'

'Then who...? How did he...?'

'How the hell am I supposed to know? Why don't you ask the fucking pigs who dragged me out of here yesterday morning and kept me locked up all fucking night for no fucking reason.'

'I'm sorry, I didn't mean to...'

'It gets better,' he said, cutting across her. 'Fuckers tried to pin *everything* on me. All these killings. Cunts. All fucking circumstantial... just picking on me 'cause we're new here.'

Michelle held her head in her hands. 'Are we going to get this wherever we go? When I agreed to come here I thought—'

'You thought what? Don't try and turn this around on me. None of this is my fault. I was just trying to look out for your fucking pain-in-the-ass daughter and stop some fucking freak from raping her.'

'I know. I—'

'It's not my fault this place is full of fucking psychos, is it? They're all out of their fucking minds.'

'I'm sorry. All I meant was—'

'I know what you meant,' he said, his voice suddenly louder. He banged his fist down on the table and Michelle jumped as much as the crockery. 'I'm doing the best I can, you know. I know you lot don't see it, but I'm trying really fucking hard here.'

'I know you are. All I was going to say was—'

'Maybe I should just stop? Maybe I should give up trying, 'cause the harder I try for this fucking family, the more fucked up things get.'

'Don't talk like that...'

'It's true though, isn't it?'

'No... no it's not, and I don't believe you really think that.' She took a deep breath, trying to block out everything Tammy had said last night and focus instead on keeping Scott calm. 'We're going through a tough time, you in particular, but look how far we've come. If you'd said to me before the inquest that we'd be living in a house like this, rebuilding our lives and sorting our family out, I'd have been over the moon. We can put things back together here, I'm sure we can.'

'Are you?'

She watched his face, waiting for any flicker of reaction. 'Please, love... please don't be like this. Everything's going to be okay. You're out of that place now. I don't know what happened to that man, but I know you didn't do it and that's enough for me, really it is. And I know it wouldn't have happened if Tammy hadn't run off. It's not your fault. Stop beating yourself up. You've got to learn to let go of stuff like this.'

He looked up at her. 'Finished?'

She nodded and swallowed hard with nerves.

Scott was still staring at her. 'They kept talking about the accident.'

Michelle's body language changed. She visibly withdrew, the way she always did whenever the subject came up. 'That's all over now... you were cleared after the inquest.'

'They were implying I might have done it on purpose, trying to make me out to be some real heartless fucker.'

'They were just doing it to wind you up. What happened was an accident. Sue and Roy should have been watching her. It could have been anyone driving...'

'But it was *me*.'

Elsewhere in the house, George started to cry. 'I'll go and see to him,' Michelle said, 'let him know you're back. He was asking where you were.' She got up and made for the door.

'Been celebrating?'

She froze. 'What?'

He pointed at the empty wine bottle on the draining board, evidence from last night that she'd forgotten to hide. 'Have a drink on me, did you?'

'I needed it to calm my nerves,' she said, thinking on her feet, hoping he'd just accept her explanation. She'd have to get her story straight and tell the girls to keep quiet about Jackie coming around. 'I was worried,' she added, still not sure he was buying it. 'Terrified. The police wouldn't tell me anything. They wouldn't let me see you.'

Scott nodded but didn't say anything.

'I'll go and see to George, okay?'

He nodded again. He watched her leave the room but remained in his chair. He felt as if gravity had increased by a factor of ten since he'd got back, preventing him from getting up. He stared at the hole in the wall he'd made on Sunday afternoon. His sledgehammer was where he'd left it, still leaning in the corner. He didn't dare pick it up. *Start swinging that fucking thing around again and I'll never stop*, he thought. *I'll reduce this whole fucking house to rubble.*

Michelle was back quickly, carrying George. She tried to show him Daddy was home, but he was cranky and tired and he wouldn't look. She waited a couple of minutes until she couldn't hold it in any longer. 'Can I ask one more question? I'm sorry, Scott, I just need to know.'

'What?'

'What happened to change their minds? How come they let you go?'

'Two things. First, I already told you, that pervert didn't die from a punch in the face and a kick in the guts.'

'Then how...?'

'How the hell am I supposed to know? You think they're gonna

161

tell me?'

'Sorry. I didn't think.'

'And second,' he said ominously, 'they did tell me something. There was another killing while they'd got me locked up. They found another body, that woman from the café. Someone raped her and sliced her up while I was locked away safe and sound in the cells.'

Michelle stayed well out of Scott's way all day, as did the girls when they got home from school. He'd hardly slept in the cell last night and yet despite spending all afternoon lying on the bed in the ground floor bedroom, he still couldn't switch off and get any rest. He could hear Michelle and Phoebe talking in the living room. He wished they'd shut their bloody noise up, but he couldn't be bothered to tell them. George waddled past the half-open bedroom door a couple of times, and even he seemed to know better. Now's not the time to be disturbing Daddy.

Scott couldn't see a clock, but it felt like he'd been lying on the bed for hours. His body ached and he needed a piss. More than anything he needed a shower to get the smell of that damn place off him. He stank of stale sweat, reeked of the disinfected cell where he'd spent most of the last day.

With more effort than it should ever have taken, he swung his legs around and sat up, then waited a second for his head to stop spinning. He stripped to his underwear and threw his dirty clothes in the corner, thinking he felt so contaminated from being in custody that he'd rather burn them than wear them again. Wearing only his briefs, he padded over to the bathroom and opened the door.

Tammy was in there, just stepping out of the shower. She was naked. 'Fuck's sake,' she gasped, frantically grabbing for her towel to cover herself up. 'Do you mind?'

Scott, his brain still working at half-speed, shook his head and mumbled something about the door not being locked. He'd been taken by surprise, hadn't stopped to think, hadn't heard the running water... and now he was just standing there. She'd been a little kid when he and Michelle had first got together, still at junior school, but Tammy was very definitely a woman now.

When he didn't move, she did. She shoved him back out and

slammed the door in his face.

She finished drying herself, taking her time, trying to calm down but just getting angrier and angrier at the way he'd barged into the bathroom without a damn care. It made it even worse when he'd just gawped at her without apology. Any decent man would have looked away with embarrassment, so why not him? And this wasn't the first time. She'd caught him looking at her before, and he'd always had an unspoken reputation amongst her friends. None of them liked being around him on their own. Katie called him a letch, said he was always undressing her with his eyes. She'd always wondered – though had never dared to say – if he'd done something to that little girl he knocked down, if there'd been more to the accident than he'd let on... There's no smoke without fire, she'd always thought, and what he'd just done was proof positive that her step-dad was a seedy bastard. She wished he'd get out of their lives altogether. She wished the police hadn't let him go.

She didn't bother getting dressed, just put on her bra and knickers and draped her towel over her shoulders. She thought she'd put a show on for him, see how he reacted...

He was lying on his bed with his back to the door, curled up like a frightened little kid. She knew he was awake, and she knew that he knew she was there. She stayed a safe distance back, checked no one else was near, then pushed the door shut behind her.

'Pervert.'

Nothing for a few seconds, then a mumbled reply. 'I'm not a pervert. I didn't mean to walk in on you like that.'

'You sure? I think you did.'

He felt himself getting tense. He scrunched up the bedding in his fists and fought with himself not to react. 'I'm sure. I'm sorry.'

'So, Sunday night, with that bloke,' she said, knowing she was playing with fire but unable to stop now, 'what was that all about?'

'Your mum was worried about you. I said I'd go and look for you. When I saw what he was doing, I lost my temper.'

'Why?'

'You shouldn't need to ask that.'

'I mean, I know the reasons you gave Mum, and probably the police too, but is that really all there is to it?'

He looked back over his shoulder, saw that she was only half-dressed, then turned back again and covered his head with his hands. 'You're family. It's my job to protect you.'

'You sure you weren't jealous? Maybe you just wanted me for yourself? I know what you really are, Scott.'

He was on her before she realised what was happening. In a single sudden movement he sprung off the bed and pushed Tammy back against the door, covering her mouth with his hand. Their bodies were close now – too close – but there was nothing sexual about this. She cried with fear when she looked into his wild eyes, but with her mouth covered she couldn't make a sound. He stared at her; no words, just his breathing - low, hard and heavy like an animal poised for the kill. It was only a few seconds but to Tammy it felt like forever. She couldn't move.

'I'm not a pervert,' he told her. 'Everything I've done, I've done for this family, it's just that you ungrateful shits can't see it. We're all out of options now, in case you hadn't noticed. There's nowhere left to go. So if you breathe a word about this, make any accusations or threats, I'll break you. Understand?'

She nodded, tears streaming down her face and over his hands. He relaxed his grip, ready to cover her mouth again if she dared cry out.

'I get it,' she said, and he backed away. 'But if you touch Mum again, I'll tell the police you tried to rape me.'

'You wouldn't fucking dare.'

She leant against the door for support, legs like jelly, doing all she could not to let him see. 'Try me.'

He just smiled. 'Go on, fuck off.'

Scott spent the night alone on the sofa in the living room. He told Michelle he couldn't sleep and he didn't want to keep her awake. She knew better than to argue.

18

It was getting really late but Heather didn't care. Dad thought she was in bed. He and Jamie were watching football downstairs, yelling at the TV so loud that they hadn't heard her slip out the back door. Chez was watching the same match at his place, so she hadn't stopped there for more than a few minutes. He'd tried to get her to stay, but she'd got more self-respect than to hang around in his kitchen waiting for a quick half-time shag. She'd toyed with the idea of trying to see Tammy earlier, but she'd decided to keep her distance. If everything Jamie's mate Joel had said was true, she'd be giving that whole family a wide berth from now on. Much of what Joel said was usually crap, but he'd been right about that Polish girl at the weekend. That Tammy was a nice enough girl, but from what she was hearing, her step-dad was a fucking nutter. Probably best to cool off a little. She'd have to give her some distance at school tomorrow.

It was a frigging pain in the arse being a teenager in Thussock. There was bugger all to do, mid-week especially. Being a girl was harder still, because girls were few and far between here. Most of the other girls on the estate stayed home most of the time, 'cause the boys here were predators, only after one thing. Having Jamie around had made it a little easier for her, but she'd had enough of all that mucking about. Chez was the only bloke she had sex with now. He was a real man (when the football wasn't on). She'd had enough fingers and fumbles with inexperienced kids to last a lifetime.

She walked back home trying to work out if she'd ever be able to afford to learn to drive. Dad kept trying to talk her out of it, because all he thought about was the cost. He did have a point, though – driving tests and lessons cost a bloody fortune, and she'd have to go elsewhere for them because there weren't any instructors in Thussock. And then there was the cost of a car and fuel and insurance and all the associated bills... she knew Dad was right, but there was one thing he wasn't taking into consideration, and that was the value of her freedom. Being able to get away from Thussock whenever she wanted and go and see the few mates she was still in contact with who'd already managed to escape... now that was priceless. She'd been thinking about maybe getting a scooter. She daydreamed about it as she walked the dark streets back home.

It was raining. Just a light mist, but wet enough to soak her and dense enough to reduce her visibility. The light from each streetlamp was little more than a hazy corona, a yellow-white flower head, and the few windows illuminated from lights inside barely made any difference at all out here. Heather plunged her hands into the pockets of her quilted purple jacket and walked a little faster. Tammy said she liked this jacket. Chez bought it for her off the Internet. Tammy said some of her friends in Redditch had jackets like it and that she'd wanted one herself. It made Heather feel good knowing she'd got one up on the girl from the city.

She wasn't that far from the estate, just near the community hall, when she heard a noise she wasn't expecting. It sounded like animals scavenging around the bins. Wait, no... she could hear something else now. It sounded like someone crying. Not sobbing their heart out or anything like that, just a low, quiet, intermittent moan; an occasional sad sob.

'Hello?'

No answer.

'Is anyone there?'

There was nothing on at the community hall tonight (there was nothing on most nights), and all the lights were off save for the yellow security light over the front door and a couple of streetlamps nearby. The small car park was empty but she thought she could see something moving over by the metal wheelie-bins at the side of the building. Probably just a fox or a rat, something disgusting like that. Or was she just imagining it? She told herself to get a grip and get home, to stop freaking herself out over nothing.

'Hello?' she called out again, just to be sure.

Someone stood up. It was a man. What the hell was he doing hiding behind the bins? Her pulse started to race but then she relaxed slightly when she realised she recognised him, though he looked completely different out of uniform. It was one of the local police; the young, good-looking one. She didn't know his name but they'd spoken on many occasions, usually when he was looking for Jamie or one of his dickhead mates when they'd been causing trouble. But this was different. Tonight it looked like he was the one in trouble.

'You okay?' she asked.

He just looked at her, didn't say anything. Concerned, she walked across the car park to where he was standing... where he'd been *hiding*. Shit, was this some kind of police operation like she'd seen on TV? Had she walked into the middle of a drugs bust or something? But there was no one else around and he wasn't trying to stop her.

'Is something wrong?'

He nodded and beckoned for her to come closer. She saw that he had tears streaking his face, glistening in the security light. Poor love. He looked so vulnerable, so frightened... afraid almost. His uniform shirt was hanging out and his hair was all ruffled like he'd just got out of bed.

'What's the matter?'

'I don't know,' he said.

'Are you hurt?'

'No.'

'Are you in trouble?'

'Yes.'

Bloody hell, he was lovely. His unexpected vulnerability just added to the appeal. She thought about Chez slumped in front of the TV at home with a can of lager in his hand and a fag hanging from the corner of his mouth. Why couldn't he be more like this man? His broad, powerful shoulders, strong features, cute hair... Heather had had sex loads of times with loads of kids, but she'd never been loved, never felt protected, never had someone make her feel wanted, not even Chez... *especially not Chez.* She looked into the policeman's eyes, so full of life, and dared to dream about how he might make her feel. But she was just a school kid letting her mind run away with itself. Nothing was ever going to happen between a girl like her and a man like him.

'You okay?' he asked, and the fact he cared enough to ask made the warmth and wanting inside her increase. She just wanted to be close to him now, to hold him and to be held.

So she wrapped her arms around him.

To her surprise, he reciprocated, holding her tight. It felt wrong, but it also felt so right.

She could feel his hands around her waist, could feel his breath on the side of her face, could smell him... She was starting to think he wanted her like she wanted him, but they couldn't, could they? What would people say? Somehow that made her want him even more. She felt herself moisten when she saw he had an erection.

Her first time had been around the back of this building with a spotty little kid at a youth club Christmas disco a few years back. It had been freezing cold. The sex had been fast and painful, devoid of any emotion or attachment – everything her first time shouldn't have been. Even now Chez was little better. Sure he told her he loved her and said the things he thought she wanted to hear, but it was still usually an empty fuck on his terms and for his benefit. She wasn't particularly experienced but, right now, standing here holding the policeman like this, staring deep into his eyes, feeling his gentle hand caressing the side of her face, she felt supremely confident. She wanted to feel him inside her so very badly.

It was wrong. It was dangerous. They were out in the open. She was much younger than him and he'd get into all kinds of trouble if anyone found out... but Heather and PC Hamilton did it just the same. They stripped, then fucked fast and hard and beautifully against the wall of the Thussock community hall.

19

Scott prised one eye open then closed it again. Then he sat up fast, panicking. *Déjà vu*. It was late afternoon but it felt just like it had a couple of mornings back... someone banging angrily on the front door, waking him up. He hadn't gone into work today, calling in sick so he could catch up with some sleep while the kids were at school. Michelle had been keeping her distance, giving him space, so who was at the door?

At first he didn't want to answer it, couldn't stand the thought of going through all that again if it was the police, but he knew he didn't have any choice. He was the only one in the house and any refusal to talk would inevitably be construed as an admission of guilt. Mouth dry with nerves, wearing only a T-shirt and briefs and shivering with cold, he walked towards the front door. He could see an outline through the frosted glass. *If it is the police again*, he thought, *I'll sue the fuckers for victimisation*. It didn't look like it was, though. There were no patrol cars with flashing blue lights on his drive this time.

When he yanked the door open, Scott did a double-take. Standing on his doorstep was Jeremy, Tammy and Phoebe's dad, Michelle's ex. 'What the hell are you doing here?'

'Sorry to turn up unannounced like this,' Jeremy said.

It was cold outside, but not cold enough for Scott to let him in. He went out instead and pulled the door shut behind him. 'I thought the agreement was you and Michelle arranged contact in advance. You're not supposed to just turn up. Why didn't you phone?'

'Couldn't get through.'

'We've got a landline now.'

'What, and I'm supposed to just guess the number?'

'You could have sent a text.'

'I did. I heard you had some grief with the police.'

'That's got fuck all to do with you.'

'I know that. I'm just here because of my kids.'

Scott remained in front of the door, arms folded like a nightclub bouncer. Jeremy took off his wire-framed glasses and rubbed his eyes.

The last thing he wanted was conflict. If it came down to a physical fight between him and Scott, he knew he'd inevitably come off second best.

'Your kids are fine. Everything's fine.'

'I'm worried about the girls. I'm worried about all of you, actually.'

'We're all right, thanks for your concern. You can go now.'

'I got this garbled message from Tammy on my phone on Sunday night when I got home... I tried calling her back but I think it was a payphone.'

'It was. She had... there was an incident.'

'What kind of incident?'

'Someone exposed himself in front of her. The local pervert.'

'Jesus. Was she...?' He didn't need to finish his question. Scott was shaking his head.

'I got to him first.'

'Thank you,' Jeremy said, and he meant it.

'I don't need your thanks. I smacked a deviant in the face because he was flashing his dick at your daughter. That's why I had grief with the police.'

Scott just wanted to go inside and lock the door and shut Jeremy out but he knew he couldn't. Physically he could, but that wasn't going to help anyone. Jeremy was a weed, always had been. A strip of piss, was how Scott usually described him. While Scott had always worked with his hands, Jeremy was a dyed in the wool pen-pusher. Dull. Boring. No wonder Michelle had left him.

Jeremy leant against his car. A year-old Volvo, it was neat and tidy and efficient and completely lacking in excitement, just like its owner, Scott thought. He offered Scott a stick of gum which he refused. Scott wasn't giving any ground.

'Bit barren out here, isn't it?' Jeremy said, looking across the road at the featureless yellow-green fields which rolled away into the distance.

'Suppose.'

'Nothing like Redditch, eh? It is lovely, though, I'll give you that. I drove through this place once when I was younger. Me and my brother were rebelling. We decided we'd just get in the car and drive as far north as we could and—'

'I'll ask you once more, why are you here, Jeremy?'

Jeremy smiled at the interruption. He'd been stalling for time, trying to break the ice and make things a little easier. It was a management technique he used all the time at work, but Scott wasn't having any of it. 'Like I said, I was concerned.'

'And like I said, you don't need to be.'

'Well maybe I need a little more reassurance? Look at it from my perspective, Scott. You pack up everything and move my kids to the opposite end of the country. Now I genuinely don't have any issues with you. We've had our differences and Christ knows you've had a lot to deal with these past twelve months or so, but you, me and Michelle have always managed to get on with each other and stay civil for the sake of the kids.'

'And that hasn't changed.'

'I didn't say it had.'

'What then?'

'The few times I have managed to speak to Tam and Phoebe since you moved here, they've sounded like they've been in a real state, Tammy in particular.'

'It hasn't been easy, I'll give you that. But like I said, they're fine. They just need to—'

Jeremy held up his hands as if to say *I surrender, don't shoot*. 'Let me finish, Scott. Don't start attacking me or defending yourself 'til you've heard what I want to say, okay?'

'Okay.'

'You always think the worst of me, don't you?' No answer. 'Look,' Jeremy continued, 'when I spoke to the girls I told them both all the things I thought I should. I said they were going to feel a little weird for a while, disorientated. Short of emigrating, you've put yourselves about as far away from your old lives as you could have and I understand that. I know why you did it and, for what it's worth, I think you've probably made the right move.'

'I don't need your approval. Look, Jeremy, you're not making a lot of sense here. You're talking a lot, but you're not actually saying anything relevant.'

'I was prepared to let it go at first,' he continued, heart pounding but remaining outwardly unaffected by Scott's thinly veiled aggression. 'It was hard, really bloody hard, but I was willing to keep my distance to let the girls get settled. I'm big enough and ugly enough to know when not to stick my nose in, Scott.'

'You sure?'

'I knew that if I'd turned up any sooner it would have done more harm than good. All the hard work you and Michelle have been doing to help them settle would have been undone.'

'So you thought you'd give it a week or so...?'

'I just happened to be passing through.'

'Bullshit.'

'See, I knew you wouldn't believe me. Fact is I'm needed at a site just outside Aberdeen later this week. I'm owed a few days leave, so I thought I'd drive up here rather than fly in for the meeting, that way I could drop in and see the girls first.'

'Like I said, you should have called.'

'And like *I* said, I've had trouble getting through. I also know you'd probably have done everything you could to stop me coming. Me being here is probably the last thing you need right now, but I'm here with the best of intentions. I know you can't see that, but it's true. I've had enough, Scott. Imagine how you'd be feeling now if you'd been separated from George and no one was telling you anything?' He paused for a response which didn't come. 'I'm planning to spend a few days in the area, reassure the girls and myself and spend some time with them if I can, then I'll move on. Put yourself in my shoes, mate... how could you not come and see your kids when...?'

'When what?'

Jeremy took a deep breath. 'When you see the town they just moved to on the news each night? When you can't talk to your children to check they're okay but you're hearing plenty about a string of murders happening where they are, and you're out of the country a lot of the time. I got back from Switzerland late on Sunday and the first thing I heard was that message from Tammy. She was beside herself.'

'And I've told you why that was. It's sorted now.'

'Like I said, put yourself in my shoes. What would you have done?'

Scott wasn't sure how to answer. A flurry of movement let him off the hook. Michelle pulled up in the car. She'd barely stopped the engine before the girls were out and all over their father. Jeremy raced towards them, grabbing hold of his youngest daughter first, squeezing her tight. 'Love you,' he said. 'Missed you.'

'Missed you too, Dad.'

'I was passing through and I thought I'd drop in on you. Thought I'd surprise you both. That okay?'

'That's okay,' she said, grinning.

Once she'd calmed everyone down and got her head around Jeremy's sudden arrival, Michelle invited him to stop for dinner, checking with Scott first. She told him she needed to go back into town and pick up something to eat but Scott volunteered to go instead. It was preferable to sitting in the house with Jeremy, making awkward small-talk and watching the kids fawning all over him. Michelle scribbled out a list and gave it to him, cornering him alone in the kitchen. 'Here you go. And can you get a couple of bottles of wine in and some beer? Something decent, okay?'

'Okay.'

'You sure you're all right about this?'

'I'm fine.'

'And you're okay with Jeremy being here?'

'If it helps the kids, I guess.'

'Good. Thanks, love. This means a lot to them. It's important.' He turned to leave but she pulled him back. 'I love you, Scott.'

20

Scott drove into town with George. There was a police cordon around the side of the community hall. A small crowd of people had gathered there, mostly school kids, held back at a distance. Scott just kept driving and didn't even look up. He didn't know what had happened and he didn't care. It was nothing to do with him and he wasn't about to give anyone any reason to think otherwise. Sergeant Ross was in the middle of it all as usual, and he could see that fucker DI Litherland too. Scott was paranoid that one of them would see him driving past and jump to another immediate, baseless, incorrect conclusion.

He parked outside the Co-op, and it was only when he had his hand on the door to get out that he stopped and realised where he was and what he was doing. This was where that McBride bloke had worked. Did the other people who worked here know who Scott was and what he'd done? For half a second he considered starting the engine again and going somewhere else, but there wasn't anywhere else and, anyway, why the hell should he? 'If they've got a problem with what happened then I'm happy to talk about it,' he told George who didn't understand and who wasn't listening anyway and who, most importantly, wouldn't answer back. 'I'll happily tell them what that pervert did and why I punched his lights out. They're wrong about me. They can all go to hell for all I care.'

He plucked his son from his booster seat, shut and locked the car, then took a trolley (*he might have left this trolley here, the bloke who died*) and loaded George into the seat facing him. The automatic doors opened as he approached and he disappeared inside, and for a few seconds the familiarity and normality of the bright supermarket interior came as a relief. He worked his way around the fresh produce first, shopping list in hand, remembering all the things Michelle always said whenever he came back with the wrong stuff: check the best before dates, get bananas that are still a little bit green, check all the apples for bruises, don't automatically pick up every offer you see; that second pack of mince might look cheap, but if we're never going to eat it you're actually spending more money, not less... Most of the time he didn't give a shit, couldn't bring himself to be so bloody petty, but it was different today. 'Can't give Mummy or Jeremy any reason to have a go at Daddy now, can we son?' he said. George just looked at him.

For a shitty little store in a shitty little town, the supermarket was reasonably well-stocked. He managed to get most of what they needed, placating George along the way with sweets. He was looking at coffee, trying to remember which brand he liked best, when he felt someone watching him. He looked back over his shoulder, and a woman looked down as soon as he made eye contact. He didn't recognise her, hadn't ever seen her before as far as he was aware, so why was she so interested in him? And she definitely was, because when he'd chosen his coffee and crossed the aisle to pick up something else, he caught her staring again. *Does she just not like strangers, or is there more to it than that? Does she know what happened with the police? Did she see them taking me into the station? Does she think I'm the killer...?*

George moaned, still hungry. 'Won't be long now, sunshine,' Scott told him. 'Got to get nice food in for our special guest. Can't have precious Jeremy thinking we don't know how to look after ourselves now can we?'

''kay Daddy.'

'We're playing happy families tonight, mate.'

''kay Daddy.'

Shit. There was another one watching him now. Another fucking busybody watching his every move. One of the women on the tills was giving him evils, looking down her nose at him, almost sneering. Bitch. And now another dozy fucker, a kid who could barely see out from under his bloody floppy fringe, was waiting to get past. Dumb little bastard. Scott was about to say something but he thought better of it. *No point*, he told himself. *You're better than all of them.*

He swung the trolley around the end of another aisle and almost collided with a family coming the other way. A man and a woman, two kids. The bloke looked shifty. Dodgy hair, even dodgier dress sense. The woman was about half his age and she was looking at Scott, *staring* at him. What the hell was wrong with all these people? Scott felt like going home, locking the door and never coming out again. He'd make sure he'd kicked Jeremy out first, of course.

'Hello, George,' the woman said, taking both Scott and his son by surprise. The woman was grinning broadly at Scott. She held out her hand. He just looked at it. 'You must be Scott,' she said.

'Yeah...' he replied, unsure, and he bit his tongue before he could follow it up with *and who the fuck are you?*

'I'm Jackie,' she said, still grinning. She waited for an acknowledgement which didn't come. 'Michelle's friend Jackie from playgroup?'

'Yeah, sorry... I'm not with it today. Nice to meet you.'

'This here's Dez,' she continued, and Dez grabbed Scott's hand and shook it vigorously.

'Good t'meet you, pal,' he said. 'Heard you'd had a bit of grief lately.'

Jackie shot daggers at her partner but he remained belligerent.

'You could say that.'

'That Graham was a freaky fucker, mind.'

'I noticed.'

'Dez, don't... not here,' Jackie said, turning to apologise to Scott. 'I'm really sorry about him. He doesn't think.'

'No worries,' Scott said. 'He was right anyway. The bloke was a freak.'

An awkward standoff followed, both sides blocking the other's way through. Scott wanted to go, Jackie wanted to know more about what had happened but didn't dare ask. Dez, however, remained completely ignorant. 'I'll tell you sumthin' for nothin', mate, this town is full of bloody odduns.'

'What?'

'Odduns. Weirdos. Freaks.'

'Don't listen to him,' Jackie said, embarrassed.

'S'true.'

'Aye, Dezzie, but your definition of a weirdo is different to the rest of us. In your book a weirdo's just someone who don't do things your way, and as there ain't no one else who does things your way, it looks like that's all the rest of us.'

Scott managed a wry smile. He quite liked this woman. Nice face, great tits, and she seemed to talk sense. Couldn't see what she was doing with this prick, though. George moaned again. 'We should go,' he said, glad of the excuse.

'Course. Oh, how's the kitchen coming along?'

'What?'

'The hole in your kitchen wall... it's going to look lovely when you're done.'

How the fuck does she know what's happening in my house? 'Not had a lot of chance to work on it this week,' he said, swallowing down his anger. It wasn't Jackie he was angry with, it was the others. He hated being kept in the dark and being talked about, and he'd have Michelle about it as soon as they got rid of Jeremy.

'Course,' Jackie said. 'I should keep my nose out.'

'You probably should.'

'Let's get on then,' Dez said, urging Jackie forward.

'Nice to meet you,' she said, pushing her trolley around the end of Scott's.

'Aye,' Dez added, ushering his kids away. 'See yous around.'

Scott watched the family walk away. *Fucking inbreds... Talk about strangers, are there any stranger round here than that bloke?* With his eighties clothes and nineties hair, married to a woman who looked young enough to be his daughter... there was definitely something odd going on there. He was wearing a frigging Dr Who T-shirt, for fuck's sake, and it was the old Dr Who at that. *Wonder where he was the night Graham McBride died? Wonder where he was when the rest of them were killed?*

Scott finished the rest of the shopping quickly, passing the family a couple more times in the next few aisles, the awkwardness increasing each time they met. He waited for an age at the one checkout which was still open. The woman who was serving barely even looked at him. *Are you this rude to all your customers, or do you feel the same way about me as I do you?* He loaded up his bags and pushed the trolley out to the car, keen to get out and get home until he remembered who was there.

21

He felt like he was a guest in someone else's house, the way they were all fussing over bloody Jeremy. It made him sick. They never treated him like this. All he did for them, and Phoebe and Tammy had barely even looked at him when he got back with the shopping. And Michelle was just as bad, checking Jeremy was comfortable and that he'd got a drink, asking if he wanted to watch TV or use the bathroom before dinner.

To his credit, Jeremy looked as uneasy as Scott felt. When he saw that Scott was back he immediately got up from his seat and offered him his hand. 'You okay, Scott?' he asked.

'Fine. You?'

'Jeremy has been planning to take in the sights and sounds of Thussock,' Michelle shouted from the kitchen.

'Good luck finding any.'

'Quite a place you've found here,' Jeremy said, grinning broadly. 'Shame I've only got a few days. It'll never be long enough. So much to see, so much to do...'

'It is a bit like that, isn't it?' Scott said, taking a beer from Phoebe who'd brought in a bottle for him and a coffee for her dad. 'We've got a brewery one way, a fracking site just over the hills behind us...'

'The fun never starts,' Tammy said sarcastically.

'I'd be interested in seeing the fracking site,' Jeremy continued. He stopped, conscious that the others were looking at him. 'What? I'm interested, can't help it. It's not a million miles removed from my line of work. I've been talking to another firm about going into partnership on a project in Yorkshire of all places. Once they've sorted out the PR side of things, of course. Have you had any earthquakes yet?' George waddled into the room. 'I can't get over how you've grown,' Jeremy said to him. 'When I last saw you, you were just a titchy little fella, not a big strapping man like this.'

Michelle came in from the kitchen and watched Scott from a distance, trying to gauge his reaction as Jeremy interacted with his son. He looked as uncomfortable as she'd expected, but at least he was keeping his temper in check. Conflict between the two men had been an issue in the past, particularly when the girls had been younger. Scott had always accepted that Tammy and Phoebe needed to spend time with their father, but he'd struggled with the realities and practicalities. In fact, it hadn't been until he'd become a father himself that he'd finally started to understand the emotions and un-spoken needs at play.

'Oh, I nearly forgot,' Jeremy said, ducking back out into the hall to fetch a plastic carrier bag. Glass bottles clinked together as he picked it up. He gave a bottle of wine to Michelle (her favourite label... she was touched that he remembered) and handed a bottle of scotch to Scott who seemed genuinely surprised. 'The best I could find on the way into Thussock, so not great I'm afraid. Supermarket's own.'

'Thanks,' Scott said, checking out the label. 'A malt. You shouldn't have.'

'Nonsense. You're both being very hospitable and I appreciate it. Understanding too.'

'Want a shot of this in your coffee?'

'No thanks, I'm driving.'

'You could stay here if you wanted a drink,' Michelle said. Scott bit his tongue and glared at her. 'We're out of beds, but the sofa's pretty comfortable.'

She might not have picked up on her husband's unease, but Jere-my did. 'What, and miss out on staying over at the Black Boy? Hell of a place, your local.'

'Something to do with a sheepdog, isn't it?' Scott said. 'You'd think they'd change the name. I thought twice about going in there for a drink, so fair play to you for spending the night.'

'I haven't done it yet,' he laughed. 'Not a lot of choice around here though.'

'You're lucky you managed to get a room,' Michelle said. 'It's not the biggest pub.'

'Don't think that was ever going to be a problem. I think I'm the only guest there right now. And judging by the state of the room they've given me, I get the impression I'm the first person they've had there in a long time.'

'Can't say I'm surprised,' Michelle said. 'Anyway, the offer's there.

If you feel like getting drunk or decide you can't stand the thought of the pub, you can bed down here.'

'I'll be fine,' he said quickly. 'I'm looking at it as an adventure. I've stopped in far worse places. At least here we all speak the same language.'

'You reckon?' Tammy laughed. 'Have you heard how they talk, Dad? I don't have a clue what they're saying half the time. I had to ask a teacher to say the same thing four times today. Made me look like a right idiot.'

'I just keep nodding my head and make the right noises when they pause for breath,' Michelle admitted.

'So you're finding the locals a challenge?'

'Everything's a challenge,' Tammy answered quickly.

'She's exaggerating,' Michelle said. 'She always exaggerates. The people are fine.'

'Those who are still alive,' Tammy said under her breath.

Michelle felt the mood in the room immediately change.

'What did you have to say that for?'

Tammy shrugged her shoulders then turned to her dad. 'You've heard about Thussock's little problem, I take it?'

'I've heard.'

'And what do you think?'

Jeremy looked around the room. Michelle was watching him, Scott was glaring at him, Phoebe was chewing her bottom lip anxiously... even George looked unsure.

'I think it's very sad and very worrying,' he said. 'But I also think you'll all be okay. Scott's here, and he's not going to let anything happen to any of you, isn't that right, Scott?'

'Absolutely.'

Another pregnant pause. Awkward. Uncomfortable.

'Right, let's eat,' Michelle said, her voice overly enthusiastic. 'Who's hungry?'

Jeremy stayed at the house until almost eleven. The evening was, for the most part, unexpectedly enjoyable and inevitably awkward in equal measure. The girls had gone up to their rooms just after ten, the initial novelty of having their dad around having worn off. He joked that they'd always liked the idea of being with him better than the reality. They made plans for him to pick them up after school tomorrow and spend a little time together.

Things soured soon after the girls had left. Scott disappeared, leaving Jeremy and Michelle alone in the living room. 'Weird, isn't it?' Jeremy said.

'What is?'

'This. The fact it feels reasonably normal to be sitting here talking like this. We've lived apart for years yet it's like we've hardly been out of the room.'

'Suppose. We spent a lot of time together. A lot of good times to start with.'

'I know, but when you think how long it's been... In some ways you've hardly changed, Chelle.'

'Is that meant to be a compliment?'

'I guess,' he said. Jeremy watched his ex-wife watching him, wondering whether he should stop talking now. He'd had a question on the tip of his tongue all evening. 'Look, if I'm out of line, tell me to shut up, but are you sure you're okay?'

'I'm fine,' she answered quickly. 'Just tired, that's all. It's been a tough few months. Mentally and physically.'

'I'm not convinced.'

'Honestly, Jeremy. Look, I hear what you're saying, but we've barely seen each other for years. How do you know I'm not always like this?'

'I hope you're not. That'd make it even worse.'

'What's that supposed to mean?'

He sighed. Did he really want to do this? Then again, could he afford not to? 'I've got a memory of one particular night just before we split up. You probably wouldn't even remember it. We weren't fighting or arguing, we were just trying to live together and failing miserably. I remember watching you watching TV and thinking, something's not right here... but I couldn't put my finger on it. It's hard to explain, but looking back I think that's when I first knew we were in trouble. It was what you weren't saying that was important, not what you said. There was no connection anymore. The spark had gone out. You looked like you were lost. Remember that tatty old armchair we had? The one Mum gave me? You were sitting on it with your knees pulled up to your chest, watching TV. You looked so small, so vulnerable... I didn't realise it was me making you feel that way.'

'What point are you making?'

'That you've been giving off the same vibes all evening.'

'So maybe it's having you around again that's making me feel this way?'

He shrugged. 'Maybe it is.'

'All due respect, like I said, we've hardly seen each other in ages.'

'You're right. But like *I* said, if you are usually like this, then that makes me even more worried.'

'Don't be. There's nothing to worry about.'

'The girls tell me things...'

'Well they shouldn't.'

A heavy silence. The two of them staring at each other across the dark room, just the creaks and groans of the tired old house around them. Jeremy cleared his throat. 'I care about you, Michelle, so I'll ask once more, then I'll shut up. Are you sure you're okay? Are the girls going to be all right here?'

'Tell you what, Jeremy,' Scott said, 'why don't you just save us all the trouble and shut up now? Seriously. I've put up with your bull-shit all night, and I've had just about enough of your fucking noise.'

'Scott, don't...' Michelle protested.

Jeremy held his head in his hands. 'I didn't mean anything by it, Scott. I just need to know. For the sake of my kids...'

'Jeremy was just—'

'Shut the fuck up, Michelle,' Scott ordered. 'Don't you take his fucking side.'

'I thought we were all on the same side,' Jeremy said, quickly getting to his feet and positioning himself between Scott and Michelle, hands raised. Fuck, how he hated confrontation. He could smell the scotch on Scott's breath from here. 'Like I said this morning, just put yourself in my shoes. I'm worried about the girls.'

'And like I said this morning, everything's fine.

'Maybe I still need convincing?'

Scott grabbed Jeremy's collar and pushed him back against the wall. Michelle tried to force herself between them. Jeremy kept his hands raised in submission, refusing to fight back. 'Then let me convince you, fucker,' Scott hissed.

'Scott, please,' Michelle said, trying to separate them. 'This isn't helping anyone.'

He remained tense for a few seconds longer, then let go and walked away. Jeremy straightened himself out, adjusted his glasses and smoothed his hair, breathing hard but trying not to let his nervousness show. 'I should leave.'

'You don't have to go,' Michelle said.

'I think he fucking does,' Scott told her.

Jeremy didn't hang around. He tried to tell Michelle it was okay and that he'd try and talk to her tomorrow, but Scott wasn't having any of it. He handed Jeremy his coat and blocked his way to any other part of the house but the front door. Standing out on the step, Jeremy turned around to try and make one last situation-saving apology, but the door was slammed in his face.

He stood next to his car and could already hear Scott yelling at Michelle. But what could he do? Part of him wanted to go back inside, but would that just make things even worse? He'd come back and try again tomorrow. Michelle was a good mum. She'd always look out for the kids. He tried to hold onto that thought.

He looked up at the house and smiled and waved to Phoebe who was watching from her bedroom window. *Don't let her see*, he told himself, *don't let her see...*

22

It wasn't even eleven, but it looked like the entire town had already gone to bed for the night. *Christ*, Jeremy thought as he drove, *how could anyone stand living in a place as soulless as Thussock?* He drove the short journey back to the Black Boy, hoping he'd come across somewhere more interesting to stop *en route*, because the idea of spending the rest of the evening alone in the cramped little box room above the pub lounge didn't bear thinking about. He travelled constantly and he'd stayed in some pretty shitty places and lonely hotel rooms around the world, but this was grim by anyone's standards. It reminded him of a week he'd once spent living on his nerves in Azerbaijan.

The room seemed stuck in the late eighties. There was no Internet, and it would probably be better to take your chances and shout from the window rather than risk the temperamental mobile coverage. The landline in the room was corded – *Christ, when did I last use a phone that wasn't cordless?* – and he hadn't been able to get a picture on the small portable TV when he'd tried earlier. He'd only wanted to catch up with the news headlines and it was only after a frustrating twenty minutes spent checking cables and fiddling with the aerial that he realised it was because the TV was an old analogue set, useless since the switchover to digital. And that, he decided, summed up Thussock perfectly: an analogue place stuck in a digital world.

With nothing else to do, the bar of the pub seemed the only option. He parked on the road outside the scruffy-looking building (damn place didn't even have a bloody car park) and locked the car. He stood outside for a few moments, listening to the silence. Ah, maybe he was just in a bad mood after the ruckus back at the house. There was a lot to be said for the peace and quiet. There was no other traffic, hardly any other noise at all, in fact. The pub wasn't far from the station and he remembered thinking the clattering of the railway would probably keep him awake all night. As it was, he couldn't recall hearing even a single train since he'd arrived. Thussock was too quiet, if anything. He was almost relieved when he saw two helicopters crawling across the sky in the distance, taillights blinking, almost in unison. And far away he heard the low rumble of a truck, airbrakes hissing. *Life goes on elsewhere...*

There were only two other drinkers in the bar tonight, a couple of men in their late fifties, both reading newspapers, sitting right next to each other but barely speaking. They acknowledged him, but that was the extent of the interaction. The landlord kept himself busy, dividing his time between the bar and the TV Jeremy could hear blaring in one of the backrooms. The noise was muffled, but he could tell it was some kind of comedy programme. Every so often the volume would swell with the laughter track, the noise sounding out of place.

It was so bad he nipped upstairs and fetched himself a book to read as he drank his pint. It was that or paperwork, and no matter how bad it got, he decided, there was no way he was resorting to doing office work in a pub at this time of night. His dedication to the company, whilst strong enough to keep him travelling all these years and intense enough to have been the cause of many of the rifts between him and his ex-wife, still had limits.

At least the beer was good. Thussock's own, no less, produced less than half a mile down the road. Ever the optimist, Jeremy was glad he'd found something positive to take with him from his time here. He'd try and pick up a crate or two before leaving. *What happened at the house is getting you down*, he told himself as he finished his first pint and got up for another. *Things aren't that bad.* What other reason could there have been? Was it a local curse or something equally ridiculous? Was this one of those bizarre isolated communities you saw in horror movies? *Abandon hope, all ye who enter Thussock...*

The second pint went down even better than the first. The drink was going straight to his head, but that wasn't a bad thing. He'd needed a drink all evening, all day if he was honest. He didn't let them see, but he found being with Tammy and Phoebe almost as hard as being away from them. He hated leaving them more than anything. *If I had my time again*, he said to himself, sounding like an old man on his death bed, *I'd never have let things get as bad as they did.* He reminded himself that it hadn't all been his fault. He and Michelle had grown apart naturally, their individual priorities and desires slowly changing the longer they were together. In the end their marriage had become a passion-free arrangement of convenience. He'd told her repeatedly that he'd done all the hours and all the travelling for her and the girls, of course, but he'd been blind to what they'd actually needed from him. The status quo at home had continued for longer than it should have. When it became clear that their close proximity but lack of interaction was having a negative effect on the girls, they'd separated then divorced soon after. No hard feelings. Regular and informal access. The best of a bad situation.

Third pint before closing time. That was what he needed. He got up again and checked his change, deciding that if there really was a curse of Thussock, he'd been well and truly blighted today. The other two drinkers had disappeared, though he couldn't remember them going. The TV in the other room was still blaring. It sounded like a war movie now, all guns and noise and stirring music. Whatever it was, it seemed to be holding the landlord's rapt attention. Watching the film was clearly more appealing than coming back and serving his one remaining customer. Either that or he'd fallen asleep in front of the box. Jeremy rapped the edge of a coin on the bar several times and coughed loudly, but his noise wasn't having any effect. He doubted anyone could hear him.

There was a girl standing next to him. Where the hell had she come from? He physically jumped and swore with the sudden surprise, then immediately apologised. 'Jesus Christ, you scared the hell out of me.'

'Sorry,' she said, her voice quiet, little more than a mumble.

'I think he's nodded off in there,' Jeremy said, his composure returning, gesturing in the direction of the TV noise. 'If he's not back in the next two minutes, I'm just going to help myself.' He was half joking, but he thought he would if he had to. They could just add it to his room tab.

The girl didn't move. She was just standing there, leaning against the bar, looking at her own reflection in the mirror behind the row of optics. Jeremy tried not to stare but he couldn't help studying her face. She was very young and attractive, her skin pale against the vivid purple of her jacket. He noticed that her legs were bare. She was either wearing the shortest of skirts or nothing at all below the waist. He looked at her face in the mirrors again, caught her looking back at him. Her lips were full and red, inviting... he stopped himself.

What the hell did they put in that beer? He made himself look else-where and rapped the coin on the bar again. *Bloody hell*, he thought, *get a grip... you're old enough to be her father.*

'Can you help me?' she asked, and there was something about her light, breathless voice which cut straight through him. He felt an immediate concern for her, an inordinate need to protect.

'What's the matter?'

'I'm really cold.'

He turned to look at her, taking a couple of subtle, shuffling steps back to increase his distance and not give the wrong impression. She did look cold. She was shivering, but that was hardly surprising giv-en her lack of clothing. He felt uneasy, not knowing what would be worse: helping this girl and risking being accused of being a pervert, or leaving her shivering. *Sod it. Look at her. Poor kid's freezing.*

Jeremy fetched his own coat from where he'd left it on the bench behind the table where he'd been sitting. He offered it to her, then carefully draped it over her shoulders, not wanting to make too much contact for fear of her – or anyone else, for that matter – getting the wrong impression. 'Thank you,' she whispered, and she laid a hand on his and smiled the briefest of smiles.

'Do you want a drink?' Jeremy asked, hearing himself say things he knew he shouldn't. 'I could get you a tea or coffee if you'd rather? Warm you up? I'll go to the kitchen and make it myself if no one comes to serve me in the next thirty seconds. This is a joke. It this what it's always like here?'

He was rambling. Nervous. Excited.

She chewed her bottom lip and nodded.

'You're funny.'

'Thanks.'

'I like you.'

'Thanks again.'

'I'm still really cold.'

She was watching him intently now. She shifted her weight from foot to foot and when she moved he caught a glimpse of the rounded cheeks of her bare backside. He felt himself getting hard. Christ, he felt his heart burning for this kid now. He knew it was wrong on every conceivable level, but he wanted her so suddenly and so desperately… A comfort fuck with no strings – that'd do him the world of good tonight. She looked to be a similar age to Tammy, a little older, perhaps, and clinging onto that thought gave him a few brief seconds of clarity. But she smiled at him again and the burning – the *wanting* – returned, even stronger than before.

She moved along the bar, closing the gap he'd opened between them. Eyes locked. He focused on the sounds of her breathing. He could smell her. Almost taste her…

'I'm staying here tonight,' he said, screaming at himself to shut up but unable to stay silent. He felt awkward and clumsy… dirty. 'I've got a room upstairs if you want to…'

She didn't give him chance to finish. She lifted herself up on tiptoes and kissed him lightly on the lips. Then again. He felt her arms wrap around him. Then once more, with even more passion this time. She slipped her tongue into his mouth, slightly rough but completely perfect. And he reciprocated, no longer able to hold back. They kissed harder now. Full-on.

Jeremy broke away and glanced around. No one here. No one watching. She took his hand and led him over to the corner of the room. He tripped over a chair, only just managing to stay upright, the sudden unexpected movement almost bringing him to his senses. *Almost.* He was thinking he should definitely stop this, that this was just about the worst thing he could possibly do on every conceivable level, and yet he couldn't do anything but go with everything this girl was doing. He couldn't stop. He didn't want to stop.

'I don't even know your name,' he said between kisses, the girl still chewing his bottom lip.

'Heather,' she said, pushing him back onto a leather-padded bench behind a table in an alcove. The bench was too narrow and he slid off, crashing onto the floor and sending the table and another couple of chairs flying. He cracked his head back but the pain faded into insignificance compared to what this perfect girl was doing to him. He'd never done anything like this before, not ever. And Christ, it felt so good and so right… inevitable. He fumbled with his fly but she was already there and their fingers fought to be first to unzip him. He could feel her feather-light touch now, and the sensations were almost too much to stand. Lips still locked, limbs still entwined, she pulled out his dripping cock and guided it between her thighs. He grabbed at her jacket and unzipped it, revealing her completely naked body beneath it. *Why isn't she wearing anything?* The question rattled around his head for the briefest of moments until he realised he didn't care. Was this a set up? Something to do with Scott? Some unfathomably crazy local tradition? Was she going to rob him? Frame him? Kill him? No, she was just going to fuck him.

His fully erect cock slipped deep inside her and they fucked harder than he'd ever fucked anyone before.

23

Scott was still in bed, sleeping off the combined effects of the scotch Jeremy had brought around last night and the absolute fucker of an argument which had continued long after he'd gone. Michelle had almost drunk all her wine and she felt like finishing the last dregs this morning, rather than sober up. Her head was pounding, both as a result of the booze and how hard Scott had hit her this time. He'd slapped her right across the face back-handed, hard enough to loosen a tooth. She swallowed down a bilious sob: a nauseating mix of hangover and fear. Getting back into something resembling the drunken state she'd ended up in last night seemed like a good idea, an easier option. Far easier than dealing with the inevitable aftermath this morning.

Same old routine, she told herself, checking her face in the mirror for marks. *Different argument, but the same old routine.*

She didn't know how much longer she could keep repeating this cycle, but equally she didn't know how to get off. *The pressure builds, his behaviour gets worse, then he hurts me.* That time he punched her in the face and knocked her out cold, that time he shut her hand in the door, that time he grabbed a handful of hair and smacked her head against the wall... she was his release valve. Hurting her made him feel better. But when he told her he was sorry and begged for forgiveness, she believed him. Every bloody single time she believed him.

She decided she'd enjoy the early morning silence for a short while longer, then go and wake him up for work. He'd be full of apologies and remorse again, no doubt, blame it on the booze or on her or on Jeremy... anyone but himself. *It'll never happen again, I swear*, he'd tell her like he always did.

She knew what Scott was. She'd known it for a long time. It still made her laugh that *she* was the one getting help! Her counsellor had been helping her identify her own faults and start working through them so she could better deal with Scott's. The pills, the therapy... all necessary because there was a part of her which still wanted this to work. *Needed* it to work. She had loved Scott to begin with – honestly, genuinely – and maybe she still did. She still believed there was a chance she could get those feelings back despite everything he'd put the family through. This move, this house, this place: all just temporary setbacks. That's what the therapist had said when she'd told him she was moving away.

The house was in a real bloody state. An absolute bloody pigsty. It pissed her off how it was all left to her again. The division of labour in this family was so bloody unfair. She gave, they all took. No, wait... that was unfair. The girls helped when they could, regularly looking after George so she could get on with everything else. This morning, though, this kitchen seemed to perfectly sum up hers and Scott's relationship. She worked hard to keep it clean and comfortable, he'd just come along with a sledgehammer and knocked a fucking huge hole in the wall.

Jeremy might have had his faults, but at least he'd tried. He'd been pretty good around the house, actually, and had enjoyed cooking. But even that had caused issues because when she wanted something quick and easy out of a packet to feed two hungry kids, he'd wanted to cook a wholesome three-course meal from scratch. They'd learnt to adapt to each other and everything had become a joint effort. Shame, then, that the spark had been snuffed out somewhere along the way. They'd ended up more like brother and sister than lovers. Looking at him last night, she struggled to remember what she'd ever found attractive about him.

It's got to be me. It must be something I do. I must be the one who always messes it up. I never give them what they want. Jeremy wasn't happy, Scott's never happy, the kids are always complaining... it must be me.

She'd started around the house too fast and too early this morning, and Michelle had already peaked. She'd been up for less than an hour, but she was ready for bed again. *I'd love to spend the whole bloody day in bed*, she thought. *Let them fend for themselves.*

There was a pounding noise outside, and it wasn't helping her head. It sounded like a helicopter, hovering over Thussock in the same way the motorway police used to buzz around the M42 and M5 back home near Redditch. This morning it was a constant, irritating, migraine-inducing noise which bored into her brain and refused to go away. She hoped it wouldn't wake the others. She walked around the ground floor of the house, looking out of all the windows, seeing if she could spot it.

She was staring out of the kitchen window, looking up into the blue sky overhead, when Jeremy appeared at the glass. She jumped back with surprise and cursed him as she tried to catch her breath and calm her nerves. What the hell was he thinking, creeping up on her like that? And what was he doing here anyway? Christ, Scott would go mental if he caught him. He'd arranged to see the girls today, but not until later. She marched outside to deal with him.

'You scared the crap out of me, Jeremy. What the hell are you doing?' He just looked at her. 'We agreed you'd pick the girls up after school, didn't we?'

He moved closer. Mumbled 'sorry.'

Something wasn't right. Michelle realised he was wearing the same clothes as last night. She remembered his cardigan, and she hated cardigans on men. Kids and old folks could just about get away with them, but middle-aged men like Jeremy definitely couldn't. She remembered thinking he looked like he was trying too hard when she'd first seen him yesterday, but that definitely wasn't the case today. His trousers were grubby and creased and his hair was a mess. It wasn't like him. 'Are you okay? Has something happened?'

'Didn't know where else to go,' he said, his voice almost too low to make out. That damn helicopter was still buzzing overhead. 'Wanted to see you.'

She looked around but couldn't see his car. 'How did you get here?'

'Walked.'

Alarm bells were ringing. Was he planning something? Was he going to try and snatch the girls and take them back with him to the Midlands? But hold on... this was Jeremy, remember? Safe, sensible, reliable Jeremy. He wouldn't do anything like that, would he? When they'd first split up, he'd immediately acknowledged the kids would be far better off with their mother and in all the years since he'd never said anything to make her think his opinion had changed. He didn't take risks, he did things by the book. And she realised that whatever his reason for being here this morning, she was actually glad to see him.

He moved a little closer, stopping just a couple of paces away, almost close enough to touch. He just stared at her. Needed her. Wanted her.

'Jeremy, love, what's wrong?'

Michelle remembered everything that had happened last night and how physically inferior Jeremy had appeared next to Scott, how quickly he'd capitulated. She'd felt so sorry for him but hadn't dared say anything. It had been like watching the nice, quiet kid at school getting the shit kicked out of him by some lump-head bully. If Jeremy was hurting or upset this morning, she didn't want him to be. She looked deep into her ex-husband's eyes and all she could see were the things that had first attracted her to him. She loved his face. She'd always loved his face but it was like she'd forgotten why and was only now beginning to remember. She could see it again now... the bump at the top of his nose, his light blue eyes, his neat ears. There was nothing pretty or particularly handsome about Jeremy, but this morning he just looked... *right*. And then she felt her legs weaken because it was as if that innocent, unspoken admission had unwittingly opened the floodgates. A torrent of long forgotten and completely unexpected emotions washed over her. Had these feelings merely been suppressed, not lost? She felt desperately sad because she'd let him go. More than that, she suddenly felt an undeniable urge to be with him stronger than anything she'd felt for him before, even during their first weeks and months together. This felt pure and basic, unstoppable and inevitable. All she wanted was to hold him close again, to feel his body against hers, inside hers...

Not a word needed to be spoken between them. It was as if a forgotten connection had been re-established between the estranged couple, transcending the need for verbal communication. There remained just inches of clear space between them.

A final moment of hesitation, one last failed sanity check, then an embrace in the middle of the yard in front of the house.

Their lips locked and hands began to move, exploring bodies which hadn't touched one another in years, hadn't wanted to. Jeremy gently pushed her up against the side of Scott's Vauxhall Zafira, his tongue exploring her mouth in the same way the girl's tongue had explored his last night, and—

—and Scott flew through the front door and pulled Jeremy away from his wife. He threw him to the ground and kicked him in the gut, hard enough to roll him over. 'Bastard,' he spat. Michelle grabbed at him and tried to pull him away, but he swung around and slapped her across the face, just as he had done last night. 'What the fuck is going on?' he demanded, standing over her as she sank to her knees, sobbing. 'Answer me! What the fuck is going on?'

Michelle looked up at her husband, then at her ex-husband behind him on all fours, struggling to get back to his feet. Her mouth opened and closed, but the words wouldn't come. 'I don't...' she said, 'I didn't...' She couldn't form full sentences, could barely even form full thoughts. Blood poured from her nose.

'You bitch,' Scott said. 'How long have you and him been planning this?'

Already distracted, he was taken completely by surprise when Jeremy barged past him to get to Michelle again, his unbuckled trousers now around his ankles, his penis erect. Too stunned to react at first, as Jeremy reached for Michelle, Scott grabbed his shoulders and pulled him over backwards. He kicked him again, focusing his full fury on the man on the ground. Michelle staggered away, heading for the relative safety of the house.

Jeremy was still trying to get back up. Scott ran at him and punched him so hard he thought he'd broken his hand, catching him full on the side of his jaw and knocking him out cold. He stood over the unconscious, half-dressed man and shook his stinging hand. There was a noise behind him. He spun around quickly, expecting to have been locked out of the house, but the noise had come from upstairs. Phoebe was hanging out of her bedroom window, and she started screaming when she saw her dad. Seconds later, Tammy came flying out of the front door. Scott caught her and carried her back inside, throwing her down the hallway before slamming the door shut then locking and bolting it behind him and pocketing the key. She scrambled back to her feet and threw herself at him, pounding him with her fists. He tried to catch her vicious, flailing arms but couldn't. He refused to hit back and instead just soaked up punch after punch until she was too tired to keep fighting.

The house was full of noise now: Michelle sobbing at the bottom of the stairs, Phoebe a few steps above her, howling too, and else-where George, forgotten, was screaming for attention. Tammy saw that Scott was distracted and shoved him away before bolting, look-ing for another way out of the house. He blocked her at every turn. 'It wasn't my fault,' he tried to say, cornering her in the kitchen. 'He attacked your mum... tried to force himself on her.'

'He wouldn't do that. You're lying again... he wouldn't.'

'It's true,' Michelle said, wiping her bloody nose, desperately trying to cling onto Scott's half-truth and avoid making any admissions of her own. She'd been as much to blame. She'd wanted Jeremy as much as he had wanted her, though now she couldn't understand what had possessed her. She felt as if she'd been violated though they'd barely touched. Conscious they were staring at her, she wrapped her dress-ing-gown around her half-naked body. Her voice was hoarse with crying and tears flooded down her cheeks, mixing with the blood. 'He was outside and I went to ask him what was wrong. He looked scared. I went to talk to him and he... I don't know if he'd been drinking or what... he was wearing the same clothes as last night and—'

'And you weren't putting up much of a fight,' Scott sneered.

'You're both lying,' Phoebe said from the corner of the kitchen, away from the rest of them.

'Did you not see him from up there?' Scott said, no consideration for her feelings. 'Trousers round his ankles, everything hanging out... dirty fucker.'

'Scott!' Michelle said.

'What? Don't you dare criticise me, you bitch.'

'Don't talk to Mum like that,' Tammy screamed at him.

'And don't any of you talk to me at all.'

Michelle looked at him and he held her gaze for several seconds. But there was no concern in his eyes anymore, no love, just hurt and hate. She moved towards him, he backed away. 'You have to believe me, Scott... I know how it looked but it wasn't like that. I really thought there was something wrong. I went out to check on him and he... I don't know what came over me.'

'Well your ex-husband very nearly did,' he said, emotionless.

'We need to talk about this. For the sake of the girls and George, we need to talk...'

'What's there to talk about? I caught you in the front yard, about to fuck your ex-husband. That's pretty much it from where I'm standing.'

'I know, and I can't explain it... it's just...'

'Just what? Come on, I want to hear this. Are you going to explain to me how it's okay that you nearly fucked Jeremy just now?'

'I swear, I didn't plan anything... But there was just something about the way he was, the way he looked at me...'

'Oh, fuck, was it love at first sight all over again?'

'Don't take the piss out of me, Scott.'

'Then don't treat me like a fucking idiot. You're telling me you just felt like having sex out in the open with your ex because of the way he looked at you? So you've not had any feelings for him for years, you just changed your mind this morning? Or was it last night? Did something happen before I came back in and caught him slagging me off? Was he touching you up while I was out of the room?'

Michelle gasped. 'Don't talk to me like that. Don't say things like that in front of the kids. You shouldn't—'

'*You're* criticising *me*? Don't waste your breath,' Scott cut across her, the contempt in his voice clear. He leant closer so that only she could hear him. 'I saw *everything*. I was watching from the moment you went out there. I know what happened. I know what you did, what you wanted to do.'

'No, Scott, I swear... I didn't do anything to...'

He grabbed her throat, squeezing tight enough to leave red finger marks, almost choking her but not quite, knowing just the right amount of pressure to apply because he'd done this plenty of times before. 'Save your breath. Go and see to George and get out of my fucking sight.'

She did as he said, running to the stairs, keen to shield her son from the chaos. On the other side of the kitchen, Tammy straightened herself up, ready to attack Scott again. 'This is all your fault...' she started to say. He lifted a hand to hit her and she cowered away, the moment seeming to last forever. He eventually lowered his fist.

'Get upstairs and get ready for school,' he said, the unnatural calm in his voice now somehow more frightening than the anger he'd shown seconds earlier.

'I don't want to go to school,' Phoebe sobbed. 'Not now, not af-ter...'

'Both of you get upstairs and get ready for school before I really lose my fucking temper. Now!'

They did as they were told, fearing for their safety. Scott could be intimidating at the best of times, right now he was downright terri-fying. Neither girl had any doubt he'd hit them if it came down to it. They'd seen what he'd done Mum enough times.

And then they were gone, and he was finally alone, left to try and make some sense of the madness of this morning. He looked out of the window at the pervert lying on the gravel by the side of the fami-ly car. *What the fuck is wrong with all these people?* He was surrounded – both in this house and in this town – by crazy people. What had he done to deserve this? A wife who cheated on him, step-kids who couldn't stand him... He thought about just getting in the car and going, but that wasn't going to happen. He had nowhere to go. He checked he'd still got the door key in his pocket, then walked around downstairs and made sure all the other doors and windows were locked too. *If I can't go anywhere, neither can they. Not until I decide.*

In frustration, hoping to get rid of some of the pent-up anger fes-tering inside him, Scott picked up the sledgehammer. It was where he'd left it on Sunday evening. He shoved the kitchen table back and began to swing at the hole in the wall. Again and again he swung the hammer at the brickwork, feeling satisfied every time a piece of ma-sonry fell, kicking rubble out of the way so he could keep swinging. He'd thought previously that he might be capable of demolishing this whole bloody house, now he thought he might actually be about to do it.

A frantic few minutes and the hole had almost doubled in size, but it still wasn't enough. He lifted the hammer to swing it around again, then stopped, feeling like he was being watched. Phoebe was standing in the kitchen doorway, dressed in her school uniform, face white and eyes red. 'What do you want?' She was almost too afraid to talk. She fidgeted on the spot, eyes on the sledgehammer, not him. 'What?' he shouted at her again, and she jumped at the noise.

'My dad's gone,' she said quietly, wincing in anticipation of his reaction.

'So? Do you think I give a shit about your bloody father after what he's done this morning?'

She was crying again now, sobbing hard, shoulders shaking. It was almost impossible to speak between the tears but she made herself do it. 'Please, Scott... I know what he did but I'm worried...'

'Then you go and sort him out.'

'I can't get out.'

'I'll let you out.'

'I think something's wrong with him.'

'I *know* something's wrong with him. Sick fucker.'

'Please, Scott... Please help.'

Scott swung the sledgehammer at the wall again, grunting with effort, then he stopped. He looked over at Phoebe. Was any of this her fault? Her sister was a genuinely spiteful and vindictive bitch, but Phoebe wasn't. She was just a scared and vulnerable kid who'd already seen things she should never have seen this morning, things which would no doubt scar her for life.

'His trousers are still in the yard,' she said, sniffing back more tears. 'And his pants...'

'Wait here,' he told her, deciding he needed to make sure Jeremy was well away from the house. 'I'll go and look.'

Scott side-stepped Phoebe then let himself out and locked the door behind him. Phoebe went to the window and watched, keeping out of sight as Scott hunted around the yard, checking under the car and around the side of buildings and walls, like he was trying to find a missing cat... She didn't know what to do for the best. She couldn't understand what was happening. She'd seen more than she'd let on, and she didn't know why her mum and dad had done what they'd done. He'd always been a good dad. He'd always looked out for her and Tammy and Mum, even after they'd split up. He'd always said kind things about her, and had never talked about Scott in the unkind, disrespectful way Scott usually talked about him. But she couldn't think about Dad like she used to now, because she had an image burned into her head that she couldn't shake: her own father, lying on his back in the middle of the yard of this horrible grey house, beaten up and bleeding, half-naked and exposed to the world.

She just wanted all of this to stop.

Scott couldn't find him. Surely the dirty bastard couldn't have got far? He climbed up onto the stone wall at the end of the drive to get a better view and looked out over the fields on the other side of the road. He could see for miles, but he couldn't see Jeremy.

He had to have gone back into town. Where else would he be? Scott picked up Jeremy's trousers so he could sort him out when he finally found him, though he didn't know why he was bothering. Sick fucker didn't deserve his help.

Scott walked back to the house then got in the car and drove towards Thussock. The roads were silent today, absolutely no other traffic about. He couldn't remember having seen a single other vehicle, not that he'd been looking.

When he reached the wooden bus shelter near to the small house where those bizarre twins lived, he slowed down. He could see movement, though he couldn't quite make out what it was at first. Wait... it looked like someone lying on the ground on the other side of the shelter, feet sticking out but the rest of their bodies obscured by the little wooden building. Hang on, there was more than one person. Had someone else found Jeremy? Were they helping him? He hoped so, because he didn't want to have to. He decided he'd just make sure it was him, throw the sick fuck his trousers, then go back and tell Phoebe everything was okay, that her dad was fine.

He parked in the bus space in front of the shelter and walked around the Zafira. Then he just stopped, struggling to understand what he was seeing. In spite of everything he'd already witnessed today, what was unfolding in front of him now was bizarre, grotesque and just... *wrong*. He'd found Jeremy all right, but there was a woman with him. More than just *with* him, she was astride him. *Fucking him*. Riding him in broad daylight, neither of them appearing to give a damn about anyone or anything else.

'What the hell is this?' he demanded. The woman – who he didn't recognise – slowly turned her head to face him but didn't otherwise react, so consumed by what she was doing with Jeremy to care, overcome with pleasure and completely uninhibited. Scott followed a trail back to the bus shelter with his eyes... her shoes, her knickers, the remains of a torn pair of tights... Christ, had this woman just been waiting for a bus when Jeremy came wandering down the road, and had they just decided to fuck on the spur of the moment? It had to have been quick and spontaneous, no time for small-talk or foreplay. Scott almost laughed out loud at the ridiculousness of it all, but the serious implications of what he was seeing were clear. There was something inherently sinister about this inexplicable public display of base emotion, something clearly unnatural about this most natural of acts. Should he stop it? Try to separate them? Or should he just get back in the car and drive home and pretend none of it was happening?

'Jeremy, what the hell are you doing?' he asked, hanging back a short distance, almost too embarrassed to keep watching but unable not to. 'Do you know what—?'

A howl of pleasure from the woman interrupted him mid-sentence. He watched as she threw her head back and looked up into the swirling white clouds overhead, groaning as she started to cum. Scott stared as she began to experience an orgasm of remarkable intensity, muscles hard in spasm, gripping Jeremy's shoulders tight. Scott could take no more and he returned to his car, head spinning. He couldn't understand why such an uptight little idiot as Jeremy would behave this way? He'd always been so reserved, so proper, overly polite... Michelle used to joke about how awkward he'd always been about sex, how it had always been safe and functional with Jeremy. Never spontaneous. Boring, even. Text-book.

Scott was about to get in the car and drive home when he noticed the woman was up and rushing away, running almost, clutching her clothes. She kept looking back over her shoulder. Was she looking at Jeremy, or looking at him? Hurrying away with shame, perhaps? She was still half-naked. Scott almost called out to her, but stopped at the last second because he didn't know what to say. He felt like he didn't know anything anymore. Nothing made sense. How could she possibly be embarrassed now after such an exhibitionist performance seconds earlier?

He noticed that Jeremy hadn't moved.

Scott could still see his feet sticking out from around the side of the bus shelter, one of them twitching. He thought about Phoebe back at the house. *How the hell am I going to explain this to her?* For a moment he considered taking Jeremy back with him. *His mess, his fault. He can do it...*

'Oi, Jeremy,' he shouted. 'Get up you useless bastard.'

Nothing.

Had he fallen asleep? Again the immature side of Scott's character took hold. Michelle was always having a go at him for falling asleep straight after sex, was this just the same thing? Was poor little Jeremy exhausted after all that uncharacteristic exertion? No way. Jeremy was a nervous little shit, scared of his own shadow, terrified of not doing everything 'by the book'. So why was he still lying there?

He walked around to where the semi-naked man lay on the grass verge, then stopped.

Fuck.

If Jeremy wasn't already dead, then he would be in the next few minutes... the next few seconds, even. His face was unnaturally pallid. His mouth moved slightly, as if trying to form his final words, and though his eyes looked directly at Scott, he knew they weren't seeing anything.

There was blood all over the grass: puddles of it under his pale white buttocks, pools forming between his spindly legs, dribbles running down his thighs.

Where the hell's it all coming from? Did that woman cut him?

Scott gagged when he saw it, almost threw up. The end of Jeremy's penis looked like it had been torn apart, as if someone had first skewered the hole, then ripped the flesh away in sections like they were peeling a banana. Flaps of skin hung uselessly over the end of the stump from which blood continued to pump in dull spurts, slowing with the weakening pace of Jeremy's pulse.

And, for the briefest of moments, all Scott felt was relief. He didn't understand what was happening, but he didn't care because he immediately knew this was what had happened to Shona McIntyre. This was what he'd seen in all those grotesque photographs that frigging detective had shoved under his nose while he was in custody. This was proof positive to the rest of them that he wasn't the killer.

The woman.

Was it her?

He reached for his mobile, but stopped. He scanned the horizon looking for the woman and spying her almost out of view, half-running into town. He couldn't be the one to tell the police, could he? They'd jump to all the wrong conclusions if he admitted to being here. No, Scott knew he had to get away from here fast. He'd phone them from home, let them know what Jeremy had tried to do to Michelle, tell them where he thought he'd gone then let them find him and his fuck-buddy... Better still, maybe he'd stay quiet and plead ignorance and let someone else find the corpse.

He got back into the car, turned a tight circle in the empty road, then drove away at speed.

'Well?' Michelle said. She was in the kitchen, waiting. They all were.

'Well what?'

'Did you find him?'

'No,' he said, because lying was easier than the truth.

'But he can't have just disappeared.'

'Well I couldn't find him.'

'You can't have looked very hard,' Tammy said.

'I looked hard enough.'

'So what do we do?' Michelle asked.

He shrugged his shoulders. 'What do you want me to do? I'm not exactly heart-broken, if that's what you're thinking. Call the police if it makes you feel better. Tell them he's disappeared. Tell them he was acting like a fucking freak.'

'Scott...'

'Tell them what you like, just don't involve me. I'm sick of getting dragged into other people's messes.'

'I'll do it,' Tammy said.

'No, I'll do it,' Michelle said. 'It'd be better coming from me.'

Tammy followed her out into the living room, leaving Scott with Phoebe. George played on the floor, oblivious to everything.

'Thanks for looking,' Phoebe said.

Scott looked at her, confused. 'What?'

'I said thanks for looking for Dad.'

He turned away. 'It's fine. Sorry I didn't find him.'

'He'll come back later, won't he?'

Shit. Is she testing me? Does she suspect? 'Sure he will.'

'He's not well, is he? There's something wrong with him. He must be sick.'

'He must be.'

Scott went to the bathroom, more to avoid Phoebe than through any real physical need. He leant against the wall, shaking with nerves. What he'd just seen happen to Jeremy made no sense at all, and yet he felt in his gut that it should explain everything. Who was that woman? Was she the cause of all of this? If so, why hadn't she been seen or caught previously? Was she the killer, or just another victim? Could it be that these weren't murders, that they were something else entirely? Some kind of infection? A killer STD passed from person to person? He laughed at the ridiculousness of it all, then sat down on the toilet and held his head in his hands, unable to think straight.

When Scott returned to the kitchen, several minutes later, Michelle was back. 'They won't do anything,' she said.

'Who won't?'

'The police. They won't do anything about Jeremy. They say someone walking off after a fight doesn't qualify as a missing person.'

'They'd know. Fucking top-notch police force we've got round here.'

Michelle stared out of the window, looking for something to help make sense of this impossible day. Maybe she should go and look for Jeremy herself? She quickly dismissed that idea, knowing full well how Scott would react. Besides, she thought that if she left this house, she might not ever come back, and she couldn't leave the kids. She glanced up as a convoy of three khaki-coloured trucks thundered past on their way into Thussock. *If they'd been going the other way*, she thought, *I might have thumbed a lift.*

This was stupid. They were grown adults. She couldn't explain how she'd felt around Jeremy this morning – maybe it was just a reaction to how she was beginning to feel around Scott? Anyway, as close as it had been, nothing *had* happened. She turned around, looking for her husband.

'We need to talk, Scott.'

'You need to shut the fuck up and keep out of my sight. You think I want to talk to you after what's happened?'

'Phoebe, would you take George upstairs please,' Michelle said, undeterred. Phoebe looked from face to face, unsure.

'But I don't want to go upstairs.'

'I need to speak to Scott. Just do it. Please.'

She grudgingly did as she was told, scooping up her little brother and his toys and carrying him out. Scott watched Michelle intently, trying to work what she was thinking, how she thought she was going to worm her way out of this mess. If only she knew what he knew. This inexplicable urge to copulate – first between Michelle and Jeremy, then Jeremy and the woman – was it pheromones or endorphins, he wondered, something like that?

The silence between them was deafening. Michelle didn't know where to begin. She was starting to wonder if she even wanted to, if it was worth the effort anymore.

'I'm worried about the girls,' she said, trying a different tack. 'They were already struggling, and now this...'

'Maybe you should have thought of that first,' he said, his spite a gut reaction. Then he thought about Jeremy, lying dead on the grass less than a mile from the house. 'Oh well, look on the bright side, eh.'

'There's a bright side?'

'There is for me. For once none of you can blame everything on me. You and Jeremy can share this one.'

'And is that all that matters to you?'

'I'm sick of being the whipping boy. Everything's always my fault.'

'That's because it usually is,' she said without thinking. She cringed inwardly, waiting for his reaction, bracing herself in case he came at her. When he didn't, she risked saying more. She knew she had to; the enormity of the moment slowly dawning on her. It was now or never: to put up with more of his shit and risk things getting even worse, or to finally make a stand and do something about it. Tammy had said as much the other night, and Michelle knew now that her daughter had been right. She'd known it for a long time. 'It's your fault we're here and in this mess, Scott. Your fault we had to leave Redditch.'

'So is what happened this morning somehow my fault too? Is it my fault I lost my temper when I saw another man trying to fuck my wife outside my bedroom window? Jeez, what a terrible overreaction on my part. What do you think I should I have done, Chelle? Fetched you a bloody condom? Cleared out of the bedroom so you two could have had the bed?'

'I can't explain this morning. I just...' she started to say before losing her nerve. *Deep breath. Can't avoid this. Have to do it.* 'I think you're the cause of all our problems. I want you to go. I want you to leave us alone.'

207

He threw himself at her and she cowered, braced for the familiar rush of pain. But he stopped, fist just inches from her face, and grinned as she shrank away from him. 'You've got this all mixed up in that empty little head of yours,' he said. 'You see, love, I'm the one who keeps this fucked-up family together. I don't know why I bother sometimes.'

'Then why don't you just stop? Leave us alone... Don't you get it? There's nothing wrong with us. There's nothing wrong with Thussock or any of the people here... it's all *you*. You're the one who's different. You're the one who's got it wrong, the one who doesn't fit in. You should just pack your stuff and—' The phone started to ring, interrupting her. She heard Tammy sprint to the living room to answer it. Michelle tried to follow but Scott blocked her way.

'You're unbelievable, you know that?' he said. 'You're deluded.'

'I think I might have been, but I'm starting to see things more clearly now.'

Tammy was in the doorway. 'It's Jackie. She's asking to talk to you, Mum. Says it's urgent.'

'Be a good girl and tell the nice lady that your mother's busy,' Scott said. 'Actually, tell her your mother's busy and ask her to stop sticking her fucking nose in other people's business.'

'Leave Jackie alone,' Michelle said. 'She's a good friend.'

'I know. I met her.'

'You didn't say.'

'No, and you didn't tell me she was round here when I was locked up, either. Have a little party, did you? Drinks with friends while I was away?'

'That's not fair, Scott,' Michelle protested, pushing past him to get to the phone. 'None of this is Jackie's fault. She came around to support me. She's just—'

'—she's just another frigging hillbilly local who can't keep her nose out of other people's business.'

Michelle ignored him and snatched up the phone, but the line was dead. She checked and double-checked it, then turned back to face him again. 'What have you done to the phone?'

'What are you talking about now? How could I have done anything to the phone?'

208

'It's disconnected.'

'It has to be you,' Tammy said. 'You pulled the cable out because you don't like Mum having friends.'

'Jesus, love, you're getting as bad as your mother. You're all paranoid.'

'I'm not paranoid, and I'm not your love,' she spat.

Scott grabbed the phone from Michelle and held it to his ear. Nothing. He tried making a call – still nothing. The screen lit up but there was no noise, not even a dialling tone. 'I give up,' he said. 'Is there nothing in this house you lot can't fuck up?'

'Come on, Tam,' Michelle said and dragged Tammy upstairs.

'Something I said?' Scott shouted after them. 'Where you going now?'

'To check on Phoebe and George.'

'But I thought you wanted to talk...'

They went into Phoebe's room and found her sitting on her bed, knees drawn up to her chest, George playing by her feet. Her face was drawn; eyes red, cheeks streaked with tears. She didn't even look up. Michelle crouched down and put a hand on her arm but Phoebe pulled away. 'Come on, Pheeb, please... don't do this.'

'Don't do what?' Phoebe said, her voice so quiet the words were hard to make out. 'I haven't done anything. It was you, remember? You and my dad. I saw you.'

'Look, if I could do something to put this right, I would. I swear, I don't know what happened or why... I think we're all under a lot of stress right now with the house move and new jobs and new schools and—'

'I've tried though, Mum. I haven't done anything wrong. When you lot were all bitching and fighting, I was just getting on with it, trying to make the most of it. None of this is my fault.'

'I never said it was.'

'You and my dad, trying to shag each other out in public...'

'Don't use that word, Phoebe.'

'What do you want me to say instead then? Cuddling? *Raping*? It was disgusting...'

'I only went out there to try and talk to him. I didn't mean for the rest of it to happen, I swear. I just—'

She stopped talking abruptly when she heard a noise downstairs. Someone was at the front door. Was it Jeremy? Tammy had the same thought and she moved fast, desperate to get there before Scott did. The door flew open before she was halfway downstairs, kicked in from outside. Hazmat wearing soldiers flooded into the house. Michelle yanked Tammy back as Scott ran at the nearest of them. They overpowered him easily, catching his arms and dragging him into the kitchen, kicking and yelling. They looked terrifying in their camouflaged all-in-one suits, their faces obscured by breathing apparatus, eyes hidden behind reflective visors.

George clung to Michelle's leg. She scooped him up into her arms and ran back to Phoebe's room, pushing Tammy ahead of her. Once inside, she turned to shut the door, only to find it wedged open by a light brown boot. The soldier forced the door open again, sending Michelle, George and the girls running to the furthest corner of the room. He had a rifle, but left it slung over his shoulder. His gloved hands were raised. 'Come downstairs please, ladies,' he said, his deep voice distorted by his breathing gear. 'Everything's going to be all right.'

Michelle thought she detected a faint Midlands accent and that familiarity, bizarrely, made her feel marginally safer. There were three more soldiers on the landing, and even more behind them. The first man led them back down to the kitchen in silence as others explored the rest of the house.

'Anyone else here?'

'No, just the five of us,' Michelle said. She felt herself relax, or was it just that she was finally giving up and shutting down? Was she relieved because there were people here now who could keep Scott under control, or was it more than that? Somehow, in the utter chaos of this day so far, the house being invaded by a horde of faceless, protective-suit wearing soldiers made things feel a little more certain. She began to think it might not just be this household which was screwed-up beyond repair. Maybe the rest of Thussock was the same too?

When Phoebe looked into the face of the next soldier, all she saw was herself reflected back. It wasn't until the soldier spoke that Phoebe realised it was a she. 'Go into the kitchen with your mum and dad, love. And don't worry, everything's gonna be okay.'

Phoebe glanced out through the kicked-in front door. The yard was full of military machinery. There was some kind of truck blocking in the Zafira, and a jeep on the road with a soldier manning the kind of massive machine gun she'd only ever seen in films before. There was another vehicle too. It looked like her old school minibus, all done up in army colours.

The entire family was rounded up in the kitchen. They stood next to each other in front of the huge hole Scott had knocked in the wall, feet crunching in the brick dust and plaster, the closest they'd been to each other all morning. There were soldiers standing either side of Scott, ready to restrain him if he kicked off again. 'What the hell's this about?' he demanded, spitting the words angrily at the intruders.

'Don't be alarmed.'

'Don't be alarmed? Fuck's sake, you break into my house carrying guns and wearing fucking facemasks and suits, and you tell me not to be alarmed?'

'Please...' Michelle said, clinging onto George with one hand and trying to hold onto Phoebe with the other. 'What's happening...?'

'If you'd like to come with us,' another soldier said, standing to one side, opening a clear passage through the ranks. *Jesus*, Michelle thought, *how many of them are here?*

'I'm not going anywhere until you fuckers tell me what's going on,' Scott said, standing his ground. His resistance didn't last long. With a nod from the commanding officer, two soldiers hauled him outside. He protested at first, struggling to get free, but there was no point.

The others were ushered out. Michelle walked across their suddenly chaotic yard, looking around in disbelief. High overhead, three helicopters circled Thussock like birds of prey, and in the fields on the other side of the road she saw a long line of similarly suited figures moving across the land. They looked like they were combing it, hunting for something. It reminded her of the people they'd seen from the hills when they'd first arrived in Thussock. And every soldier she could see – every last one of them – was armed.

They were loaded into a van. She sat down with Tammy and Phoebe, George perched on her lap. Scott was a few seats ahead, still seething. He made fleeting eye contact with the others, but that was the limit of their communication.

The back of the van was more secure than she'd expected: a metal division between those in the front and their passengers behind, just a small rectangular hole cut into it at driver's eye level. It was stiflingly hot and claustrophobic. *Dogs die in hot cars*, was all she kept thinking.

Scott pressed his face against the glass and watched the soldiers crawling over his property. They were everywhere now – visible in all the windows, checking the garage and outbuildings, disappearing around the side of the house and rummaging through the garden, sticking their noses into places he hadn't even looked yet. What the hell were they after? After what he'd already seen this morning, he didn't want to know.

The back of the van was slammed shut and they began to move. Michelle looked over at Scott, hoping for some reassurance but getting none.

Minutes later and they neared the bus shelter, travelling as part of a convoy with other vehicles. Scott was less concerned with all the military might now, more worried about how the girls would react if they saw their father's butchered body lying on the verge. He didn't know what to do. Did he try and distract them, or not bother and just let Tammy and Phoebe see Jeremy lying there in his blood-soaked, naked glory. He cursed himself. *Should have thought about this*. He was sitting on the wrong side of the van. If he'd sat where Michelle was he'd have been able to block their view. As it was, he had no chance.

Except it didn't matter.

Jeremy's body had gone, a grubby crimson-brown stain on the grass the only indication he'd ever been there. There were more soldiers here, a crowd of them gathered around the back of a military ambulance.

Fortunately there was enough of a distraction on the other side of the road to keep Michelle and the girls looking elsewhere. The van lurched to a halt opposite the cottage where the twins lived. More soldiers surged towards the house, a replay of the procedure they'd followed at the family's home. When they hammered on the front door it was opened almost immediately, no need to force entry. Scott watched as the twin who answered instantly crumbled with fear. She disappeared from view momentarily, pushed back into the house, followed by ten hazmat-suited soldiers, only to reappear a short time later, hand in hand with her sister, walking together like frightened little kids. The back of the van opened and the two of them climbed inside.

The routine was repeated again a few minutes later. Scott didn't recognise the older man and woman being bundled into the van this time, but Michelle clearly did. He acknowledged both her and the twins. 'What's going on Dr Kerr?' one of the twins asked, sobbing with fear, barely able to speak.

'I wish I could tell you, Jeannie. Anyone else have any idea?'

'They took us from our house, same as you,' Michelle said.

'It's Mrs Griffiths, isn't it?'

'That's right.'

'We met at the surgery last week.'

'Yes. These are my daughters, Tammy and Phoebe. That's my husband Scott in front of you.'

Scott looked over his shoulder and Dr Kerr nodded.

A couple more stops and the van had almost reached capacity. As they drove further into Thussock, the doctor tapped Scott's arm. 'Any ideas?'

'Not a clue. You're a GP, right?'

'Your GP, I believe. Your wife came into the surgery to register the family. It's not usually like this round here.'

'I've only got your word for that.'

'We've never had anything like these deaths before... all of this must be something to do with the murders.'

'I'm not so sure they were murders,' he said.

'Well they're not suicides,' the doctor replied, 'I can tell you that much. I saw a couple of the bodies myself.'

'Me too. Listen, can I talk to you in confidence?'

Dr Kerr looked concerned. He patted his wife's hand and smiled at her. 'Give me a minute, love,' he said and he changed seats, shuffling up next to Scott. 'What is it?'

Scott checked Michelle and the girls were out of earshot. He leant closer to the doctor and kept his voice low. 'We had an... incident at the house this morning.'

'What kind of incident?'

'My wife's ex-husband turned up... he practically forced himself onto her.'

Dr Kerr was confused, his weather-beaten brow furrowed. 'Sorry to hear it, but what's that got to do with anything?'

'They don't know this yet,' he warned, 'so keep it to yourself, right?' The doctor nodded, and Scott continued. 'We had a fight and I left her ex lying in the yard while I went to sort out the wife and kids. Things were crazy, you can imagine. Little while later, one of the girls notices he'd gone...' Scott paused, unsure. Had he really seen what he thought he'd seen earlier or just dreamt it? Was he as mad as he now sounded? 'I went out in the car to look for him.'

'And?'

'And I found him behind the bus shelter. He was with another woman.'

'Who?'

'Don't know. Never seen her before.'

'What do you mean, with her?'

'What do you think I mean? He was fucking her. The two of them, at it out there in the open without a frigging care.'

'And did they see you?'

'She did, but it didn't bother her. They finished what they were doing then she got up and pissed off.'

The doctor was struggling. 'So this friend of yours—'

'He's no friend of mine.'

'—this chap then... your wife's ex-husband... where is he now?'

Scott paused again, forced to question his own sanity once more. 'He's dead.'

The doctor seemed less surprised than he should have been. 'Go on.'

'It was frigging horrible. Made no sense. It was like the woman had mutilated him when they were... you know... The end of his dick was all mangled... blood everywhere.'

'Is the body still there?'

214

Scott shook his head and gestured at the soldiers. 'This lot took him away. Maybe that's what this is all about. Like I said, the kids don't know. I'll tell them when the time's right, but it'd be too much for them to take right now.'

Dr Kerr nodded. Scott watched him and wondered what he was thinking. *He probably thinks you're a crank. He thinks you're as mental as you sound.*

'All these deaths...' he said to Scott, his voice only just audible. 'All along we were looking for someone to pin the blame on.'

'I know. I was that someone for a while.'

'I'd heard. But what you've just told me has confirmed what I'd been thinking for a while, something I couldn't get the police to accept.'

'And that is?'

'That perhaps they should have been looking for some*thing*, not someone.'

'I don't get you.'

'I think we're dealing with some kind of parasite or disease.'

'That's transmitted sexually?'

'Exactly. Sergeant Ross called me out last night when they found the last body.'

'Which body?'

'Young girl, Heather Burns. I only saw her in the surgery last week.'

'What happened to her?'

'Much the same as all the others, I expect, but I don't know for sure. Sergeant Ross called me back before I'd even left the house. He told me not to bother, told me there were already people at the scene. They'd taken the investigation off him. He was fuming.'

'Who?'

'The same people who've just rounded us up, I presume.'

'So where was the body?'

'She was found in the bar of the pub.'

'Jesus. That's where Jeremy was staying last night.'

'Jeremy? Is that—?'

'Michelle's ex-husband.'

'Then it sounds like your wife had a lucky escape this morning.'

215

'This is too much. I mean, I knew this place was fucked-up, but honestly...'

The doctor remained stony-faced. 'Doesn't matter how it sounds, fact is, it's happening. Trace it back... did you hear about the police officer? Mary McLeod from the café? Poor old Graham, and that Polish lady.'

'I heard.'

'All the time they were looking for the person or persons who was doing this, but there might never have been anyone. I know how this must sound, but I think the killer – the germ or parasite or whatever – remains invisible until it's too late.'

Scott felt strangely reassured. As far-fetched as it was, he'd thought similar. 'So where do you think they're taking us?' he asked.

'No idea. Somewhere isolated, perhaps? I think they'll want us out of the way until they can round it up, stop it being passed onto anyone else.'

'Until they round *her* up,' Scott said, correcting him. 'The woman who had sex with Jeremy, she must be the one who's carrying it now.'

'Unless they find her corpse.' The doctor took off his glasses and rubbed his eyes, then leant closer to Scott again. 'You do realise the implications of this, don't you Mr Griffiths? If no one sees it being transmitted, the damn thing could be inside anyone.'

25

The van stopped again, and all those inside knew that this was the end of the line.

School.

Tammy thought she was going mad when she realised where they were. She pressed her face against the window and watched as armed guards opened the school gates and allowed the van through. It was a bizarre collision of the normal and the surreal: the banality of the out-dated school campus, now alive with military activity, their equipment everywhere. Right in the middle of the netball courts, near to the temporary classrooms, was a helicopter, and it didn't take a genius to identify stockpiles of guns and missiles. What the hell was going on?

They'd reached some kind of checkpoint, manned by more soldiers, this time armed with clipboards, pens and tablets rather than guns. Scott craned his neck to see what was happening. At the front of the van paperwork was exchanged, lists of names compared... were the people of Thussock being processed? 'Looks like I was right,' Dr Kerr said. 'They're rounding everyone up.'

'I guess.'

'My money's on that fracking site. Must be something to do with that. Problem is they never fully investigate these things before someone gives their high-powered friend a grant and tells them to get on with it, do they? It's always profit before people, you know?'

'I don't reckon this has got anything to do with digging holes in the ground.'

'You never know though, do you? I was dead against it from the start. I got on all the committees and went to all the public meetings, but did it make any difference?'

'I doubt it,' Scott said, wishing he'd shut up.

'Damn right it didn't. All the objections were just dismissed. It was an absolute bloody whitewash. You'd think they'd be legally bound to act on objections, wouldn't you, but you'd be surprised.'

'Nothing surprises me anymore.'

The doctor was about to say something else when the van juddered forward again, processing complete. It followed the narrow road towards the main school buildings, then curved sharply to the left.

A few rows behind, Phoebe watched with wide eyes as they drove deeper into the campus. She'd almost been on the verge of getting used to this place, but every last shred of familiarity had been stripped away today. There was the assembly hall which doubled-up as a gym, and the Portakabin classrooms, freezing cold even on warm days, the uncomfortable temperature keeping her awake during Maths. There was the dilapidated technology block and the music rooms, and the playing field and—

—and this looked less like a school now, more like something out of a science-fiction film. The relatively new leisure centre towards the back of the site had always seemed out of place, but now it looked positively alien. It was surrounded by armed guards, and much of the car park space had been filled with camouflaged temporary buildings. As she watched, another van similar to this one drove away from the leisure centre. Parts of the angular building were covered in heavy-duty plastic sheeting, like someone was trying to shrink-wrap the place.

The van stopped again. The driver turned in a tight circle, then reversed back into the space the other vehicle had just vacated. There was a delay, probably less than a minute but which felt inordinately long, before the back doors were opened and the van's passengers were asked to move out, politely but very firmly, by more faceless military personnel.

The doctor returned to his wife. Michelle and the girls waited for Scott. He walked with them in silence.

The gap between the back of the van and the leisure centre door was several metres wide. Big enough, Scott thought, to be able to make a run for it if he wanted to. But even though the barrels of their rifles were pointing at the ground, there were enough armed guards around to deter anyone thinking about trying to make a break for freedom.

Dr Kerr was just ahead of them. 'Is anyone going to tell us what's going on?' he demanded of one of the soldiers. Scott couldn't hear what the reply was, but it was clearly insufficient as far as the doctor was concerned. He continued to rant, oblivious to the proximity of their weapons, sounding increasingly angry, winding himself up but, it appeared, no one else. None of his questions or demands seemed to warrant even the most cursory of responses.

When they reached the inside of the leisure centre, Tammy stopped walking, dumbfounded. It looked as if the entire population of Thussock was already here, that they were late to the party. She remembered how this room had felt like a vast, cavernous space when she'd first come in here, bigger than the rest of the school combined. Right now, though, it felt uncomfortably cramped. It looked like something out of a film, one of those old disaster movies, she thought, or maybe something she'd expect to see on the TV news after an earthquake or tsunami. The floor was covered with row upon row of people lying on metal-framed camp beds or sitting on thin foam mattresses and bedding rolls. Thussock had seemed like such an insignificant place in comparison to Redditch, but the sheer volume of people gathered here in close proximity made it feel horrendously overcrowded. She was feeling claustrophobic, and the fractious atmosphere wasn't helping. People were uncertain... afraid. Considering how many people were trapped in here, it remained unexpectedly quiet. There was a constant low hubbub of subdued conversation, but little other noise.

'Chelle!' someone shouted. Michelle looked up and saw that Jackie, Dez and the twins were camped on the far side of the huge room, leaning up against the back wall. There was a space next to them. Without waiting for anyone else, Michelle marched over to her friend. The girls sat down in silence, still in a state of shock, but Scott remained where he was, reluctant to follow. His heart sank when Dez got up and walked over to him. There was no escape, no way of shaking him. Between Dez and Dr Kerr (who'd also followed them across the gym and who was setting up camp with his wife just a couple of metres away), he imagined he'd be struggling to breathe if they were stuck in here for any length of time.

'How long have you been here?' Scott asked Dez.

'Couple of hours.'

'And have they told you anything?'

'Nothin'. You got your pack yet?' Dez pointed to a half-demolished mountain of cardboard boxes in the diagonally opposite corner of the hangar-like room. More were being taken away as Scott watched. 'You get a couple of pillows and sheets, some water, a bit of food, and this,' Dez explained, pulling a laminated card from his pocket and handing it over. Dr Kerr intercepted it. He adjusted his glasses to read it, flipping it over first, holding it up to show Scott the biohazard symbol printed on the reverse.

'Residents of Thussock... We apologise for any inconvenience. A biological concern has been identified in the immediate area.' He stopped and looked from Scott to Dez and back again. 'A biological *concern*? Who wrote this garbage?'

'What else does it say?' Scott asked.

'Blah, blah, blah... not a lot really. It's all just bullshit and flannel. All very vague... all residents are required – *by law* – to remain on these premises until such time as the hazard has been successfully contained and neutralized.'

'And that's it?'

'Pretty much.'

'Well, there's not a lot we can do for now,' the doctor said, and he handed the card back to Dez, then ambled back over to sit with his wife.

Scott realised Michelle had gone. He looked around and found her on the other side of the leisure centre with Jackie and Tammy, collecting boxes. He watched her every move.

Bottles of water, pillows and a few chocolate bars kept the girls and George occupied temporarily. Michelle walked over to Scott. 'Mind if I sit here?'

'If you want,' he grunted.

'What's happening, Scott? You've been talking to the doctor... what does he say?'

'He knows as much as I do. Nothing. You see the card?'

'This thing?' she said, picking one out from her cardboard box and studying it. 'Doesn't say much, does it?'

'Not really.'

'Look, Scott, I just—'

'Do me a favour, Michelle, just don't even talk to me. In fact, just stay away.'

26

The last time Scott had seen Barry Walpole, the two of them had almost come to blows over the death of Ken Potter. Barry had been full of anger then, ready to defend his late friend's dubious honour. He'd been a formidable creature that day, all piercing eyes, bulging veins and flared nostrils. Not now, though. Today Barry was a shadow of his former self. He was quiet and subdued, timid almost. Scott didn't even notice him there until he almost tripped over him on the way back from the bizarrely heavily guarded toilets. 'Strange how they've got armed guards round the toilets, isn't it?' Barry said. His voice was drained of all its former energy. He was sitting cross-legged on a mat, holding a frail-looking old woman's hand, his other arm around her shoulder, his size dwarfing hers. He carefully let her go and stood up. 'You all right, Scott?'

'I'm okay,' Scott replied, perfunctory. 'You?'

'I'm all right. Mother's struggling, though, aren't you, Mum?' The old lady barely looked up. 'You been here long?'

'Few hours. You?'

'Since first thing. I was only just out of bed when they started hammering on the door. Requisitioned a load of stuff from the yard, they have. Buggers. You got any idea what's happening?'

'Not a clue,' Scott answered quickly. Having seen what happened to Jeremy he felt sure he probably knew more than most but he couldn't bring himself to explain. Besides, he thought, what good would it have done other than to push everyone closer to the edge than they already were?

'What about Doc Kerr? I saw you with him. Does he know anything?'

'If he does he isn't saying. It's all just speculation right now. Look, Barry, I have to go. I need to get back.'

'Course you do. Got to look after the people nearest to us, eh Scott?' he said, crouching again and giving his mother's hand another tender squeeze.

'Absolutely.'

'Sorry,' Barry said unexpectedly.

'Sorry for what?'

'For being so hard on you after Ken...'

'No problem. You weren't to know. None of us were.'

'Right. Okay. Hopefully see you back at the yard in a couple of days when all this has blown over?'

'Yep. Almost looking forward to it, Barry.'

'That's the spirit. Look after yourself, lad.'

'I always do. You too.'

Scott continued back across the hall, watching his family as he weaved between the rest of Thussock's refugee-like population. People had continued to be herded into the leisure centre continually through the day, but their numbers had reduced to a mere trickle now. Space was at a premium, the narrow gaps between each family's individually claimed area of floor steadily reducing. In places it was difficult to get through.

Scott didn't feel scared, he decided, just uneasy. He didn't like not knowing, not being in control. He sat down next to Michelle, not knowing what else to do. As much as they'd pissed him off today, his family was all he had left.

'The atmosphere's changed in here,' she said. 'Can you feel it? It's like there's a storm brewing. It's making my head hurt.'

'What do you expect?' he said, still not able to find it in himself to be civil. 'They've dragged everyone out of their homes at gunpoint and locked them in a school gym. Hardly going to be a fucking party, is it?'

She chose her next words carefully. The last thing anyone needed was Scott kicking off and causing another scene. *Keep him sweet. Keep everything together. Keep it all ticking over like I always do.*

'What do you think's going to happen?'

'How am I supposed to know?'

'What are they trying to protect us from?

'You've read the card, same as I have. Biological hazard.'

'I know that, but Dez said he was talking to the doctor... he was saying something about this being something to do with all those deaths... about them being linked.'

'Yeah, that's what he reckons.'

'So are we going to be okay, Scott?'

222

'Well there are plenty of soldiers around. Don't know what good all those guns'll be against a bloody biological hazard though.'

'And are *we* going to be okay?'

'You tell me.'

She was about to speak again when Phoebe interrupted her. 'I still can't see him, Mum.'

'Can't see who?'

'Dad. If they're bringing everyone here, then he should be here too, shouldn't he?'

Michelle stood up to comfort her daughter and help her look. Scott lay back and stared up at the high roof of this expansive gym, counting metal struts and ceiling tiles, doing everything he could not to get drawn into their impossible conversation. He wished he hadn't found Jeremy. It would have been easier not to know. He'd have to tell them at some point, and then they'd—

—a sudden commotion erupted on the far side of the leisure centre, near to the rapidly depleting stack of supplies. Scott got up fast, scrambling to his feet. He couldn't see much through the sudden chaos. Many other people were up now, though most remained defiantly rooted to their own pockets of space.

It was different on the other side of the gym. There people were trying to get out of the way, both from whatever it was that was happening and also from a mass of soldiers who were wading through the crowds. Their weapons, this time, were held ready to fire.

A bubble of space had opened up around a woman lying on the floor. Her body was convulsing, limbs flailing, kicking and lashing out. All around her people were trying to get away, grabbing at their bedding and supplies, desperate to move but finding their progress impeded by other people all doing the same. Two soldiers without weapons, wearing slightly different suits – medics or scientists, perhaps, Scott thought – approached the woman writhing on the floor.

'I'm not getting involved,' Dr Kerr said, appearing by Scott's side. 'It's Edie Fitzpatrick. She's epileptic. That's all this is. They'll realise soon enough.' Scott just looked at him and the doctor anticipated his unspoken questions. 'I know, I know... Hippocratic Oath and all that... Thing is, they'll help her and I know she'll be all right. They know who we are and I'm sure they've access to as much medical information as I had, more probably. Until someone tells me exactly what's going on here, I'm not helping anyone.'

'Don't blame you, Peter,' another voice said. Scott thought he recognised the man, though he wasn't immediately sure where from. Then it dawned on him. It was Sergeant Ross, out of uniform. Strange how much attention he'd previously paid to the uniform, not the man, Scott thought. 'Mr Griffiths,' the police officer said, acknowledging him.

'Sergeant.'

'Care to tell us what's going on here, Dan?' the doctor asked.

'I was going to ask you the same question.'

'Hold on,' Scott said. 'How can you not know? You're the bloody police, for Christ's sake.'

'This hasn't been a typical investigation...' the sergeant began to explain.

'You can say that again. Fucking amateurs. You arrest me, spend a day trying to get me to confess to crimes I know fuck all about, then just turn me out again without a frigging word.'

'What was I supposed to do? Like I said, Mr Griffiths, this hasn't been a typical investigation. We thought we were looking for a serial killer, and you have to admit, you gave us more than enough cause for concern...'

'You treated me like a bloody animal. You'd decided I was guilty before you'd even—'

'That's enough,' the doctor said, scalding both of them. 'Don't you think we've enough to worry about without fighting amongst ourselves? How much do you know, Dan?'

The sergeant rubbed his eyes. He looked around then answered Dr Kerr in hushed tones. 'Not as much as I should do. You know what it's like yourself, Peter, we're at the arse-end of nowhere out here. It still takes forever to get the information you need. It shouldn't, but that's how it is.'

'What kind of information?' Scott asked.

'Test results. Forensics.'

'It would have helped if you'd listened to me,' Dr Kerr said, clearly disgruntled.

'I know, and I'm sorry.'

'I said we were missing something crucial. All along I was trying to say that...'

'I know you tried, and I've apologised. With the benefit of hindsight we—'

'But you just dismissed everything I told you. Bloody hell, Daniel, the gender of the victims should have made it clear.'

'Gender?' Scott interrupted. 'What's that got to do with it?'

'Male, female, male, female... it's what we were saying earlier. This thing is a parasite, transmitted sexually.'

'We were almost there,' the policeman said. 'We'd found foreign DNA traces on all the bodies, but we didn't spot the pattern.'

'What pattern?' Scott asked.

'On most of the bodies we found traces of the DNA of someone else, but we didn't know who because none of them were on the database. It took us a while to work it out... longer than it should have. The DNA belonged to the next person to die, you follow? But there were never any signs of a struggle, that's what threw us. Just blood and genital mutilation.'

Dr Kerr took off his glasses, breathed on the lenses, then cleaned them on his jumper. 'Scott here saw an attack today. Tell him, Scott.'

'I wouldn't call it an attack,' he said, picturing Jeremy and the woman. 'It looked like...'

'Like what?'

'Like consensual sex, just out in the open. Two people having sex, oblivious to everyone and everything else. It was after they separated, though... it was like he'd been torn apart. Just like all the others.'

'Who?'

'My wife's ex. Jeremy Williams.'

'He was staying at the pub last night, and I'll put money on him having been with young Heather Burns,' Dr Kerr whispered. 'It's like I said, some kind of parasite. Will you listen to me now?'

'Explain,' Sergeant Ross said.

'The parasite needs a body to survive. When it's taken what it needs, it has to find another host. What Scott saw this morning, what you've seen the aftermath of, was that transmission.'

'So what you're saying,' Scott interrupted, 'is that this thing needs blood or whatever, and when it's taken what it needs from one body,

225

it's passed on to the next through sex?'

'That's exactly what I'm saying.'

'You make it sound like a vampire,' he laughed, unable to quite believe what he was hearing. The doctor looked serious.

'Vampyrrhic. That's actually a pretty good way of describing it.'

'I'll go get a fucking crucifix,' Scott said, and he almost walked away from the ridiculous conversation.

'I'm glad you said that, Doc,' Sergeant Ross admitted. 'I'd been thinking along the same lines myself. I thought it was just me going mad. Do me a favour, you two, keep a lid on this. People are already scared. If word gets out, this place'll be out of control.'

'So what are you going to do about it?' Scott asked.

'Me? What can I do? Have you not noticed, we're all in the same boat here. I'm not in charge anymore. The investigation was taken out of my hands, shall we say. I'd tell you who by, but I honestly don't know. Like you lot, first I knew about all this was a knock on my door from a soldier who's face I couldn't see. All I could see was his bloody rifle and I wasn't taking any chances.'

Mr Renner, the school pastoral teacher, spotted Tammy and Phoebe in the crowd and came over to speak to them both. He told them about Heather, though Tammy had already suspected something had happened. She'd seen Chez sitting alone with his head in his hands and had feared the worst. Mr Renner told her where she'd find Jamie and she went to look for him. He was sitting on a bench at the side of the gym with Joel. Tammy positioned herself between the two of them, hoping they'd distract her with pointless rubbish and immaturity, but fearing they were already past that.

'Got anything to drink?' she asked hopefully. Joel shook his head, Jamie didn't even look up.

'I can't take no more of this,' Joel said, getting up. 'You deal with him.' And with that he was up and gone, relieved to be away. Tammy cautiously put her hand on Jamie's leg.

'I'm sorry, Jamie. I'm really, really sorry...'

He lifted his head and looked at her, wiping his eyes. 'We thought she was with Chez. Dad was doin' his bloody fruit tryin' to find her. We called Chez and he said he thought she was with us.'

'What happened?'

'She was all fucked up, Tam. Like the others...'

'Where?'

'The pub.'

'My dad stayed there last night...' She stopped herself. She didn't want to think about what might or might not have happened in the Black Boy. Did it have anything to do with what happened to Dad this morning? Did he have anything to do with what happened to Heather? He couldn't have, could he?

Jamie wasn't listening. He couldn't take anymore of this in. He reached out for Tammy and held her, pulled her close. And she responded. All she'd had from pretty much everyone since first arriving in Thussock was constant grief, and this sudden unexpected physical contact seemed somehow to make it all a little easier to cope with. She held him tight, then tighter still, both of them sobbing as they leant against each other, his face buried in her chest. Huge amounts of previously suppressed emotions were released, let out at long last after having being locked away for too long.

Tammy kissed the side of Jamie's face. He looked up at her. Oh, those eyes... those deep brown, hurting eyes... she'd thought him good looking the first time she saw him outside the Co-op, a class apart from the other boys, but she'd not wanted to get too close because he was from Thussock and she didn't want to be here and because it felt like there was a world of difference between them and... and none of that mattered now. She'd just been looking for excuses before, avoiding reasons to form connections with this hellish place. Jamie looked so pale and drawn, racked with pain, and yet he was still attractive. She felt his hands on her and it made her feel alive. She really needed to be held like this... to be wanted. They parted for a moment, then kissed – soft, light and unsure, then stronger. Eyes closed now. Tongues touching, lips locked. She reciprocated his every move, finding such unexpected comfort in his touch and—

—and they separated when someone screamed. Tammy pulled back and felt her bladder weaken. The space around the bench where they'd been sitting had emptied, people scrambling away from them in absolute terror as soldiers rushed towards them. Hundreds of them it looked like, sprinting through the crowds with their rifles raised, all of their weapons pointing at her and Jamie. Jamie slipped off the bench in panic, landing on his back with a sickening thump and winding himself. Stunned, he lay there helpless as they surrounded him.

Tammy couldn't see what they were doing to him. There were hazmat suits all around her now too. She tried to look for Jamie, but all she could see now was her own terrified face reflected back in the visors of the soldiers encircling her. 'Name?' one of them demanded.

'Huh?'

'Tell me your bloody name?'

'Tammy Williams,' she answered, voice shaking.

'Did you have intercourse with this man?'

'What?'

'Have you had sexual intercourse with this man?' he shouted, pointing at Jamie, still on the floor, still surrounded.

'No.'

The soldier took a step back. Tammy remained exactly where she was, feeling as if her legs would buckle with nerves at any second. The rest of the leisure centre was silent. It was as if everything and everyone else had frozen. Everything except Scott. He shoved his way through the stationary crowds to reach Tammy, only to find his way forward blocked by more armed guards. The harder he fought to get through, the tighter they closed ranks. He pulled back a fist, ready to punch, but a soldier dismissively shunted him away then raised his rifle.

Scott froze.

The stand-off was unbearable, the pressure increasing by the second.

'No reaction, Sir,' a mask-muffled trooper shouted.

'Clear,' another soldier confirmed, and all of the faceless, suited figures stood down. Scott pushed his way through them to get to Tammy who'd dropped to her knees now, sobbing. He picked her up and no matter how much she hated him and how sick he was of her, they walked back to Michelle together.

27

The waiting was endless, unbearable. It was late now, dark out-side. Their interminable incarceration had lasted most of the day and showed no signs of ending anytime soon. Frustrations were beginning to show. There were occasional glimpses of trouble, only for those involved to immediately separate when military interest was aroused. Much of the bad feeling seemed to be down to the dwin-dling level of supplies. What had appeared to be a virtual mountain of cardboard when Scott and Michelle had first arrived had been re-duced to a few remaining boxes. There was a sudden change in mood when a door opened and the stocks were replenished. The smell of hot food temporarily soothed the tensions within the leisure centre.

There was an initial crush but the ever-present threat of military intervention kept things moving with civility. Scott fetched enough for him and his family. He found himself sitting close to Dez, Ser-geant Ross and Dr Kerr as they ate.

'Can't say they ain't lookin' after us,' Dez said.

'They can stick their fucking food,' Scott said, poking with a plas-tic spoon at his dish filled with some kind of meat stew. His stomach was churning. 'I'd rather be hungry and out of here.'

'I don't think you would,' Dr Kerr said. 'They're keeping us safe until they've got this thing under control.'

'Like hell.'

'Much as I hate to admit it,' Sergeant Ross said, 'I think you're right, Doc.'

'I know I'm right.'

'I'm not so sure,' Scott said.

'Why not?' Sergeant Ross asked.

'Think about it... why are they really keeping us here? Why would they want the whole of Thussock locked up in one room?'

'To keep us safe,' Dez quickly volunteered. Scott looked at him in disbelief.

'You're so bloody naïve. It's never about us, it's always about *them*. If the doctor's right and there is some kind of fucking weird, previ-ously unheard of, sex-starved parasite-thing running loose around here, where do you think it is? Do you think there are even more soldiers outside trying to hunt it down?'

'There are. I seen them in the fields.'

'Yes, but the bloody fields are empty. If this is a parasite, then it's almost certainly going to be in here, isn't it? It's where the people are, not where they *aren't*. Those soldiers out there weren't looking for the parasite, they were looking for *us*, the people of Thussock. They want us where they can keep tabs on us.'

'He's got a point,' Dr Kerr agreed.

'Wait... didn't someone say you seen an attack this mornin'?' Dez said to Scott. 'Can't you find who it was? Point her out or sumthin'?'

'I've looked and I haven't seen her. Anyway, who says she's still the carrier? She might have had her wicked way with someone else. It could be any one of us by now. Could be you, Dez.'

His words had a noticeable effect on the others. They all stopped to consider the implications of what he'd just said.

'So it has to be about finding the carrier and isolating them now, doesn't it?' Sergeant Ross said. 'That's what all this is about. They're waiting for them to show themselves.'

'So can't we jus' find them?' Dez suggested. 'Dob them in?'

'And how are you going to do that?' Scott sighed. 'Fuck's sake, if it was that easy, don't you think they'd have already done it? They don't know, that's why we're all left hanging.'

'This is all well and good,' the doctor said, 'but what if it's some-one we know? What if it is one of us or worse still, one of our fam-ilies? You were the one who had a close encounter this morning, Scott. How do you know your wife wasn't infected?'

'Because I dragged the dirty fucker off her and kicked the shit out of him before he could get near her. And I saw him infect someone else, that's how.'

'And are you sure you weren't infected?'

'I'm sure I didn't get fucked, if that's what you mean.'

'But we don't know for sure that this thing is only transmitted sexually, do we?'

'No, but the only contact I had with Jeremy was to drag him away from the house and punch him in the face. I didn't share a drink with him, didn't kiss him...'

'And was this morning the first time you'd seen him?'

Scott paused. 'No. He came around last night. He had dinner with us. I swear, everything was normal back then. He'd only changed this morning. His behaviour was completely different...'

'I don't think you're infected, Scott,' Dr Kerr said, sensing the other man's patience was wearing thin. 'For the record, I don't think your wife is either. But you can see the point I'm making here, can't you? We just don't know. We don't even know if there's just one of these things or whether there are more...'

'Jesus,' Scott said under his breath. He hadn't thought of that.

'Think about it... there are hundreds of people in here, how do we know how it'll react to these numbers? Maybe it behaves differently in crowds... maybe it divides or reproduces...'

'I'm getting out of here,' Dez said, suddenly agitated.

'How?' Sergeant Ross sighed. 'Don't be an idiot, Dez.'

'I'm not an idiot. I jus' think...'

'But you don't think, do you? Never have.'

'There's no need for—'

'There's no need for what? Fuck's sake, do you understand what's happening here? They're playing it all light and friendly, giving us food and water and trying to make it like everything's going to be all right, but our lives might be on the line here. Scott and the doctor might be right. Your life, Jackie's life, your kids' lives... Do you think they're going to let any of us go until this thing gets found and neutralized?'

'Who says they're gonna let us go anyway?' Scott said, fuelling the flames.

Dez was beginning to panic. 'I'm not stayin' here. You can all piss off. There's no way I...' His voice trailed away. They were all looking at him. *Staring* at him. 'What?'

'Calm down, Dez,' Sergeant Ross said, wishing he was in uniform. 'You're making me nervous.'

'Calm down! You're tellin' me to calm down at a time like this...'

All still looking at him. All uneasy. All starting to think the same thing. Scott vocalised their concerns. 'Is it him?'

'It ain't me,' Dez said quickly, almost laughing at the preposterousness of it all, then almost pissing himself with fear when it dawned on him they were deadly serious. How could they think it was him? 'Come on, Doc... Sarge... you both know me. You know it ain't me...' The longer they watched him, the more he began questioning himself. He tried to remember where he'd been recently, who he'd been with, how they'd behaved... then common-sense kicked back in. 'You've both known me for years,' he said with a little more certainty in his voice. 'If there's anyone you wanna worry about, it's him.' He turned and looked directly at Scott.

All eyes shifting. Slow, subtle, shuffled movements away from the others. The doctor shook his head, exasperated.

'Bullshit,' Scott protested. 'I already told you—'

'That you had a physical encounter this morning with a man who was infected and who's now dead,' Sergeant Ross said. 'Dez is right, we hardly know you.'

'An' you arrested him,' Dez continued, grabbing the sergeant's arm. 'You wouldn't a done that if you never had good reason. He was there when them others died. Jackie told me. It's him... he's the one.'

More definite movement now. Whether their actions were subconscious or not, they were all trying to put distance between themselves and Scott. Or was it distance between themselves and each other?

'You've got this all wrong,' Scott started to say before Dez cut across him.

'That's what a carrier would say. Ain't that what a carrier would say? It wouldn't wanna get caught out. It wants to hide and keep killing.'

Scott shook his head. 'Are you completely fucking stupid? We're talking about a parasite, not a murderer. It's not killing or even thinking about killing, it's *feeding*.'

'Same difference.'

'No, it isn't. If I'd had contact and I'd been carrying it, wouldn't I be dead now? I'd either be dead or trying to fuck someone. I wouldn't be sitting here talking like this with you, you bloody moron.'

A moment of silence. 'He's right,' the doctor said. 'We need to take a step back and calm down, not let our emotions get the better of us.'

'It's like *The Thing*, ain't it?' said Dez, relaxing slightly. 'Remember that?'

Scott, Sergeant Ross and Dr Kerr just looked at him. 'Bloody idiot,' the sergeant said. 'Don't you know when to give up?'

'I'm serious. Did you see that film, *The Thing*?'

'Long time ago. Why?'

'Because this is like that, isn't it? All those people trapped together. One of them's an alien, but they don't know which one. They might not even know it themselves. You see it, Doc?'

'No. Doesn't sound like my kind of film.'

'There's this bit when they're trying to work out which one of them it is,' he continued, oblivious to how infuriating he'd become. 'They figure out a test, an' they all sit round in a circle while everyone has it done.'

'I remember,' Scott said. 'Can't remember what happens though.'

'What do you think happens? The bloody monster doesn't wanna be found out. It goes apeshit.'

'How exactly is this helping, Desmond?' Dr Kerr asked.

Dez paused. His face dropped. 'Sorry. Bit nervous. All I was thinkin' was why ain't they doin' sumthin' like that?'

'It's a fair point. Maybe they will. Maybe they just haven't worked out the test yet?'

'Should be pretty easy though, shouldn't it?' Sergeant Ross said. 'All they have to do is look at the last body. The carrier's DNA will be on them somewhere. Or in them.'

'Sounds too easy,' Scott said. 'So why aren't they doing it? Because you're right, if they can work out who the carrier is, they should be able to check us all then isolate that person.'

'Maybe it's not that straightforward,' the doctor said, struggling to keep up with the increasingly surreal situation. 'There could be any number of reasons why. Maybe they're waiting for an exchange. Maybe they can only stop it when the parasite's in the process of passing from host to host?'

'You think that might be the case?'

'It would explain why they over-reacted when your daughter was with that lad,' he said, looking at Scott. 'If I'm completely honest, I don't know what to think anymore.'

'It's all down to perspective, isn't it?' Sergeant Ross said. 'We look at things from our point of view, don't we?'

'I don't follow,' Dez said. 'Don't talk in riddles.'

The sergeant's shoulders slumped forward, like he was carrying an immense weight. 'Something Mr Griffiths here said a few minutes ago that we all just glossed over. Who says they're planning to let us go? We've assumed they'd shut us all away in here to keep the parasite out, but maybe the opposite's true? What if they've got us rounded up because they're trying to keep it *in*? Who says our safety matters to them? We might just be bait. Expendable.'

'You think it's like a worm or sumthin'?' Dez asked. 'You think you can see it? You ever seen *Rabid*? Wait, no, not *Rabid*... *Shivers*. It's about this sex slug. Goes crazy in a block of flats in Canada in the seventies an'...'

They were all looking at him again. 'Shut up,' Scott said, and this time he did. There followed an awkward moment of quiet, only disturbed by the low hubbub of conversation elsewhere.

'It would make a good weapon, wouldn't it?' Sergeant Ross said.

'Come on, Dan,' Dr Kerr sighed. 'Are you serious? Now who's scaremongering?'

'I'm serious. Think about it. All those invasions they've spent billions of pounds of our money on over the years... this thing would make wars like that a hell of a lot easier and cheaper. Just drop the parasite in and let it do what it apparently does. If the area can be contained, it'll just keep killing and being passed on from person to person until there's only the final carrier left.'

'Stupid idea,' the doctor scoffed.

Scott didn't agree. 'No more stupid than anything else I've heard. I think you might be onto something. That'd explain why we've got the army here and not the NHS or Environmental Health.'

'So what are we going to do?' Dr Kerr asked. 'Do we just sit here and wait for this thing to show itself. If it's in here with us, surely it's only a matter of time before it needs a new host? There's never been any longer than a couple of days before kills... maybe that's how long each new body can sustain it for.'

Sergeant Ross looked around the crowded leisure centre. Some people appeared to be getting used to their incarceration, accepting everything they were being told with blissful ignorance. They were reasonably comfortable, well fed and watered... Others clearly remained unconvinced, defending the independence of their own little areas of space, perhaps only deciding not to fight or protest for fear of the heavy-handed military response they'd already seen demonstrated.

'Way I see it is this,' he said. 'We don't have much in the way of options right now. This place is probably surrounded. We certainly are, anyway. Stay alert and keep your wits about you. Stay close to your families and make sure they don't mix with anyone you don't know. Hold onto your own, lads. Don't let anyone else get too close. Bottom line is this – if this parasite or whatever is being passed from person to person, and all the people of Thussock are in here with us, then it's only gonna be a matter of time before it shows itself.'

28

Phoebe was standing up, looking out over the heads of the unsettled crowd, still desperately searching for her father. He had to be here somewhere, didn't he? Michelle pulled her down but she shook her mother off. 'I'm going to go and find him,' Phoebe said.

'You can't, love. You have to stay here with us. It's not safe.'

'But what about Dad? He's on his own.'

'After what happened at the house he could be anywhere. If he was here he'd have found us, wouldn't he? He's probably left town. He'll be in touch soon, I'm sure he will.'

'He wouldn't have left, not with all this going on.'

'Listen to your mother and shut up,' Scott said, his voice detached and unemotional. Michelle pulled Phoebe closer and held her as she cried. She watched Scott, and she wished she could tell him exactly what she was thinking like she'd tried this morning. She wished she could be honest with him and tell him to fuck off and leave them alone, to take a frigging hike and never come back again... but she knew she couldn't. Not yet. She knew him better than he ever gave her credit for. She knew he had a better understanding of what was happening in Thussock than he was letting on. She and Jackie had watched him and Dez and the others talking, watched how they grouped together in a secretive huddle and spoke in whispers the way men do. *They know,* she thought.

'Why can't I go?' Phoebe asked again, not giving up.

'Because it's too dangerous.'

'How is it dangerous? We're locked in here, aren't we? I'm only going to be walking around this one room. You'll be able to see me. It's not like anything's going to happen with all those soldiers around.'

'No.'

'I'll go with her,' Tammy said.

'I said no.'

'This is bullshit,' she said.

'Watch your language.'

'You just don't want us to see Dad because of what happened this morning. You're embarrassed, aren't you? Ashamed...'

'That's not true.'

George was sleeping with his head on Tammy's lap. She gently moved him and got up. 'I'm not waiting around here. I'm going to find him. And if I can't find him, I'm going to...'

Scott was on his feet in seconds. He held her arms and pushed her back against the wall, suddenly aware of sounds of movement and concern all around as people scurried away.

'Scott...' Michelle hissed at him. 'Soldiers.'

He looked over his shoulder and saw that his actions had aroused plenty of interest. A couple of soldiers were approaching, swinging their weapons off their shoulders in readiness as they moved towards him. He pulled Tammy back down and she yelped with pain.

'You're not going anywhere,' he told her, 'not yet. It's too danger-ous. You have to trust me.'

'Trust you?'

Michelle positioned herself between her husband and her daugh-ter and looked straight at Scott. 'I've had enough of this.'

'We've all had enough of this...'

'You know exactly what I mean, Scott. All this bullshit. All this pretence. You know what's happening here, don't you?'

'We're in danger, that's all you need to know.'

'So how come you're the one who gets to decide how much the rest of us need to know?'

'Because I'm the one who has all the responsibility, that's why. Because I'm the one who keeps this family together.'

'You control us, Scott. You stop us breathing and try to stop us thinking for ourselves. You don't keep this family together, you just won't let any of us go. That's what all this is about, isn't it? It's all a bloody power trip for you.'

'For fuck's sake, now's really not the time for one of your domes-tics.'

'One of *my* domestics? Jesus.'

'Listen, this is serious. That warning about a biological hazard... it's true, but it's a hell of a lot worse than they're letting on. If you have to know, and I'm guessing you won't shut up until you do, there's some kind of parasite on the loose.'

Michelle laughed involuntarily. 'That's the best you can come up with?'

'It's the truth. It's passed from person to person. It's passed through sex.'

She laughed again. 'Bullshit.'

'Think what you like. Why else do you think Jeremy was all over you this morning? Don't flatter yourself, sweetheart, it's because he was infected, not because he fancied you.'

'You're a heartless bastard.'

'Maybe,' he said, shrugging his shoulders nonchalantly. 'Thing is, getting through this is going to need someone with a little backbone. As soon as I can I'm going to get us out of here and away from everyone else.'

'What about Jackie and Dez and those others you were talking to?'

'What about them? Fuck 'em.'

'Hang on... if what you're saying's true, surely the army are trying to protect us from this thing? So shouldn't we just stay in here? Wouldn't they be trying to isolate or quarantine it?'

'Clever girl. Yes, they are. But I'm not having them quarantine *us* along with it.'

'But wait, Scott... shouldn't we stay here? They'll find out who's got it sooner or later and deal with them.'

'We're not taking that risk.'

'But if we try to get away, will they not think we might be infected?'

He shrugged his shoulders. 'Maybe. We're not waiting here all night to get caught like sitting ducks, though.'

'There you go again, making decisions for the rest of us...'

'Like I said, somebody has to do it.'

'What happened to *us*?' Michelle said, tears stinging her eyes, keeping her voice low so as not to involve or upset the girls more than they already were. 'We used to be a couple... a partnership.'

'You're the one who tried to fuck your ex this morning,' he said coldly.

'But that was to do with this, wasn't it?' she said. 'Christ, what happened to Jeremy? How did he—?'

'Don't know, don't care.'

239

Michelle watched Scott closely... studied the way he did what he could to avoid looking at her. 'You're lying.'

'Listen,' he said, voice ominously low, 'I've had enough of you. Just keep your bloody mouth shut and do what you're told.'

'Not anymore, Scott,' she said, her throat dry, body shaking with anger.

'What did you just say?'

'I said not anymore. I can't take this. You do what you want to do like you always do. The kids and I are staying here.'

'You don't have any choice.'

'There's always a choice. I could—'

A scream rang out from the far end of the cavernous room and everything stopped. For a single, heart-stopping moment, barely anyone moved. Scott stood up as a few trickles of movement threatened to become a stampede of desperate people, all trying to get away from whatever it was that was happening. More and more folks were getting in the way of him now, crisscrossing, blocking his view. He pushed them away, moving further forward until he was at the outermost edge of a roughly semi-circular bubble of space which had formed around the disturbance. And then he saw it.

It had been a woman who'd screamed, but it was a man's body he saw slumped against the leisure centre wall, stripped to the waist. It was only when his blood-stained hands twitched that Scott realised he was still alive. As other people tried to get further away, Scott was one of the few who moved closer.

Soldiers swarmed out into the crowds, blocking his view again momentarily. When they moved, he saw that the man had, somehow, managed to flip himself over onto his front. He was using the wall to haul himself up. He recognised him. Christ, it was Warren from Barry Walpole's yard.

'Stay where you are,' a soldier barked at Warren, aiming his rifle directly at his head and circling him at a distance, kicking rolls of bedding and people's possessions out of the way. One arm outstretched, Warren leant against the wall, barely able to support his own weight. He was bleeding. Scott had been so focused on his pallid face that he hadn't seen the streaks of blood running down the inside of his thighs from the eviscerated stump where his penis used to be. And now he was almost upright, the blood-flow increased, the trickling becoming a gushing, then a flood. Warren pushed himself away from the wall and staggered a few steps forward, hunched over, painting the wooden gym floor red. Then he collapsed, hitting the floorboards with a nauseating thud.

At first stunned silence; an uneasy malaise.

How did no one see this happening? How did they not know?

Then absolute chaos.

As panic erupted, Scott turned back and ran straight into Michelle. 'What the hell was that? What just happened?' she demanded.

'Oh, so you believe me now?'

He grabbed her arm and dragged her back through the imprisoned population of Thussock. She tried to stop herself but was unable to find anything to hold onto. She slid along the smooth wooden floor. 'Scott, stop!'

He saw more soldiers appearing, moving towards a mass of desperate people trying to force their way out through the entrance to the leisure centre through which they'd all originally been admitted. He yanked Michelle's arm again. 'We're getting out of here.'

'How?'

He couldn't answer, but he knew he had to find a way. The carrier of the parasite was trapped here with them now, of that there was no doubt, but who was it? Probably a woman, but that barely narrowed the field. Already he could see troops dividing those people they could reach, separating them into males and females. The air was filled with screaming and crying, then with shouted warnings as brutally divided families fought not to lose sight of those they loved.

'We're getting out of here,' Scott said to Tammy and Phoebe who were already on their feet. He bent down and picked up George, then turned to Phoebe. 'We need a way out. Is there another way out of here?'

Trembling, she nodded and gestured, barely managing to lift a shaking hand and point towards the corner of the room where a fire exit had already been forced open by someone else. Scott looked back across the gym. Soldiers. Coming their way. No time to waste. But now Michelle had hold of him and was trying to pull him back the other way.

'It's not safe out there,' she yelled.

'Doesn't look too safe in here.' He pulled his son close, holding him so tight it clearly hurt. The boy writhed in his father's arms. 'George is coming with me, so I suggest you follow.' He looked at Tammy and Phoebe. 'Stay close.'

Gunshots.

For a heartbeat – no longer – everyone froze again. Scott spun around and from the dust and debris now falling like snow from the high ceiling, he figured they'd just been warning shots. Rather than calm the situation, though, they had the exact opposite effect. The threat of the soldier's weapons clearly paled into insignificance alongside the horror of whatever it was that was loose in the leisure centre; the fear of the unknown far worse than the fear of being shot or beaten. Several people rushed the military lines, Sergeant Ross included, and were felled with a hail of bullets.

Enough. Scott ran for the exit which was, thankfully, being almost completely ignored by almost everyone else. 'It'll bring us out by the playing field,' Phoebe said, shouting over the sudden carnage.

Another round of gunfire. George was screaming, his noise deafening Scott. Tammy winced at the echoing cacophony inside the gym and put her hands over her ears. Phoebe shoved her towards the exit and they piled through the fire door. Scott kicked it shut behind them, keen to stem the flow and mask their escape. The more people who followed, the worse their chances of getting away unnoticed.

It was cold and wet outside, and the sound immediately changed. The noise coming from the leisure centre became muffled, then was almost completely drowned out by the tumultuous soundtrack out here: the sounds of people being rounded up and fighting back. Jeeps, gunshots, warnings being shouted through loud-hailers, a helicopter drifting overhead which was clearly tracking people down with an intensely bright searchlight. Scott pressed himself against the side of the building they'd just escaped from while he considered their options. 'We should go back,' Michelle said. 'What's the point of running? They'll know it's not us who's sick...'

'Are you out of your fucking mind? You think they're just going to give us the all clear then let us go home?'

'Why wouldn't they?'

242

He shook his head in disbelief and pointed into the chaos. 'The world don't work like that, Chelle. They won't let any of us go now. They're hunting people down... look!'

She followed his gaze down the side of the leisure centre building and saw a white-haired woman trying to get away. She'd somehow managed to escape, squeezing out through an unexpected gap in the chaos, but she was struggling to keep going. A soldier was in close pursuit, almost matching her speed even though he was only walking. Michelle looked away as he grabbed the woman by the waist and dragged her back towards the leisure centre, frail legs kicking and hoarse voice screaming for help.

Scott looked from face to face. 'If we run now, they'll see us and they'll catch us. We need to lie low, then make our move when things calm down. Where do we go?'

The girls tried to think, to visualise, also trying not to panic. Tammy couldn't get her bearings at all, but Phoebe could. 'The temporary classrooms,' she said, pausing mid-sentence as more gunshots echoed around them. 'Over by the netball courts. They're about halfway between here and the school gates.'

'Show me.'

She crouched down and led them away from the leisure centre, taking them through a dark and narrow gap between two more buildings, then pausing to check her bearings. She took a sharp left, still crouching, half-running, only stopping when she reached the edge of the next block along. Scott looked over her head and could see across the playground to the Portakabin classrooms. It was relatively quiet there. Plenty of activity overhead and behind, but nothing in the direction they needed to go. 'Wait here,' he said, but none of them did. Michelle kept them moving forward together, bunched up tight. They held back slightly and ducked down as he forced the door to the nearest classroom. It flew open with barely any effort, just as flimsy as it had appeared. Still carrying George, Scott held the door and the others squeezed through. 'Get down,' he told them. 'Stay low and stay away from the windows. We'll sit tight, then get out of here.'

The five of them crammed into the corner of the room furthest from the door, hiding behind desks and chairs and holding onto each other for warmth and support, differences temporarily put to one side. 'So what now?' Michelle said. 'Or didn't you think any further forward than running out into the middle of a bloody war-zone?'

He glared at her, the anger in his face illuminated momentarily by a flash from the helicopter's sweeping searchlight. 'I told you, we're getting away from here. Getting away from whatever's doing the damage back in that place.'

'And you think they're going to let us get away?' Michelle continued. 'You think they're just going to let us sneak out by the back door?'

'We already have.'

'No we haven't. We're still trapped, in case you hadn't noticed, just in a different building.' She stopped talking and held her breath as a group of soldiers thundered past the classroom. She lowered her voice again. 'How is this helping any of us?'

'I'm doing a damn sight more than anyone else, in case you hadn't noticed. If it wasn't for me we'd be—'

'Back home in Redditch?' Tammy said, wrong-footing him. 'A million miles away from whatever's going on around here.'

'What the fuck is wrong with you lot?' Scott said, the volume of his voice rising the angrier he became. 'I should have just—'

The classroom door flew open again, and another group of figures crawled up the steps on their hands and knees. Scott braced himself to fight, to defend his territory and kick out these intruders. But wait... he recognised them. 'Saw you lot gettin' away,' Dez said, shoving Jackie and the twins towards Michelle, the girls and George. 'Figured you looked like you knew what you were doing.'

'Think again,' Michelle said.

'We're just trying to keep one step ahead, that's all,' Scott said.

'It's madness out there,' Dez said, on his knees now, his eyes just above the wooden windowsill, surveying the chaos. 'Never seen nothin' like it.'

'Keep your bloody head down,' Scott yelled at him. 'And get away from the fucking windows. You'll bring them straight to us.'

'Doubt it. They're too busy tryin' to sort out what's happening in the gym. Anyway, the helicopter's probably got us on infra-red.'

'So why don't you just piss off and hand yourself over? I didn't ask you to come in here. If you're staying, you do what I say. Now get your bloody head down.'

'All right, Scott, man... no need for that. All the trouble's out there. Don't want anything kickin' off in here.'

Time crawled. The world beyond the flimsy walls of the prefabricated building continued to be full of noise and activity; a constant, muffled din. Most sounds were indistinguishable, the noise occasionally punctuated by things they were able to make out more clearly, sounds of suffering and panic that they didn't want to hear. It seemed the worse the noise got, the louder it became.

Dez tried to talk to Scott and plan a way forward, but he had nothing. And the frustration and the fear combined to leave both men feeling increasingly lost. Scott's helplessness manifested itself as anger. By contrast, Dez tried to remain positive for the sake of his family. 'We might'a made a mistake here, Scott.'

'What?'

'I don't reckon we're gonna get far like this.'

'So what are you saying? Give ourselves up?'

'Least we'll have a chance of talkin' then. What good's this doin' us?'

'I can't believe I'm hearing this.'

'An' I can't believe *any* of this. Look, mate, this ain't just about us. We've both got families to look out for.'

'What the hell do you think I'm doing?'

Dez's silence spoke volumes. 'I don't know, man... There's a lotta firepower out there. Seems to me we might not have a lotta options.'

'So you're just going to hand yourself over? Hand your kids over?'

'I never said that...'

'You didn't need to say it. Jeez, what kind of a man are you?'

'One who knows when he's beat. One who knows when what he's doin's gonna cause more harm than good.'

'You're fucking pathetic.'

'That's fuckin' rich. You don't even know—'

Their argument was truncated by the classroom door flying open again. A soldier scrambled up the steps then shut the door behind him and leant against it, facemask pressed up to the glass. What the hell was he doing? Whatever it was, Scott quickly realised he hadn't yet noticed there were other people in the classroom. He went to get up. Michelle grabbed his arm but he shook her off. He gestured for Dez to go the other way around the outside of the small, dark room. Dez's scrambling movements were more obvious than Scott's and as the trooper turned around, panicking, Scott lunged at him and grabbed him from behind, taking him by surprise. Dez ripped off his facemask. Jesus, he was little more than a kid.

'Don't hurt me,' he begged. Stripping him of his breathing apparatus had stripped him of his bravado too. He looked broken, close to tears. 'Please don't hurt me, mate. I'm on your side. I'll help you.'

'Bullshit,' Scott said. 'Why should we believe you? You've rounded up the entire town and held us prisoner for most of the day. Why should we believe anything you say?'

Scott pushed the soldier into an empty corner and squared up to him for the first time. He had a pistol in a holster, no rifle, but he made no attempt to reach for it. 'I was just looking for somewhere to hide, same as you.'

'Ask him what's going on,' Jackie shouted. The soldier looked startled. He hadn't realised there were others there. His demeanour changed when he saw there were kids too.

'We were just following orders,' he said, his voice full of emotion. 'We didn't know...'

'Didn't know what?' Dez asked.

'What we were dealing with. What *you* were dealing with. They didn't explain. They just told us there'd been a chemical spill in the town and that we had to round everyone up and keep them safe, that's all.'

'And you believed that?'

'Wouldn't you? Ask yourself, mate, what's more believable here? Some bullshit story about a chemical spill or the truth?'

'And what exactly is the truth?'

The soldier looked around with frightened eyes, wishing there was more light so he could see how many people he was up against, and at the same time praying for the darkness to swallow him up. He licked his lips and took a deep breath, figuring he had nothing left to lose. 'They don't know where it came from. They don't even know what it looks like. Fuck, they're not even sure what it is yet.'

'What's he talking about?' Tammy asked.

'It's a parasite,' the soldier explained. 'We were laughing about it when we first heard, 'cause it sounded so bloody unbelievable, like something out of a horror film. It found the perfect way to make sure it kept itself alive – making people have sex. No one's gonna say no to a quick fuck, are they?' He grinned, the strain and surreal desperation of the moment beginning to show.

'Wait,' Tammy said, looking at her mother. 'Is that what happened to Dad this morning...?'

'I don't know...' Michelle answered.

'It has to be, doesn't it? So what happens to them?' she asked, demanding an answer from the soldier. 'Once they've got this thing inside them, what happens?'

'It takes what it needs,' the soldier said, still watching Scott's every movement, 'then it discards the rest.'

'What do you mean, *discards*?'

'Did you not see what happened to that fella back there? It forces its way out. There's not a lot left when it's finished.'

Tammy stared into the darkness, letting the full enormity of what she was hearing sink in. Her dad was dead. She didn't need any further confirmation, she just knew it. The lack of any comfort or explanation from either her mum or Scott was enough to convince her she was right. She began to sob. Next to her, Phoebe wailed.

'Keep the bloody noise down,' Scott hissed at them both.

'You bastard,' Michelle said. 'You absolute, heartless bastard. You knew all along, didn't you? You let them spend the day thinking he was okay, worrying about him... and all the time you knew he was already dead.'

'What else was I supposed to do? I'm trying to keep us all together here.'

'Like hell. You've never given a shit about anyone but yourself.'

Scott grabbed the soldier by the collar of his protective suit. Focusing on him made it easier to shut out the rest of the unwanted noise. 'Why did you keep us isolated? That's the real question.'

'Because isolating everyone in Thussock meant we'd isolate the parasite too.'

'I get that, but why? Was it for our benefit, or yours?'

'Why else would they do it?' Jackie asked.

'To keep *it* safe,' Scott answered quickly.

Michelle laughed with disbelief. She'd seen and heard it all now. She looked at the young soldier, waiting for him to start laughing too, but he didn't. His expression remained unchanged. 'I swear I don't know,' he said. 'We was just told to stop people getting away, that's all, but it all went tits up when people started panicking. That's why I'm here. I wasn't gonna be a part of that. I couldn't. And...'

'And what?'

The soldier paused, choosing his words, knowing he'd said too much already. 'And something wasn't right. Something changed.'

'What do you mean? What changed?'

'I don't know, I swear. You ever been in the forces? It's just something you learn to pick up on. Usually happens when things are about to go shit-shaped.'

'What the hell are you talking about?'

The soldier shook his head, struggling. 'The orders changed, and no one would say why. We felt it filtering through the ranks. There was a shift in focus. The priorities were changing...'

Scott had had enough. 'That's it. I'm getting us out of Thussock right now.'

'How?' Dez asked.

'You'll never do it,' the soldier said. 'They won't let anyone get away.'

'So why exactly are you here again? Surely you'd have been better off staying with the military?'

'It's fucking chaos out there. They won't notice me missing.'

'So once they've caught this thing, they'll leave the rest of us alone, right?' Michelle asked.

'I suppose,' the soldier said. 'All they're interested in is—'

'Are you serious?' Scott interrupted. 'You really think they'll just let people go back to normality after this?'

'Depends,' Dez said. 'If they still think this was just a chemical spill or sumthin' like that, why not? They can't make a whole village just disappear.'

'They probably could,' the soldier said ominously, 'but they won't want to, not unless they have to.'

'So we can just stick it out here with him, can't we?' Michelle suggested, nodding at the soldier. 'Wait 'til it's all died down out there, then give ourselves up. We're not infected, so they're not going to care. We act dumb, tell them we just hid when it all kicked off, then tell them he found us. He'll look good, we'll be safe... we might all get out of this still.'

'She's right, Scott,' Dez said. 'Play our cards right an' we might all be okay.'

'Do you have any idea how naïve you both sound?' Scott said. 'Just listen to what you're saying.'

'And can you hear how cynical you've become?' Michelle said. 'You're not interested in anyone but yourself, are you?'

'Shut the fuck up and—'

'Quiet!' The soldier's voice abruptly truncated Scott's outburst. He raised his pistol and aimed it at Scott. 'All of you shut up. She's right, we can do this. Stay quiet, stay calm, and we'll all get out of this in one piece.'

29

Scott was at the end of his tether. They'd been cooped-up here for over an hour now. He was sitting with his back to the door, holding George while Michelle consoled Tammy and Phoebe. The madness outside wore on, though to a lesser extent now as more of the population of Thussock, those who'd escaped and run blindly into the night, were rounded up. The longer Scott spent trapped in here, though, the harder it was to sit still and do nothing.

They were wrong, all the others.

Between them they'd agreed to sit tight and wait until everything had died down outside before giving themselves up, but giving himself up just wasn't in Scott's nature. And if they did surrender, he doubted the military would be as welcoming as the rest of them seemed keen to believe. The others were naïve, stupid even. He couldn't afford to lose control, not now, not with so much at stake. He needed to get out of Thussock.

There was a lull outside. Time to move.

The soldier was sitting on the other side of the door to him. Scott reached across and tugged at his sleeve. He sat up with a start. Christ, had he almost been asleep? 'What's your name?' Scott asked, voice low.

'What?'

'I don't even know your name.'

'Gary Waites.'

'Can I trust you, Gary?'

'Sure you can. We're all in this together now, far as I can see.'

'Good man. Listen, I'm worried.'

'You ain't alone.'

'Something's not right here.'

'Things haven't been right around this place for a long time now.'

'No,' Scott said, shaking his head and lowering his voice again, 'I'm not talking about in Thussock, I'm talking about in *here*.'

Gary looked concerned. 'Like what?'

Scott paused. Should he do this? He was running out of options. 'Have you seen anyone who's been infected with this thing yet?'

'I ain't seen nothing. Just a couple of the bodies and that guy in the leisure centre, why?'

'Because I have.'

'And?'

'And I didn't think about it until just now... that bloke who turned back there, I knew him. Used to work with him. His name was Warren.'

'So?'

'Like I said, it didn't mean much at the time, but I was watching him just before it happened and he looked... different.'

'Why are you telling me this? What are you saying? You think I'm infected?'

'No, no... it's not that. I respect you, mate. You've come in here and nailed your colours to the mast and I respect that. No, it's not you, it's *them* I'm worried about.' He surreptitiously gestured towards Dez and Jackie at the other end of the room. They were sitting in the opposite corner to Michelle and the girls, their twins safe between them.

'What about them?'

'I think...' he began before stopping again and clearing his throat, nerves getting the better of him. 'Look, I might be wrong, but I think I know what I'm talking about. I found one of the bodies last week and this morning we had an infected bloke hanging around by our house...'

'Just say what you're thinking,' the soldier said, pulse racing, hints of desperation and panic in his eyes.

'I'm trying to tell you I think I know what people look like when they've got it in them. I've seen them. It takes its time to show itself, but I'm starting to think... Look, it's that woman over there... I think she might be infected.'

The fear in the soldier's face was clear now. He lowered his hand towards his pistol. Then he paused. 'Are you sure?'

'I'll be honest, mate, not a hundred per cent. But I don't know about you... I don't want to take any chances. My missus and my kids are in here, you think I'm going to risk them? But that woman... she's got the same kind of look about her as the guy at the house this morning and the bloke who turned just now in the gym. I've been watching her. I tell you, if I'm right, I don't reckon it'll be long now...'

'So what do we do?'

'What can we do? Just be ready for when she turns I guess.'

Gary sat back, weighing up his options. What was it his commanding officer had said? *Be wary of anyone showing any signs of sexual activity. Watch out for displays of physical contact... we don't know how fast this thing moves.*

He went for his gun again. Scott grabbed his arm. 'What are you doing?' he asked, his whispered voice full of feigned concern.

'I'm going to talk to her. Find out where she was before she came in here, who she was with.'

Scott relaxed his grip and let go. *Perfect. So easily manipulated.* Gary got up and walked over to Dez and Jackie. Dez looked up. 'Problem?'

'Split up.'

'What?'

'You heard me.' He raised his pistol. 'Both of you get up. Move away from each other.'

Jackie started to panic. She grabbed the kids and reached out for Dez at the same time. He tried to pacify her then scrambled to his feet, blocking the soldier's way through. He put his hands up in submission. 'Look, mate, I dunno what this is about, but you've got the wrong idea about us... we just—'

'Shut up,' Gary ordered, and the volume of his voice was enough to panic everyone in the classroom. Scott picked up George in the confusion and made for the door.

'What's wrong with you?' Jackie said, sobbing, still trying to pull her family closer together. 'Dez ain't done nothing wrong...'

Gary looked from Dez, to Jackie, then back again. Dez made another move. Gary shoved him back and aimed the pistol at his chest. 'Don't, man...' Dez said, mouth dry. 'This is fuckin' crazy...'

The soldier was frightened. Confused. He didn't know what to do now. He didn't know how to stop this, didn't know which of these strangers he could trust and who he couldn't. 'Which one?' he asked, looking around for Scott. 'Which one is it?'

Scott remained low behind a desk, clutching George close to his chest. Michelle and the girls were crawling towards him.

At the other end of the room, Dez moved forward again, but Gary was having none of it. He raised his pistol level with Dez's face. 'Don't move,' he yelled. 'Don't you fucking move!'

'Wait, wait, wait...' Dez protested, terrified. 'You got this all wrong.'

'I've got nothing wrong,' Gary said, 'I know what's going on here. It's one of you two... one of you is infected.'

'I swear we're not. We never went anywhere near anyone who—'

'Shut the fuck up!' Gary screamed, but all his noise did was make matters worse. Dez pleaded with him, Jackie wailed with fear, the twins both began to cry...

In the midst of the chaos, Scott bolted for the door with George. Michelle had no choice but to follow, Tammy and Phoebe close behind. She tumbled down the steps, losing her footing and falling onto the tarmac, scuffing her hands and knees but barely noticing the pain through the fear. Scott tried to move but she grabbed hold of his shirt and pulled him back. She could hear shouting inside the classroom from which they'd just escaped, five desperate voices fighting for space.

'What the hell are you doing?' Michelle demanded.

'Getting us out of here,' he said, brushing her off and starting to run.

'Are you completely out of your fucking mind? Do you know what—?'

A flash of light and a single gunshot from the classroom silenced her.

Tammy and Phoebe were already running. Michelle sprinted after the rest of her family, then overtook Scott and blocked his way through. 'What the hell did you just do?'

'What I had to do to keep us safe.'

'Keep yourself safe, more like.'

'You're out too, aren't you?'

'But Jackie and Dez... the kids... you engineered that... you made that happen...'

'Fuck 'em. And fuck you, too.'

He pushed past and ran on with George. Michelle knew she had to stick with him if she wanted to stay with her son. The sound of another two shots inside the classroom sealed the decision.

The outside world felt wholly alien now. There were still a couple of helicopters high overhead and whilst quieter than before, a never-ending buzz of noise continued to come from around the leisure centre. Michelle watched the rest of her family run on ahead, feeling bizarrely detached from everything now, almost as if she was watching events unfold on TV. Only the fear and the cold air and spitting rain reminded her she was still alive and a part of this. She watched Scott and wanted to wrestle George from him and take the kids away. *I don't know you anymore. Don't know if I ever really did. We'll never be safe as long as we're with you.*

They waited in the shadows between two more imposing school buildings until she caught up. 'Move faster or you'll get left behind,' Scott said, his voice detached and unemotional. He looked around for Phoebe. 'Which way now?'

She couldn't immediately answer, could barely even think straight, traumatised with fear and struggling to make sense of her surroundings. She looked around again, then gestured down the side of the next school block. Scott sprinted along the wall of the building, using it both as cover and support. He stopped at the furthest corner, gesturing for the others to stay low and almost overbalancing with his son, then looked ahead.

Nothing. It was clear.

Most of the chaotic activity was still concentrated around the back of the school, the area from which they'd escaped. From here Scott could see the main gates. He'd expected to see a mass of soldiers and equipment there, but posts had clearly been abandoned in haste. Michelle grabbed his shoulder and swung him around. 'You're going to get us all killed.'

'No, staying here will get us all killed.'

'We're not safe.'

'That's why we're leaving. We can do this. We're gonna run for the hedge over there, then follow it around to the gate and slip out the front. There's no one there. We'll get out, find a car, then get as far away from Thussock as we can, right?' Scott looked into each face in turn, waiting until he'd seen something positive – a nod, a mumble, some kind of definite agreement, no matter how slight – before he

255

moved.

Just a few steps away from cover and Scott was on his face on the ground, George squashed beneath him, screaming. He picked himself up and put his hand over his son's mouth, trying to stop his noise. 'Shh... they'll hear us.'

'Is he okay? George, love, are you okay?' Michelle asked, trying to get closer. Scott turned his back on her.

'I tripped, that's all. Keep moving.'

He looked back and saw that none of them were following. Phoebe and Tammy were standing around something he couldn't make out in the darkness. *What did I just fall over?* He went back and saw it was the body of a woman, facedown. A pool of blood glistened around her naked crotch, steam still rising. Her torn, blood-soaked knickers were around her knees. 'Was she...?' Tammy started to ask.

'Infected?' Scott interrupted. 'Probably. None of our concern. We need to move.'

He shifted George in his tired arms, struggling with his increasingly heavy weight, and ran on. Phoebe still wasn't following. 'Come on, Pheeb,' Michelle shouted at her.

'Does this mean it's got out?'

'What?'

'This woman... does this mean the parasite-thing got out of the leisure centre?'

'Obviously,' Scott said, 'but it doesn't make any difference. As long as we keep away from everyone else we'll be fine.'

'But it does, though, doesn't it? It *does* make a difference.'

'Listen to me. We're going to just keep doing what we're doing and get out of Thussock. We can worry about all this later.'

'But wait,' Phoebe said, still refusing to move, 'I don't get it. There was ages between all those other people dying.'

'So?'

'So why is it getting faster? Is it getting hungrier? It's not long since it got that man in the leisure centre, is it?'

'I don't know. Does it even matter? Just shut up and move, for Christ's sake.'

She still wasn't going anywhere.

'Does it mean there's more than one of them now?'

Shit. She might be right.

'We need to go,' Scott said. This time he kept running, giving the others no choice but to follow.

And it was far easier to get away than any of them expected. A final breathless dash across a patch of open space and they'd made it beyond the school gates.

30

The silence away from the school was somehow more frightening than the noise they'd left behind. Thussock was deserted; a ghost town, devoid of all life. Although the lights in most buildings remained unlit, the street lamps enabled the family to see more than enough. It was as if the entire place had been frozen like a paused DVD. Wherever they looked they could visualise the exact moments when people's lives had been unexpectedly interrupted during the course of the long day now ending. Cars had been abandoned in the middle of the road. The doors of many shops and houses had been left open. A stray dog mooched around for its missing owner, edging forward when it saw Scott and the others, then yelping with panic and running away in the opposite direction. Scott stepped over a river of water flowing into the gutter from a hosepipe which had been left running for hours. Nearby, a courier delivery remained incomplete, the back of a truck half-full of boxes left wide open, its contents untouched. A rain-soaked child's pushchair lay on its side in the middle of the pavement, its young passenger long gone. Thussock felt eerie and unsettling, as if someone had casually flicked a switch and erased the entire human race save for this one dysfunctional family left skulking through the shadows, avoiding the light as if they were vampires.

They'd been walking unchallenged for almost a quarter of an hour when Scott stopped. He changed direction and led them down a dark alleyway. 'Where are we going?' Michelle asked, talking in whispers despite there being no one else around to hear.

'Back to work.'

And Michelle began to slowly make sense of their surroundings. She'd never seen it like this before, but she was sure this was close to where she'd dropped Scott off on those few occasions he'd actually managed an uninterrupted day's work at Barry Walpole's yard.

He handed George to Michelle and told her to wait near a solitary street lamp by the entrance to the yard, out of plain sight but where he could still see them. Scott then jogged across the yard and forced his way into Barry Walpole's caravan-cum-office.

He'd triggered the alarm. Scott made straight for the metal key cabinet mounted on the wall by Barry's desk. He broke into it quickly with a screwdriver, nerves and the shrill alarm noise combining to keep him moving at speed. Keys flew everywhere as he prised the door open and he dropped to his hands and knees and scrambled around on the grubby floor, feeling the constant noise boring into his brain now, clouding his already confused thoughts. And then, right under the desk, his outstretched fingers found what he'd been looking for. He snatched up the keys to the truck and ran back outside.

His family had gone.

'Michelle,' he shouted, but he could hardly hear himself think over the never-ending klaxon. Where were they? Had he pushed Michelle too far with what he'd done to Dez and his family? He hadn't had any choice. *It was them or us... it was the only way.* He ran over to the truck, no longer sure if he even believed himself.

No time to waste. Helicopters overhead. Easier to find them in the truck. Then again, maybe he should just leave alone? If it wasn't for George, he thought, he probably would have.

He started the engine and pulled away, accelerating hard down the driveway, figuring Michelle would most probably have tried to get home as there was nowhere else left to go other than back to the school. He'd barely made it halfway to the road when Phoebe jumped out at him from the shadows, scaring him senseless. He slammed on the brakes, virtually standing on the pedal to bring the tired old truck to a stop. Michelle got into the front with George as Tammy and Phoebe clambered onto the flat-bed behind. 'Drive,' Michelle yelled at him once she was sure they were safe. He swung around a sharp left turn, then accelerated again. She was confused. 'You're going the wrong way. You should have turned right for the house.'

'We're not going to the house.'

'What?'

'I told you, we're getting out of Thussock.'

'You're not thinking straight, Scott. Everything we own is back at that house. I'm not saying we should stop and pack it all up, just get a few essentials. Our documents, some food and drink, clothes...'

'No.'

'For Christ's sake, it's on the main road out of Thussock. It's the most obvious way out of here.'

'Exactly. That's why we're going this way.'

'But what about the girls? They'll freeze on the back of this truck.'

'They'll be all right.'

Michelle didn't bother arguing. What was the point? When had he last listened to her, anyway? Maybe if he had, they wouldn't all be in this fucking mess.

Scott was pushing the truck harder and harder, braking then accelerating, driving like a fucking maniac. The road began to climb – Michelle felt it rather than saw it – and from the shapes of the dark silhouettes on either side, she worked out roughly where they were. They were driving over the hills behind their house now, retracing the route Scott had taken that Saturday afternoon when they'd first arrived in Thussock.

As the road reached its peak then began to descend, Scott braked hard, bringing the truck to an unexpected, juddering halt. Michelle clung onto George with one hand and steadied herself with the other. In the back, both Tammy and Phoebe lost balance and lurched forward, falling against one another and butting heads, yelping with pain. 'What the hell are you doing?' Michelle screamed at him, but he didn't answer, he just left the truck. Incensed, she picked up George and followed him out. He'd stopped a short distance ahead and was standing on the white line in the middle of the road, staring into the distance. 'I can't handle this, Scott. You need to...' She shut up when she saw what was up ahead.

Just beyond the fracking site was a blockade. Scores of soldiers. Plenty of firepower. And it wasn't just the road, she realised: the blockade stretched for as far as she could see in either direction. 'They've sealed us off,' Scott said, sounding numb, barely able to believe what he was seeing. 'The bastards have sealed off the whole bloody town. We're not going anywhere.'

31

They didn't have any other choice now. Other than surrendering themselves to the military, going back to the house was the only option left.

Scott parked the truck on the grass at the side of the house rather than on the drive, hoping to make it less obvious that they'd returned. Phoebe ran to the door but Michelle called her back. It was still open from where it had been kicked in by soldiers this morning. *This morning*, she thought, *was it really only this morning?* Was this day ever going to end? 'I'll go first,' she said, but Scott had other ideas and he pushed her out of the way. She followed him in and flicked on the hall light. He immediately switched it off again.

'Too dangerous. Don't want anyone knowing we're in here.'

'You really think anyone cares?'

He wasn't going to discuss it. He grabbed her wrist tight and pulled her closer. 'You leave the fucking lights alone and you do exactly what I tell you, got it?'

He handed George to Michelle, made sure the girls were inside, then propped the broken door shut with an upturned shoe rack. 'I need the toilet,' Phoebe said. He glared at her.

'Be quick, then get into the living room. I want all of you in the living room, got it? You stay out of sight at the back of the house.'

Michelle ushered Tammy through. Scott waited for Phoebe to finish, then made sure she followed. He went into the kitchen and grabbed a little food and drink, pausing at the window. It appeared deceptively calm out there now, but he knew it was just an illusion. They were trapped between the chaos at the school on one side and the military lines securing Thussock on the other. No man's land.

The girls were sitting on the sofa, George perched between them, while Michelle anxiously paced the other end of the room. There were no street lamps visible here, but the intermittent moon provided a little illumination through the French window. Scott dropped an armful of food onto the coffee table then shut the door. The silence in the room was ominous, the tension unbearable. Tammy stared straight ahead. George looked from face to face, hoping for reassurance from someone but getting nothing. Michelle chewed her nails and watched the others, Scott especially. Phoebe was sitting with her hands in her lap, eyes wide with fear. When she spoke there was a noticeable waver to her voice. She was right on the edge. 'What are we going to do?'

'I don't know yet,' Scott answered quickly, getting in fast before anyone else could speak. 'For now we're just going to sit tight and wait.'

'Wait for what?' Tammy demanded. Michelle felt her guts tighten.

'No, Tammy, this isn't the time.'

'Then when is?'

'Your mother's right,' Scott said. 'Shut up. No one will have expected us to come back here, so we wait for the situation back in town to get sorted, then we leave. Simple. As long as we stay away from everyone else, there's no chance of any of us getting infected by this damn thing.'

'Unless one of us already has been.'

Tammy's words silenced all of them. She couldn't be right, could she? Scott and Michelle individually tried to work their way back and remember if any of them had been left alone long enough to have been infected. They couldn't have caught it from that body on the grass outside the school, could they? It was all too much for Michelle. The idea of one of her girls being violated... she couldn't bear to think about it. 'No one's been infected...' she mumbled. 'We can't have been.'

'So all we've done,' Tammy said, not letting go, 'is leave one prison cell to end up in another. We might as well have stayed at the school, or even in that Portakabin. Oh, but we couldn't stay there, could we, Scott, because you screwed that up as well. You got Mum's friend and her family killed.'

'We don't know what happened. Anyway, they weren't my concern.'

'And we are?'

'You're my family.'

'But we don't matter really, do we? As long as you're okay, that's all that's important. You don't give a damn about anyone but yourself.'

'Tammy, please...' Michelle begged. 'Don't...'

'No, come on,' Scott said, goading her, 'let her have her say.'

Tammy stood up, face to face with her step-father. 'You just keep backing us into corners.' She looked at Michelle. 'Can't you see it, Mum? We had our freedom back in Redditch, until he screwed up and we lost that. You keep making our world smaller and smaller, Scott, adding more and more restrictions. You brought us here to the middle of nowhere and you even managed to fuck that up.'

'If it wasn't for me—'

'If it wasn't for you, everything would be okay. You think you're above it all, don't you? You think you're more important than everyone else. The army dragged us out of here this morning. *The bloody army!* And even that's not enough to stop you. Now look at us, stuck in a single shitty room in this shitty house. Like I said, from one prison cell to another. What's next? Seems to me there's nowhere left to go now. We're stuck here. We'll probably die here.'

'Don't say that,' Michelle protested. She tried to get to Tammy but Scott wouldn't let her through. He held her back.

'You just don't get it, do you?' he said to Tammy. 'You're all fuck ups, the bloody lot of you.'

'I don't have to listen to this.'

'But you do, don't you? Because it's not up to you, it's up to *me*.'

Tammy stood her ground, tears of anger running down her face. 'This was our last chance, Scott, don't you get it? I'm not going to let you drag us all down anymore.'

She went for the door but he caught her shoulder and pulled her back, throwing her down onto the sofa, crushing George who yelped with pain. 'Leave her alone!' Michelle screamed and she threw herself at Scott. He spun around and caught her by the throat, fingers digging into her neck. She tried to speak but couldn't, choking on her words.

'Stop it!' Phoebe yelled.

Scott let go of Michelle and pushed her away but she came at him again, arms flailing. He swung out as she launched herself at him, punching her in the face. Stunned, just adrenalin keeping her moving now, she lunged at him again. He punched her for a second time, a quick, brutal jab. She swayed momentarily then dropped to the ground, out cold.

When he looked around, Tammy had gone. Phoebe ran to help her mother but Scott stopped her. 'Get up to your room and don't move,' he ordered. 'Take a step outside this bloody house and the same'll happen to you. Got it?'

She scooped up her little brother and held him close, cowering in the corner until Scott had gone.

The front door was open but he couldn't see Tammy. Little bitch. Where had she gone? He ran out to the road and ducked down instinctively when a military helicopter thundered overhead, flying low on its way out of Thussock, filling the air with pressure and noise. He couldn't see Tammy anywhere. He ran back and did a quick circuit of the outside of the house... nothing.

'I know you're still here,' he shouted over the wind and the fading helicopter noise, certain she was hiding nearby. 'You're on your own now, you hear me? This family's better off without you. Don't bother coming back, dumb little bitch.'

Breathless, he looked up and down the length of the back garden once more then went inside. He stood in the hallway and listened to the silence. He could hear Phoebe and George upstairs, but other than them, nothing.

Thank Christ for that.

The unexpected quiet was blissful. No one shouting at him or accusing him of anything for once. No one arguing or trying to tell him what to do... Why couldn't they have always been like this?

He knew what he had to do now. Tammy leaving had made it all that much easier. 'The key to staying together and surviving now,' he told Michelle who remained facedown and motionless on the living room floor, 'is keeping apart.'

Scott fetched himself a can of beer from the fridge and knocked it back in a couple of quick, gassy gulps, then he picked up his toolbox from the corner and carried it to the living room. Michelle was beginning to come around. Her face was a mess. He regretted that – he always did – but it had been necessary. She had to learn. She needed to know her place in this household and this kind of thing was just going to keep happening again and again until she got it right. It wasn't like she hadn't had any warnings. He'd told her over and over. When was she going to stop talking and start listening?

266

'Scott...?' she mumbled, though she was drifting in and out of consciousness and it was difficult to speak through the blood and spit and broken teeth.

'Be quiet, love,' he told her, standing over her. 'It's gonna be all right.'

She tried to get up but couldn't. She slurred another word. Or was it a groan? He couldn't tell.

'I don't like hurting you,' he said, 'but it's not my fault. You bring it on yourself. You could have avoided all of this.'

'I'm sorry...'

He left her lying in the middle of the room.

'Stay there and get your strength back. I'll check on you later.'

She tried to protest but couldn't. She could barely move. Her body was a dead-weight, nothing working how it should have. All she could do was watch as he shut the door.

The hammering startled her. It seemed to go on forever, the noise hurting her already throbbing head, but it stopped eventually, the door nailed shut.

Phoebe was crouching at the top of the stairs, George just behind her. When they heard him coming they ran back into her room and hid on the far side of the bed. He appeared in the doorway. 'You here?'

'We're here,' Phoebe answered, sitting up slightly so he could see her.

'Good girl.'

'Where's Tammy?'

'She's gone.'

'What about Mum?'

'Your mother's fine. She's downstairs.'

'What was the banging?'

'You know how this thing spreads, don't you Pheeb?'

She nodded but didn't want to say. 'Yes...'

'So the safest thing is for us all to stay in the house but keep apart from each other, right? You and George should be okay 'cause you're just kids, but it's different for me and your mum. You understand?'

'Think so.'

'Good girl,' he said again.

He shut the door, picked up his hammer, and took a handful of three inch nails from his pocket. Just as he had downstairs, he worked his way around the edge of the door, hammering the nails through the door itself at an angle and deep into the frame.

He was dripping with sweat by the time he'd finished, his hands and arms heavy and numb. He leant against the door. 'All done,' he shouted to Phoebe. 'It's for your own good. I'm just doing what I have to do to keep us all safe.'

32

It might have been hours later, it might have only been minutes. Scott wasn't sure. He was sitting in the hallway in almost complete darkness, leaning with his back against his bedroom door. The house was still largely silent, but the noise outside had increased again. There'd been more traffic on the road, pretty much all of it heading out of Thussock now. He'd seen some of it from the kitchen window. It had looked almost exclusively military.

'You there, Scott?'

He sat up fast, not sure if he'd imagined Michelle's voice. He moved towards the living room, crawling through empty beer cans. 'I'm here.'

'Let me out, love.'

'You know I can't.'

'But I'm scared in here.'

'And I'm scared out here. This is the only way to be sure, you know it is.'

'My face hurts. I think you broke my nose.'

'I'm sorry.'

'I'm tired of this, love. I'm tired of you hurting me.'

'I had to do it. You know that.'

'I know.'

'You were hysterical. You were scaring Phoebe and George.'

'I know.'

'It won't happen again.'

'You said that last time.'

'This is different.'

'You said that last time too.'

'I mean it, Chelle. You believe me?'

A pause, then 'I believe you.'

Scott looked up at the door. He wanted to see her and he thought about opening it, but he knew it was a risk he couldn't afford to take.

'Are the kids okay, Scott?'

'They're fine.'

'Can I talk to them.'

'They're in their rooms.'

'What about George?'

'He's with Phoebe.'

'Okay.' Another pause. 'What are we going to do, love?'

'You keep asking me that. I don't know... I'm not sure. I think we should just stay here like we planned.'

'I thought I heard more helicopters.'

'You did.'

'If they're going, shouldn't we go too?'

'If they're going then that's a good thing, isn't it? It means they're clearing out. It means it's over.'

'I don't know, love... I'm not sure.'

'Trust me.'

Another pause, then 'Can I come out and talk to you? I really want to see you.'

'I already told you, Chelle. You have to stay in there. We have to keep apart for now, just until we're sure it's safe...'

'But how will we know?'

Her questions were starting to annoy him. He could feel himself tensing up again.

'We'll know.'

'But, Scott, I just think—'

'Shut up,' he yelled suddenly, and he banged his fist against the living room door in anger. He heard her sob. 'I'm sorry, Chelle... I didn't meant to shout. Just be patient. Just do what I say, okay. I'll go and see if I can find out what's happening later.'

She might have spoken again, but another helicopter drifting overhead drowned out her words.

Scott needed to pee. He went to the bathroom and emptied his bladder. He washed his face with ice-cold water. *I need to stay focused.* He leant his head against the mirror and breathed in deeply, trying to stay calm and in control. What did he do now? Had he truly backed them into a corner here like they'd said, or was there still a way out? The waiting was unbearable.

When he went back out into the hallway, Tammy was there. 'Jesus Christ,' he gasped. 'What the hell are you doing? You scared the shit out of me.'

'Sorry,' she mumbled. In the low light he could just about make out her face. She was crying.

'What are you doing back here?'

No reply.

'Where've you been?'

Still nothing.

'You've got a fucking nerve coming back after what you said to me. You've no fucking respect.'

'Sorry,' she said again. 'I was wrong.'

Scott shook his head. In a night filled with impossibility, this was the hardest thing of all to take. 'Wait... you're apologising? Fuck me, I've heard it all now.'

She didn't react. She didn't even move other than to lift a hand and wipe her eyes. She cleared her throat. 'I should have listened to you. I was scared... I didn't know where I was going out there. I just ran and ran... almost got lost.'

'But you come back?'

'I wanted to see you. I felt so alone out there... there was no one looking out for me, no one protecting me. It made me realise I'd been stupid. I know I've been a bitch to you, Scott, but...'

'What?'

'But when I was out there, completely bloody terrified, I realised how much we all need you. How much *I* need you. All along you've been trying to keep this family together, but I just couldn't see it. I was angry. I was stupid.'

He leant back against the wall and stared at her. 'Why leave it until now? You could have made this all so much easier for everyone.'

'I know,' she said, and she took a step forward. 'I wish I could have the time again.' He could see her more clearly now. Her skin was pale, porcelain-like, her hair falling in soft curls down either side of her face. She'd been a little kid when he and Michelle had first got together; a snotty-faced rebel full of resentment and spite. Christ, she'd made things difficult for all of them. And though he'd certainly noticed it before today, her gradual transformation was now complete. She was a woman now, her emotional maturity finally catching up with the physical changes her body had undergone over the last few years. 'I wanted to make it up to you, Scott,' she said.

271

She started to unbutton her shirt, letting it fall back off her shoulders. He stared at her pert breasts, not sagging like her mother's. Cellulite and stretch-mark free skin. Her young, inexperienced body. He checked himself. The dulling effect of the beer faded quickly. Was she playing him? 'Do you think I'm fucking stupid?'

'Nope,' she said, and she bit her lip as she watched him watching her.

'This is bullshit.'

'It's not, I swear. I'm sorry.'

And then he remembered. He cursed himself for being so easily distracted. 'Wait... this isn't right... Did you see anyone else while you were out there?'

'What do you mean?' Her voice was light and airy, strangely soothing.

'You know exactly what I mean. Are you infected?'

She laughed. A cute nervous giggle. 'I didn't see anyone else. I got halfway to Thussock then turned back because I was scared and I didn't know what else to do.' She took another step closer, almost touching him now, and took his hand in hers and held it against her chest. Her breasts felt so smooth, so soft and so cold. 'We might not have long left. I wanted to come back and show you how sorry I am. I wanted to make it up to you.'

She stood on tiptoes and kissed him gently on the cheek, then pulled him into the kitchen. He followed at first, then stopped and pulled back, yanking his hand from hers. 'You're infected.'

'I didn't see anybody out there, honest I didn't.' She hopped up onto the kitchen table and sat and watched him. He was holding back, obviously unsure, and she wasn't surprised. She'd expected this. Yet more traffic thundered past outside. She opened her arms to him. 'Come on, Scott... please...'

He grabbed her wrist when she lunged for one of the knives in the knife block on the table. She screamed with pain as he twisted her arm around behind her, forcing her up onto her feet and pushing her against the wall. He pressed his full weight against her. She was right, he did want her, had done for a while, but it was too late for that. 'You dumb fucking kid,' he said. 'Did you really think I'd fall for that bullshit?'

She screamed again, sobbing now for him to release her. 'You're hurting me... please.'

'Do you think I care? After all the grief you've caused?'

'It wasn't me, it was—' she started to say and he yanked her wrist upwards again, threatening to pop her shoulder from its socket.

'You're all as bad as each other,' he whispered, his mouth just millimetres from her ear, his weight crushing her. 'I don't know how I managed to stay sane living with so many moaning, miserable bitches.'

'Let her go, Scott.'

Scott looked around, surprised. Michelle was standing in the kitchen doorway. Christ, she looked bad. One side of her face was lumpy and misshapen, her right eye black and swollen, almost completely shut.

'How did you get out?'

'You said we'd need double-glazing, remember?' she said, her voice slurred and her words hard to discern. 'You were right. I forced the French window open. Now let her go.'

'Fuck you,' he said, turning back to face Tammy.

'No, Scott, fuck *you*.'

Michelle smacked him on the back of his head with the claw hammer he'd used to seal up the doors. He let go of Tammy and slowly turned around, almost tripping over his own feet. He lifted a hand to his head and looked at the blood on his fingers, glistening in the half-light. He looked confused. Hurt. 'Chelle, why did you—?' She swung the hammer around again, shattering his jaw. Scott crumpled to the ground and she reached for Tammy's hand and pulled her away. 'We're going. Find the car keys.'

Without waiting for her response Michelle ran upstairs to get the others.

Ten minutes and she'd managed to prise open the bedroom door and get enough of their stuff together. They loaded it into the Zafira, still more helicopters circling overhead as they worked. The road out of Thussock was a steady stream of traffic now, an exodus. The military retreat told them all they needed to know.

'Where are we going, Mum?' Phoebe asked.

'Home.'

'What, to—'

'Redditch, yes. *Home*, home. We'll go and stay with Granddad.'

'What about Scott?'

'What about him?'

She started the engine, waited for another truck to pass, then pulled out onto the road. She glanced back in the rear view mirror at the house they were leaving and felt relief, nothing else.

They'd barely driven more than half a mile when they followed a bend in the road and reached the military blockade. The other vehicles had made it through, but she was unidentified and was flagged down. Guns and soldiers everywhere. For the briefest of moments she wondered if Scott had been right. Should they have stayed back at the house? Had she made a huge mistake?

Familiarly faceless figures appeared at every window. A solider opened her door and pulled her out. George began to scream. 'Follow me,' a voice barked. 'All of you, now!'

Too tired, outgunned and outnumbered to even think about resisting, Michelle pulled her children close and did as she was told. The family were pushed roughly into the back of a large trailer which began to move, a lab on wheels from what they could see. There were no explanations as DNA swabs were taken from the inside of their mouths and blood samples drawn, but they were beaten now, way past the point of being able to resist. The vehicle began to pick up speed, part of a convoy heading south.

It felt like forever but it could only have been a minute or two later when one of the faceless figures took off her mask. 'All clear,' she said. 'Lucky escape there, Mrs Griffiths.'

'Lucky?' Michelle said, still struggling to speak with a mouth full of broken teeth.

'Yes, lucky. You managed to get away before the accident.'

'What accident?'

'The accident at the fracking site.'

'When?'

The woman paused, glanced at a colleague, then looked at her watch. 'Anytime now.'

*

Two low flying jets raced over the convoy, travelling in the opposite direction, back towards Thussock. And in the distance, the infected town died. A moment of silence, then a series of explosions and chain reactions tore the place apart. From the fracking site to the leisure centre, from the centre of town all the way to the grey house on the road south out of Thussock, the place was consumed by fire, heat, and intense white light.

FIFTEEN MILES SOUTH OF THUSSOCK

The van juddered to a halt. 'What the hell are you doing?' the soldier in the passenger seat said.

'Just checking. Christ, can't you hear her? They'll have our bollocks if we don't get her back in one piece.'

'You know what they said.'

'Yeah, I know what they said.'

Before the other man could argue – as he usually did – the driver climbed out and walked around to the back. He slid the viewing panel across and looked at her through the wire-mesh. 'You all right there, Jackie, love?'

She was more than all right. She was bloody gorgeous. She sat in the corner of the cage just looking at him... wanting him.

But he'd seen enough tonight to know better. The noise from the explosion which had destroyed most of Thussock was still ringing in his ears. He slid the viewing panel back across.

'Everything all right?' his mate asked.

'Perfect.'

FALRIGG

'Told you sumthin' like this was gonna happen,' Arthur had said to his wife before he'd set out this morning. They'd known something had been wrong in Thussock all day yesterday. Bloody army had stopped them getting anywhere near the place. He'd missed his doctor's appointment because of the road blocks. Inconsiderate buggers.

When they heard the explosions last night, ten of them had set out from the village to try and see what had happened, to see if they could help. They'd made it as far as the first of the peaks before being turned back. They'd seen all they'd needed to see, mind. It had been the fracking site, all right. Arthur had been telling people from the start that place was an accident waiting to happen. It was some kind of chain reaction caused by gas deposits buried underground, Jock had said. It was all over the news now, of course, but Jock had heard first. His son was a teacher at a school in Glasgow. If anyone knew what had happened, it'd be him. Probably no bad thing that Thussock had been wiped off the map, though, after everything that had gone on there over the last couple of weeks.

Still, life goes on.

Arthur found her by the stream which ran along the bottom edge of his lowest paddock. Poor thing looked like she'd barely managed to get away in time before the town had gone to hell last evening. She'd been caught in a blast, that much was clear, and quite how she'd lasted this long, he didn't know. He didn't think she'd be alive much longer. Maybe the water had helped keep her alive, or the shock, perhaps.

Her legs and the right side of her face were badly burned. Some of her clothes were fused to her flesh. She'd no hair left on one half of her scalp. That was what upset him more than anything. She'd probably been a good looking woman before this, he'd thought. She'd groaned with pain when he'd lifted her up and laid her down in the back of the Land Rover. The dogs had gone crazy, but he'd just shooed them away. Bloody animals.

She watched him through her one good eye, the left eye blistered and burned, glued shut with discharge, and she reached out for him with the one hand that still worked. She pulled him closer until he could feel her breath on his face, then closer still until their lips met.

ALSO BY
DAVID MOODY

the acclaimed autumn series
www.lastoftheliving.net

"A head-spinning thrill ride"
Guillermo del Toro

www.thehatertrilogy.com

The author of the best-selling HATER and AUTUMN books
delivers his final word on the living dead.

"As demonstrated throughout his previous novels, readers
should crown Moody king of the zombie horror novel"
—*Booklist*

Includes THE COST OF LIVING ("A truly superb post-apoc-
alyptic story" —*DLS Reviews*) and ISOLATION ("a must have
for zombie lovers and people who love stories with exceptional
characterisation... not to be missed" —*BookBloke*) and more...

"British horror at its absolute best" —*Starburst*

"Straight To You deserves to be ranked alongside such classics as The Stand and Swan Song." —*Ginger Nuts of Horror*

The sun is dying. The temperature is rising by the hour. The burning world is in chaos. Steven Johnson's wife is hundreds of miles away, and all that matters is reaching her before the end.

Every second is precious. Tomorrow is too late.

"An engaging and heart-breaking read – Moody is the go-to-guy for extraordinary stories starring ordinary people" —*Wayne Simmons, author of Plastic Jesus and Flu*

"Trust is a slow-burner and all the richer for it. The layers of characters and details of the story play out perfectly when matched with an ending you're not likely to forget. It's also an outstanding novel, delivers in more ways than one, and is worthy of a place on the discerning fan's bookshelf. 10/10."
—*Starburst Magazine*

www.trustdavidmoody.com

If you are the original purchaser of this book, or if you received this book as a gift, you can download a complementary eBook version by visiting:

www.infectedbooks.co.uk/ebooks

and completing the necessary information (terms and conditions apply).

Lightning Source UK Ltd.
Milton Keynes UK
UKOW05f1150191114

241836UK00002B/17/P

9 780957 656345